A SOLDIER ENTERED the alcove. The girl fell to her hands, swung her leg out, and caught the guard's ankles. He flopped to his backside and the girl stood to bring her heel onto his neck with enough pressure to render him unconscious like the others.

"I wasn't sure I'd remember how to do that," the girl admitted.

Vex choked, laughed, choked again. "Who *are* you?"

She took a moment to steady herself, but when she looked up at Vex, she smiled.

It was the smile Nayeli gave when she was about to suggest blowing someone up.

"I'm Adeluna—Lu," the girl told him. "Former soldier of the revolution."

Also by Sara Raasch

Snow Like Ashes

Ice Like Fire

Frost Like Night

These Divided Shores

THESE
REBEL
WAVES

SARA RAASCH

BALZER + BRAY
An Imprint of HarperCollinsPublishers

Balzer + Bray is an imprint of HarperCollins Publishers.

These Rebel Waves
Copyright © 2018 by Sara Raasch
Map art © 2018 by Jordan Saia
Interior art © 2018 by Michelle Taormina
All rights reserved. Printed in the United States of America.

ISBN 978-0-06-247151-2

19 20 21 22 23   PC/LSCH   10 9 8 7 6 5 4 3 2 1

First paperback edition, 2019

To O—you rebelled from the start. Never stop.

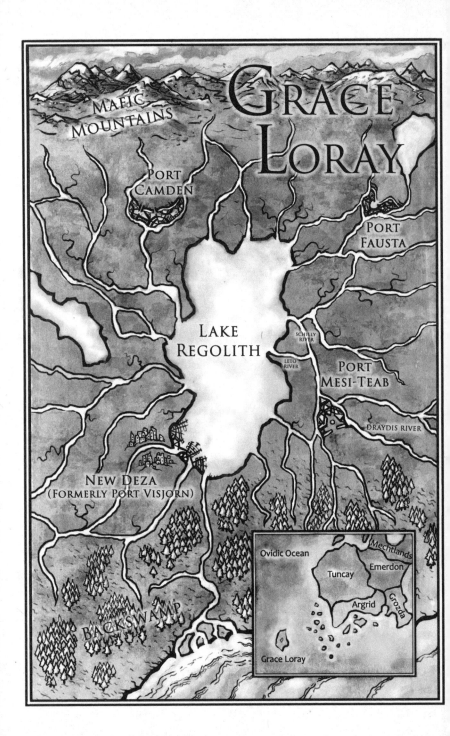

Hemlight

Availability: extremely common

Location: sand deposits along river edges

Appearance: small white seeds on long
   white stems

Method: friction: the seed is rubbed
   between the fingers and thrown

Use: combustible

Prologue

BENAT GALLEGO WAS thirteen when he watched his uncle and cousin burn to death.

He had told himself it would be no different from the other burnings. Anxious onlookers would pack the cathedral's lawn, trampling the grass as they fought to see the spectacle at the end of the yard. Monxes, Church servants clad in heavy black robes, would scurry around the pyres, adding wood, supervising the soldiers who secured posts and readied chains. And Ben would watch in quiet horror from the shadow of Grace Neus Cathedral, the stained-glass windows in its towers feeling far too much like the Pious God's judgmental eyes.

But as Ben stood in the yard, soldiers blocking him from the raucous crowd, he knew this was different. It had been different from the moment his father had passed the sentence—not just as Asentzio Elazar Vega Gallego,

King of Argrid, Eminence of the eternal Church, but as a man condemning his brother for heresy.

Ben's mind refused to reconcile the sentence with the happy memories he had of his uncle Rodrigu. The man who had chased him and his cousin Paxben around the palace when they were younger, long limbs like sticky spiderwebs catching Paxben in a delirium of giggles; the man who had pinned the silver Inquisitors seal to Ben's tunic in front of the reverent royal court a month ago.

That Inquisitor ceremony had been the proudest day of Ben's life. He had stood in the cathedral, ready to join the society that judged crimes by the Pious God's doctrine. Paxben would have been inducted when he was thirteen, and one day would take his father's place as the High Inquisitor, while Ben would be king and leader of the Church like his own father.

That was an impossible dream now, destroyed by Rodrigu's sins.

Ben's chest bucked, a sob threatening to send him to his knees.

"Your uncle and cousin are traitors," Elazar had told him. *"Traitors to Argrid, for giving money to the rebels on Grace Loray. Traitors to the Pious God, for dealing in the Devil's magic that comes from that island. For that, we must expunge their souls."*

"But he was my teacher," Ben whispered now, as if reliving the conversation could change the present. "He taught me about Grace Loray's magic. He taught me which plants were good and which were evil. He *knew* evil. He can't be a tool of the Devil. He can't be."

Around him, the crowd's noise united in one chanted hymn:

"Purity, to live a life divine. Honesty, that our souls may shine. Chastity, a pureness sure. Penance, humble and demure. Charity, to share his heart. The five pillars of the Pious God, ours to embrace, ours to start."

Ben's lungs filled with lead. He'd sung this hymn beside his cousin during services. Paxben had always been pitchy, but once he realized how hard Ben had to fight to keep from laughing, he started making his voice squeak on purpose. They'd stand side by side, Ben trying to sing around his chuckling, and Paxben squawking so off-key that Ben imagined the statues of the sainted Graces covering their marble ears.

The hymn ended, shattering Ben's concentration. He forced his eyes open.

His uncle was being led out to the first pyre. His cousin would soon follow.

They had been caught buying and selling harmful magic from Argrid's colony of Grace Loray. Rodrigu had connections to the rebels there. He'd encouraged the spread of the Devil's magic in Argrid. And he'd roped Paxben into it.

Ben looked over his shoulder, running his tongue across salty lips. On the steps of the cathedral, his father stood in vibrant orange robes that symbolized Grace Aracely, the saint who embodied the Pious God's pillar of penance.

Elazar stared at the unlit pyres with utter conviction in his eyes. No remorse. No sorrow.

A gust of wind brought the heady stench of soot, ash, and embers that permanently lingered in this yard, a tribute from decades of purging evil. Ben faced the pyres, because he was Benat Elazar Asentzio Gallego, and he would take his father's place one day. The Pious God had chosen him to lead.

But I loved Rodrigu. I loved Paxben.

I loved them both so much that it must make me evil, too.

❖❖❖

At eleven years old, Adeluna Andreu had been a soldier for a year.

The dim New Deza tavern was filled to the rafters with patrons—which in this area of Grace Loray's capital meant stream raiders. Their body odor mixed with the humidity, and as Lu ran an oily rag over an empty table close to the rear exit, she held her breath.

"We need to know if the raiders are willing to join the revolution," her mother had instructed as she readied Lu to leave the safe house. *"We've heard rumors they are gathering, but . . ."*

"I don't bring back rumors. I bring back information," Lu had said, parroting the words her parents had taught her. The other children of the revolutionaries had watched her with wide eyes between the stairwell railings, and their fear straightened Lu's spine even now.

She would bring back the right information. She would do whatever her parents needed her to do to send the Argridians back across the ocean, where they belonged.

Raiders bellowed drunkenly at a nearby table and Lu jumped, fingers clenching around the rag. She could feel the ghost of her father's hand on her back, encouraging her to pick up any information she could grab like scraps dropped from the patrons' plates.

One table seemed to be the focus of the room's attention. The other raiders cut their eyes to it every so often, keeping their weapons handy and their postures alert.

Lu eased closer to that table, wiping her rag on the bar along the back wall.

"Which way you leanin'?" asked a pale man with sharp blue eyes, crocodile-skin bracers, and wooden toggles in his blond beard. "The rebels been pesterin' you too, huh?"

"Can't get rid of them," said a round man with golden-brown skin and wide, dark eyes. Lu saw a tattoo on his cheek—two vertical dots over two horizontal ones.

That was a symbol of the four gods worshipped by the Mainland country of Tuncay. And Lu had seen people like the blond man all over New Deza, the center of the territory that the Mecht stream raider syndicate had claimed on Grace Loray.

When settlers first arrived, this empty jungle island, so far from the Mainland, had sat unclaimed by any king or emperor for more than a century. It was a place of possibility and freedom—until Argrid made the island its colony.

Four raider syndicates arose in response, made up of the immigrants from the other countries who called Grace Loray home: the Mechtlands, Tuncay, Emerdon, and Grozda. The separate syndicates protected their own from Argrid with blood and pistols, Lu's parents said—but the revolution was about all the groups on Grace Loray starting their own country together. And until now, the raiders hadn't wanted to unify.

But Lu was looking at people from two of the four syndicates, talking with each other.

Her pulse galloped.

"The Church has burnin's up at their missions. Burn the plants; burn the *people*," the Tuncian was saying. He took a swig from a stein. "I knew Argrid'd go and turn on us, but what's stopping the revolutionaries from overthrowing Argrid and ruling Grace Loray just as bad?"

"I don't trust 'em." The Mecht raider stood and slammed his fist on the table, sending his own stein of ale toppling in a waterfall of amber liquid. "*I'd* rule Grace Loray better than any revolutionaries. Us Mecht raiders should take control!"

The Tuncian flew to his feet. His raiders surged around him, but the Mecht had a crew to match—swords sang out of scabbards, pistols cocked and aimed.

Lu dropped her rag and shot out the back door as insults flew—"Like hell will we let Mecht barbarians take over!"

"Tuncian whore, where are your four gods now?"

The noxious tavern birthed Lu into the midnight streets of New Deza. Every building around her glistened in the humidity, the dozens of rivers that crisscrossed the island polluting the warm air with the staleness of water. But that wasn't what made it hard to breathe—it was terror that choked Lu as she scurried across the cobblestones.

Her father stepped out of the shadows between faint streetlamps. Tom's tricorne hat shielded his eyes, but his smile was sad as his head pivoted from her to the shouting in the tavern.

Lu needed to recount what she'd heard. But all she could say, as a pistol fired within the tavern, was "Why won't they help us stop Argrid, Papa? Don't they want peace?"

With the raider syndicates' numbers, the revolutionaries could finally push Argrid out of Grace Loray. The war would end, and Lu wouldn't have to go on missions, and the children of the other rebels wouldn't have to cower in fear of Argrid deciding they should be cleansed—

Her father chucked her under the chin. "Getting the raiders' support was a weak hope, sweetheart. There are other things we must do to end the war."

Lu's heart sank. "You have another mission for me, don't you?"

Tom's face flashed with remorse. But when he smiled at her, it was proud.

Lu clung to that pride like she clung to hope. Even as

her throat closed. Even as she could already smell the iron tang of blood.

The raiders weren't willing to do what needed to be done to end the war. But she was.

Lu's hands fisted, her fingers gone cold despite the island's heat.

"There's my Lulu-bean." Tom kissed her forehead. "I can always count on you."

❖❖❖

Devereux Bell was thirteen, and that was the only thing about him they didn't say was evil.

They'd had to tie him to a chair to stop him from trying to escape. He could see the scratched hinges on the door from his latest attempt—courtesy of a nail he'd pried from his cot.

Vex hadn't expected it to work. It'd just felt good to let them know he was still trying.

The bell that hung over this mission—*prison*—announced the hour in six sharp tolls. A choir started singing on one of the floors above, voices carrying into the lonely cells. Hymns about honesty and chastity, purity and penance, and other things Vex willed himself to ignore.

The scratched hinges groaned as the door opened. The hall's flickering torchlight filled Vex's cell and he dropped his head, hands balling so the rope over his wrists squealed.

When a jailer stopped in front of him, Vex whipped his head up and spat in the man's face.

The jailer wiped the spittle from his cheek with the sleeve of his black robe. "Another night has done nothing to sway your heart, herexe."

Herexe. Heretic, in proper Argridian. It reminded Vex of where he was, in a hell created by Argrid on Grace Lorayan soil.

Vex bowed his head, greasy hair swinging as he gulped down sour air so humid it was more like drinking than breathing. He knew what would come next. More jailers would gather and pray over him or recite scripture. It'd been that way, every day, for . . .

He couldn't remember. And that was downright funny. Vex chuckled.

"This is humorous to you, herexe?" the jailer pressed.

"I'm young," Vex said, stretching back in the chair. "But you're not. And I'll make it my life's goal to watch this job kill you."

Other cells up and down the hall stirred with rebels and anyone else Argrid had caught with Grace Loray's magic. "You are weak," the jailers' voices carried as they chanted in other cells. "You are evil. You have proven susceptible to the Devil's temptations. May the Pious God cleanse you. May the Pious God save what is left of your soul. You are weak. You are evil. . . ."

Vex's jailer let out a soft sigh of disappointment and started pacing. Vex shook the hair away from his uninjured eye. His wound hadn't bothered him since his imprisonment—what need did he have for two working eyes when the prison's routine was so predictable? But now he felt at a disadvantage, able to follow the jailer only from the left.

The jailer stopped, considering. "The Pious God has a plan for souls that do not yield."

Panic swept from Vex's head to his toes. The look on his face must've said enough.

"Not a pyre." The jailer smiled. From the folds of his robe, he withdrew a leaf in a vial.

A Church jailer, responsible for punishing people caught with the Devil's magic, *had magic*?

But the jailer didn't explain. He opened the vial and tugged Vex's head against the chair. Vex cried out, but his open mouth was a mistake—the jailer shoved the leaf in.

Vex swallowed. He couldn't help it. The bitter leaf broke apart as it slid down his throat.

Every muscle in his body begged for release. Vex screamed, his blood gone to rapids in his veins, tendons in each limb threatening to come apart under his restraints.

"You are weak," the jailer prayed. "You are evil. May the Pious God cleanse you." Words, empty words, and *pain*. "May the Pious God save what is left of your soul."

I

AS NEW DEZA'S mission bell sliced ten consecutive chimes into the steamy morning air, Lu bounced on the toes of her worn buckle shoes. The treaty negotiations between the Democratic Council of Grace Loray and the Argridian delegation would be starting again at the castle, yet here she was, stuck in the market that hugged the western edge of the lake. But one more purchase, and she would have all she needed to stop at the infirmary before heading to the castle to resume listening to the draining debates that had filled the past month.

That thought quelled her anxiety. Perhaps she shouldn't be in *such* a hurry.

"It is not worth more than six galles," Lu told the vendor with a table of wares on the deck of his steamboat. The boat on his right offered coconuts, green bananas, and large, spiky jackfruits from farms throughout the island;

the boat on his left sold handmade leather goods from tanneries in the north. But this vendor sold botanical magic.

The man dropped a crate on the deck, making the vials of plants clink as the boat listed. "There's been a rush on Drooping Fern. Twenty galles."

"A rush," Lu echoed dully. The back of her throat tickled—oh, the irony of haggling over a plant that caused unconsciousness when she could easily fall asleep right here. She'd spent too many nights in a row sitting with Annalisa in the infirmary.

The vendor squinted at her. "You know what Drooping Fern is, don'tcha? One whiff of its smoke could lay a grown man out for hours. If yer looking for help wif sleeping, apothecaries in the nicer parts of town grind up tonics for fancy things like you."

That was precisely why Lu had come to what she suspected was a raider stall. The law-abiding sellers of magic offered either individual plants with mild uses like skin protectants and appetite suppressants, or more dangerous plants diluted and blended into tonics like relaxing potions or strength-enhancing brews. Combining plants into elixirs was delicate, often time-consuming work that only a select few undertook, and it would have been too much hassle for Lu to convince a respectable seller that she knew what she was doing with a raw ingredient as potent as Drooping Fern.

Had Lu any other choice, she would not have been so eager to buy botanical magic from someone who had stolen it out of the island's riverbeds. Riverbeds that belonged, now, to the Grace Lorayan Council.

The threat of a storm made the air harsh, tasting of rank river water with the added bitterness of electricity, of a spark about to light. A cluster of half-dressed girls and boys sauntered past the end of the dock, whistling at sailors and vendors.

Lu tucked stray pieces of black hair into the knot at the back of her head, fighting to regain her composure. "If I wanted to spend fifty galles on a single dose of what the apothecaries mislabel a *sleeping tonic* but is actually weak chamomile tea barely infused with Narcotium Creeper, then yes, I'd be in the more respectable parts of Grace Loray. But I can't imagine you'd survive long in this profession if you made such inquiries of all your customers, *raider*."

Lu might have regretted speaking so rashly, but the vendor clearly had made up his mind about her, too. With the wooden toggles in his long blond beard, his pale skin, and the decorative pieces of fur on his clothing, the vendor was clearly part of the Mecht syndicate that had claimed the area from New Deza down to the southern coast as their "territory" on Grace Loray.

"I wanna make sure you ain't getting in over your head," the vendor said. "I can't go selling to anyone for so little, least of all to someone who might hurt herself wif magic."

"Hurt myself?" Lu whipped out her copy of *Botanical Wonders of the Grace Loray Colony*, the reference book penned by the island's first settlers. "Your bloodshot eyes say you are aware of Narcotium Creeper's hallucinogenic properties— but did you know it can be combined with your overpriced Drooping Fern to create a tonic that—"

—will help my friend get some sleep. She's dying up at the infirmary, and this is the only tonic that might help—

Lu stopped, desperation getting the best of her.

Clusters of Grace Lorayan soldiers moved across the muddied wharf, passing the end of Lu's dock. The next dock over supported oceanworthy craft, and one, a three-masted ship, bellowed a horn of greeting before lowering its gangplank.

An immigrant ship from the Mechtlands, the northernmost country on the Mainland, carried those who fled their country's clan wars for Grace Loray's freedom.

The vendor waited until the soldiers had passed before he surged toward Lu over his table of wares.

"Quiet, girl! You Argridians are too good at gettin' people in trouble."

Offense surged hot into Lu's chest. "I am not Argridian. I am *Grace Lorayan.*"

"What does that even mean, sweetheart? You look Argridian. Maybe Tuncian, too. Means somewhere along the way, you owe yourself to one of those countries, just like I owe myself to distant clans in a war-torn icy wasteland, no matter that we're on this island. Ain't no one *from* Grace Loray. Now, *Argridian*, you gonna buy something from me or not?"

Lu's vision went red.

When Grace Loray had been discovered centuries ago, an uninhabited island with magic in its waterways, this land had stood for possibility.

When immigrants from the Mainland had flocked here, it had stood for freedom.

When, after two hundred years of tentative peace between the five Mainland countries, Argrid had claimed the island for itself and called it Grace Loray after one of its saints, this land had still managed to stand for hope.

And when, after fifty years of calling Grace Loray their colony, Argrid's Church had decided magic made people impure and pushed them away from the Pious God, this island had stood for resistance.

That was what it meant to be Grace Lorayan. To believe in what this island used to be, and what it could be again. A country of unity, of acceptance of its wonders, of *hope*.

Lu was not Tuncian, and she was most certainly *not* Argridian, no matter that her mother's heritage had given the Tuncian golden hue to her brown skin, or that her father's heritage had given her the sharp Argridian angles of her features.

Her parents were Grace Lorayan now. And so was she.

"How can you stand here"—Lu leaned closer to the raider—"and sell magic freely (albeit illegally, as we both know you are a criminal) while dismissing the blood and sacrifices that went into giving you this freedom?"

The raider scoffed. "Oh, and you understand the sacrifices made, little girl? How old were you when the war ended, eh? Nine? Ten?"

"I was twelve when the revolutionaries overthrew Argrid," Lu told him. Her grip tightened on *Botanical Wonders*, the cover worn and soft under her fingers. "But I was Grace Lorayan long before that. And I will be Grace Lorayan long after you realize that the Council provides the protection and security of your syndicate, only better."

The raider syndicates began when Argrid first turned this land into the Grace Loray colony. They protected their own on an island where one oppressively religious country had broken the unspoken rule of peaceful cohabitation. The syndicates worried that Argrid's colonization would mean oppression.

And they were proven right when Argrid's Church started cleansing people.

But the revolutionaries won the war and formed the Council to enact laws, levy taxes, spread jobs and growth and assistance—to help *everyone* on this island. Grace Loray had no need for raider syndicates anymore. It was a country now.

The raider's top lip curled. "You know what? Fine. Take the Drooping Fern for six galles, and get away from my boat."

Lu buried her thoughts, her anger, her sadness. She plunked the money into the vendor's outstretched palm.

"Thank you," she said.

He rolled his eyes. "Just let me carry on my business in peace."

Lu took her purchase and turned down the dock.

No one wanted to interrupt this man's business. The Council merely wanted him, and all raiders, to contribute to Grace Loray as a whole, functioning country, not four separate raider syndicates all vying for resources and warring with each other.

As she slipped the Drooping Fern into her satchel, Lu looked up, cradling her book, her finger worrying at the bullet hole in its cover.

The new Mecht immigrants had gathered near the market stalls. One child knotted her fingers in her mother's petticoat. *Hope,* her wide eyes said. *Wonder.*

Lu's heart ached. What would that family do once their hope wore out? Not everyone who immigrated to this island from the Mainland joined the syndicate that operated for their country of origin. And many raiders had given up their lives of crime once the Council had presented the chance to be Grace Lorayan. The island was alive now in citizens and immigrants with jobs, proper housing, and respectable, productive Grace Lorayan futures.

But almost a century of loyalty to syndicates could not be countered entirely.

Regardless, the Council would bring order. They would complete this peace treaty with Argrid. And Lu looked forward to focusing on something innocent—like botanical magic concoctions.

Lu closed her fingers tighter around *Botanical Wonders*, the mud of the shore pulling at her shoes as the market crowd enveloped her. Her hand dipped back into her satchel, to the vial of Drooping Fern.

But she found another set of callused fingers there already.

"Oh," said the owner of the fingers, his lips curling into a smile. "This isn't *my* satchel."

Instinct got to Lu before she could react in a more proper, ladylike way: she wound her fist and socked the pickpocket in the nose.

The boy snapped his head back with a howl. He cupped his face, one wide, alarmed eye gaping at her, the other covered by an eye patch and a tangle of black hair.

"You hit me!" he cried, sounding honestly shocked.

He wasn't much older than her, his features windbeaten and dark, so he likely wasn't part of the local Mecht syndicate. His clothes were tattered, and the hand he had against his face showed a glossy branded *R* behind the curved *V* and crossed swords of Argrid. The brand Argrid's Church gave to those they captured and *cleansed* of magic use.

As those details swept over Lu, so did dread. She had assaulted someone.

Vendors and customers stared. Two of the soldiers who

had been overseeing the immigrant ship suddenly focused on her.

Lu looked back at the pickpocket. With the sharp points to his features and the russet hue to his brown skin, he looked Argridian, which annoyed her beyond her dread. Her father was Argridian, as were many of the former revolutionaries. Though they had all fought to be accepted as law-abiding Grace Lorayans, others, like this boy, encouraged the hatred most felt toward Argrid.

The boy patted his nose, hands coming away covered in blood. His dress was familiar, the eye patch in particular—

"Devereux Bell?" Lu realized, and the boy's eyebrows vaulted toward his hairline. "You're trying to look like Devereux Bell?"

A notorious raider known the island over by his missing right eye—and the fact that he wasn't part of any raider syndicate. The only moral beacon most raiders had was loyalty to their syndicates. But Devereux Bell's renown came from being one of the few raiders who dared to sail and thieve with only his crew on his side, successfully operating as an unaligned raider longer than anyone, more than a year.

Successful meaning he had neither yielded and joined a syndicate nor been killed by one.

Children mimicked his missing eye when they pretended to be the infamous brigand. The raider syndicates hated him for stealing magic from their territories without paying dues; Grace Loray's Council despised him for much the same reason, but they had never caught him, as he knew the island so well that he could escape even the heaviest pursuits.

The boy smiled, teeth red. "Who wouldn't want to be the most dreaded raider on Grace Loray?"

The soldiers were nearly upon them. The boy hadn't noticed. Lu cut her eyes to them, something the raider was sure to note.

But he continued to smile at her. "Who are you?" he asked.

The soldiers descended on him, each grabbing an arm.

"Causing the lady trouble?" one bellowed.

The boy's smile waned when he looked up at the soldiers. "Oh, take me away," he trilled. "I dare not strive to again see the light of day."

Lu and the soldiers raised three pairs of eyebrows in confusion. But the raider was still smiling pleasantly. Was he mad?

One of the soldiers cleared his throat. "I beg your pardon, miss—he won't bother you again."

Lu nodded absently. The soldiers hauled the boy away, and as well as he could with one eye, the raider winked at her, blood rushing down his face.

A sharp chime carved through the air, bells echoing the time. Ten thirty now.

Lu flexed her sore fingers and cut to the left, where the soldiers headed to the right, toward the castle that sat on a cliff over Lake Regolith. She was even more grateful now for her planned visit to Annalisa in the infirmary before she had to return to the treaty negotiations—it would give her heart time to come out of her throat.

But Lu looked back at the soldiers and the raider one last time, their group shuffling through a crowd of people in sweat-dampened neckerchiefs, salt-rimmed tricorne hats, crocodile-skin ornaments over tattered breeches and mud-soiled hemlines. Most were citizens of this island, good Grace Lorayans staffing Council-approved stalls or receiving shipments of plants from soldiers, working just as hard as the people who had spilled their blood to give them freedom.

This island had come far since Argrid's rule. All the protection and support that the syndicates offered, the Council could provide; all the freedoms that raiders thought they had in disobedience would be so much more sustainable in unity. And boys like that raider, who wasted their days pickpocketing, could become something that would benefit themselves and society.

Grace Loray was a country of second chances. So Lu believed, with all her heart.

✷✷✷

Of all the cities on Grace Loray, New Deza most represented the island's history. The place had started as a

Mecht settlement called Port Visjorn, for a type of white bear sacred to the Mechtlands, until Argrid picked it as their capital and renamed it in their own image. One-story cottages from the original Mecht settlement cowered beside six-story Argridian apartments, wood structures sulked against stone ones. It was chaotic to look at, and more than a little sad to see an obvious reminder of Argrid's fondness for inserting itself where it wasn't wanted.

But there was something comforting about New Deza. As if it said, *Hey, I survived the revolution—you can too, and you're probably far less mangy than I am.*

Which was why Vex had picked it as the port he'd get arrested in. He liked this city.

But he hadn't expected his mark to *hit him*. He'd thought she'd scream or struggle over her bag, enough to rile soldiers into arresting him—but he had not expected the girl to be so goddamn accurate with her fist.

By the time the guards tossed Vex into a communal cell under New Deza's castle, his nose was *still* bleeding. He chose a spot where his uninjured eye could watch the rest of the cell, but since he had to keep his head tipped back, he couldn't get a good look at who was in there with him. He heard voices—gruff, male—and had a moment of panic when he had to choose between not bleeding to death and getting a look at his cellmates.

He should've expected the girl to be aggressive. What had drawn him to her was the bullet hole in the cover of the book she was holding—it was clearly a memento of the revolution. Most people wanted to heal from the war's scars and move on, but here this girl stood, in the middle of the marketplace after having outright *yelled* at a vendor who was clearly a raider, holding a relic of the war in her arms.

Vex had walked up to her and stuck his hand into her satchel. And only realized afterward what an asinine thing that had been to do. The girl had to have endured the worst of the war, if she had mementos with bullet holes in them, and he'd assaulted her without a single thought of what other scars she might have.

Vex closed his eye. Both his crewmates had told him his plan was idiotic. Nayeli had smacked him. Edda had told him that if he got arrested, the soldiers would toss him into a communal cell and someone was bound to recognize him.

"What good'll that do, huh? What if the Council realizes they've got Devereux Bell in custody? You won't have to fear Argrid, because Grace Loray will hang your ass."

Though Argrid may have lost the war with Grace Loray, some Argridian lowlifes still lived on the island. And they thought a stream raider of Argridian ancestry with no syndicate to support him should have some *allegiance* to his country of origin. Or so Vex's blackmailers continued to say every time they threatened to hurt him or his crew unless he stole magic for them. Over, and over, *and over.*

What the hell did Argrid need with magic anyway? Let them find some other raider to harass. Vex was done.

But getting imprisoned was the only way Vex could get the Argridian bullies off his back. He needed time to think of how to lose them for good, so he and his crew could return to their far more noble goal of buying the biggest, nicest, most well-fortified mansion on Grace Loray and staying the hell out of everyone else's way.

Vex sighed and choked on the blood running down the back of his throat.

An hour passed before he could lower his head. Nine other prisoners were in here with him, all raiders, one so old he looked like a pile of dead rags and white hair in the corner. Magic may have been legal now, but stealing and reselling it, passing nonmagic plants as magic ones, or threatening people who refused to pay dues in syndicate territory? Still illegal, though most had to choose between that and starvation. Being an honest sailor cost a lot—your own boat, supplies, *taxes*. It was far easier to join up with a syndicate and let them take care of you in exchange for things you could actually give, like time and loyalty.

In New Deza, most of the raiders were part of the Mechtland syndicate headed by Ingvar Pilkvist. Not one of Vex's favorite people. But then, none of the four raider Heads were.

Vex looked his cellmates over again, but this time, he caught one's eye.

Damn it.

The man had greasy brown hair and tattered clothing over more tattered clothing, held up by a thick crocodile-skin belt. "What're you looking at, Argridian trash?" he snarled.

Of all Vex's shortcomings—not that there were many—the one he hated most was how damn Argridian he looked. He couldn't get rid of the reddish hue to his skin or the sharp angles of his face that made people instantly classify him as *one of the enemy*, even if he'd been as victimized by Argrid as everyone else.

Vex smirked. "Hey, didn't you arrest me a month ago? Aren't you a soldier?"

The inmate's wrist had no brand, but that didn't mean he wasn't a raider. Just meant he hadn't had the pleasure of going through the Church's rehabilitation.

Vex kicked out his legs and leaned against the wall as leisurely as he could manage. He had the attention of the cell, everyone looking at him like he'd be a fun way to pass the time.

The greasy cellmate huffed. "What're they doing now, roundin' up Argridians? Hell, the Council lets those ones from Argrid in for peace talks, so they make up for it by arresting the dregs?" He paused. Squinted. "Wait. Aren't you—"

"You're almost *too* mangy." Vex cut him off. "Like you're trying to fit in. Isn't he?"

A few of the other prisoners moved closer.

"You a soldier?"

"He's here to spy on us! Get our confessions when we think we're alone!"

"I AIN'T NO SOLDIER!" the man bellowed and snatched Vex upright. "Yer Devereux Bell! Saw him make off with a crate of Healica from the docks last month! It's him!"

Shit shit shit.

Nayeli was insufferable enough when she was right. But Edda was worse.

"How long did it take 'em to notice ya? Uh-huh. I thought so. Brilliant plan, Captain."

The rest of the prisoners twisted to Vex. The old man in the corner hadn't moved. Yeah, he was probably dead.

"You're Devereux Bell?" one repeated, disbelieving. "Yer so . . . young."

Another grabbed Vex's arm. "Head Cansu'll have a thing or two to say to you!"

Vex hung his head. *Great.* Not only were raiders from Pilkvist's syndicate in here, there were ones from the Tuncian syndicate too.

The first prisoner tugged on Vex's collar. "No way— Head Pilkvist'll deal with him!"

Vex could use this to his advantage, get the raiders fighting each other. But as he lifted his head to say something nasty about Pilkvist, the door to this wing of cells ground open. Half the prisoners retreated to the back of the cell. Four stayed to surround Vex.

"What's the trouble?" a guard shouted.

Vex held his breath. The prisoners wouldn't be stupid enough to respond, would they?

"It's Devereux Bell!" said the one who'd claimed him for Cansu.

Vex groaned. Apparently, they *were* that stupid.

"It is him!" the greasy man confirmed, shaking Vex.

"They'll take credit for finding me, and it'll become a Council matter," Vex whispered to the greasy man. "You won't have a chance in hell of handing me over to Pilkvist."

The man's mouth dropped open. "I—uh—no, no, it ain't him!"

"You said it was!" Cansu's raider chirped.

Vex gave the first man a look of horror. "*What* did you say about his mother?"

Cansu's raider shoved Vex aside to glare at Pilkvist's raider. "You better shut yer mouth! The Mecht syndicate don't know when to quit!"

The greasy prisoner gaped. "I didn't say nothing!"

But Cansu's raider threw a fist. Chaos caught—legs kicked, knuckles broke open lips.

Vex dropped back onto his bench. Would this be enough

of a distraction to make the guards forget the prisoners' claims? He doubted it.

The cell door flew open and a half dozen guards rushed after the rowdiest prisoners. One made for Vex, looming over him with crossed arms.

"Devereux Bell?" he asked.

Vex looked up, smiled, and batted his eyelashes. "Who?"

The soldier clamped his hand around Vex's throat. Vex choked, and before he could remember any of the defenses Edda had taught him—something about bending the attacker's wrist, or his own wrist, or maybe a thumb?—the soldier ripped off Vex's eye patch.

A sheet of cold swept over Vex's body, pinning him to the bench like a shackle. He knew what the soldier was looking at: two scars in the shape of an X through the socket where his right eye had once been. His own memento of the war.

The soldier grinned. He released Vex but kept the eye patch in one beefy fist.

You are weak came voices that Vex could never get out of his memory. *You are evil.*

He saw the men who had thrown him into the custody of the Church during the war. He saw the smirks on the Argridian soldiers' faces as they delighted in purging Grace Loray's shores of *scum* and *impurities*. He saw the monxes in the holding cells where he'd spent four months, and his throat thickened with the memory of plants, poison, forced into his body. When he finally did pray, it wasn't for redemption—he prayed that if there *was* a Pious God, it would show mercy and let him die.

The eye patch dropped onto the stones at his feet. Vex snatched it up and yanked it on, and the world settled enough that he heard the soldier's order.

"Put him in solitary till we can figure this out. Don't need no more fights."

Vex kept his hand over the patch as if he could weld it to his skin.

This was not an ideal situation.

2

BEN LEANED AGAINST a pavilion in Argrid's capital, Deza, willing himself not to vomit.

He was on land, but the slosh and sway of the water lapping at ships in the wharf in front of him made his stomach spasm. Though the actual cause of his current state was the drink last night, the spicy one the barkeep had called o Golpe de Veludo do Inferno—the Velvet Punch of Hell. It was living up to its name now, in both its aftereffects and the fact that stumbling back to the palace last night, drunk off too many of those damn things, had landed Ben a shift on the Inquisitor patrols this morning.

Overseeing defensors, Church soldiers, as they patrolled inbound ships had once been one of the esteemed responsibilities of the Inquisitors. Now it was a cushy "punishment" for sinful youth.

Ben pinched the bridge of his nose and took a long draw of the salty bay air.

"My patrol stopped a diseased ship from coming into port last week," a voice carried. A duque's son, one of the half dozen royals in the tent behind Ben—though, for the life of him, Ben couldn't remember the boy's name. "Not quite as exciting as finding illegal magic, but it is useful work."

A goblet clinked. The scent of floral wine perfumed the unventilated tent.

Another boy groaned. Ben recognized that particular grumble—it came from a conde, a count, named Claudio, a year younger than Ben, who'd been in a few of Ben's classes on Church etiquette and history growing up.

"I swear," Claudio groaned, "most of these searches are so *boring*."

"They aren't meant to be entertaining," said the duque's son. "They are reparation for our sins."

"We didn't do anything wrong, Sal," Claudio countered. *Salvador*—that was the other boy's name. "So your parents caught us kissing. We're betrothed, for the Pious God's sake. It shouldn't matter."

The rest of the group gasped.

"Calm down," Claudio moaned. "We didn't do anything *that* bad. We aren't real sinners, like the rest of you heathens."

Someone cleared their throat, reminding Claudio that the Crown Prince was one of the aristocrats serving on the

Inquisitor patrol. One of the *heathens*.

Silence fell.

Ben massaged his temples and looked back. Velvet chaises and overstuffed settees created a circle for the handful of nobles, all fancied up in silken breeches, polished gold buttons and beads, lace neckerchiefs and jeweled hair nets—styles befitting a Church service, not a dockside search for magic.

Ben shook his head. He swore he saw at least two of each of these people. *Damn that drink.*

He tugged on his collar, wanting to rip down the pavilion walls and let in a breeze. But it would show the world around and remind the aristocrats here of true problems. With the walls up, the elite could sit in ignorance as too many guards had to stand watch to keep the desperate at bay—the sick who lined up outside of hospitals, the poor who begged along the streets.

"This duty used to mean something," Ben mumbled to no one in particular.

Salvador squinted. "Are you all right, my prince?"

The rest of the Inquisitors leaned forward, some concerned, others intrigued.

Ben met their eyes, fighting a hiccup. But his reputation was no secret.

Even our prince falls for the Devil's temptations, Argridians said. *Poor Prince Benat—he overindulges, he is promiscuous! He serves Inquisitor patrols to cleanse himself. If our divine prince can be so seduced by evil, yet be redeemed, then there is hope for our own brittle souls!*

Ben imagined it all as a clumsy waltz. How many missteps could he take in one direction, back, forward, before people stopped crying *poor Prince Benat* and started crying *heretic*?

Caught drinking—he served a week of Inquisitor patrols, and the Church forgave him, like any other aristocrat. Sex—if rumors spread, another week of patrols, and all was atoned for.

But being caught with Grace Loray's magic? Speaking favorably of certain plants? Unforgivable.

Ben brushed off their concern. "I'm fine," he snapped.

Claudio sat up straighter, his dark eyes flashing. "My parents pray for you at each Church service. They pray that our country is strong enough to undertake the Pious God's most difficult tasks."

Ben lifted an eyebrow. "Are you saying I'm not already strong, Conde?"

Claudio's face went red. He hadn't thought Ben would call him on it. He'd thought he'd sulk off, simpering and shamed that he was as prone to sinning as the rest of them.

"Of course not, my prince," Salvador jumped in, putting his hand on Claudio's knee. "What he means is you're an example to us. Your resilience against evil gives us hope that we, too, can overcome any sin."

"Even being dumb enough to kiss your betrothed in

your father's study," a girl next to Salvador whispered.

Claudio whipped a frilly pillow at her.

Ben faced outside again, enough of a dismissal to get another conversation going. Claudio and Salvador threw themselves into it, doing their best not to look at Ben, still at the door.

In another time, Ben might have joined their conversation, something frivolous about the next Church holiday. He might have joked about what had landed him on this patrol, or given Claudio and Salvador tips on how not to get caught.

But Ben couldn't get Salvador's words out of his head.

Argrid wanted him to be strong, to inspire them; but they wanted him to fall as well, because the Pious God rewarded those who sacrificed—and what bigger sacrifice than to give up an ordained leader?

The Argridian people had cheered for Rodrigu's and Paxben's deaths. They had *begged* for them.

Pious God above, his head hurt.

"Prince Inquisitor? Your presence is needed."

Ben turned. Jakes Rayen stood at attention on the dock, his defensor uniform billowing in the wind, showing the ivory crest of Argrid: the curved *V*, cupped hands for a willingness to lead a life of purity; the *X*, representing crossed swords, to protect that life. Jakes yanked the uniform straight, tugging the collar down, showing the flushed bronze skin along the top of his chest, a few bristly hairs that Ben knew ran all the way down to the soft skin below his stomach.

Ben's body sang with heat that had nothing to do with the warmth of the day. Part of the reason he was glad to have Jakes in his guard was because he looked so good in that uniform.

"Is it a diseased ship, Defensor?" Ben asked, but he knew Jakes wouldn't have come if it were that simple.

Jakes frowned. "No," he said. "Raiders."

A few of the Inquisitors groaned, jealous that Ben's patrol had found what would release him from duty for the rest of the day. He ignored them and followed Jakes out into the sun.

The raider ship was a steam-driven frigate moored at a dock that embodied Argrid's despondency now. The planks were brittle and ill patched, with barnacles and grime sticking to the posts and along the edges. Ben walked behind Jakes up the dock, stepping where he did so as not to fall through the weak wood.

Ben paused at the base of the gangplank. More of his defensors swarmed the deck, some hauling a chest overboard, taking such care that he immediately knew its contents. He almost asked them to lift the lid so he could see the vials of magic inside. Could he still name the plants, as Rodrigu had taught him?

A different memory came, though—vicious monxes, and his own father, smacking him across the mouth when he dared say something positive about magic after Rodrigu's burning. The only thing important to know about magic now was that it was a sin, all of it—and his sins would be wiped away as soon as he gave the necessary speech to the raiders.

"Are you all right?" Jakes asked, falling in step as Ben started up the gangplank. Then, realizing they were within earshot of others, added, "My prince?" Then repeated, louder, "Are you all right, my prince?"

Ben cut him a smile. "Nice recovery, Defensor Rayen. But I'm fine."

"*Fine* here meaning *both drunk and hungover?*" Jakes whispered.

"Oh, Defensor, your flirtation doth take my breath away."

Jakes's eyes flashed wide. "Shh—" But he cut off his shushing and ducked his head. "I don't want to give those vultures"—he motioned back toward the Inquisitors tent—"a reason to cause trouble for you. Even if the nobles of court look down on a royal and a guard, I have to believe the Pious God, at least, can forgive us."

A year as one of Ben's defensors, yet Jakes was still the earnest orphan who had come to Deza desperate to serve the Pious God.

Ben exhaled, almost a growl. "I have enough experience dealing with the gossip and macabre interest of the court. Let them try to spot another heretic in the Gallego family—they will find nothing irredeemable in me. Sex before marriage is a sin, but not a condemnable one."

Jakes bowed his head, and Ben hated the formality of it, though it was necessary. There were some things in Ben's life that crossed political lines more than religious—and the fact that the heir to Argrid had maintained a relationship with a commoner for ten months now was borderline reprehensible.

Argrid allowed a measure of freedom among nobles to choose their own partners—so long as those partners were also of nobility, to not be *unequally yoked*. Elazar hadn't forced Ben to find a partner yet, but if he knew that Ben had given his heart, his soul, and most of his waking thoughts to one of his guards, who until his post as a defensor had been the orphaned son of a merchant, well . . .

Ben did his best not to think about what his father would do. His relationship with Jakes was just one more thing he had to keep staunch control over.

Ben made his voice lighter, but it sounded pained to his ears. "You know I don't think of you as a sin. . . . I mean, I'm not ashamed of us."

Jakes cocked his eyebrows. "You should be. I'm not even a captain, for the Pious God's sake." He smiled.

Ben winked at him and pressed forward to keep from taking Jakes's hand.

The morning heat was slightly more bearable on the ship's deck. Ben tugged at the thick velvet of his sleeves as he neared the line of raiders kneeling amid a circle of defensors. He didn't know how anyone managed to survive the conditions of Grace Loray to leave in the first place. The island was a week's sail away, and supposed to be hotter and more humid than Argrid's sweltering capital.

The salt-seasoned wind did its best to steal Ben's hat, thrashing the feather against his face. Four of the raiders looked Argridian: varying shades of russet and brown skin, black hair, angular features, and dark eyes—not uncommon, since any raider who dared sell magic here tended to blend in. But the last raider, a Mecht, drew Ben in. Blond, pale, and brutish, he embodied everything Ben had heard about that country's clans and their endless, bloody wars.

The Mecht looked up, his glare biting with an intensity that Ben recognized.

The Eye of the Sun flower gave the temporary ability to control fire. Only the Mechts had figured out how to harness its power—and, more, how to make Eye of the Sun permanent. Eye of the Sun warriors became infernos in human skin, living proof that botanical magic was the Devil's work.

Before Ben could ask if this Mecht had undergone the ritual to absorb the flower's abilities, the raider exhaled, smoke streaming from his nostrils.

"Bárbaro diaño," a defensor spat. *Barbarian devil.*

A few others muttered prayers. But Ben smiled.

An Eye of the Sun warrior. Fascinating. The only ones he'd seen before had found themselves dragged back to

Argrid as examples by Church missionaries for refusing to accept the Pious God. Their executions had been through pistols, not flames.

"How is it that an Eye of the Sun warrior has come to be in Argrid?" Ben asked.

"He ain't our regular crew," said one raider, most likely the captain, his voice thick with the Grace Loray accent that trilled his *r's*. "Picked him up as a hired hand in the Mechtlands, not a month ago. If he's the reason for all this, take 'im."

The Mecht snarled to the deck.

It wasn't that simple. The captain knew it. The Mecht knew it. And Ben did, too, his stomach squeezing as the boat rocked.

Jakes walked past him, discreetly brushing his hand along Ben's hip as he joined the other defensors to circle the raiders.

Ben pressed his hands to his chest, wrists together, fingers cupped upward in the stance of prayer. The defensors on deck did the same.

"Our Pious God, show us the ways of purity, honesty, chastity, penance, and charity," Ben prayed. "We thank you for opening heaven to those created of the Devil's hellfire and evil. May you purge our lives of temptations so we may reflect your pillars. Praise the Pious God."

"Praise the Pious God," echoed everyone on deck, save for the raiders.

"You have been detained by the Inquisitors of His Majesty's Church of Argrid," Ben continued, addressing the raiders now. "Unholy items have been found in your possession. If you do not repent, the Church will purify Argrid of your irredeemable soul."

The Church had written this speech so detainees would have fair opportunities to repent. Everyone caught with plants was guilty, and admitting it was the only thing that could save their souls. They would still be rehabilitated for a time, but they wouldn't burn.

Fair had had a different meaning under Ben's uncle—back then, the accused were assumed innocent until the Inquisitors passed a sentence based on careful analysis of Church doctrine. Were their sins rooted in magic? If so, did they have evil plants that had been proven dangerous, or did they have pure magic used for healing or growth?

But Rodrigu's betrayal had destroyed the luxury of assuming people were innocent. After his death, the Church had disbanded the remaining Inquisitors, and those who resisted had been burned as well. The only duty of the Inquisitors that the Church hadn't eliminated was searching inbound ships, but they had bastardized even that duty by giving it to careless aristocrats.

"I won't repent for made-up sins." The captain spoke again. "My crew 'n' I are as innocent as you are, especially with that group from Argrid in Grace Loray right now. You wanna condemn us for stuff yer own men are negotiatin'—"

"Quiet!" a defensor snapped. "You're speaking to the Crown Prince!"

Ben bit his tongue. *You're right,* he wanted to tell the captain. The Church still ordered the arrest of anyone carrying Grace Loray's botanical magic, even when a contingent of Argridian diplomats was negotiating a peace treaty with the island's ruling Council.

When Ben's uncle and cousin had tried to change the Church's stance on magic, Ben had watched them die. Anyone who supported the war had been exterminated as well.

Ben didn't have much hope that a new treaty would change Argrid.

Another of the raiders dared to chuckle. "The Prince. You ain't as good-looking as they say, but maybe if you were the one kneeling . . ."

Jakes punched the man so hard he flipped into the raider beside him. The movement caused a distraction, and just as Ben registered that, the Mecht raider did, too.

The Mecht flew up and slammed his body into Ben. Though his wrists were lashed to his back, that didn't affect the strength of the man's muscles—or his Eye of the Sun.

Ben careened toward the ship's railing, the Mecht shoving with every bit of anger he had repressed as he knelt. The Mecht's face was so close that when he breathed, heat brushed Ben's forehead, his senses flaring with ash and flame.

Memories ruptured in Ben's mind. His uncle and cousin writhing on pyres. *Screams.*

Panic overtook him. His spine connected with the railing, and the Mecht exhaled a stream of fire that Ben dodged instinctively. He jerked to the left, the flames biting over his shoulder, and the Mecht stepped back in surprise. Ben regained enough control to plant his feet and jam his elbow into the Mecht's stomach. The fire cut off as the man let out a strangled cough.

"Bring the barbarian down!" a defensor shouted.

"Hold!" Ben countered. He flung himself up to sit on the railing while hooking his leg behind the Mecht's knees. The Mecht buckled, thrown off balance, and as he dropped, Ben rammed his other leg into the man's stomach. This laid him out across the deck, with the defensors training a dozen different weapons on him.

Ben eased off the railing. "This is the evil forcing him to lash out," he barked. "This man will still have the opportunity to repent, along with the rest of you. I beseech you all: see through the Devil's corruption in your hearts, repent, and choose freedom. Otherwise, you will burn."

Had Ben saved the raider now only to have him die in front of a jeering crowd later?

Though he didn't care. If raiders wanted to burn, let them burn—Argrid offered a way to survive, if those convicted weren't so proud.

Three defensors dragged the Mecht away as others moved toward the rest of the crew.

Ben tugged his hat lower, the deck spinning.

Jakes bumped his shoulder. "This will please your father."

"Why?" Ben honestly wanted an answer. "I did nothing. Ever since the Church did away with any real due process of justice, I have no use."

Jakes's eyes widened. "You're going to be king someday—"

"Of a country built on ashes and fear. I—" *I don't believe magic is evil. And I miss it.*

He'd never be drunk enough to say that. Especially not to Jakes.

A low hum came from Jakes, the lilt of a Church hymn. A tic of his—when he was nervous, or anxious, or thinking too hard about responsibilities that should have been Ben's alone.

"If the treaty with Grace Loray happens," Jakes said, "we won't arrest every sailor from there. Evil won't be as easy to identify. They'll need Inquisitors to judge cases again."

Ben sighed. "Wishful thinking, Defensor."

The Church had ultimate power now. Any treaty with Grace Loray would mean more of this, only on their shores. Patrols. Purity. *Cleansing.*

Did Grace Loray know what was coming for them?

3

THE STABLES PROVIDED the quickest route to the infirmary's Shaking Sickness wing. Lu hurried down the aisle, stirring up dust as she passed drowsy horses flicking their tails in the heat.

A little boy plunged down in front of her, hanging by his knees from a rafter. "Gimme yer plants!"

Lu screeched and dropped the parcel in her arms.

"Oh, Lu!" Teo said. "You're not the nurse."

Her surprise eased into a laugh. "And I have no magic plants for you to steal." She bent to salvage the treat she had picked up on her way here. The filling in one of the pastries had leaked, making the parchment wrappings sticky, the air overly saccharine with sugary coconut against the sweet smell of straw. "Yet you are quite fearsome—tell me, raider, who are you?"

Though she knew—Annalisa's brother always chose to

be the same raider no matter the game.

He isn't the first boy I've encountered today who's pretending to be Devereux Bell, Lu thought.

Teo swung up, grabbed the beam, and plummeted to the ground, surprisingly nimble for a six-year-old boy. "I'm Devereux Bell!" he confirmed, closing one brown eye and stabbing his fist into the air. "Uncatchable! Undefeated! So scary I don't need any syndicate to protect me!"

"Among other things," Lu added, but she smiled at his delight. "As I said, Mr. Bell, I am but a simple lady. May I interest you in a treat instead?"

Teo dove to his knees, leaning over the two small pastries she managed to recover.

"Luuuuu," he sang. "Can I have one?"

"Yes."

"Anna gets the other one?"

"Anna gets the other one."

He moped. "But you don't get any."

Lu passed him the largest pastry. "I already had one, Tee, but you're sweet to worry."

"Teo Casales—oh, there you are!"

The nurse he had been playing with appeared at the stable's door. Her smile struggled to hide her fatigue, brought on from too long tending Grace Loray's needy.

When Annalisa fell too ill to care for herself, she had insisted on staying at the infirmary where she had volunteered, the one that served the impoverished of New Deza.

"If I have good days, I can lend a hand," she'd said.

If it gives you hope, Lu had thought, *then anything.*

"Lu brought treats!" Teo leaped up to show the nurse.

Lu rose and smoothed the hair away from his face, freeing the black strands that stuck to his cheeks as he chomped a mouthful of the chocolate-covered pastry. Whether his skin's red undertones were from childish exertion or an Argridian heritage was almost difficult to tell.

Almost.

"Why don't you go out to the garden?" Lu told him. "I'm sure they could use help."

The nurse nodded when Lu looked up for encouragement.

Teo's eyes widened. "Maybe we'll find magic plants! I know they're only in rivers. But maybe. You never know."

Lu smiled. Garden plants had their uses but didn't offer the guaranteed and unnatural effects of Grace Loray's magic. And even if the infirmary could grow healing magic plants, none had any effect on Shaking Sickness.

Lu had spent enough time looking.

"Maybe," she told him. "The gardeners will appreciate your help regardless."

Teo took off but slammed to a halt and looked back. "Thank you for the treat!" he called, and resumed running, the pastry clutched in both hands.

The nurse's expression tightened. "Have you brought more treatments today?"

Lu's lips straightened. "Soon." She wouldn't be able to

create the sleeping concoction with the ingredients from the market for a few days. "What's the count?"

As if Lu might have forgotten how long Annalisa had been in the hospital. But she always hoped she miscalculated.

"Twelve days, miss." The nurse bit her bottom lip. "We lost another this morning. A man who had been here for"— she wrung her hands—"ten days."

Shaking Sickness was as mysterious as Grace Loray's magic. No treatments, magical or otherwise, affected it; it didn't spread from person to person; some patients suffered with it for years, others were taken in days. The only predictable thing about it was that it manifested in tremors at first, which eventually deteriorated a person's bones until they could no longer stand or walk on their own, confining them to an infirmary bed. Once that happened, it was a matter of days before the disease claimed its victim.

Annalisa had gone into the hospital twelve days ago.

The nurse pushed her wrists together, fingers cupped upward. Lu recognized the motion as one used by followers of Argrid's Church.

Her nose curled. How people could still believe in the Church on Grace Loray, after everything that toxic religion had done here, was beyond Lu.

"I pray for the Casales children," the nurse said, speaking of Annalisa and Teo. "And for your soul as well."

Pray all you like, Lu wanted to tell her. *Your god would never accept my soul.*

"Thank you," Lu said through gritted teeth. She moved past with the remaining pastry. Annalisa would tell her to give it to Teo, but it would make her happy for a moment.

Moments were all they had now.

The war had seemed like a fun game at first: taking school lessons in the lower decks of steamboats and sleeping in blanket-filled cellars, always on the move, waking up in new places and around new people. But the illusion came to a crashing end when Lu was whisked out of a cellar one morning, her mother, Kari, screaming orders to their soldiers, with Tom grasping Lu's hand and yanking her around sprays of cannon debris.

Lu learned that when Tom sang her to sleep at night, it was not always to comfort her—it was to cover the moaning of their soldiers upstairs as others dug bullets out of their limbs. And when people called her mother *Kari the Wave*, it was not because she so loved the ocean, as she told Lu—it was because she had single-handedly led dozens of armed rebels into an Argridian headquarters to steal their battle plans, sunk a fleet of enemy steamboats, rescued prisoners from a damp mission basement, and performed dozens of other acts that kept the rebels afloat.

None of this was a game. The war was a necessity. And as Lu got older, she became a part of that necessity, more than the other children of the rebels. Like Annalisa, they believed in the fun of revolution long after she had learned the truth.

"It'll end soon!" Annalisa had often declared. *"My mother promised."*

My parents have never promised me that, Lu thought. But she would smile, and play with the other children, and use their innocence as fuel when her parents sent her on missions.

But she was with Annalisa for the war's end. Lu tried not to remember the day, for many reasons. It served as a definitive break—before that day lay the war and her duty as a soldier; after it, peace, and her duty to help her parents build a functioning country.

There was no place in her new reality for the children she had grown up alongside. Only months after the revolution's end did Lu's mother ask, *"Why have you not seen Annalisa? You two were once friendly."*

Looking at Annalisa was like reliving the sacrifices of the war. Lu had been glad to have other children to motivate her during it, but it was finished. Annalisa had escaped unscathed. What more could there be?

Sickness, apparently. After Annalisa and Teo's mother, Bianca, died of Shaking Sickness and Annalisa came down with the same illness, Lu had stumbled back into her life. She had kept a war from hurting Annalisa—she would not let something as small and useless as a disease harm her.

Or so she had tried. And still tried.

Now Lu reached Annalisa's wing. The peeling plaster walls surrounded a dozen patients in cots, most of Mecht ancestries thanks to New Deza's position in the declared territory of the Mecht syndicate. Only the impoverished hospitals needed entire wings dedicated to Shaking Sickness—it struck mostly the poor. However Shaking Sickness happened, Annalisa had probably gotten it, like Bianca, from helping those who refused to help themselves. This was Annalisa's reward for being more selfless than Lu could hope to ever be: a death sentence.

Annalisa's dark eyes dropped to the pastry as Lu approached. "You smuggled that past Teo?"

Lu sat next to her, knotting her petticoat and shift around her legs to block bedbugs from making a meal of her. She ignored the stench of the foul bedding, the muffled screams from the surgery wing, and the occasional retching of other patients.

"He insisted you have it," Lu said. "A generous little boy, that one."

Annalisa picked up the pastry. Her arm's splint reached only to her wrist, leaving her hand free. A few bruises decorated her fingers, but Lu forced herself to overlook them.

"Have they finalized the treaty yet?" Annalisa asked.

Lu bit down on her lip. The Council was weeks from approving the treaty, according to Lu's mother. The war might have technically ended five years ago, but this would ensure it was truly, finally, over.

Lu fought the unease that had been filling her since the Argridian diplomats had landed. She didn't want to think of them. She yanked open *Botanical Wonders*, the cover creaking as much as the cot. The descriptions from Grace Loray's earliest explorers stared up at her, along with her own scribblings, and she dove into the distraction.

"Where did we leave off last time? The Digestive plant?"

Annalisa hesitated, her finger coated in the pastry's rum glaze. Her eyes widened and her face broke out with sweat. Violent tremors clacked her teeth, and she dropped the pastry, a shaking spell rushing over her, limbs twitching so she looked as though she was trying to fly.

When it passed, Annalisa pressed her forehead to Lu's arm, tangles of black hair falling around her face. The patients in the other cots didn't glance over, so it wasn't shame that made Annalisa turn away. It could have been pain—though her body occasionally released tremors, her internal organs were in a constant state of convulsion. That was part of why she was covered in blankets despite the heat. She didn't want Teo seeing the yellow and blue marks on her limbs.

"Digestive," Lu tried again. "Purple stems with magenta leaves. Found in the peat bogs of Backswamp. Consuming one stem sates hunger for seven days. Based on that"— Lu forced a smile—"when would be the most inopportune moment to take it?"

Annalisa lifted her head. A vein in her eye had burst,

streaking red around her dark iris.

"Will you never give up?" she asked. Bianca had fled from Argrid when Annalisa was ten, and painful fits let the accent Annalisa had grown up with sneak through.

I fought in the revolution to keep people like you happy, Lu thought. *If I can ease this suffering of yours now, somehow, someway—no, Annalisa. I will not give up.*

"Digestive." Lu nudged her, emphasis heavy on the word.

"Fine, fine." Annalisa let her head fall back against the wall, her dark hair sliding off her neck. "Digestive. If it sates hunger for days, then . . . then the most inopportune moment to take it would be the day before the Mild Season Festival. Think of all that food you'd be unable to eat. Roasted aubergine and pig-tail stew—and, oh, the smoked fish! It would be torment."

"Then we'd best get some for Teo before the next festival. Remember last year? He ate fistfuls of that imported whipped sugar and vomited all over the Emerdian trader's booth. You had to buy two dozen stone rings and a whole stack of Emerdian leather hats because he ruined them."

Annalisa's grin froze. "Lu," she said.

Lu's hands tightened around *Botanical Wonders*, her finger finding its way to the bullet hole in the back cover.

"You've done so much already. But you'll take care of him? Teo, I mean."

"It won't come to that."

"I'm all he has. When I . . . I need to know he'll be cared

for." She took a breath. It did little to steady her voice. "His Argridian heritage is as undeniable as mine. If he ends up on the streets, a child his age, with obvious enemy blood? Even if the Council signs a treaty, prejudices like that don't die. He'll be—"

"Stop." Lu laid a hand on her arm. "He isn't Argridian, and neither are you. You're Grace Lorayan. You'll be cared for, and so will he, and you don't need to worry about such things."

Annalisa's smile matched her bloodshot eyes. "The island is so simple from your view."

"Why shouldn't it be?" Lu's tone was harsher than she'd intended, but words spilled out from behind her unease. "Why shouldn't we be one country working toward the same goal? Why shouldn't we put our past ills behind us? If everyone agreed to live by the laws of this new country, we would have a fresh start. We could stop fearing people with Argridian blood, or assuming those who look Mecht or Tuncian or Grozdan are raiders, because we would *all* be Grace Lorayan. We wouldn't even need a treaty to ensure that Argrid wouldn't attack us again. We would be so strong in our unity that they could never hurt us."

Lu stopped, gasping. Annalisa put a hand on Lu's where she gripped *Botanical Wonders*. The book mocked her now, that she thought a game could distract from the meeting that awaited her.

"Lu," Annalisa started, voice cautious. "Are you—"

"Anna!"

Teo's squeal made the inhabitants of the wing stir. He hurried down the aisle, his black locks once again sticking to his sweaty face, proof he had been out toiling under the sun.

"Anna," he whispered when he got to the foot of her bed, remembering her rule in the infirmary—soft voices. "Did Lu give you the pastry? Isn't it delicious?"

Annalisa grinned. "So delicious, Tee. I doubt I can finish it—help me?"

He crawled up onto the bed, squishing in on her other side, his hands leaving streaks of chocolate syrup on the already-stained bedding.

His eyes brightened when he saw the book on Lu's lap.

"Lu! You brought the magic book!" he cried, and patients groaned at the volume.

Lu grinned and passed it to him. "You'll be better at this game than I am one day."

"I'm good at *every* game."

"Oh, are you?" Annalisa nudged him. "Prove it, little man."

Footsteps thudded toward them on the warped floorboards. Lu rose, expecting nurses rushing to attend a patient, but a lone nurse slid to a stop at the foot of Annalisa's bed.

"Miss Andreu," she gasped. "A runner brought a note

for you, but news is already spreading. They've caught him! He's being held at the castle."

"Caught who?" Teo asked.

Lu took the proffered note as the nurse smiled at him. "A stream raider. But not *any* stream raider—one who isn't with a syndicate. It's—"

Disbelief squeezed Lu's throat, making her voice high as she read the name in her mother's note. "Devereux Bell."

4

NEW DEZA'S CASTLE provided the best view in Grace Loray. Argrid had built it decades ago, high on one of the ebony cliffs that jutted over Lake Regolith. The port spread out beneath it like a sand deposit, cut apart by narrow rivers that infused the air with gray plumes of steamboat fog. Beyond, the view dissolved into the crisscrossing waterways that split Grace Loray into a bedlam of soggy swamps, dense jungle, and ramshackle ports, capped by the dormant volcanic mountains in the northern distance.

Normally, the enchanting view would immobilize Lu. But today she found her anxiety too potent to be cleansed by beauty, and she stopped on the highest of the stone steps that led to the castle's doors, clenching and unclenching her fists.

Beyond these doors, the Argridian negotiation awaited. And now, the fate of Devereux Bell.

Suspicion tasted sour on her tongue. But no—it was a coincidence that her pickpocket had resembled Devereux Bell. The most notorious stream raider on Grace Loray certainly would not have *failed* to rob her, nor was he so young, and—surely it was not him.

On that brittle yet resolute thought, Lu opened the castle doors.

Lu's memories of the months following the revolution were patchy, filled with the haze of relief and joy and the chaos of victory. But a few events had seared into her brain: playing with a little dog in a free and safe New Deza market; Tom fixing her hot chocolate, the decadence of the treat making her want to weep; and walking with her parents and other revolutionaries through this castle entryway with the surrendered Argridians.

The castle's empty entrance hall fanned out with glittering windows on either side of the door, the domed ceiling and marble floor accented by sea-glass chandeliers and gold conch shells. Towering white-and-gold doors marked the courtroom, well oiled so they did not give Lu away as she slipped into the ongoing meeting.

The long room's newly polished black and white tiles glinted in the light of chandeliers. Pillars framed two sections of wooden pews, facing a dais with a table and chairs for the Senior Councilmembers—the four people who oversaw voting and motions of the twenty-four general councilmembers seated in the pews.

One of the Seniors, Lazlo Spits, flipped to a fresh page in his ledger. "Motion passed," he declared, and made a note. The attendees showed little reaction, so the bill must not have been controversial.

General councilmembers and other politicians took up the first several pews, while the rest were open to the public. Lu knew most of the members the same way she knew Annalisa and Bianca, from back when they had all been rebels. In the first row were five people who had fought under Kari at the ambush of an Argridian storehouse on the coast; off to the left sat two women who had snuck into a Church mission with her mother and freed two dozen captive rebels.

Now the women were stoic in linen jackets and airy petticoats, the men in brass-buttoned coats and tricorne hats, all with brown skin and dark features. No one would have guessed that they had once been insurgents.

The Argridian delegates at the front of the room focused on the Seniors. Lu purposefully ignored them and the hum of discomfort that came at their presence. *Enemies,* instinct told her. Years of being taught to fear and fight them could not be quelled.

Lu slipped into one pew and sat, exhausted, next to her father.

Tom smiled. The Argridian red tone of his skin gave him a permanent warmth in his expression, always close to smiling or winking at her.

"We didn't mean to pull you away from Annalisa," he whispered. "I know you only recently rekindled your friendship with her. Madness, that two people can survive a revolution, yet an illness can strike them down within two years of each other."

Bianca may be dead, but Annalisa is still alive, Lu wanted to say. "I don't mind," she lied. But which location would be less miserable—the infirmary, watching her friend suffer, or here, a stone's throw from Argridian diplomats who had slaughtered people on her island? "Especially not for the arrest of an unaligned stream raider. What do we know?"

"Bell was in the dungeon with common criminals, and other raiders betrayed his identity."

"What of his crew?"

Tom shook his head and opened his mouth to say more as Lazlo banged his gavel.

Like everyone around her, Lu sat up straighter. She had proven herself during the revolution by catching details from enemies, as those with something to hide often lowered their guard around children. Her parents relied on her now for the same reason—with her mother as a Senior Councilmember and her father as a general councilmember, they trusted her to hear what might otherwise go unnoticed by officials.

"The next item deviates from our negotiations," Lazlo said, "but if our guests allow, we will sentence a convicted criminal and return to proceedings within the hour."

Lu's mother spun on Lazlo. "The accused has not yet been convicted. We have not even interrogated him," Kari stated.

"What would be the point?" Lazlo consulted his ledger. "Devereux Bell is the suspect in more than three dozen counts of theft from Grace Loray. Witnesses say he stole Variegated Holly from the castle's own stockpiles; he was also seen taking two boatloads of Hemlight, and the vessels as well; he has impersonated members of the Council—I could go on. The syndicates at least hold to certain levels of honor and do not steal from under our watch. An unaligned raider like Devereux Bell deserves no sympathy. We must condemn him immediately and return to the far more pressing matter of the treaty."

"Bell deserves to be aware of the reason for his sentence," Kari countered. "Our Argridian guests do not expect this country to cease proper procedures for them."

One of the Argridian diplomats rose from the front pew. No, not one of them—the only one who mattered. Milo Ibarra, a favored general of the Argridian king.

Lu's body went stiff. When Argrid had stopped calling Grace Loray a colony and started calling it an abomination, Milo had overseen its cleansing. Now here he was, a human embodiment of the war, returned under a banner of peace.

"Of course not, Mrs. Andreu," said Milo, straightening his silken overcoat. "We are most eager to bear witness to how Grace Loray handles stream raiders, in fact."

Kari's brow furrowed. "Handles?"

"Once we finalize this treaty, threats to Grace Loray become threats to Argrid. It is no secret that raiders are a danger." Milo took a step forward, hands behind his back. The chandeliers flared light on his greased black hair, the steep Argridian slants of his jaw and nose. "The raiders deal in the most dangerous botanical magic and spread such hazards to their corresponding Mainland countries."

"All botanical magic trade with the Mainland is now tightly controlled," said Lazlo, shifting in his chair. "The Council has binding trade agreements with Tuncay's empress, Emerdon's queen, and fifteen of the twenty Mechtland clan lords. And, after this treaty is finalized, we will be proud to add Argrid to that list as well."

Milo's expression was sardonic. The Argridian treaty had not yet touched on what magic, if any, would be approved for legal sale in Argrid.

"Treaties between governments will not stop criminals, Senior," Milo responded. "The stream raiders' threats extend beyond magic trade. They encourage disunity by holding to their countries of origin—Emerdon, Tuncay, the Mechtlands, and Grozda—and funneling impoverished immigrants between nations, which spreads diseases due to their destitution and unsanitary lifestyles. I understand you have tolerated them because of an ill-made promise during the war, but promises should not excuse crimes."

Those around Lu shifted awkwardly, shame pinking

their cheeks for the pestilence of stream raiders. But Lu was overcome with rage at Milo for ignoring why they had made a promise to the raiders at all.

"If you mean to change a way of life, you must offer a benefit the old way could not," Lu's mother had said. *"Something more valuable, or that would solve a more immediate problem."*

Over the course of the eight-year war, Kari and the other leaders had tried numerous times to get the raiders to join forces with them. Neither Argrid nor the rebels had numbers on their side—Argrid because they were used to enacting obedience through the threat of damnation, and the rebels because they were only made up of those rare people willing to risk their lives for freedom.

But toward the end, Argrid overtook a rebel headquarters. The revolution leaders, finding their safe house and the assets therein compromised, grew desperate. They didn't have the numbers to retake the safe house from the majority of Argrid's forces—and so Kari and a handful of revolutionaries told the stream raiders that if they helped end the war, they would have a place in the new government. The raiders, eager to have unmatched control over Grace Loray, agreed.

Despite months of negotiations after the war, the raider syndicates scoffed at the proposed system of laws, demanded anarchy, and retreated to their declared territories when they did not get their way.

Unity with the raiders should have happened. Without

laws keeping them in check, they were what Milo said: a constant source of danger and threat, a drain on the economy.

"That promise was not ill made," Lu's mother said. Lu smiled—trust Kari to always advocate for Grace Loray's best interests. "The raiders' support allowed peace to come between Grace Loray and Argrid. Their existence speaks to cultural differences we should embrace, and we will treat raiders, including Devereux Bell, as the worthy citizens they are."

Milo scoffed. "The only thing criminals like Devereux Bell are worthy of is death, Mrs. Andreu. I have been under the impression that you wanted us to see Grace Loray as a functioning nation, not as an embarrassment."

Lu's hands fisted around the strap of her satchel, her mind echoing with a childlike plea.

Leave, please leave, get off my island, leave us in peace—

Kari's golden-brown skin paled, the only sign of her displeasure, and she didn't engage Milo further. The rest of the Seniors remained silent, whether in fear or shame Lu wasn't sure.

A moment, and Kari waved to a soldier standing by a door behind the dais.

"Bring in Bell," she said in the voice that reminded everyone of her moniker during the revolution: the Wave. She could break with unstoppable fervor and be completely unmoved, no matter the opposition.

The mood of the courtroom changed. People rose,

angling to see the doorway. Lu couldn't help but think of Teo, how he would have reacted to Devereux's entrance with the same desperate curiosity.

The soldier opened the door. Another entered, blocking the man behind him, trailed by a final soldier. Two more followed—which felt extreme for the guarding of one man, chained at the wrists and ankles with irons that rattled, but Devereux Bell's notoriety made them cautious.

The men stopped in front of the Seniors, the soldiers blocking Devereux from view of the room. A waist-high beam with an iron loop at the top had been set into the floor before the dais. One soldier linked Devereux's wrist manacle to the post, and the soldiers stepped to the side.

Devereux Bell, his back to the room, stood like a man well aware of the power he wielded, leaning his weight casually on one leg. He was wiry but tall, and his dress was what one would expect of a raider: threadbare pants, knee-high boots, his shirtsleeves rolled to the elbows, in varying shades of black and speckled with patches and stains. Unlike most men, he did not wear his hair tied back—the black strands hung loose to his shoulders.

Collecting botanical magic from Grace Loray was not without its dangers—most plants grew deep in the riverbeds, and only explosives could dislodge the rarest specimens. This resulted in wounds like the one Devereux was known for: his missing right eye. He pivoted his head to the left, a glance over his shoulder, but all Lu could see were the muscles in his jaw. Was he smiling?

He looked straight ahead again.

Kari gaped. Even Lazlo looked flustered, his eyes shooting once to Milo, who stood close enough that he could make his voice heard should he wish to weigh in.

Lu realized how hazardous this trial would be. Milo would be satisfied only if the Council proved its authority over raiders by condemning Devereux Bell to death—a sentence the Council had not yet passed on anyone. What would it mean to the Council's tentative peace with the syndicates if their first death sentence was a raider? But would it come to that?

"Devereux Bell—" Lazlo began.

"Vex," Devereux countered.

Lazlo gave a look that said he was not, despite how appropriate it might be, going to call the raider *Vex*.

Lu shifted. Exhaustion from so many stresses in one day made her falter. She steadied herself on her father's arm. Tom gave her a questioning look, but she shook her head.

"You are the suspected perpetrator of forty-two counts of piracy against the Grace Loray Republic, ranging from black-market trades to theft," Lazlo began. "How do you plead?"

Devereux snorted. "Only forty-two official counts? Damn, I just lost a bet."

Lu's grip on her father's arm tightened. That voice. The flippancy.

It was Kari who asked, "Only forty-two? How many should we have on record?"

"That's a loaded question. Might as well ask how long I want to be imprisoned. Though, if it means getting to see such a fine specimen again, I might confess everything."

Lazlo banged his fist on the table. "How dare you speak so about a woman of such esteem!"

"Presumptuous, sir. I meant you." Devereux made a crude gesture with his arm and fist.

Kari dipped her head while the rest of the Seniors dissolved into outrage. Lazlo jabbed a finger at Devereux but said nothing; his jowls swung, but again, he said nothing; spit flew, and still, he could not think of a retort to the raider's insinuation.

Lu's exhaustion crept over her in a horrifyingly unexpected way.

An effervescent sensation started in her belly, and before she could gather her wits enough to reason that it was *not* funny, seeing Lazlo so flustered—she laughed.

All attention swung to her, four rows from the front with her hands over her mouth.

Devereux turned at long last, searching the crowd for the laugher. He didn't find her straightaway, allowing Lu time to study him, and her suspicions were confirmed.

Devereux Bell had tried—and failed—to pick her pocket that morning.

She knew now what had troubled the Seniors. The

crimes Devereux had committed, the way he had spent the past year escaping justice—everyone had expected to find a weathered outlaw, but this man couldn't have been older than twenty.

Kari put her hand on Lazlo's arm to pull his attention away from Devereux—and Lu, now. The motion woke Lu out of her trance, and the weight of her actions settled on her.

The Seniors regrouped around her mother. The rest of the room expressed their disdain for Lu's outburst with snide expressions—none more so than Milo.

Lu willed herself to look at him. His scowl mirrored those around him, but it held disgust. To him, she was a lady who had breached propriety. Nothing more, nothing less.

Lu exhaled, but relief didn't come. She glanced at Tom, who stared at Devereux.

"Father?" she whispered.

He shook his head and clasped her fingers. "Too much excitement for you, Lulu-bean?"

He hadn't called her that in five years, since the revolution. Since he had entrusted her with special missions that not even Kari had known of, and tapped her nose with a smile.

"You're my Lulu-bean—you can keep a secret so well it's as if you've taken a magic plant that sealed your lips. I trust you. You can do this."

All the blood in Lu's cheeks rushed for her heart. "Are you all right?"

Tom nodded before she finished the question.

Was her father unsettled because he shared an ancestry with Devereux? She had been annoyed by it in the marketplace too, that someone of Argridian descent would encourage prejudices that were so difficult for people like her father to overcome.

When Lu faced the front again, she found Devereux watching her.

She glared back at him, and he started in response.

"Our law states that crimes such as those committed by Devereux Bell are punishable by death," Lazlo declared. "I move for death by hanging. Is there a second?"

✥✥✥

Vex grinned. The girl was here. She wore the same nondescript gown from their encounter this morning, but she held herself differently, shoulders hard and chin level as if she one day intended to rule something.

But Vex's nose still smarted where she'd hit him. And she'd laughed at his joke—then glared at him. Not an annoyed glare like the ones he'd received from Nayeli and Edda more times than he could count. One that said, in no uncertain terms, *murder*.

She was getting more and more interesting by the second.

One of the Seniors—Lazlo, a guard had said—was talking again.

". . . death by hanging. Is there a second?"

Vex spun forward. *What? Already?*

"Seconded!" a councilmember called from somewhere behind him.

Another of the Seniors leaned forward. "Are we certain that this is Devereux Bell?"

Vex sighed. "It's my hair, isn't it? People always expect me to be blond."

The courtroom doors bounced off the walls and a different voice intervened. "It's him."

Vex shifted with the rest of the room to look at the new guest: Ingvar Pilkvist, Head of the raider syndicate that called New Deza its home port.

Pilkvist had the pale skin of those with Mecht ancestry, but if his hair had been Mecht blond, that had been years ago. Wooden beads decorated the gray clumps that hung to his lower back, and he wore a vest of crocodile skin holding dozens of knives, but the rest of his image countered the usual undertakings of stream raider syndicates—stealing magic, selling the most dangerous plants, murdering whoever got in their way. Pilkvist's was the face that first drew people in, a caring grandfather who promised fairness and security.

Pilkvist stopped at the front of the room. He'd brought three lackeys with him, all glowering at Vex. One had an odd-looking scarf of crocodile skin looped around his neck—

Shit. Not a scarf. An actual crocodile hatchling hissed on the raider's shoulder. Vex swallowed and forced himself to smile at Pilkvist.

"Milkfist! It's been too long. When did we last see each other—a shipment of Aerated Blossoms was involved, aye? I've been meaning to pay you back for it."

Pilkvist ignored him, but Vex caught a flush along his cheekbones. "I move that you turn Devereux Bell over to me," Pilkvist said.

"The Council is not in the business of giving prisoners to the raider syndicates, Head Pilkvist," one of the Seniors said.

"The Council isn't in the business of keeping its promises either." Pilkvist heaved forward, and the Council soldiers matched him. Pilkvist's raiders grasped their weapons.

"Head Pilkvist," another Senior tried. "Please—"

"No," Pilkvist said. "When you dragged my syndicate into Grace Loray's revolution, you promised we'd have a say in our government. Five years, and all you've done is ignore our demands and steal our money. Stop pretending we're not separate."

One of the Seniors, a man with a blotchy face, huffed. "We have stolen nothing from criminals."

"The Mainland trade. You take syndicate money with every boat of magic you sell."

"A Council-run trade assures that any funds from botanical magic benefit the people of Grace Loray, not just the individual syndicates," countered the other Senior—a woman, who looked calmer than the blotchy man. "The magic trade should have been legal and government controlled from the beginning of Grace Loray's founding. We have done nothing but restructure this island into a functioning—"

"Functioning. Sure. You call lettin' the syndicates fester into poverty *functioning?* Whaddya expect us to do now that the Council controls the trade with the Mainland? Least you can give me is rightful say over Devereux Bell. He's a raider, and he's *mine* to deal with, Andreu."

Wait. Andreu, as in *Kari Andreu?* The infamous Kari the Wave, who'd come up with the guerrilla-style attacks that had chipped away at Argrid's more formal-style military during the revolution? Kari the Wave, who had personally planned more than a dozen of the rebels' moves against Argrid—taking storehouses, sinking ships, freeing people in missions—and *hadn't lost any* of the attacks she'd led? *That* Andreu?

This could be fun.

"Go screw a smokestack, Silkcyst," Vex cut in.

Unlike Lazlo, Pilkvist didn't blubber—he backhanded Vex across the face. *Ow.*

"Head Pilkvist!" said Andreu. "You will not bring violence into our—"

"This urchin," Pilkvist cut her off, and when Vex righted himself, a fist met him in the gut, "is an insult to every syndicate. He is a pest who must be eradicated"—Vex recovered from the second blow and Pilkvist readied for a third—"and he is mine to eradicate!"

Andreu appeared beside Pilkvist and grabbed his arm, her face red, her cream-colored skirt slapping Vex's boots. Behind her, soldiers moved in, weapons drawn. Pilkvist's raiders lurched forward a beat, and the crocodile around the one's neck clacked its jaw.

Vex tasted blood. He had to focus on the pain to keep from smiling—it'd been way too easy to turn the room upside down.

"This is how you allow trials to operate?" came a voice from the front row of pews.

Vex sought it out—a councilmember with slick black hair and a glossy overcoat. One of the Argridian diplomats.

A completely unwelcome gush of terror made Vex croak.

Andreu released Pilkvist. "I move we reconvene in one week," she said to the other Seniors, "to allow time for deliberation."

Relief spiraled through Vex. A week was better than nothing.

He looked over the crowd, found the girl again, and winked at her.

One of Pilkvist's raiders pulled out a pistol and clocked him on the base of his skull.

✦✦✦

Devereux dropped to the tiles, his manacled hands keeping his body dangling from the post.

Head Pilkvist gave a tight bow. "A pleasure doing

business with you, Kari the Wave."

Kari's nostrils flared as though she wanted to say more, but she held back. The raiders left, trailed by the soft hissing of the small crocodile.

Milo stood. "You allowed raiders to treat you with disrespect—and ones from the Mecht syndicate at that? They are barbarians! Have you any control over your country?"

The courtroom drew a breath, and Lu thought that, if they could, everyone present would burrow into the tiled floor.

Kari whirled on him. "You will not pretend to understand the operation of this island."

It was a rebuff, that Argrid had misunderstood their colony when they had controlled it.

Milo waved his hands. "We have accepted that Grace Loray holds to different standards of purity than we do, but surely your government has a registry of immigrants? Use that to begin restraining those who may have joined a syndicate and ensure that they cannot do harm to this government—or ours by extension, once we finalize this peace treaty. If you—"

Milo stopped, turning his head as he surveyed the slack-jawed Council.

"Oh," he breathed. "You *don't* have a registry?"

"It would be better to invite the raider Heads to a discussion and foster peace with them," Kari said, but Milo didn't acknowledge her.

"An addendum to our treaty." He waved Lazlo to write and Lazlo, dumbstruck, grabbed his pen. "Argrid demands Grace Loray eradicate stream raiders and the threat they pose to both our countries, first by condemning this Devereux Bell outlaw to death."

"Eradicate the stream raiders?" Kari echoed, nausea visible on her face. "They are citizens of Grace Loray. They are numerous and well armed, and as Pilkvist mentioned, they already resent the Council for restructuring Mainland trade. What you are suggesting will lead to civil war."

"And what you have tolerated is mutiny. Without definitive action to prove that Grace Loray values order over crime, Argrid cannot, in good conscience, link itself to this island via a treaty."

That speared Lu in the chest.

Lazlo called for a discussion on Bell's sentence and Milo's proposition. Councilmembers shouted objections; others cried agreement. Milo didn't move from where he stood in front of the Seniors, as though each opinion needed to go through his ears first.

Dread crept over Lu, darkening her vision, but she sucked in a breath and shook her head to clear it. Argrid had sought to cleanse the island and now demanded that Grace Loray continue their work.

It didn't matter what Milo wanted, or how they had gotten here. Lu might not have agreed with the syndicates, but they surely did not deserve to be *eradicated*. The Council would negotiate a better resolution, and the Argridians would leave. There would be no need for rash action or—forbid it—civil war with the raiders.

Lu was a lady now, a politician like her parents, fighting with her words and diplomacy. She would never again have to fight for Grace Loray in any other way.

5

THE VIEW FROM Elazar's office had been breathtaking once. The cathedrals had stood tall, beacons for the lost, and the Inquisitors' university headquarters had gleamed. Shops had boasted lavish imports from neighboring countries: pungent spices from western Tuncay; polished gems and intricate weaponry from Grozda; extravagant leather wardrobes brought across the northern valleys from Emerdon; furs and wooden baubles from the distant, war-torn Mechtlands. Citizens had looked up at the palace, hands lifted in thanks to the Pious God for blessing Argrid with a holy king who had brought them prosperity.

Their fields and forests offered exports of cash crops and lumber. Their coast gave them abundant hauls of sea life and easy access to trade. Ben had been a child, but he had soaked up these lessons from proud monxes, excited to be part of such a prosperous, anointed country.

But Argrid's military had never required many of their funds before—so when it became clear that the threat of burnings was not enough to keep the Grace Lorayan colonists in line, Elazar had been forced to reallocate the funds from Argrid's exports. Buildings crumbled into disrepair; shops were boarded up; hunger and poverty struck the outlying villages and flooded Deza's poorer districts. Twists of smoke rose where infected belongings had been burned to prevent the spread of disease.

As Ben stood at the window the afternoon following his Inquisitor patrol, he watched passing citizens lift cupped hands in reverence to the holy Eminence King who guided them through this struggle.

His breath streaked across the glass. Sometimes he envied Grace Loray's democracy. Better to have a country of people who participated in their ruling rather than people who took everything from their king as truth.

Such unwavering belief, however, was the reason Argrid had never needed a strong military before the revolution. The threat of hell was enough to thwart any dissent.

The door to Elazar's office opened and shut. Ben's awareness piqued, but he didn't turn.

A chair slid out. "You disappoint me, Benat."

Ben faced his father. Elazar sat at a desk with bookshelves behind him displaying Church tomes and statues of the Graces. Grace Aracely, for the Pious God's pillar of penance; Grace Loray, for the pillar of purity and the evangelist who centuries ago began the mission to purify what became his namesake island; and more.

The oddments gave Elazar consequence, even when he wore a silk shirt, cravat, and breeches instead of his ceremonial robes. Though Ben couldn't remember his father ever being anything less than imposing. His black hair had just given way to gray, and his smooth brown skin merely looked more lived-in than Ben's finer features. Years of bearing the title name of Elazar, of balancing the politics of kingship with the religious guidance of Eminence, fending off evil and uprisings—none of that had worn on Ben's father. Everything he'd done, he'd done at the bidding of the Pious God. There was no better reason.

No safer excuse.

"How so?" Ben put the desk between them, hands behind his back.

Poor Prince Benat, people would say once they heard that his father had, yet again, summoned him to berate him. And after an Inquisitor patrol, no less.

Elazar lifted a dark eyebrow. "You showed up at your patrol hungover. You allowed the condemned to speak, which is the reason they felt free to attack you. Things could have ended in disaster had your defensors not been able to restrain the raider."

"With all due respect, that wasn't—"

"And shortly after you stumbled back last night in a fog, the ambassadors from the Mechtlands left." Elazar rose, knuckles on the tabletop. Ben's father hadn't beaten him in years, yet Ben fought an instinctive recoil. "I needed you here, helping me convince the ambassadors to give Argrid the loan that will repair our military from the Grace Loray disaster. The world is changing. It is not enough to sway people's souls with truth; missionaries are only as successful as the armies behind them. You abandoned your country for your own desires."

"I was there for the emissaries of the Emerdian queen," Ben returned. "And the representatives from Grozda, and the empress's viceroys from Tuncay. I was there when they scoffed behind our backs that Argrid was broken and unable to hold on to our assets. How would it have been different with the Mechts? Clan wars deplete their own country's assets—I couldn't watch them sneer at us all the same."

Elazar lifted a hand, silencing him, and Ben flinched. Elazar didn't react.

"I've allowed your . . . lapses because I hoped you would find the Pious God's path and become a beacon of healing to our people on your own," Elazar said. "But I was wrong to assume you would not need the same guidance as others to reach a state of purity. I am sorry. I have failed you as your Eminence."

"Fantastic. I suppose I should— Wait. What?"

Ben had had this meeting with Elazar at least a half dozen times. Elazar reprimanded him, Ben argued, and Elazar would sentence him to Inquisitor patrols or a month in a monastery. Their people rejoiced as Ben served out his sentences. Their prince making reparations encouraged them to atone for their own sins.

Elazar's apology stopped Ben cold.

"Much of your rebellion stems from a lack of responsibility," Elazar said. "It is time I pass on to you some of the duty you will one day hold in my place. Despite their barbaric tendencies, the Mechts have agreed to assist us. With that aid, I give you the task of developing a cure for the diseases plaguing Argrid."

Ben's anxiety turned to outright dread. "*The* diseases? All of them?"

"Yes. Influenza. Boils. But particularly Shaking Sickness."

Shaking Sickness. A disease with no known cause or cure, one that pulled people apart from the inside.

See? the devout said. *Evil will rip you apart.*

"The contingent in Grace Loray is close to finalizing the peace treaty." Elazar's voice was guarded. "The Grace Lorayan uprising came because they wanted independence. They have independence now—but still, we fear for them. They cling to the Devil's ways. We have the chance to approach them with cleansing again, in a new way:

"I want you to develop a healing potion with Grace Loray's botanical magic."

Ben gawked. Memories raced through his mind, of his uncle teaching him about Grace Loray's wonders, of him and Paxben reciting the names of plants that were evil.

The rebels on Grace Loray had revolted due to evil magic tainting their minds and souls. So Elazar said, and so Ben had believed, until *all* magic became evil and Elazar had overseen the burning of his brother and nephew without hesitation.

Then Ben felt the smallest seed of understanding for the Grace Loray rebels. For their freedom. For their staunch connection to magic when his own world became so restrained.

Had Elazar truly just said he wanted Ben to use magic? Was this a dream?

"How," Ben started, his mouth tasting of ash, "will using their evil cleanse them of that evil? And why me? Why would I be able to do anything?"

Elazar's eyes narrowed. "You question the task that the Pious God has outlined for you?"

Ben's breath caught, his body tensing as it had during so many lessons after Rodrigu had burned and the Inquisitors had been stripped of any real power. *"Everyone must understand the importance of the Pious God's pillars, especially the pillar of purity,"* Elazar had told the monxes who tutored Ben in his father's stead. *"Treat him as any other pupil. Show no restraint. He must learn what is right."*

"No," Ben stammered. "I do not question you. I—I just—"

A smile carved through Elazar's disdain. "As Eminence,

you will face many things that teeter between sin and salvation. Questioning your tasks is wise, but know your limits, Benat."

Ben's heart skittered.

"Before the war with Grace Loray escalated," Elazar continued, "the Church allowed healing magic. You studied it once, and as my ordained heir you are protected from its temptations. Use the University to develop a cure for the diseases plaguing our country."

Elazar came out from behind his desk. Ben stood his ground, thinking over everything he'd done or said—but nothing was worthy of a beating.

"If you can cure the Pious God's curse with the thing Argrid fears," Elazar said, "you will show Grace Loray that the Pious God accepts their magic. The world will see that we are capable of adapting. I will ease the transition in the Church and government, but you will win our people by alleviating their ills. I admitted that I failed you, and I admit now that—"

"Father." Ben cut him off. He couldn't hear more. Elazar had said too many impossible things already.

Every year, on the holiday honoring the Pious God's pillar of chastity, people made pilgrimages to cemeteries. The day celebrated abstaining from impurities, living *without*— but it had also become a day to remember those the Pious God had removed from the earth.

Elazar and Ben would trek to the royal cemetery, where Ben's mother was entombed alongside dozens of Gallegos in sealed stone coffins. In the stillness of the crypt, Elazar would choke back tears as he told of how Ben's mother had died in childbirth with Ben's younger sister. How Elazar's parents had died before that, from a plague; and how Elazar's two older brothers had died as teenagers, passing the burdens of the title-name Elazar to Ben's father and Rodrigu to Paxben's father.

"*Ours is a family of tragedy,*" Elazar would say. "*The Pious God ordained us in blood.*"

Ben had always believed his family were servants to a higher calling—until he'd watched Rodrigu and Paxben burn. For all his power, Elazar hadn't saved his brother and nephew. *Hadn't,* not *couldn't,* a distinction that Ben had begun to see more and more: The Church hadn't given any of the people they burned on Grace Loray a chance. They hadn't explained why magic was suddenly considered the Devil's work. They hadn't tried to save the Inquisitors when the public demanded their power be stripped.

Ben had been faking prayers since he'd watched his uncle and cousin burn. He sinned obviously so those who looked for weakness didn't have to look too hard. He knew *exactly* where the line was between irredeemable and forgiven, and he'd spent so long living within these boundaries that he'd forgotten how confined he was by the Church's dogma.

But here his father stood, telling Ben his country needed him to work with magic again.

A childlike part of Ben cried out before he could reason through it.

"All right," Ben said. "I'll do it, Father."

By the time Ben got to the University, it was late afternoon. A half dozen defensors accompanied him, including Jakes, who carried the chest from the raider ship—once contraband, now supplies.

They left the carriage and horses in the stables outside the University complex. Ben was barely aware of their progress, unable to take his eyes off the chest.

The initial high of being commanded to work with magic again had worn off as soon as Ben had left his father's study. Ben had to be drunk, or passed out in a tavern, dreaming of things that *could not* happen. Had Elazar truly changed his stance on magic? Argrid desperately needed assistance—looking at the city confirmed that no amount of praying helped.

Maybe Elazar had changed. Maybe the treaty with Grace Loray would bring acceptance.

Thinking it felt impossible.

Ben trailed two of the defensors through the gates that opened into the University complex, the pale bricks of the perimeter wall worn from centuries of standing. His eyes tore from the chest to latch onto the sign arching over the entrance. Protesters had scratched through it years ago, but Ben could see the words as though they were etched in his skin.

Universidade Rodrigu.

Rodrigu, a family name given to the second son of the king, as the name Elazar was given to the first son. The first son was destined to be the king and head of the Church; the second, when there was one, became the keeper of knowledge and the High Inquisitor.

After Rodrigu's execution, defensors had purged the University of anything associated with magic: all copies of the text he had used, *Botanical Wonders of the Grace Loray Colony*; his research; his stores of plants. Ben hadn't been here since just after Rodrigu's and Paxben's deaths, but the University looked like the rest of Deza now: decrepit.

Weeds streamed out along the courtyard's walkways. Trees and shrubs, long in need of trimming, nodded in the wind. The main building, a huge ivory structure with dozens of branching wings, was covered with graffiti of the Church symbol in broad strokes.

"Set up a patrol," Ben said as his defensors opened the doors for him. He stepped inside, his eyes lifting to the ceiling, where a glass dome let in hazy light. "Summon the University's overseer. I'll need to speak with him to find the laboratory and other supplies."

Men broke off to do his bidding, but Ben was already walking toward a door on the left. He remembered the

University as well as he remembered every plant Rodrigu had taught him. All the information sat in his mind, locked in a box covered in ashes—but he wouldn't let anyone know he remembered these sinful things so well. Not yet.

He heaved his shoulder against the door, knowing he'd find the laboratory behind it.

Tall windows lit an oak table littered with empty vials, mortars and pestles, shattered glass, and broken clamps, all beneath a film of dust and cobwebs. The delicate bouquet of plants still fragranced the air, earthy and bitter, the smell of long nights and his uncle's laugh and Paxben crossing his eyes at him through the warped glass of a beaker.

Ben felt as if he'd been in the room as recently as yesterday. Rodrigu had stood in that corner, grinding plants; Paxben had sat at the table, kicking his legs on the stool; Inquisitors had scurried around the room, making tonics, filing reports.

"They're testing plants," Rodrigu had said.

Paxben had scrunched his nose in disbelief. *"How do you test something for evil?"*

"The tests reveal the effect. If the effect causes harm, it is evil."

Jakes entered the room and dropped the chest onto the table. Ben jumped.

None of the other defensors had followed Jakes in, leaving them encased in sunlight, surrounded by ruin.

Elazar had planned the delegation to Grace Loray a year in advance—how long had he been planning Ben's assignment? He knew how much Ben had loved his uncle and cousin, so Elazar had to know how much this—*magic*—meant to Ben. Did he want to free Ben from living a lie, and bring acceptance to Argrid, and reignite peace with Grace Loray?

"Have you heard anything?" Ben asked Jakes. "Have any of the defensors . . . have there been rumors of magic? Are others meant to report my actions?"

Elazar had briefed Ben's defensors on the delicate nature of this project before they'd left for the University. But Ben had long ago accepted that members of his personal guard would always be more loyal to the king than to him.

Jakes gave Ben a sympathetic smile. "I hadn't heard anything until today."

"Would you have, though?" Ben nodded toward the rest of the University. "My whole guard knows we're involved. If something is afoot, they'd keep us both ignorant."

Jakes frowned. "What do you think is happening?"

Ben shrugged, feigning nonchalance. "I'm afraid, I suppose." He flicked a broken piece of glass across the table. "All who dabble in magic end up beyond reach. As you said."

"The king and the Pious God ordained this task. The Devil's touch will not corrupt you."

Ben laughed, dry and sad. "You put too much faith in me, Jakes."

And I don't know how much further I would fall without you.

Ben gasped. He wanted to pour out the unworthiness

that gnawed at him whenever they went to services and he watched Jakes sing hymns, his eyes closed in reverence. That was what had first drawn Ben to him—Jakes embodied the devotion Ben hadn't felt in years.

Jakes took Ben's arm, his face alive with piety.

"You know I came to Deza after my family died. My parents of influenza. My sister and her children of Shaking Sickness. But I really left because I couldn't—" Jakes stopped. "My parents and sister believed in this country. In making it better. So I left to serve Argrid. The Pious God has me in your service as he has you in his service—because we are the best tools for his tasks."

Ben parted his lips. He wanted to tell Jakes the truth. That a cure that could have saved his family wasn't in a blessing from an absent God—it was in that chest. Ben had watched Rodrigu perform a test in this room, using botanical magic to cure a patient of influenza within a day. Prayer might work, but magic was *always* effective.

Except against Shaking Sickness. For now.

Ben said other impossible words instead. "The Mechtlands."

Jakes squinted.

"If there were no responsibilities. No Pious God, no higher calling. We'd go to the Mechtlands," Ben said. "It would be cold, and barren, and a raving warrior would probably kill us. But we'd build a hut. You could teach me how to fish. We'd never have to deal with . . ."

Ben waved at the University around them. At Argrid. At the Church and his father.

Jakes pulled the sun from the window to his smile. "Give a guy a chance, would you?"

"Apologies, Defensor. I'll try to be more repulsive."

"That's all I'm asking."

Ben faced the chest. He opened it, hoping it would make him feel steadier. Vials of botanical magic stared up at him, each nestled in a snug velvet compartment.

Awacia. Healica. Aerated Blossom. Then—a brown flower. He struggled. Cleanse Root? One of the most powerful plants, capable of healing both internal and external wounds.

"Defensors and protesters destroyed most of the University's resources after my uncle's heresy," Ben said. "We'll have to find someone to assist us. Someone to . . ."

Take the blame, Ben wanted to say. Even with Jakes believing that this mission was right, Ben wouldn't admit that he could name the plants in this chest, and was already piecing together how he could use the Healica and the Cleanse Root—

No matter how his new responsibility tempted him, Ben was playing a dangerous game with people who would cry *Heretic!* at the slightest provocation.

"We need someone who understands magic," Ben said. But the ones who knew anything were priests and defensors, who only used their magic to condemn people.

A moment of silence in which Ben heard Jakes humming

softly to himself. He didn't recognize the hymn, but that was unsurprising—Jakes knew far more than Ben.

Finally, Jakes said, "The raiders. Maybe one could help us as a way to cleanse his soul."

Ben nodded, the idea gaining traction. He knew which raider to ask, too. The one who had already proven himself familiar with magic.

The Mecht warrior.

6

THE COUNCIL MEETING devolved into arguments fueled by Milo and the Argridian diplomats, who offered occasional suggestions that bordered on insults. The room was on the edge of combustion—should they please the raider Head or the Argridians, or deal with Devereux in some other way? Should they act on Milo's proposed bill to eradicate the stream raiders, or take another stance with Devereux's sentence? The decision would be definitive. Too definitive.

If the Council killed Devereux Bell, it would mean war with the raiders—Head Pilkvist would take it as proof that the Council wouldn't negotiate, and the Argridian contingent would push for the Council to act on Milo's bill to eliminate raiders. If the Council gave Devereux to Ingvar Pilkvist, tensions with Argrid would spike and the peace treaty would dissolve—the Argridians would be outraged that the Council had complied with the demands of criminals.

Devereux's fate would anger either the raiders or the Argridians.

Neither threat was preferable.

In the row ahead of Lu, a councilmember called out in favor of Devereux's death—thereby endorsing the bill to eradicate stream raiders. Lu blanched, leaning closer to her father.

"Either we kill Bell and strike a match on the fuse of civil war," Lu whispered to Tom, "or Ingvar Pilkvist kills Bell and the Argridian treaty likely disintegrates."

Tom's lips puckered. "Much is riding on one boy. Apparently Bell was caught in the market, assaulting a lady? A foolish mistake for someone with his reputation to make, especially at such a time as this."

Lu's cheeks heated, but her embarrassment was alleviated by her father's implication. "You think this might have been planned?"

"We don't have enough information to make assumptions." Tom's gaze turned to the door through which the soldiers had dragged an unconscious Devereux Bell. "If only there were someone with a proven talent for getting information out of people. Someone Devereux Bell might not be expecting."

Tom looked at her again, a spark in his eyes. He was being coy, and she wanted to respond in kind, to joke about how capable she had been during the war. But a hole opened in her stomach, and she looked to the front of the room, to Milo, in a heated debate with Kari again.

"I'm not that person anymore," Lu whispered. "I don't have to be."

Tom took her hand and drew her focus back. "No, darling. You would not be going after him as a spy or a soldier. You would be only questioning him, and as a politician."

Lu weighed that. As a politician. Not as someone who would go with weapons tucked into her stockings or escape routes planned.

She smiled, soft and true, and squeezed Tom's hand. That was all she needed to excuse herself from the meeting—everyone was so distracted that she simply walked down the aisle.

All Senior Councilmembers held apartments in the castle, where they stayed during particularly long sessions, so Lu stopped at her family's apartment to gather supplies before she slipped down to the castle's dungeon.

The two soldiers on duty snapped to attention as Lu entered the alcove that linked the wings of the dungeon. A ring of keys jostled at one's hip, the only keys that opened the four doors branching off this bare room.

One of the soldiers stepped forward to intercept her.

She tugged at her satchel. "I've brought some supplies for Mr. Bell. He may be more likely to cooperate if we show him a few courtesies."

The soldier's eyes brightened. "Ahhh. Come to gawk at the notorious raider?"

The other soldier smirked. "I bet Bell's got lovers in every port. Careful, miss—criminals only lead to heartbreak."

The first one muttered, "And diseases."

The other soldier snorted and covered it by coughing.

She had anticipated this. Lu adjusted her satchel over the dress she had changed into. The scarlet gown crested over narrow panniers that gave the skirt a fashionable drape from her hips, complete with a bodice stitched in a golden vine motif and bell sleeves accented by ruffles. Feigning lovesickness had been the second excuse she had planned.

With a delicate sigh, she patted her cheeks. "Oh no, an innocent visit, truly. . . ."

The soldiers shared another chuckle. One shrugged, unhooking the keys from his belt. "Eh, he's restrained well enough. No danger in a short visit."

"Maybe danger's what she wants." The first soldier winked at her.

They unlocked one of the iron doors that led from the alcove. A hall appeared before Lu, the stone floor slick from the moisture of humidity, iron bars designating each cell. Two other soldiers stood outside a cell on the left. When the door squealed, they glanced over.

The soldier who opened the door grinned at them. "Bell's got a visitor." He looked at Lu. "Been a quiet few days as far as serious crime, so you've got no other prisoners to worry about."

Lu started down the hall, her silence stoking more chuckles as the door closed. The guards outside Devereux's cell stepped out of earshot yet were still close enough to intervene if needed.

Bell was in one of the cells with a window, and the evening cast moonlight through; tapers in the hall lit all else. He was conscious now, spread out on the bench beneath the window, one leg crossed over the other, his foot bouncing. His eye was closed, his arm bent to cradle his head.

Lu stepped closer to the bars. "Mr. Bell," she said.

❅❅❅

Vex heard the door to his wing open and assumed it was someone come to interrogate him, so he stayed reclined, kicking his foot in the air.

But the voice that said his name was infinitely more interesting.

Vex grinned and rolled his head to face the hall. A few cuts from Pilkvist's beating burned at the movement, but his grin stayed when he saw the girl outside his cell. She wore a fancy red dress that pulled out the golden tones in her brown skin and made her hair glossier in the light from the wall sconces.

"Now *this* is a surprise." He flailed his legs into the air and spun off the bench, but his gut reminded him that he'd recently been punched in the stomach.

As he wheezed, the girl said, "You were given nothing for your injuries."

Vex looked up. "Have you come to tend my wounds?"

She moved something over her shoulder—a satchel, the one he'd tried to steal from—and pulled out a jar of ointment.

Vex's eye widened. "Seriously? But if you insist I disrobe, I must ask the same of you."

The girl held the jar to her stomach. "I have matters to discuss with you, Mr. Bell."

He wrinkled his nose. "Just Vex."

"Vex. Truly?"

He grinned again. "Deeply."

She stood close enough that if he was against the bars, they'd be nearly chest to chest. He took a step forward, not realizing until then that she might not appreciate being so close to the man who'd scared her half to death in the market. Would she have come down here if that were true?

This would tell him how much he'd hurt her. If he needed to make amends.

He sauntered over and rested his elbows on one of the horizontal bars, a dare in his eye.

The girl lifted a thin black eyebrow but didn't move away. She wasn't much shorter than he was, and the angle allowed for a certain vantage point that Nayeli liked to use during cons. It was why she spent so much money on the *really nice* silk stays. They *lifted* and *pushed* certain things *higher* and *tighter* and—

Vex swallowed, fighting a shudder, but it came anyway and he swallowed again.

"What could you want to ask me, Miss—" He waited.

"Andreu."

"Andreu? As in the daughter of Kari the Wave?"

The girl was unruffled. "The daughter of a Senior Councilmember, yes."

Vex grinned. "I figured you weren't the typical riffraff who shop from raiders, but I never would've guessed you were the daughter of someone important. I know how to pick my marks."

The muscles in the girl's jaw bulged. She glanced at the guards, but they didn't have much interest in their conversation.

"A matter you would be wise to keep to yourself, lest you wish to bring the Council's wrath upon you," the girl whispered.

A coil of black hair brushed her collarbone. She had a bit of Tuncian in her, which gave her skin that golden hue, but maybe a little Argridian, too.

"It is only due to my compassion that you aren't dead already," she said.

"Ah. So I'm indebted to you?"

"In a way."

His smile flared. "What do you want in exchange for

your assistance, Miss Andreu?"

"I picked up many things from your display in the court-room, chief among them your disregard for the severity of your circumstances."

She waited, eyebrows raised, and Vex rolled his eye.

"Of all the things we could be doing . . . fine, milady." Vex shoved back and swept his arm in a dramatic bow. "Shockingly, you're not the first person to accuse me of wanting to be here, and I'd bet what's left of my reputation that you won't be the last."

"What's left of your reputation?"

"I've become the most notorious unaligned raider in Grace Loray." He pressed back against the bars. "What possible reason do you think I'd have to ruin that? While I'm flattered your people think I'm a criminal mastermind, I'm here against my will, Túa Alteza."

Your Highness, spoken in the fancy language of Argrid's upper class to see if she reacted to it with the same haughti-ness Argridian bullies showed. Though he'd dealt only with men, that didn't mean his blackmailers wouldn't send a girl to get something out of him. Actually, they should've sent pretty girls to sway him from the start.

But she didn't flinch. "You were caught, alone, in the market. You didn't try to run."

Vex groaned. "Do you have any idea how many times I've repeated this story since I got put in here, Princesa?"

The girl cringed.

"As with most aspects of raider life," he began the lie he'd sculpted, "things got dangerous, and I got separated from my crew. Stopped in the market to gather enough supplies to find them. Saw a certain young lady, who shall remain nameless, and figured she'd have a few dozen galles on her, and—" He rubbed his bruised nose with a smirk. "She surprised me. It was stupid, but it was an accident, Princesa."

The girl pursed her lips. She definitely didn't like that title.

"You have to see the curiosity in this." She tapped the jar on the iron. "Your reputation is that you have avoided capture because you know Grace Loray better than anyone. Surely you would not lose your own crew."

Vex grimaced. If her mother was a Senior Councilmember, maybe she wasn't an Argridian agent—but had the Council sent her here?

"Is this why you came here?" he asked, letting his irritation show. "The Council thinks I'll spill my secrets to a pair of pretty eyes and tightly pulled stays?"

The girl smiled as if he'd given away something important. "I already know your secrets."

"Do you now?" He echoed her smile, making his slier.

The girl leaned in. She smelled like . . . plants? He inhaled again, thrown by the scent. Yeah, he knew dried botanical magic when he smelled it.

The girl spoke. "I think the Argridians told you to get yourself captured so your presence would create dissension in the Council and help Milo Ibarra's proposition pass. Whatever is planned, Mr. Bell, I'm here to tell you that I will not let it progress further than this."

He blinked, thrown again—this time by her certainty. She cared about this island in the same way Edda cared about keeping their crew safe. Like it was a sacred task she'd been born to.

The girl was right, though. Sort of. Should he tell her? *"I am actually getting blackmailed by Argridians to sell them magic. Which I did. But I didn't do this. I mean, Argrid didn't ask me to get arrested, but I did do it* because *of them—no, wait—"*

Yeah, better to lie.

"You think I'm working with Argrid?" Vex laughed. "Please. I'd forgotten our beloved mother country had paid us a visit until I was shackled in your courtroom."

"Then perhaps it was not an elaborate scheme. Perhaps all you wanted was to create unrest in the government that would lead to easier targets and bigger payouts."

"Which would be difficult to capitalize on if I was imprisoned. Or dead."

"Ah, therein lies the true purpose of my visit."

The girl lifted the jar to the neckline of her bodice. Vex's eye dropped to it and he cursed himself, but he was already looking at her cleavage, and the girl was *watching him* look at her cleavage, and—damn it, she'd intended all this, hadn't she?

"I'm prepared to make you a trade," the girl said. "This jar's contents for an answer."

Vex tipped his head. "I thought I was already indebted to you."

"That debt will remain. This is separate."

Huh. "Go on."

"The Healica's ability to soothe skin ailments should heal your wounds in less than a day." The girl pressed her palms on either side of the jar. "Do we have an agreement?"

It was odd for a politician's daughter to know anything about magic beyond how sailors gathered it from the riverbeds and sold it. The upper class relied on apothecaries and merchants to tell them what to take and how to take it.

"You're willing to trust me?" Vex pressed. "Even if I'm as awful as you think I am?"

"Is that a yes?"

He bobbed his head, his gaze not breaking from hers.

"There are three possible outcomes to your current situation," the girl started. "The two that will lead to strife involve your death: either the Council kills you and angers Head Pilkvist, or Head Pilkvist kills you and Argrid is angered. The only way you will survive is via the third option—so whatever plan you or Argrid had to bring unrest to Grace Loray will not come to fruition."

Vex frowned. What would Argrid get out of his death?

What had she said earlier—some kind of proposition from one of the diplomats? That couldn't be good.

"The third option," the girl continued, "will be unpopular, but may pass more easily if you cooperate. Will you either pay the hundreds of galles in fines you owe or work off your debt under our supervision?"

Vex's smile stiffened. She was seeing if he'd take an out instead of choosing to stay here and keep stirring up trouble. To prove whether or not he was here with a nefarious plan.

He'd never intended to stir up trouble. He'd wanted only to make it too difficult for his Argridian pursuers to reach him until he figured out some brilliant way to get rid of them.

But it'd be nice if the Council didn't kill him first.

"How would I work for you?" he asked. "Bleed taxes out of the impoverished?"

The girl drew back. "No one bleeds taxes out of Grace Loray's—"

"Yeah, yeah. 'It's for the good of the country; we operate for the people.' Point is, you want me to work for the corrupt system I've built a reputation working *against*."

The girl's mouth bobbed open as if she couldn't see anything wrong with what he'd said, save for the one word he knew she'd latch onto.

She held steady, didn't so much as tremble. "Grace Loray is not corrupt. But yes."

He bowed his head. "Fine. If that's the price of freedom."

He reached for the balm, but the girl kept her fingers around it, surprised by his answer. He stopped, his hand close to her bodice's neckline. The brand on his wrist was shiny in the light from the sconces, Argrid's crest tangled with the rough *R*.

"If that's all, Princesa." He closed his fingers over her fist, brushing the lace along her neckline. A lightning bolt shot to his gut. "This is mine?"

The girl's lungs hitched, and she released the jar. Vex's grin widened.

He unscrewed the lid. The jar held some sort of ivory paste.

"There are no princesses here," the girl said, regaining herself. "I am a politician."

Vex frowned at her, one finger bent toward the ointment.

"While it may be in your nature to lie, raider"—she leaned closer—"it is in my nature to control the truth. I never said the contents of the jar were healing balm."

Vex shook his head. What? She'd said—

She'd said that a balm would heal him. Not that that balm was actually in the jar.

He yanked his finger back. "What's in the jar?"

"Maybe healing balm. Maybe poisonous oils from Digestive leaves." She curtsied. "Lovely speaking with you."

Damn it. She *had* played him. The tight stays, her body

against the bars of his cell, every goddamn word from her had been some careful game meant to shake him up.

The girl got a few steps away before she glanced back at Vex.

He tipped the jar against his forehead in a salute. "Fair play, Princesa."

She spun around before he could read anything else on her. The door to the soldier's alcove opened, and she was gone.

7

BEN'S CARRIAGE STOPPED at the base of the Grace Neus steps. He didn't get out right away, his fingers digging into the velvet-covered seat.

Grace Neus Cathedral was the heart of Deza. Its stained-glass windows were riots of scarlet, lavender, and orange; over the front doors stood statues representing the five pillars of the Pious God: purity, honesty, chastity, penance, and charity. Beneath them, wallowing in the Devil's fiery hell, were depictions of debauchery, overindulging, whoring, and other impurities. High atop it, as on every cathedral, sat the symbol of the Church carved out of white stone: the curved *V*, cupped hands beseeching the heavens.

For all its beauty, the cathedral was also the site of Deza's holding cells. Beneath the sanctuary where choirs sang and congregations gathered were those struggling to purify their souls. Church servants branded the successful and released them; the unsuccessful, well . . .

People packed the cathedral's yard, some singing hymns and swaying with their wrists pressed together, hands cupped in the Church's symbol. Others cried, "Nos purificar!" *Purify us.*

The only place that wasn't clogged with onlookers was the circle at the south end, so seasoned by the burned bodies of those who had refused to repent that Ben wondered if it would ever be anything but a black stain on the ground.

The door to his carriage opened. Jakes's watchfulness turned to concern as he leaned in. "Have you changed your mind?"

Ben didn't respond. Jakes pulled the door at an angle, blocking them from the crowd as he put his hand on Ben's thigh. "We don't have to do this."

Jakes's sympathy brought Ben back to his duty here. Not to watch the daily burning that the crowd had gathered for. Not to stew in memories. He'd come to gain access to the raiders who had been detained, particularly the Mecht.

Ben wrapped his fingers around Jakes's, squeezed, and jumped out of the carriage.

A line of defensors stood between the crowd and Grace Neus, a half circle of navy tunics and feathered hats. Beyond them, nobles clustered across the marble steps— Claudio, his arm linked through Salvador's, and a few other aristocrats from that morning's Inquisitor patrol. They watched him, hopeful and judgmental and a dozen other conflicting, exhausting things.

Someone broke off from a group of priests, causing everyone on the steps to turn like banners following a breeze.

"Benat!" Elazar declared. His white and scarlet Eminence robes brushed the stones. "I expected you to be at the University."

"I've come on that business. If I may speak to you—"

A cheer drew the crowd's focus. Ben clenched his fists and turned, holding his breath. Across the long yard, defensors led out the condemned in wrist manacles.

"Nos purificar!" people cried as soldiers tugged sacks over the heads of the doomed.

Then, "Burn the barbarian!"

Ben squinted at one of the prisoners—huge, blond, and unmistakably Mecht. The man's head vanished under a canvas sack.

"The raiders." Ben spun to Elazar. "They can't be burned already?"

Elazar's face was heavy from years of yanking too many souls from the brink of destruction. "The raiders you arrested are guilty of too many crimes. The Pious God demands we commit their souls and bodies to hell."

Ben remembered the Mecht attacking him, the fire parting his lips, smoke on his breath.

"Father." Ben stepped closer. "Everyone deserves a chance to choose the Pious God. Give them that—the Mecht was defending his captain. You would have done the same."

"Do not compare the Eminence King to these vile sinners!" a priest shouted. His voice cut like a dull knife would through flesh and grabbed all attention—the nobles; groups throughout the crowd, looking up at their leaders with wide, curious eyes.

Ben could pull Elazar aside, ask for a private audience. But hymns continued as soldiers tied the condemned to stakes. They'd shoot the Mecht—the Eye of the Sun kept him from burning, but they could purify his soul in other ways.

"Father," Ben tried before the deaths could be carried out. "I need the Mecht warrior my patrol captured. He has knowledge of magic that—"

Ben's own words died in his mouth before Elazar shot him a stunned look.

The Crown Prince had asked to pardon a prisoner because of magic.

Ben's body broke out in a cold sweat. He was reminded yet again of why Argrid had never had need of a large military force before the Grace Loray war: because all it took was one word, one whisper of unforgivable sin, to subdue the entire population.

The priests around them gaped, their hands going to positions of prayer that might as well have been raised fists. Nobles started to whisper *magic*, a word none of them wanted to be caught with but everyone wanted to say.

Elazar straightened, and Ben swore he felt the crack of knuckles on his jaw already, the blood spilling over his tongue.

"Benat is correct," Elazar said, loud. "Ours is a God of mercy."

He leaned to whisper to a nearby priest, who lifted trembling hands.

"By order of Crown Prince Benat, they shall be spared!" the priest announced.

The whole yard went silent.

Heretic was all Ben could think. *Heretic, heretic—*

Days after Rodrigu's and Paxben's deaths, Ben had wept to go to Grace Loray. He'd heard stories of crowds there overpowering priests and saving the condemned; of guerrilla-style fighters descending on prisoner transports; of the entire country rising up against the Church.

Why did Argrid want to murder people? Why did Ben's country take comfort in atrocities padded with words like *ordained* and *righteous*?

He'd asked those questions of his monxe teachers, and of Elazar. All he'd gotten in response were bruises and, eventually, a broken jaw.

Ben's pulse throbbed in his neck, his chin aching where the bone had snapped under his father's hand all those years ago. Eyes from the crowd and nobles bored into him, as hot as fire. Murmured words of shock and horror clumped at his feet, as deadly as dry kindling.

"Nos purificar!" the people began again, and other prayers they seemed to send not to the Pious God but to Elazar, standing on the steps, unmoving.

"I gave you this task," Elazar said for only Ben to hear. "You know its delicate nature. It has been less than a day, and you are already causing unrest. Was I wrong to trust you?"

Ben shivered and bowed. His fear crested and broke upon him.

Can Prince Benat be forgiven for this? he already heard people whispering. The Pious God was clear about magic now. There was only one end: death.

Which was why Elazar had ordered him to make a healing potion: to banish beliefs that stifled their country, to end the extremism and violence.

Ben looked at his father. Was that what Elazar wanted? Was it possible for him to have changed from someone who had condemned his brother and nephew and beaten his own son to someone who wanted tolerance?

Defensors led a new group of prisoners out. The first nine were gone, sent back to the holding cells. The crowd's hysteria rose again, glad that someone would die, proof that evil would be expunged. A few eyes stayed on Ben, though, full of hatred and fear.

Elazar had his hands to his chest, his lips moving in a prayer Ben caught only pieces of.

". . . give these souls to prove our penitence. We pay for impurities in blood. . . ."

Elazar would do anything to serve the Pious God. *Sacrifice* anything. Either the job Elazar had given Ben was what he promised it to be—an improvement to their country—or Elazar was trying to make the sacrifice Ben had felt looming over him for the past six years.

The royalty gave hope to Argrid while they were alive. But Ben had seen the impact of dead royals—Rodrigu and Paxben had burned and brought desperation for safety at any cost, and unchecked power for the Church.

What could a dead prince bring?

Ben retreated, stumbling into Jakes. There was a breath of space between them, so when Jakes asked, "Are you all right?" only Ben heard.

Jakes took Ben's elbow regardless and pulled him down the steps. At the far end of the yard, flames fed on dry wood, racing to gobble up the tarnished souls before they could taint this country any longer. A noise filled the air, a scream that could never be unheard.

Priests said it was the sound of evil being driven out.

In a fog, Ben wound up back in his suite in the palace. The soft glow of the fireplace's flames was meant to make his rooms welcoming, but it only stung his eyes.

He marched past it, stopping to drop his hands to the top of his desk and let out a howl.

A hand clamped his shoulder. The door to his suite was shut. He and Jakes were alone in the firelight and the curtained darkness of the sitting room.

A better prince would have ordered Jakes away long ago. A better defensor would have apologized for crossing the line between noble and servant.

"You're supposed to make them question, to change their minds," Jakes tried.

"Am I?" Ben looked at him. "It feels like heresy."

Jakes smiled. Ben spun even more. "Heresy—or hope."

The firelight behind Jakes shone between the strands of his hair. The room pitched, the paintings on the walls and the dark cherrywood furniture throbbing with each flicker of flame.

Jakes was humming. That hymn, and Ben still couldn't place it.

"What is that?" Ben whispered. "That hymn you sing when you're nervous."

Jakes smiled. "I'm not nervous." His face went rigid. "And it isn't a hymn. My sister used to write songs. It was one of hers."

Ben pulled back, his brow pinching. "You never told me that."

"You never asked."

He didn't say it accusingly, but Ben's heart still bucked with shame.

"Why do you love me?" Ben asked. "I'm selfish. I'm distracted half the time. The Pious God demands chastity until marriage. I'm bad for you in every way possible."

Jakes's face softened. "My sister used to say you could tell a person's character by what they considered their weaknesses, rather than their strengths." His smile was brittle. "You're my weakness."

The firelight heaved, and Ben grabbed Jakes to steady himself. That touch was all he needed—Ben followed the sway of the flames to nestle in the fold of Jakes's neck.

If working with magic sentenced him to burn, he hoped this smell—the one that clung to Jakes's neck, right here, ginger spiced soap and bitter salt in the sweat on his skin— filled his final moments.

He tangled his hands in the folds of Jakes's shirt, getting drunk off the sweetest wine.

8

LU DID NOT get a chance to speak to either of her parents until the next morning. The Council had been in session when she left Vex's cell, and Tom was one of the council-members at the front of the room, shouting and arguing, making it impossible for her to inform him of what Vex had told her. When Kari and Tom at long last returned to their apartment, bleary and exhausted, Lu was slumped across her desk, half-asleep working on the tonic for Annalisa.

But finally, the new day dawned. Sunlight streamed through each window Lu passed as she made her way to the castle's dining room. Alongside the warmth of the soft white light, Lu felt something familiar, and it made her steps heavier.

The war against Argrid had begun when she was too small to remember. Every time Lu had gone to pick up information on the street or in rooms where one tiny girl went overlooked, she had felt she would burst with the certainty that this would be it. This piece of information, which as a child she had not truly understood—numbers of troops or the location of a battle—would end the war. Later, when Tom sent her out on bloodier missions, everything she did was because of the certainty that she would make things better.

She felt that same certainty now. Vex was willing to cooperate—which likely meant he was not involved in a larger plot with Milo, which further meant there might not have been a plot at all. Lu may have been a fool to believe a raider, but his response had seemed sincere.

A just-as-familiar feeling of dread rose when Lu eased open the dining room's door—not once had her certainty as a child resulted in the war's end.

The dining room overlooked the lake, giving a miraculous view that Lu had once believed showed the whole of Grace Loray. Glass panes along the outer wall opened to let in waves of fresh lake air and sun-kissed billows of humidity. The table down the center held dozens of seats, and servants kept a smaller table off to the side fresh with fruit and pastries as visitors staggered in throughout the morning.

General councilmembers and a few of the Argridian contingent were present. Milo was not.

Lu's parents sat at the main table. She took a chair across from Kari, Tom next to her, and let their presence serve as a reprieve.

Tom smiled at her over a cup of steaming Awacia, one of the most popular of the commonly used plants. It caused alertness and kept the taker awake for extended periods of time when dissolved in water. The earthy scent painted the air as he offered her his plate of food.

"We didn't wake you when we left this morning, did we? You seemed as exhausted as if you'd been testing that sleeping tonic on yourself. You haven't, have you?"

Lu yawned in response and took a saltfish fritter. "Of course not, Father. When does the Council reconvene?"

"Don't worry about that," Kari said. "You'll return to the hospital? Tell Teo if he doesn't stay with us tonight, I'll drag him here myself. A hospital is no place for a healthy child."

Lu managed a smile. "I will see if the promise of sleeping under the same roof as Devereux Bell will tempt him, but I doubt even that will pull him away from his sister." She paused. "Speaking of—was a decision reached regarding Mr. Bell's fate?"

"Hardly," Tom sighed. "The Argridians refused to move forward with our treaty unless we agree to hang Bell. A move most of the Council was none too pleased with."

"I spoke to him," Lu said, picking the crispy breading off the saltfish fritter. Oil glistened on her fingers.

Kari's eyes were on the door behind Lu. "Who, sweetheart?"

Lu looked at Tom. He hadn't told Kari about her meeting with Devereux?

Raised voices broke through their conversation, drawing the attention of all in the dining room to the door. Lu spun as Branden Axel, captain of the castle guard, shoved his way ahead of the fuming Argridians.

Kari was on her feet immediately. Lazlo was the only other Senior present, and he joined her as she moved around the table to intercept Branden.

"Captain?"

Branden extended a closed fist to Kari and peeled back his fingers. Lu shot up from her chair, her eyes falling on the handkerchief that fluttered open across Branden's palm. Inside, a ribbon looped plants in a bundle, their color indicating that someone had dried and steeped them.

Kari shook her head. "What is this? What's happening?"

"An outrage!" an Argridian behind Branden shouted. "It's beyond condemnable—"

Kari ignored him. "Captain, what—"

But it was Lu who said, "Drooping Fern?"

Branden looked at her. "That's what it is? How do you know?"

Lu's face heated at the accusation in his tone. *How would a politician's daughter recognize a dangerous plant on sight?* But he might have been only anxious for the angry delegates behind him.

"I've studied *Botanical Wonders*," she explained, not mentioning that she had Drooping Fern in her room at that moment. But she hadn't steeped her supply—the plant was effective only when burned and the smoke inhaled.

"Drooping Fern? One of your despicable plants?" the Argridian spat. He looked liable to punch something, his hands in fists, everything tense. "Not only is he gone, he was *poisoned*?"

A wave of silence fell over the room. Lu went immobile as her mother asked, "Who is gone?"

"General Milo Ibarra," Branden answered.

A beat, and the room exploded, questions overlapping in a tangle of anger.

Lu balked. *Milo is . . . gone?*

Kari raised her hands for silence that didn't come as Branden offered more details. "The general hasn't been seen for hours. The teapot on his table was upended, revealin' the Drooping Fern. In his tea."

Those details did nothing to soothe the room—in fact, the anger and questions grew. Why Milo? Who would do such a thing?

And, loudly, over and over: How dare Grace Loray allow this to happen?

Lu's gut cramped. She pulled at Branden's arm to see the Drooping Fern again, and she got one good look before her mother spoke.

"Captain Axel, have your men search the premises," Kari tried. "We will bring to light whatever has happened!"

"This abduction was no coincidence!" one of the Argridians countered.

The Drooping Fern hadn't been burned. If it had, the plant would have been charred, unrecognizable, or at least singed in part—but the plant Lu had seen was whole, if not damp.

Either someone had intended to use the plant to knock Milo unconscious but hidden it in the teapot after changing their plan, or the Drooping Fern had been placed there to make others think he had been drugged.

Lu glared at the Argridians, her gut twisting with wariness.

Councilmembers gathered, talking with heads together, and Tom swung away to join one group.

Lu took his arm. "Father, it wasn't—"

"Lu—I can't—"

"Listen!" She forced him to look at her. "Drooping Fern isn't administered through drinking. It must be burned and inhaled—"

Lazlo lifted his hands. "Silence! Order!"

Another Argridian diplomat leaped onto a chair. "Yes, you'd love for us to be silent! Why else would the man leading the charge against your island disappear?"

"Enough, sir!" Kari shouted. Lu froze. Her mother rarely, if ever, raised her voice. "You will not accuse Grace Loray of such a crime!"

"An Argridian has gone *missing*! This is why we demanded you rid your island of stream raiders. They have no respect for authority and have clearly abducted the general to protest the proposed bill. The raiders are a danger to you, and to Argrid as well, and we will not be silent! Non máis silencio!"

The other diplomats picked up his chant in proper Argridian, an obvious rebuff of the Council: *"No more silence!"*

"While I'm concerned for General Ibarra," Kari said, "I am also concerned that we have misplaced our outrage. This could be a misunderstanding—"

"Then where is Ibarra?" an Argridian shouted.

"The raiders took him!" another exclaimed, as if they each took turns carrying the cause. "Head Pilkvist was here yesterday making threats! Who else would use a dangerous plant like Drooping Fern? This is why we must eliminate them. This is why we must take action!"

That chant started up again: "Non máis silencio!"

"We will investigate Ibarra's disappearance!" Kari tried. "But we will do so with careful deliberation!"

Lazlo faced her. "If we discover that Ibarra was indeed abducted by raiders, what would you have us do—deliberate as well? Particularly now, when we are so close to peace with Argrid, and the raiders jeopardize that! Perhaps Ibarra was right—perhaps it is time to take action against the raiders!"

"If Drooping Fern in tea is the only cause to believe Ibarra was abducted," said Tom, "and there is no other proof, one might ask why our Argridian delegates have leaped so quickly to fury."

"What are you saying?" shouted one delegate.

"I'm saying"—Tom took a breath—"if this abduction was staged, and Ibarra had a hand in his own disappearance to further Argrid's causes—what would you have us do then?"

Kari's eyes went round in horror. Lu jerked back, hips slamming into her chair.

The moment Tom made that accusation, the Argridians erupted in fury again.

"How dare you!"

"You would accuse us of treachery!"

"ENOUGH!" One Argridian stood above the rest, arms spread. "When we agreed to this treaty, we believed we could have peace. You undermined every bill we proposed, and you undermine us when we call for justice!"

A few Argridians peppered the air with enthusiastic agreement.

"I say enough!" he continued. "Prove your dedication to peace—regain control of your island. We will be silent about these dangers no longer! Non máis silencio!"

"Non máis silencio!" the Argridians echoed.

The Seniors and councilmembers stared, some shocked, others fearful.

Lu had grown up with arguments such as these, and fear such as this. They had left the same feeling on her skin, tingles of urgency and action. But it had been more than five years since she had felt this—and all it had taken was two days to stoke such incendiary attitudes again?

Lu paused. All this had happened in two days. Milo's plan to oppose the stream raider syndicates; his abduction. Did Devereux's capture fit into it? There was still the matter of the Drooping Fern—drinking it in tea could not have made Milo unconscious.

Something more was at work. Was Argrid behind this? Was Milo?

Sweat trickled down Lu's spine. The Grace Lorayan and Argridian delegates had spent the past month negotiating for peace—why would Argrid throw that away? The revolution had drained them; their country was nearly bankrupt, and Argrid had lost many soldiers, too. Grace Loray was not the only country that would be damaged by another war—

The pieces snapped into place, and Lu gasped. With Grace Loray at war with the raiders, with *itself*, Argrid would be free and intact. The island would crumble, leaving it open for Argrid to do with it as they willed.

Lu surveyed the room, seeing it as if from a distance. The shouts for justice, the divide between the Argridians and the Grace Lorayans.

"Non máis silencio!" the Argridians chanted. "Non máis silencio!"

✿✿✿

Vex had never cared much about politics. As an orphan during the war, he'd only cared what reactions he could get from people and how he could use those reactions in his favor. Which, someone told him once, was how the governments of the world operated—through manipulation.

He'd nearly behaved. He wasn't *manipulating* anyone. He stole only from people who were awful; he didn't overcharge when he sold plants; and he'd never gone to the lengths other raiders did when someone wronged them. It was why he'd never joined a syndicate. He was, for all his obvious humility, better than them.

But what good had that done him?

"You hear about the commotion?" A new soldier came to relieve one of the two guarding Vex that night, and he jutted his chin at his comrade in greeting. "One of the visiting Argridians is missing. That general, Milo Ibarra."

The other guard's eyebrows shot up. "What? How?"

"Abducted, they think." The new guard folded his arms and cut a look into Vex's cell. "The day *after* he proposed a bill to get rid of stream raiders."

Vex stayed where he was, reclined on the bench again. But every muscle stilled as he strained to listen.

"Shit," the other said. "Wasn't Pilkvist here just yesterday? The Council thinking Ibarra got snatched by him?"

"Maybe, but it'd be awful obvious, wouldn't it?"

Vex rolled his eye. *Duh*, but also, Pilkvist wasn't that resourceful.

"Bet it was a raider, though. Another syndicate, or even filth like this one." The new guard kicked the bars to Vex's cell, and Vex flinched. "Hate to say it, but Argrid was right—we need to clean up this island. My pop's storefront got a rat problem a few years back. Getting rid of 'em was a struggle, but it'd have gotten worse the longer we waited. Gotta eradicate vermin before they *really* get out of hand."

Vex forced his eye to stay on the dingy ceiling.

He'd heard the word *eradicated* before. The Church had spewed it—*eradicate evil magic; eradicate those who use it; eradicate the impurities from your soul.*

A pressure built in Vex's chest, but he didn't let himself shiver or fall into memories that were always one slip away from consuming him. Memories of the war, of soldiers seizing him and declaring him a heretic and other words he was too young to understand, much less *be*.

He knew Argrid wanted Grace Loray back. Why else would they put so much effort into exploiting raiders? Why else would they have noted Vex's faults when he was in that damn prison years ago and used them to blackmail him?

They knew they'd lost the war because of their weak military. This way, they'd break the Council, split the island apart, and make it easier to take control. Prayers and hymns and pyres would choke this island of free markets and magic-filled rivers.

Vex had known all along. Ignored it, because all he had was his smart mouth, Nayeli's penchant for explosives, Edda's muscles, and their steamer, the *Rapid Meander*. How could they fight an empire? They could barely keep Argrid off their own backs, and all they'd wanted was to carve out a home away from Grace Loray's mess and Argrid's too. Away from war and cleansing.

But listening to that guard say *eradicated*, Vex should've done something. He should've . . . he didn't know. What would that girl have done? She'd cared so much about this island in that one conversation that he'd almost fallen in love with her for her passion alone.

She'd have done something by now. She wasn't some useless unaligned raider, living off notoriety for things that didn't matter.

❄❄❄

Lu's balcony door swung open.

She pushed herself upright, wincing as the muscles in her neck spasmed. Beneath her, the pieces of her sleeping concoction were arranged over the top of her desk. Mortars and pestles; empty vials; two cloths on which she'd laid out the Drooping Fern and Narcotium Creeper. She had felt so smug when she'd thought of the glass bell jar, the perfect vessel in which to trap the Drooping Fern's tranquilizing smoke. She had lit a leaf and placed it under the glass, intending to infuse the Narcotium Creeper with it and create a tonic.

She had been tired, though, and clumsy, and all it had taken was one jab of her elbow. The bell jar had toppled, releasing its smoke, and she hadn't had the foresight to put Awacia within reach to neutralize the Drooping Fern.

Unconsciousness had taken her.

Lu leaned back in her chair, digging the heels of her palms into her eyes. That was the problem with Drooping Fern—it caused unconsciousness, but not *restful* unconsciousness. She was no more refreshed now than she had been before she had fainted on her desk.

Wait—what had awoken her?

She blinked around her dark room. The gauzy curtains over her open balcony doors rippled in the heady midnight breeze. Beyond, the murmur of Lake Regolith's waves infused the lull. Had the wind pushed the door open? She had shut it tight since Milo's abduction. . . .

Lu flew upright, barefoot on the cool marble tiles, heart racing. All she wore was a thin shift, and its airiness made her feel naked as the eerie sensation of being watched crept down her back like a bead of sweat.

Someone was in her room.

Lu had spent the day after Milo's abduction in Council meetings, leaving to attend Annalisa in short snatches. Waiting, hoping for word of a resolution, but all the Council and the Argridians agreed on was that they didn't agree on anything.

Milo is unaccounted for, her terror whispered. *No one knows where he is. . . .*

Lu scrambled over her desk, sorting through vials whose labels she couldn't read in the blackness. The sensation of being watched grew, and Lu grabbed a handful of the vials, intending to smash them on the floor.

But a voice stopped her cold.

"Lu? I'm sorry, but . . ."

Soft shoes padded on the marble; hands tugged at her nightdress.

Lu saw it, then. Teo was always climbing on things, hanging from rafters in the barn, far too nimble and quick for his own good; his agility—and sorrow—could have propelled him up the two stories to her balcony.

An aching hole opened in her gut as Lu fell to her knees, the vials of plants tumbling to the floor. She cupped Teo's face, but it was too dark to see him—she could feel him, though, the tears on his cheeks.

"She's . . . gone, Lu," he gasped. "Like mama. They're both gone. . . ."

He toppled into her, sobbing.

It's all right, Tee, she tried to tell him, but she could only hear Annalisa, from long ago.

"It'll be all right," Annalisa had whispered as they huddled under the bed, stomping boots and gunshots filling the safe house. *"It'll be all right, it'll be all right, it'll be—"*

Fingers had bruised Lu's arm and yanked her out from under the bed. The attacker flung her into the shelves that lined the room. Books rained around her, and as she heard the pistol click, she grabbed the nearest one and raised it like a shield.

"It'll be all right," Lu had said, repeating those words

because she couldn't fathom anything else as she stared into the pistol's barrel. *"It'll be all right—"*

The war had ended that night. But nothing had been all right.

Lu prodded at the ache in her heart, at the weeks of watching Annalisa deteriorate. She didn't feel anything other than a sobbing child in her lap and an emptiness that made her blink dumbly as light filled her room.

Kari swung through the doorway, a thin robe wafting around her nightgown. She didn't say a word as she knelt and curled her arms around both Teo and Lu, the scent of coconut rising through her loose black hair, gone to thick curls in the humidity.

The smell swept Lu away, for a heartbeat, for a breath.

Kari had learned the concoction from her own mother, a Tuncian immigrant: Healica, to restore the skin; coconut, to mask the Healica's odor; and various spices from Tuncay that were said to do everything from increase energy to ward off negative thoughts. Lu was overcome by the nutty, rich aroma, which made her recall falling asleep in her mother's lap as a child.

Tom stepped into the room, and over Kari's shoulder, Lu watched him rest a lit candelabrum and pistol on her desk.

The comfort of the moment broke. Lu stared at the weapon, every nerve screaming, *No! Get that away!*

Decorum didn't matter, though—let there be a dozen

rifles in her room, let her world be nothing but weapons and blood again.

None of this mattered. Annalisa had died, just like Bianca had died. Lu hadn't been able to save her.

Tears came, gushing down Lu's cheeks on sobs.

Kari pressed her lips to Lu's forehead. Deep in her throat, she started to hum, stroking Teo's back. Lu recognized the song as one from the revolution. It had become Teo's favorite since Bianca's death.

"Dirt and sand, all across the land; the currents are ours, you see," Kari sang like a lullaby. Teo quieted, his small body spent. *"No god, no soldier, no emperor, no king, can take my current from me."*

Lu had listened to the revolutionaries sing this in the cramped darkness of safe houses, voices soft and breathy.

"Flow on, my friends, flow on with me; together we flow as one," Lu started to sing along, her voice muffled in Kari's shoulder. *"No god, no soldier, no emperor, no king, can erode what we have done."*

9

THE WHISPERS ABOUT Ben grew.

Prince Benat frequents the University, he heard as he passed nobles in the halls, as he sat in pews during crowded Church services. *Does it have anything to do with the incident during the burning? With . . . magic?*

That word followed him like a shadow. Guards drew up to straighter attention when he neared. The aristocrats on the Inquisitor patrols gave him wide berth, their eyes saying they were watching him fall, judging the distance until he hit the ground, placing bets on whether the impact would shatter him or if there was a way, any way, he could be forgiven.

Elazar didn't rescind his order for Ben to make a healing potion with Grace Loray's magic. He didn't have guards waiting to bar Ben from the University or destroy his plants. But surely, after the reaction at Grace Neus Cathedral—the fear, the rumors—Elazar would reconsider?

Every time Ben looked at his father, he saw the spark and spasm of the flames that had killed Rodrigu and Paxben. The unyielding way Elazar had stood on the Grace Neus steps, as though the screams of his brother and nephew would not keep him awake that night, because the Pious God had commanded it.

Ben didn't trust that Elazar wouldn't one day watch his son's death with the same coldness.

When he was younger, Ben had been jealous that Paxben would grow up to take Rodrigu's place. Now Ben *was* in Rodrigu's place. He was trusted to sort plants—*Healica, safe, used to cure any internal or external wound; Narcotium Creeper, evil, a hallucinogen that encourages the Devil's evils of overindulging and intoxication.* With the loan from the Mechts that had bought vials and mortars and other equipment, Ben had all he needed to prepare the plants and combine them into one tonic, maybe, or test them in different preparations—but he needed some modicum of protection to do so.

Which would cause the worst repercussions: dragging the Mecht to the University, or Ben going about his research alone? Either would bring scrutiny. The first, because the citizens of Deza knew the Crown Prince had pardoned a condemned raider, and now he was working with him. The second, because if Ben admitted to having a deep knowledge of Grace Loray's magic, he would be proving himself to be what people had labeled Rodrigu and Paxben: heretics.

Would any number of healing tonics soothe Argrid's hatred? Would it make peace with Grace Loray possible? Would it lead Argrid to tolerance?

Ben was trapped, grinding magic plants as he hunched in the back corner of the laboratory, too afraid to act, too afraid not to.

After three days of working on Elazar's task, Ben had managed to break down most of the plants in the chest from the raider ship. Some were in a paste; some a powder; others didn't need to be broken down. That he could remember, at least, from what Rodrigu had taught him.

But now that Ben had these ingredients, what to do with them? How to make them cure Shaking Sickness? Should he figure out some way to make them more potent, or combine them to see if their effects paired well? He didn't have an endless number of plants, though. And whom would he test them on—would he be able to find any willing participants before Argrid became impatient with rumors of their prince at work on the Devil's magic?

Ben sighed and packed up vials of plants.

A knock, and Jakes entered. "My prince, your carriage is—"

A door slammed in the hall, followed by braying voices.

The University's entryway was narrow, with paneled wood and natural lighting. Defensors who had patrolled the entrance stood near the laboratory door, but they were outnumbered by what looked to be normal citizens, not University servants. Bodies poured through the open doors, some holding lanterns that shot unstable light around the walls.

Ben had only seconds to absorb it. As soon as he appeared in the doorway, people whipped to face him.

"Príncipe Herexe!" they cried. *Heretic Prince.*

The title stunned Ben immobile. The flashing flames in their hands. He couldn't think.

The crowd dove for him over the defensors who shouted for order. Jakes cursed, barring the doorway with his body.

"You play with evil while the true danger grows every day!" one protester bellowed, his lantern shaking. Ben caught glimpses of the man's crazed eyes as he listed with the crowd. The defensors had subdued a few of the intruders, but others came through the doors, and more stood out in the yard beyond, shouting threats in a wave of noise. "You are as covered in Grace Loray's evil as your uncle was! We won't stand for corruption!"

"I'm trying to help you!" Ben pleaded. He clamped his fingers on Jakes's shoulder, his own frenzy a living animal he couldn't tame. "I'm trying to stop the evil! I'm *trying!*"

"So you claim," the man barked. "But Rodrigu claimed to be helping Argrid too, while he was secretly bringing Grace Loray's evil into our country and freeing the monsters who peddled it. You are continuing Rodrigu's work here, and soon the raiders will rise from their den of sin in Grace Loray to spread their depravity into Argrid. We will be lost because of *you*!"

"Enough!" Jakes roared, and slammed his fist into the protester's jaw.

The man was launched back. The protesters grew more hysterical. Fists flew, legs kicked, voices tore the air to pieces with cries of Príncipe Herexe!

"Get the prince to safety!" one defensor called to Jakes.

Jakes pushed Ben toward one of the doors on the far wall that led to corridors and other exits. But Jakes's back was to the crowd, and the protester flung himself through the line of defensors and into the laboratory. Ben yanked Jakes back as the man swung the lantern at his head, and the two of them flattened to the table behind them, barely missing the blow.

The protester's eyes went to Ben's work. Without a pause, the protester raised the lantern and smashed it onto the tabletop.

The glass shattered and heat roared in a burst of flames, feeding on the piles of supplies and harmless documents Ben had scavenged from Rodrigu's old stores.

Ben twisted to the side, watching the fire spread. This dusty space provided plenty of fuel, and in one breath, flames covered half the table.

Jakes dragged Ben by his shirt toward the door at the

rear of the room. The protester saw their attempted escape and took a step toward them, but flames raced down the table legs and over the floor's cracked boards. The man shouted and stumbled back, defensors finally regaining enough control to grab him from behind.

Smoke clogged the room, obscured anything Ben might have been able to see. The fire was spreading too fast, as if it, too, disapproved of what Ben was doing.

Jakes had the door open, but Ben wrenched out of his grip. The chest of magic was still on the table.

"Ben!" Jakes screamed, the crackling fire trying to drown him out.

Ben snatched the chest seconds before the inferno reached that corner of the table. He turned, not dwelling on the sight of the laboratory in flames.

Jakes shoved him through the door and slammed it behind them. The two ran down empty halls, but smoke followed, from new sources now—other protesters had seen the fire and added their own lanterns to the blaze.

Ben and Jakes looped through other wings, trying to put as much distance between themselves and the front of the University as possible. Finally Ben shoved open a side door, dumping him and Jakes in an empty northern courtyard. Night nestled over the unkempt shrubs and chipped fountain as if it had no idea of the destruction paces away.

Ben collapsed on a bench next to the fountain, hacking ash and smoke.

Jakes fell in beside him. "We can't stay here," Jakes said, his voice grating on a raw throat. He wheezed, coughed into his fist. "We have to get you somewhere safe."

Ben gripped the chest. From the distant western wing that housed the laboratory, flickering orange still glowed. The soft, ethereal haze in the blue-black night was almost pretty.

He shoved the chest to the ground. "God, I was so stupid to think it might not come to this. Stupid to think I'd have time . . ."

Jakes dropped to his knees to take Ben's hands. Soot streaked his face, blood trickling from a cut on his forehead. "You knew this would happen? Why?"

Numbness rushed over Ben. "It happened before." He coughed, tears dredging up ashes. *Rodrigu. Heretics burn, Jakes, we burn—*

"Then we know." Jakes didn't ask for clarification. "We know to take precautions now."

"What? You're—you want me to continue?"

Jakes frowned. "You don't? Your father gave you this job. The Pious God condoned it, and it will bring about a stronger Argrid. Why should you stop?"

Ben had a thousand reasons why he should stop. He'd repeated those reasons to himself since Rodrigu's and Paxben's deaths, to keep himself alive, to tamp down his misery. Every one stemmed from fear and self-preservation.

But Ben saw the flames in the distance, smelled his

uncle's university burning, and he knew none of his reasons mattered. Argrid needed the tolerance that would come from his work as much as they needed a peace treaty with Grace Loray. They needed to dislodge this fear.

Shouts came from the western wing of the University. Screaming. And that title, a chant on the wind, a summoning to hell: Príncipe Herexe.

10

LU AWOKE TO Teo's soft snoring. Her eyes were raw but she pried them open, and sure enough, he was curled in a tight ball, sound asleep next to her. For how long, though, she didn't know; he had awoken every hour last night in tears. Not that Lu had slept much herself—memories haunted what sleep she had managed.

The revolution had separated her and Annalisa more than not, shoving them together in safe houses or steamboats with other children. Lu had held Annalisa's innocence as some sort of lighthouse to guide her, reminding her of what she was fighting for.

They had been together the night the revolution ended, in the safe house when Argrid overtook it. The soldiers hadn't found Annalisa—but they got close. Too close. After that, Lu vowed never to let a consequence she deserved threaten someone innocent again. She would take the repercussions;

let people like Annalisa be happy.

But now Annalisa was dead, no matter how Lu had once protected her, or thought in some misguided part of her mind that doing so would atone for the terrible things Lu had done.

Lu closed her eyes, focusing on Teo's breathing. When she opened them again, her attention fell to her desk. The morning sunlight from the balcony doors gleamed on the barrel of Tom's pistol.

There would be little chance to mourn Annalisa. The Council was in upheaval, Vex's fate still to be determined, Milo's fate to be avenged. Who was behind this turmoil?

Teo whimpered in his sleep. Lu pulled the blanket to his chin, and when he calmed, she slipped out of bed.

The pistol stayed on the edge of her vision until she opened her bedroom door and left.

Tom and Kari stood by the overstuffed couch near the windows that gave a view of Lake Regolith's western coast. When they had first been given these apartments, the three of them had cuddled on that couch, looking out at their island, not saying a word. Just holding each other.

Lu grabbed the memory as though it was the only buoyant thing in her sinking world.

Until Kari's harsh whisper brought her back to the present.

"We can't tell her. Give her time. I may yet be able to stop it."

Tom grunted in protest. "Better that she find out from us, before—"

"Find out what?"

Tom and Kari spun to her, surprise pulling their features.

"Adeluna." Kari crossed the room and drew her into a hug. She wore her regular attire now, a cream-colored gown with lace edging on the bell sleeves and hem, her hair tucked back into a braided knot. Her skin glistened with that Tuncian oil blend, and a fresh wave of spiced coconut enveloped Lu in a velvet cocoon.

The pull to unravel was overwhelming. Lu drew back.

"What happened?" she pressed.

"Nothing, sweetheart—"

"There was a vote early this morning," Tom said, kicking his buckle shoe in idle frustration on the floor tiles. Kari shot him a look, but didn't do more to stop him, as though she knew the inevitability of it. "On Ibarra's addendum to our treaty, that we eradicate the stream raiders. It passed."

The tile floor shifted, or perhaps the island itself quivered far beneath Lu's feet.

"What?" Lu asked. "How? Were you there? Did you—"

"The Argridians have been using the news of Ibarra's disappearance to foster fear, saying any authority figure could be next so long as the raiders think they are outside the law." Tom's voice was worn. He slammed his foot still with a shake of his head. "The Council sent out search parties for Ibarra, set up alerts in every port, and called for information from posts across the island—but the Argridians say it isn't enough. They gathered only the councilmembers who would vote in favor of their bill. They had the support necessary to pass it—more than half the councilmembers and two of the Seniors. It's done."

"It isn't done." Kari forced Lu to look into her eyes. "What we are negotiating is a *draft* of a treaty. Nothing has been signed. I will fight this—" She looked at Tom. "I will *fight*. You will too, Tomás. We will keep treaty negotiations going as long as it takes, stretch out the talks while we figure out some way to undo this. Peace with Argrid is not worth civil war here."

"How long?" Tom asked. "How long will Argrid tolerate justice being delayed?"

"We won't stop searching for Ibarra," Kari said. "We'll do everything we can to find him. But accusing the raiders without proof isn't justice."

Tom sighed but didn't press further. The Argridian delegates wouldn't care about nuances. They would demand action. And what would happen when news of Milo's disappearance reached the king? A messenger had already left, no doubt. The Council had weeks, maybe a month, before a higher power added his weight to the call for action.

All Lu felt, watching her beautifully angry mother promise that war wouldn't again come, was empty. Annalisa's death had sucked Lu dry of every drop of emotion.

Argrid wanted Grace Loray to tear itself apart. They

wanted the island to be as it once was, trapped beneath the constant threat of death. Ports controlled by curfews, people shot outright on the streets for any number of offenses. Rivers clouded with blood as soldiers tossed bodies out of the holding cells of Church missions. Hangings, and burnings when the humidity allowed—death, everywhere. But this time, the government Lu had fought so hard to put in place would be the one behind it.

Argrid would get the cleansing they wanted. But Grace Loray would be the one to do it.

Kari rubbed her hands up and down Lu's arms, and she realized her mother had been telling her something. When Lu blinked up at her, Kari's face fell.

"Tomás, send our best to the Council," Kari said. "We have other responsibilities today—neither of us will be—"

"No!" Lu almost shouted, remembering Teo sleeping nearby. But the panic of Kari or Tom not being at any Council meeting, now more than ever, planted desperation in her. "Grace Loray needs you."

"You need us more," Tom said as he came around the couch, and Lu swallowed a sob.

"Go. I'll be fine. Besides, today is—" She thought for a moment. "It was to be the first day of Devereux Bell's interrogation. Though I suppose now—"

Kari's jaw worked, and she looked at the ceiling. "They'll move to kill him. Soon."

Vex's fate was as good as sealed—even if the treaty was

not yet signed, the Argridians could push for his hanging. They had gotten the Council to approve Milo's proposition. Vex would be dead by week's end.

The likelihood of him being an Argridian pawn faded more and more. Would Milo have bothered with Devereux Bell's imprisonment and the theatrics of his trial if Argrid were planning to stage an abduction? Doubtful.

The barest plan sprouted in her mind. If Lu could call it a plan—her idea was one part logic, five parts madness.

Devereux Bell knew Grace Loray better than any other stream raider on the island. At least, that was his reputation. He would be dead soon—which meant he was a man with nothing to lose but much to gain. And he had already proven he was willing to make deals.

"Reports of the search for Milo will come in today as well," Lu pressed.

"Yes," Tom said. "We've already received some. Nothing new, as of yet."

"Nothing at all?" Lu asked. "Isn't that suspicious—"

Kari put her hands on Lu's cheeks. "Not now, my sweet girl. We worked too hard for peace here. I will fight this until Argrid concedes, or until we reveal their plot."

Lu heaved a sigh. "You think they've planned this, too."

Kari pressed her lips together and glanced at Tom. "We have councilmembers, loyal to us, who are looking into it. They are investigating the Drooping Fern and attempting to trace it, as well as other leads. But not now—care for

Teo." She kissed Lu's forehead. "And yourself."

Lu swallowed. *No more tears; please, no more tears.* "Yes, Mother."

Kari jerked away, as though to linger would break her resolve. Tom took her place, pressing a kiss to Lu's forehead while Kari gathered her notes for the meeting.

"I know it may be tempting, with your knowledge of magic, to seek easy salves for grief. . . ." Tom paused. "You're stronger than any magic you think you need, Lulu-bean."

She stiffened. "You've called me that more this week than you have in years."

Why stir up the memories that nickname brought? Memories of Kari weeping while she thought Lu slept, telling Tom how she hated that life had forced them to use their child as a spy. Memories of Tom teaching Lu how to defend herself with a blade. Memories of him waiting for her after missions, holding her while she trembled in his arms.

"Lulu-bean," he'd said. *"I'm so sorry. . . . I'm so proud of you, Lulu-bean. . . ."*

She snapped her head to the side as though to dislodge the memories. That time was finished. The things she had done, the acts she had committed, had brought about peace. And they had been Tom's doing, as he had told her. She was not at fault—the fault was with him.

How many times had she repeated that to herself?

Now Tom smiled. "Do you remember the dog you used to play with after the war?"

He waited until she nodded.

"We would go to the market," he said. "It would jump all over you. It made you so . . . happy." He paused, eyes tearing. "That is how I wish you to be. My happy Lulu-bean."

Lu's eyes dampened. "Father—"

But he cut her off with another kiss on her forehead, and her parents left.

Again, the urge to crumple under grief nearly undid her. Her parents were always able to drag her true emotions out regardless of how well she pushed them down.

It was the final urging she needed to slip back into her room, where Teo slept.

Lu's parents had their own people looking into possible conspiracies, but Argrid had likely expected such retaliation and accounted for it. But no one expected Lu. And no one would expect her to enlist the help of the most notorious stream raider on Grace Loray to find Milo Ibarra.

Her parents were the leaders, coordinating and strategizing. But Lu was the soldier.

The thought of being that person again, coupled with Tom calling her *Lulu-bean* still so raw on the air, shot horror through her. She looked at her hands as she had done during the war—sometimes, they were covered in blood. But most of the time, they were clean.

No. Lu knew the truth. It baffled her that her hands could ever look clean. Even in a midnight alley, when it had been self-defense against a drunken man who had followed her from a tavern where Tom had sent her to spy, and the night had been so black that all color was gone in the nothingness—she could still feel it, in the crevices between her fingers.

Blood.

Was the current upheaval punishment for Lu thinking she could have peace? To tease her with getting so close to a place where she could while away her days making magic concoctions, only to rip it away as a cruel reminder that she had done nothing to deserve such a life.

Annalisa was dead. Grace Loray was being threatened. Lu may not have been deserving of peace, but others were, and she would do what she had done during the war: fight for them.

First, a change of clothes—no stays, not even a shift, and her loosest jacket and petticoat.

Next, vials and vials of plants. Combinations she had made over the years, everything from explosives to healing balms, as many as she could fit in her satchel. Then, a note.

The repercussions of my actions should fall on me alone. I act without the provocation of my parents or Mr. Bell.

Writing it unraveled the facade she had worn since the war had ended. It could destroy her parents' positions, despite stating that they were not involved. The Council would see that a Senior's daughter had freed the criminal at the center of this mess.

Lu crumpled the paper and started again.

In the wake of Annalisa's death, I realize the brevity of life—and I must follow my heart with Devereux. Mother, Father, forgive my defiance. This is what I have to do.

She nearly retched writing the lie. But the result would be less troublesome—the soldiers would corroborate her earlier visit with Vex, and the conclusion would be that she had absconded with a raider to escape her despair over Annalisa's passing.

No politics. Nothing but sympathy for her parents or anger that they had been lax with their daughter.

Lu left the note on her desk, checking over her shoulder to make sure Teo slept.

At the back of her armoire, buried beneath shifts and petticoats and silken things she had armored herself with for the past five years, sat a bag Lu had tried to forget. She eased it out, the weapons within clanking, and Teo groaned in his sleep. Half of her hoped he would awaken and ask the questions that would stop her.

"Lu, what are you doing? What's in the bag? Are you leaving me too?"

Lu swallowed her regret, told the servant cleaning up the breakfast spread to watch over Teo, and slipped out of her family's suite.

There were two explanations for Milo's disappearance: either he had staged it, or he had been abducted—unlikely, given that the outcome had aligned in Argrid's favor, and no other parties had made demands or claimed to have him. Regardless of the cause, the Council would blame the raiders, and war would come. What, then, could undermine Argrid's attempts at painting the raiders as villains that the Council should eradicate?

If a raider brought Milo back to court, not as a captor but as a heroic savior.

If Lu got Devereux Bell to seek out Milo Ibarra, find him, and drag him back to the Council, the Argridians would have to admit gratitude—or their conspiracy would be revealed. The raiders would also have to be grateful, for saving them from another brutal war and proving their innocence. It could lead to the raiders swearing fealty to Grace Loray's Council, after the proof of the benefits the Council could offer that syndicates could not.

Argrid may have expected people like Kari or Tom to send spies in search of the truth—but they would not expect a girl to ally with a raider and use his channels to seek out places an Argridian might be hiding on this island.

Devereux knew Grace Loray better than anyone—and Lu would make him find Milo Ibarra.

She hurried through the castle, not letting herself think on what this meant. That she was willingly searching out Milo. Did Argrid want revenge for the revolution? Were they seeking to reclaim Grace Loray? No matter. Lu would find Milo. The treaty would dissolve, and Argrid would at long last leave Grace Loray *alone*—possibly in a peace stronger than it had yet seen, if the raiders complied and unified with them.

This would be good. This *had* to be good.

Two guards stood at attention in the soldiers' alcove, the same two who had been on duty when last she had visited.

"Back again, Miss Andreu?" one jeered. They knew her now.

"It was Adeluna!" they would tell her parents. *"Your daughter attacked us. . . ."*

Lu adjusted her satchel. The looseness of her clothes hid her fist in the folds of her petticoat—and the long, thin reed she had clasped in her palm. "Would it be too much trouble to see Mr. Bell? I hear he is to be on trial, and— I mean, I'm sure he has gotten little support—"

The soldier chuckled, his hand going to the ring on his belt. He fingered one key in particular—black, longer than the others. It was all she needed.

The proper lady was gone. She needed to be a soldier now.

She lifted the reed to her lips and blew. The contraption's end opened, releasing some of the Drooping Fern smoke trapped within. A cloud of gray haze fanned around the first soldier's face, then the second as Lu shifted the reed to him.

They didn't have time to gape at her—they inhaled, and went down.

Lu covered her nose and mouth, the Drooping Fern hovering in the air, and grabbed the key ring from the soldier's belt.

❊❊❊

With each day that passed without a member of Vex's crew appearing, he doubted his plan to avoid Argrid in jail. Well, he'd doubted his plan the moment he'd been recognized in the communal cell, but he *really* began to doubt it when three days had passed and he hadn't gotten even a coded message about an imminent rescue. He, Nayeli, and Edda had managed to save each other from every raider syndicate on the island, as well as other Council prisons—this one should've been no different.

When the door opened again, Vex was sitting on the bench, elbows on his knees as he rolled possible escape routes through his mind. And came up with a grand total of zero plans.

He hung his head on a long groan.

"Miss, we can't allow you in here today."

Vex whipped his head up. The girl was standing in front of his cell, pouting at the guards.

"Oh, the other men said it would be all right." Her voice was more feminine than when she'd talked to Vex—Nayeli did that whenever she wanted to sway men to do her bidding.

The girl had something planned.

Her hands were behind her back. When a soldier stepped

forward to intercept her, she lifted a reed and blew a cloud in his face.

The soldier dropped. The girl spun around him and blew the last of the smoke in the final soldier's face. He fell, joining his comrade in what would be a long nap.

By this time, Vex was standing, hands out, his brain making a long, high-pitched shrieking noise.

The girl held up a key ring. "General Ibarra is missing," she said to him. "The Argridians used his abduction to pass a bill to eradicate raiders on Grace Loray—and your death will be one of the first. You can either stay and die, or you can come with me."

Vex rubbed his eye. "I'm hallucinating. You drugged me too."

"If I drugged you, you wouldn't be aware until the effects had already taken hold."

In the time Vex had known her, this girl had been a common market patron, a levelheaded politician's daughter, an expert in botanical magic, and now . . . an assassin, by the looks of it. The guards weren't dead, but she didn't seem at all moved by what she'd done.

"What do you want me to do?"

"To prevent war, I want you to help me find General Ibarra—and learn the truth of what happened to him."

"Wait—you want me to help you rescue one of the politicians who want me dead?"

"If a raider saves him, it will be harder to garner public support against them," she said. "And you know Grace Loray better than anyone. You know parts of this island I don't, where a missing man might be. And you have access to, shall we say, *unsavory* fellows who might hear news that would not reach respectable society. Regardless of my reasons, I'm offering you a chance at freedom. Why are you hesitating?"

Vex smiled, but the expression was cold. "I'm trying to figure out what would possess one of Grace Loray's prim daughters to make such a deal. You know what they say about me, right? Or did my unfettered charm and dashing good looks make you forget that I'm *a criminal*? What's to stop me from leaving you once we get out of this castle?"

The girl held up the empty reed. "I'll give you any botanical magic concoction you desire. Concoctions that other raiders haven't yet dreamed of."

Vex gave a disinterested shrug. "Drooping Fern is so common in my profession that you'd have to give me boatloads of those reeds to make it worth even a hundred galles."

Her nostrils flared. "That balm I gave you," she said. "You used it?"

Vex straightened. Obviously he had—his face was healed, the bruises and cuts gone.

"You know it was not Digestive Death." She rummaged through her satchel to come up with another jar. "This, however, *is* a poison. Sweet Peat. Consumption dissolves anyone's internal organs, but what many don't know is that its effects can be used on . . . other things."

She tossed the key ring away before tipping the jar's contents onto the lock. The poison started to eat the metal; in seconds, the lock was a foaming blob on the floor.

Vex let out a whistle. He'd come across Sweet Peat before, and he'd always destroyed it. The poison was so powerful, with no plant to neutralize it, that he didn't trust it to be resold—things like Sweet Peat almost made him understand why the Church had condemned magic.

But he had never heard of it being used like this. Escaping cells, breaking into safes—a single jar of stuff with that potential would go for a couple hundred galles to the right raider.

He could almost hear Nayeli's excited squeal. Forget retiring in a mansion somewhere—concoctions like this could let them buy a whole goddamn *port*.

"With this kind of magic, you could be extremely wealthy yourself," he said.

The girl slid the jar back into her bag. "I deal honorably. Unless the situation calls for it."

He beamed at her. "Wicked princesa."

"Politician."

"I don't know why you keep bragging about that."

"Your answer?" she pressed.

It was a way out. If he got enough magic to let him and his crew retire somewhere nice and fancy on top of it, he'd be a fool to pass it up.

But damn it if this girl didn't poke at his feelings of guilt and responsibility. Her plan sounded sane enough: find this Ibarra fellow, return him to the Council.

Vex almost told her the whole truth—but he doubted she'd work with him if she found out he did have Argridian connections. He *was* being blackmailed by them, but still.

He nodded. The girl didn't waste a beat and started up the hall, pulling her black curls into a knot. Vex strode out of the cell. The melted lock hissed on the stones. *Damn.*

When he got into the soldiers' alcove, his mix of shock and awe only increased. The two other guards were unconscious—and the girl was *stripping off her dress.*

Enough reasoning broke through for him to note that there was another outfit under her gown: breeches, boots, a black shirt and vest, and holsters for all manner of weapons strapped across her torso. But everything in Vex's body went rigid.

"You took off your dress," he stated. He should've been more concerned by the goddamn arsenal on her chest, but his brain wouldn't let the other fact go.

She frowned. "I didn't take you for someone who cared about decorum."

Footsteps slapped the staircase. Vex jerked toward the sound, but the girl moved first.

A soldier entered the alcove. The girl fell to her hands, swung her leg out, and caught the guard's ankles. He flopped to his backside and the girl stood to bring her heel

onto his neck with enough pressure to render him unconscious like the others.

"I wasn't sure I'd remember how to do that," the girl
admitted.

Vex choked, laughed, choked again. "Who *are* you?"

She took a moment to steady herself, but when she
looked up at Vex, she smiled.

It was the smile Nayeli gave when she was about to suggest blowing someone up.

"I'm Adeluna—Lu," the girl told him. "Former soldier
of the revolution."

Rhodofume

Availability: fairly common

Location: clay deposits in riverbeds

Appearance: bushy flowers that contain
brown pods

Method: pod is thrown and strikes a hard
surface

Use: smoke screen

II

"SOLDIER," THE RAIDER repeated. "During the revolution. *You were a soldier during the revolution.*"

Lu clenched her jaw, already regretting divulging that information, and took the stairs leading out of the dungeon's alcove. Vex followed.

"How?" he asked, not bothering to lower his voice until she shushed him. "You were a kid during the revolution. There's no way you could've been a soldier."

Lu stopped in the middle of the staircase and spun around. Vex didn't recoil, even now that he knew what kind of person he stared up at.

"Should we talk or escape?" she said. "At this point, I almost do not care."

Vex waved her on. "Fine, Princesa. You won't hear another word from me."

"I doubt that."

"Ah, see? We know each other so well already."

Lu resumed walking—stomping—up the stairs. They reached the landing, a long hall that ran parallel to the Council's courtroom. Four doors lined the walls: two led into the courtroom, one led to the castle's entryway, and one to servants' halls.

Only two of the doors would provide escape. The entryway, though, was almost as risky as hauling Vex through the courtroom itself.

The servants' halls. Out the kitchen. Or a window—yes, a window.

Plan formed, Lu launched herself out of the stairwell, sprinting for the door on the right. Vex followed, and despite his senseless chatter before, he moved silently now—she had to glance back to assure herself that he hadn't run off.

If he does? What will you do?

Lie was her instant response. *Claim our elopement went sour. And figure out some other way to save Grace Loray.*

Lu opened the servants' door. An empty hall branched out before her, lit by a line of first-floor windows that offered a jarring drop to the kitchen gardens. Beyond them, Lu could see the wall that surrounded the castle grounds, the blue sky bright above.

She raced ahead and yanked on the first window. It slid easily—too easily. The glass slammed into the casement above with a bang that echoed down the hall.

Lu held her breath as Vex leaned beside her. His

seriousness surprised her, so she didn't immediately notice that he was looking not out the window, but back down the hall.

Lu whirled, willing herself not to reach for her weapons.

But when she saw who it was, she wheezed. "Teo?"

He stood on the threshold of the servants' hall. "Lu. Where are you going?"

Teo's eyes went to Vex. For a moment, the joy on his face was such a welcome reprieve from his grief that Lu didn't care what had caused it. Let him be happy.

"Lu!" Teo squealed. "Devereux Bell! What are you doing? I want to come!"

Lu shushed him but urged him forward and closed the door behind him. "Teo—I need you to go back to my room. Please, I cannot explain now, but—"

"*No.*" He stomped his foot. "I saw your note. I can read, you know."

The blame was heavy in his tone.

Anna left me. Mama left me. Now you're leaving too.

Lu's heart weakened. "Teo." She bent and took his hands. "Trust me, all right? I promise, I will return as soon as I am able. I . . . there's something I have to do."

Teo ripped out of her grasp, studying Vex. "With him? I'm coming. I followed you this far, didn't I? I can do this! You shouldn't be alone. All right? No one should be alone."

Warmth gathered in Lu's eyes, tears on the edge.

On the other side of the door, hinges shrieked.

The contingent sent to gather Vex for the Council.

Panic broke through, but Lu knew what to do with panic—she focused on her plan, just her plan, and breathing, just breathing.

Out the window. Through the garden. Over the castle wall. *Go.*

"Teo, return to my room," Lu ordered.

Teo exhaled, the chirp of a scream starting to escape. Lu dove for him, but a pair of arms swept in.

Vex lifted Teo and settled him on his hip. "We haven't met. I'm Devereux Bell."

Teo gaped, wonderstruck. "I'm Teo. Casales. I'm Teo Casales."

"Now, Teo Casales"—Vex looked back to the window—"how good are you at climbing?"

"The best!"

"Glad to hear it. It isn't too far, but you think we can make it?"

"Stop!" Lu grabbed the window. Vex leaned halfway out, Teo clinging to his neck, the two of them peering down the single-story drop. "He isn't coming," she stated.

Teo sulked. "Devereux Bell wants me to come."

"You think we have time to get him back to your room?" Vex nodded toward the door.

The soldiers were no doubt in the alcove by now. They had seconds. Less than that.

Teo beamed at her, victorious.

Vex didn't give her a chance to argue. He hefted Teo onto his back, the boy's legs looping Vex's waist and his arms around Vex's neck.

"Hold on, kid," he said, straddled the window, and jumped.

Lu squealed at their descent, but it was only a heartbeat before they hit the grass.

Vex looked up at her, grinning. "Coming, Princesa?"

"Yeah, Princesa—are you coming?" Teo echoed.

Behind Lu, someone shouted. The soldiers had found the bodies in the alcove.

She jumped out the window after the mad raider and a giggling Teo, making sure they both saw her scowl as she pushed ahead of them, into the garden.

On their way to the wall, they passed a group of servants, harvesting sweet potatoes. Soldiers would question them.

"It was Bell, yes!"

"He abducted Miss Andreu? And the young Casales boy?"

"No—it was Miss Andreu who led the way!"

Lu burst through the kitchen gardens' gate with more force than necessary. The closest exit would be at the stables, one of the first places the guards would look. Or they could climb the wall and descend the rocky, perilous cliff to Lake Regolith and make their way along the coast until they reached a traversable beach. . . .

They would have to risk the stables.

Lu followed the garden's fence through the compound, straining to hear any sound from the castle. Every minute counted down in her mind, making her desperate. But Vex kept pace with Teo on his back, and in seconds they huddled against the largest barn.

"All right." Lu leaned around the corner, eyeing the space between them and the open gate. "There are five soldiers—two on the parapet of the guardhouse, three on the ground."

Vex nudged Lu. When she gave him a look, he held out his hand.

"Weapon, please."

"No."

"I said *please*."

"No."

"If we have to fight, I'll need—"

"*No.*"

Vex huffed. "What, you're the only one who's allowed to go around knocking people out? My life is at risk, Princesa. Let me fight for it."

"You lost that privilege the moment you—"

"Um. Lu?"

Lu looked at Teo. He stared up at the castle.

Then she heard it—the signal bell, tolling high and fast.

"Shit," she cursed.

Vex and Teo gaped at her with identical expressions of horror. Lu sighed, a thousand things she wanted to do warring in her mind, but she settled on pointing at Vex.

"Follow me. Do exactly what I tell you." And she walked out from behind the barn.

Vex stumbled after her. "What are you *doing?*"

One of the tricks she'd learned during the revolution—if she acted as though she belonged, people overlooked her. At least a half dozen times, she had strolled out of fortified places she'd had no business escaping from.

The three soldiers on the ground spoke with a newly arrived soldier, who was no doubt relaying news of Vex's escape. But they would be looking for a single prisoner, not three people, and not with a child.

The gate operated on a system of weights and pulleys, mainly an iron chain that attached to a crank at the base of the guardhouse. The crank sat next to the talking soldiers. Lu clamped her fists, thinking.

She approached the open gate, walking as though she were a servant leaving after a day's work. Vex hunched behind her, letting his hair hide his face and distinguishing features. Teo clung to him, eyes wide, but all Lu heard from him was a softly whispered song.

"Flow on, my friends, flow on with me—"

The revolution song.

Two paces, and they'd be outside the castle.

"Miss Andreu?"

Lu froze. The gate was above them. She batted her hand against the small of her back as she rotated, signaling for Vex to continue on. This wasn't an outcome she had considered—if she got caught, but Vex escaped with Teo.

If that happens, drown me now.

Lu dredged up a smile as one of the soldiers pulled away from the others: Branden, the captain of the guard.

She cursed again. But noted his position, right in front of the gate's crank.

Branden blushed as he registered her irregular clothing. "Um, Miss Andreu, what're—"

He looked past her, to Vex, slumping down the road with Teo on his back.

Before Branden could piece anything together, Lu pulled the most harmless thing she could out of her satchel—a sack of Variegated Holly that she had altered into a sound grenade. The white and green leaves were usually ignited to create explosions, but this sack contained Holly leaves that Lu had softened by soaking in concentrated Sweet Peat. A stalk of Hemlight within would ignite upon impact, and the Variegated Holly leaves would rupture in a cacophony. Harmless, but loud.

"Captain," Lu said, taking steps backward. "I am sorry."

Branden paused in front of the gate's crank.

Lu smashed the grenade to the ground. The impact lit the Hemlight, releasing first a spark—but it caught the Holly, and the whole sack ruptured in one great, trembling *BOOM!* that sent Branden flailing back. He hit the crank, releasing the gears, and the gate above groaned, creaked, and plummeted into the dusty road with a resounding *thunk.*

But Lu was already on the other side, racing down the road with Vex and Teo.

✼✼✼

Vex had a feeling he'd have to get used to Lu leaving him in equal states of shock, horror, and, if he was being honest, attraction.

The castle bell warred with the shouting guards fighting to reopen the gate. Vex hooted into the air, not breaking stride.

"How did you do that?" he asked. "Variegated Holly, right? But it didn't kill him—damn, Princesa, you're an enigma. You have to explain this to me."

"I do not have to explain anything," Lu threw back, winded. "I will give you the altered Variegated Holly, but I never promised to explain how I make—"

"That's not what I meant."

The narrow path dumped them onto a larger road. To the right, it led to the castle's main entrance; to the left, New Deza. Lu guided them to the left, and Vex matched her as she slowed to a walk alongside the traffic of the port. Humidity made everything sticky, but Vex found he didn't mind the heat or the stench of bodies that greeted them from New Deza.

Vex shifted so he could lace his fingers under Teo to create a more comfortable seat for the kid. "I meant how you know *any* of this," he continued. "You're the daughter of politicians, but you can escape from a dungeon in less than—what, ten minutes? Shit, Princesa, you waste that talent listening to Council meetings?"

"She didn't waste anything!" Teo leaped to her defense, kicking with enthusiasm. The kid was stronger than he seemed—he sent Vex teetering, his boot sinking into a puddle of oily water on the side of the road. "She tried hard to help my sister with the magic. Didn't you, Lu? Tell him!"

Vex watched Lu for clarification. She winced, pivoting to let parcel-burdened maids edge past her through the crowd.

"That doesn't matter." Lu stopped outside a cobbler with its shutters thrown open to welcome a nonexistent breeze. "I freed you from the dungeon, raider. Now it's your turn—how do we find Milo Ibarra before Argrid convinces the Council to start a civil war?"

"Oh, good. At least there's nothing important riding on this."

Lu didn't laugh.

Vex's initial thought was *Yeah, how do we find Milo Ibarra?* But hey, he'd take it step by step, like he always did. The first thing they'd need was transportation out of the port. Even if someone in New Deza would help them, their descriptions would be all over the city in less than an hour. Was the *Rapid Meander* docked where he'd left it before he'd gotten arrested? Eh, it was worth a shot.

Vex jostled Teo. "Hang on, kid—it's gonna get rough." He met Lu's eyes with a smirk. "See if you can keep up."

And he took off, cutting into the crowd, looking back to make sure Lu hadn't lost him. She was on his heels—looking far from pleased.

They darted down cobblestone streets, pressing between horse-drawn carriages that crossed bridges over canals. After Vex led them down the fourth road where they'd had to step over a Mecht raider half-lucid on Narcotium Creeper, Lu shoved his arm.

"Is there a more civilized route we could take?" she demanded, eyes cutting to Teo.

Vex shot her an incredulous look. "Sure. Let's go an hour out of our way to hit the three pretty boulevards of New Deza. Do you want a tour or do you want to get out of here?"

Lu balked, but her irritation deflated. "There are more than three routes that are less—"

She stopped, but Vex knew what she meant and let her know with a smirk.

"Less raider-infested? This port may be a different place than it was during the war, but that doesn't mean it's *nice* now."

Lu's annoyance returned. "I am done listening to you insult this island and its governing. It *is* a nice place now, no matter what you believe. I saw it at its worst, and while it may not yet be at its best, it is far from—"

Vex cut a face Nayeli often used to shut him up—eye rolled back in his head, tongue out as he mimicked how she was talking. Lu shrieked, but he picked up his pace, pushing down another alley.

Soon enough, Vex stumbled out onto a pretty promenade that ringed the northern part of New Deza's docks. He gave Lu a look that said, *Happy now?*

Cafés and shops lined the road, filled with fancy people dining or throwing away galles on lavish knickknacks. Vex had no use for what Nayeli called the *sickeningly expensive* area of New Deza. He didn't pause at any of the stores, even when Teo choked him and cried, "Chocolates!"—he raced down the tide wall's steps to the docks.

"Here we go." Vex stopped on a pier that ran from the northernmost military docks all the way to the southernmost merchant docks. Market stalls sat up against the tide wall, vendors peddling magic and other goods brought in by the boats anchored throughout the harbor.

At any moment in any port market on the island, vendors and buyers alike did their best to be nonchalant around soldiers. Part instinct from Argrid's years of oppression; part self-preservation due to illegal activity they didn't want coming to light.

The people here should have bustled from stall to stall, avoiding eye contact with soldiers while going about their day as perfectly normal citizens, thank-you-very-much.

But every soldier on patrol had a wide bubble of space between them and any patrons. Women with bulging sacks of the day's purchases huddled on the side of the road, waiting for two soldiers to pass, and only then did they scurry on their way. A vendor hurled a tarp over his wares to close up shop before a soldier walked by. The castle bell, tolling in the distance, made people flinch and shoot worried eyes at the nearest guards.

Lu grabbed Teo's leg to keep from losing them in the press of people. The stench was worse here than higher in the port, with body odor and various food items gone rancid.

"What's here that will help us find General Ibarra?" Lu asked.

Vex nodded at the crowd. "Anything seem strange to you?"

Lu looked. She frowned. "Is this a trick? What am I meant to see?"

Vex rolled his eye. Maybe he was imagining things. All this talk of an Argridian plot and a staged abduction had gotten into his head.

He shook it off and waved at the vessels on the docks. Most were multistory paddled steamboats for sailing the deep waters of Lake Regolith; others were masted ships that had navigated the larger rivers from the Ovidic Ocean.

"Pick one," he said.

Lu balked. "We're going to steal a boat? One of *these* boats?"

Her voice rose, but she stopped when she saw him smiling at her.

"You're joking."

"Yes. Payback for not giving me a weapon."

Lu's frown darkened, but Vex waved his hands in surrender. "Seriously, though," he continued. "My boat should be down—"

A body slammed into Lu, knocking her so hard that her hand on Teo's leg was the only thing that saved her from getting sucked away into the crowd. Vex had a brief moment of annoyance—*Damn it, don't have time for a pickpocket*—before he saw who it was: Nayeli.

He smiled. Good. His crew had probably guessed that the castle's bell was because of his escape and had stationed themselves around the docks in hope that he'd show up.

Nayeli's voluminous black curls made her eyes look larger and even more terrifying as she pointed at Lu in an unspoken question of *Need me to kill her?*

Vex smirked and shook his head.

Lu righted herself and whirled on Nayeli, who wiggled a knife in her hand.

Lu patted her holster, felt the missing blade, and snarled.

Oh, these two would be fun together.

Vex pouted. "Why'd *she* get one of your weapons and I didn't? That doesn't seem fair."

Lu lunged and Nayeli ducked to the side, slipping away with a giggle. Vex opened his mouth to explain, but Lu grabbed his arm and yanked him along in the chase. He went, his laughter drowned out by the hubbub of the crowd.

Nayeli wove down the pier, ducking around stall patrons, leaping over parked wagons. Every so often she glanced back—not to see if she'd escaped, as Lu would think, but to make sure Lu pursued. She'd pause before blind turns, linger if traffic held them up.

They were almost to the dock where he'd left the *Meander* when Lu slammed to a halt outside a fish shop. Barrels of thrashing catfish made the air salty and sharp, and the look on Lu's face gave Vex a vivid image of her dunking him in one of those barrels.

"Who. Is. She?" Lu demanded. She tightened her fingers around Vex's arm.

"Ow, ow, *ow*—"

He teetered, Teo squealed, and Lu released him.

"Nayeli!" Vex shouted. Then, to Lu, "She's . . . well, she's Nayeli."

Explaining her would take too long.

Lu drew in a breath that no doubt would have carried a piercing remark, but Nayeli slipped in, Lu's own blade pressed discreetly to her ribs.

"Shhhh." Nayeli held a finger to her lips. "It isn't nice to yell."

Lu blinked at her. "Unless you wish for me to break your hand, *return my knife*."

Nayeli presented her with the hilt. "Are we ready? It's down that dock. Oh, he's so cute!"

She launched herself at Teo, whose face went scarlet.

"Are we ready for what?" Lu asked.

"What do you mean 'for what'?" Vex echoed. "You freed me in order to use my connections to find that Argridian, didn't you? Well, meet one of my connections."

Lu glanced at Nayeli. "She's part of your crew."

Vex nodded. He watched as Lu noted the area. Not the dodgiest section of the wharf, but not the nicest, and sure as hell not one claimed by the Mecht syndicate.

"Your boat is here," she guessed.

For an answer, Vex started down one of the docks. The crowd thinned out the moment they stepped onto the wooden planks, the wood thumping under their boots. They passed at least a half dozen steamboats moored to wooden pillars before Vex cut a quick look at Lu, who stared forward, her face blank.

"How is your boat here?" she asked, too calmly.

Vex unwound Teo's arms from his neck and tipped backward, depositing him onto the dock. "You can walk now, kid—we're almost there."

"We are?" Teo's excitement was so tangible, they could bottle and sell it.

Nayeli giggled. "You'll love it! Who are you?"

She took his hand and led him on as he told her and shot questions right back at her—the boat's name, its size, its speed. Lu's hand on Vex's arm stopped him from following, her touch softer than moments ago. That gentleness was more intimidating.

"How is your boat here, Vex?"

He tried his best to look offended. "I had my own escape in the works, thank you."

"You were able to contact your crew—the one you had lost when you pickpocketed me in the market? How did they get to you?"

"Why would I tell you? What if I need to escape the castle's dungeon again?"

"Planning to be arrested a second time, are you?"

"If it serves me."

Lu stepped closer. Vex almost pulled away, then realized this was the closest she'd stood yet. A shiver came from the center of his stomach, spreading out, down his arms.

He stayed where he was.

"I may not know what game you're playing, but believe me, I will find out," Lu started, her chest brushing his. Seagulls screeched over the roar of the pier's crowd. "As much as I don't know you, raider, you don't know me. You have no idea what I am capable of."

Vex considered. "You're right—I don't know you. But I know who you want to be, Princesa, and that might be more dangerous to you."

Lu's gaze didn't break from his. "If anything you do interferes with finding Milo and returning him to the Council, I will use that Sweet Peat concoction on something dear to you."

She slid her knee up to the area she meant, a light graze

that didn't hurt—quite the opposite.

Vex twitched, creating a spasm in his torso that rocked him forward, bumping into her. An unbroken strand of curse words flitted through his head. He should not be so attracted to someone so set on maiming him.

He closed his eye for a second, for composure. When he looked at her, he let himself fall away, his humor and cockiness gone.

"I won't betray you," he told her.

She held, her eyes flitting over his face, waiting for his earnestness to break. It didn't.

"Fine," she said. "Now where's your boat?"

12

THAT VEX COULD go from secretive to sincere in one breath was infuriating. When he crooked his elbow to her and said, "Milady," Lu gave an unimpressed stare and marched down the dock.

Ahead, his crew member Nayeli stood on the deck of a steamboat, her arms out to Teo on the dock. He hesitated and looked back at Lu, briefly losing his adventuring spirit.

She smiled, grateful he could get her to, grateful she had someone whose life depended on her, reminding her of what was at stake.

But beneath that gratitude, she felt disgust at herself.

She was bringing a six-year-old into untold danger. Few of the things she had done during the war with Argrid had made her feel this . . . soulless.

Teo took her hand, and his tight grip pulled her back to herself.

"Aboard, Captain Casales!" Nayeli said, swaying like the clouds, constant bright motion that Lu suspected could all too easily give to storm. Her wild black curls accented golden skin and a softly rounded face that said she was a good part Tuncian. Unlike Vex's, her hand was free of a raider brand, which only meant that Argrid's Church had never captured her.

Lu squeezed Teo's fingers and analyzed Vex's boat.

The vessel was small, built for no more than five or six people. Red cedar had been polished and sealed for the bottom, giving the hull a dark berry color. The floor and interior were planks of teak in varying hues, depending on the state of restoration. The deck held a stack of crates tied to the starboard railing, a hatch, and, tucked up under the smokestack, the pilothouse. Within it, Lu could see a wooden helm and a table covered with maps and charts, tidily arranged.

Vex stopped beside Lu. "Breathtaking, isn't she?"

Lu couldn't keep the shock out of her tone. "This is your boat? And by *yours* I mean—"

"I didn't steal her." Vex leaped from the dock and landed beside Nayeli. He patted the hull, his pride undeniable. "Welcome to the *Rapid Meander*, Princesa."

Lu snorted. Nayeli and Vex shared a questioning look before eyeing her, and Lu swallowed the quip she had been about to make. Their love for this boat was clear—best not to insult them before Vex had fulfilled his end of their arrangement.

Lu stepped onto the deck. As she reached back for Teo, her eyes caught something up the pier. The crowd moved with the normal bustle of midday, but two flickers of intensity peeked through like fish breaking the surface of a lake.

The closest one sprinted up the dock, footsteps hammering on the planks.

"Soldiers coming!" the woman shouted as she ran.

She dove aboard, and Lu's presence made the woman teeter, blink, and glare. The wrinkles around her eyes said that her normal expression was a glower, but her height made her intimidating even without any expression.

The woman's slight accent cemented the impression that she was from the Mechtlands. She was tall, well muscled, her hair yellow and her fair skin ruddy in a way that made the white brand on her wrist stand out.

The haphazardness of Vex's crew wasn't a surprise. They were unaligned, after all, but it still left Lu in a state of awe. One of the reasons unaligned crews were so rare was that raiders with different heritages seldom got along, let alone well enough to be crewmates.

Vex motioned between her and the Mecht woman. "Edda, Lu. And that's Teo."

Introductions complete, the deck unraveled in a flurry of motion.

"Nayeli! Unmoor the *Meander*. Edda—the furnace have enough fuel for now?"

Edda gave him a cutting look that said, *Do you have to ask?*

"Excellent. Oh, Princesa, you might want to—"

Lu had snatched Teo into her arms the moment Edda had raced down the dock, but at Vex's words, she sat him on the deck.

"What do I need to do? Will we make it away from the pier in time?"

Edda paused, climbing the pilothouse. "The pier? They're coming on steamboats, barricading the harbor."

But Vex connected it first. He pulled out a spyglass and moved to the port side, rocking the *Meander* as he planted his foot on the railing and lifted the glass toward the pier.

Lu followed, directing him to the pocket of intensity she had seen in the crowd.

After a beat, Vex lowered the spyglass. "What was it you said earlier? *Shit?*"

"Who is it?"

"It seems Pilkvist has found us." Vex flew back into the pilothouse, attacking the gears and nobs along the wall. "Nayeli!"

"Unmoored!"

"Edda?"

"Waterway is clear!"

Lu shouted over the chaos, "What do you need me to do?"

"Nothing!" Vex yanked on a lever, twisted the wheel,

and sent the *Rapid Meander* heaving away from the dock.

Lu toppled backward. Teo clung to the bow, screeching as the boat glided for the open waters of Lake Regolith. But through the roar of the *Rapid Meander*'s engine came a sharp burst of sound that Lu knew by heart: gunfire.

Lu clawed her way across the deck and pulled Teo down.

He dropped onto his backside. "Lu, raiders are chasing us! We're on Devereux Bell's boat! And we're raiders now, too!"

Lu ignored him to look over the railing. The *Rapid Meander* sailed across the narrow expanse of water between their dock and the next one. Through the gaps between the moored boats, Lu saw men running up the dock, barely keeping pace as Vex punched the boat faster.

Their appearance marked them as raiders—tattered clothes, weapons across their waists and up their chests, various traits speaking of Mecht affiliation: blond hair here, wooden toggles in another's beard, boots made of crocodile skin. One fired a pistol, the shot landing in the wall of a boat. They'd never be able to aim with the steamboats in the way—but once the *Rapid Meander* cleared the docks, it would be open for the few moments it stayed within firing range.

Lu scrambled in her satchel. Sweet Peat . . . Narcotium Creeper . . . ah, finally.

Sometimes Grace Loray's botanical magics worked well as they were. In this case, an unaltered Variegated Holly leaf would be fine.

Lu bent onto her knees. Teo hunched next to her, suppressing giggles into his palm.

The part of Lu that had spent her childhood doing this—fighting to survive, not just live—had propelled her to this precipice, where she was holding a deadly botanical plant and staring at her friend's brother.

In that moment, she saw herself, younger, staring up at her father with an innocence she had lost because of situations like this. She saw herself holding a pistol, and she could still hear the echo of the blast, see the spark that had punched light into the shadows of the jungle even though her father had sworn it would be dark.

"That tree, Lulu-bean, there," Tom had told her. *"Wait for movement. I'll force him out. This isn't on your shoulders, you hear me? Fire at the first movement. You won't see a thing, I promise."*

Lu froze now. The only thing she could move was her eyes, which she lifted as the boat sped on, until they barreled into open water. The Mecht raiders stumbled to the end of the dock.

Cold sweat beaded across Lu's forehead. The leaf in her hand weighed more than she could bear, and her fist sank to the deck.

I'm doing to Teo what my father did to me.

I don't regret that life! It helped the war!

But—her heart broke—*I wouldn't wish it on anyone.*

Something thumped behind her. Lu whipped around to see Nayeli on a stack of crates, holding a fistful of plants.

"Everyone, remain calm," she announced. "I'm about to blow some shit up."

"Nay!" Vex shouted from the pilothouse. "We've a kid here now, all right?"

"Sorry. I'm about to *chaotically rearrange* some shit up."

"That wasn't the problem—" Vex started to say at the same moment Lu cried, "Don't—"

But Nayeli waved her hand by her ear. "Can't hear you. Explosion's too loud."

She reared back and let a bundle fly. It smashed onto the dock, but all that came was a series of pops and sparks that caught the raiders' clothes—Hemlight. Relatively harmless, not lethal, it leaped to life in flashes of orange that kept the raiders well occupied as the *Rapid Meander* flew beyond reach.

Up the harbor, a Council boat approached, the sigil of Grace Loray rippling beside the smokestack. It was no doubt forming the blockade Edda had mentioned, the one full of ships searching for Vex. But he and his crew would be far enough away by the time it reached these docks.

The *Rapid Meander* blew by other boats. One cluster looked, at first glance, to be another Council patrol. The largest vessel in the group of six flew Grace Loray's flag— but before Lu shouted for Vex to avoid them, she realized it was an extraction group, one Council boat keeping watch as the half dozen civilian craft anchored around it sent divers into the lake to mine magic plants. Bubbles pocked the surface of the lake, marking diving bells far below.

Even so, Vex steered the *Meander* away from the group. Twelve or more Grace Loray marines often manned patrol boats, making sure law-abiding citizens accounted for every plant taken from the lake or riverbeds.

But no one gave the *Meander* a glance, and Vex pushed the boat faster, taking them east, away from New Deza.

Lu melted to her knees, calming enough to go over her mistake. Why hadn't she thought of Hemlight? Why had she gone for a plant that would kill the raiders? Was that truly her instinct again, after all these years?

No, she told herself. She hadn't reached for a lethal plant when confronted with Branden at the castle's gate. She could find Milo without losing herself.

Lu shook it off and stood, leaving Teo to stare at the water in fascination as she walked up to the pilothouse's window. Through it, she fixed Vex with a stare. "What next, raider?"

⁂

Vex could feel Edda glaring at him from behind. Lu glared at him ahead. Off to the side of the deck, Nayeli folded her arms, waiting, though not glaring. Yet.

Lu wanted him to use his resources to find the missing Argridian. Only one thing came to mind, one group who had access to the single best tool on the island for locating people.

But going to them for help would really, *really* piss off Nayeli.

Vex cleared his throat. "Introductions," he said instead. "Nayeli's our resident diver and detonations specialist. If you need anything retrieved or blown up, she's your girl."

Nayeli beamed and winked at Lu.

"And Edda." Vex motioned over his shoulder. "Our muscle and engine expert."

Edda scowled. "You haven't said who *she* is."

Vex studied Lu for a beat, thinking. "She's . . . an investor."

Lu blinked, probably surprised he hadn't said something unsavory. "I'm Adeluna," she added. "Lu. I've hired your captain to find Milo Ibarra, a missing Argridian general."

Edda's brows rose. Her eyes slid to Teo, bent double over the bow, screaming, "A shark! A shark! I saw a shark!"

There were no sharks in Lake Regolith.

Edda's emotion sputtered into sympathy. "Ibarra your husband?"

Lu gagged. "*No.* He's—"

Vex handed the wheel over to Edda, but he paused halfway to the hatch. Sure, Ibarra was an Argridian diplomat, but Lu's revulsion seemed . . . personal? He waited, but she froze as if she either couldn't figure out the next words or couldn't force them out of her mouth.

Edda shrugged. "Keep your secrets. But know that if you

endanger this crew, I'll throw you overboard."

Teo whipped back from the railing. "No, you won't!" he declared. "I won't let you!"

A grin stretched Edda's lips. Vex teetered back a full step. Edda only ever smiled after a satisfying brawl—and *that* smile wasn't *this* smile, soft and nearly sweet.

"Edda. You all right?" Vex asked.

Edda's smile vanished. "Brave kid," she said, and focused on the horizon.

Vex chuckled. The hatch door banged into the deck with a *thud*, and he dropped down the ladder without a word.

A quick scuffle abovedecks, and Teo came hurtling through the hatch. Vex scrambled to catch him, and the squirming kid landed a stray kick to his temple.

"Ow!" Vex plunked Teo to the floor and rubbed his head. His vision blurred for a second.

Damn—with his strength, the kid would make a good raider.

"Sorry!"

Lu climbed down the ladder with more grace. She dropped beside him and took note of Teo first, then their surroundings.

The hall was so narrow, Vex could touch both walls with his elbows. Two of the three doors were open, showing bunks in each. The space was dark and cramped and smelled of fire—either Nayeli's fault or the engine—but god, there was no better place in the world.

"My bunkroom," he said, motioning at it. "Nayeli and Edda's bunkroom. Privy's in their room. Through here, we have—" Vex kicked into the last door, a thick iron barrier meant to withstand the engine's heat. "Engine room."

He ducked inside. He'd spent the better part of two years on this boat, but the warmth of the well-fed engine slapped him upside the head. Lu followed and staggered back, gasping—he gave her an apologetic shrug.

Against the right wall, a pile of coal sat in a bin, while the furnace glowed orange in the opposite wall. A cot was tucked up in the corner where Edda slept during long night trips.

That gave Vex an idea. Oh, Lu would hate this, but he wasn't sure he'd forgiven her for the *This balm might heal you, or it might be poisonous. Have a good day now.*

"Coal, furnace." Vex pointed out the things as he said them. "Coal goes into furnace, boat functions."

"What?" Lu asked.

Vex pointed again. "Coal. Furnace."

"Why do you—" Realization hit Lu. "No! I am not shoveling fuel for your boat while—"

"While what, Princesa?" Vex propped his arm on the open door, its short height letting him bend close to her. The heat of the engine room brought out sweat on his brow, and he saw it on Lu too, beads of condensation rolling down her face. "We aren't a quarter of the way across Lake Regolith. I doubt Pilkvist will leave his territory, and

I'm guessing the Council is still searching New Deza, but the more space we put between *your* pursuers and us, the better."

Lu winced, didn't tremble or shudder or anything that showed weakness. No doubt she'd stirred up considerable chaos when she'd freed him.

"They aren't after *me*," she said, regaining herself. "And that's your plan? Sail us into Lake Regolith—and then what? I hired you for a purpose, and I expect you to deliver, *raider*."

She glanced back at Teo, who was busying himself by singing some soft, mildly depressing song and seeing if he could hop from the doorway of one bunkroom to the other.

Lu leaned closer to Vex, which shocked him enough that he almost missed her question. "You're Argridian," she whispered. "Is that how you will find Milo? Do you have connections?"

Let's not delve into that particular detail yet.

"No, Princesa. I'm going to use . . . other means. Ever met Cansu Darzi?"

Lu shook her head.

"Good. She's a pain in the ass. But she's the head of the Tuncian syndicate in Port Mesi-Teab, and they have a certain magic that might help us find Ibarra."

"There's no botanical plant that can serve as a tracker—"

"Not a tracker. It's—well, it's complicated. Trust me. I may be a *raider*"—he said it with exaggerated disgust—"but

I adhere to a certain standard of integrity. Since *you* broke *me* out of jail, I'm guessing you don't have anything to contribute to this search. So be useful."

He waved at the furnace again, and when Lu looked at it, Vex shot out into the hall. He got halfway to the ladder when he noticed Teo behind him, walking in a jolting, awkward way.

Vex blinked. Was the kid trying to mimic his walk?

If so—did he really walk that weirdly?

He looked back. Lu stepped out of the engine room, already frowning.

"Eh, c'mon, kid," Vex said. "You know how to navigate?"

"No!" Teo chirped.

"Never too early to learn."

Vex hefted Teo up and attached him to the top few rungs of the ladder to avoid frantic scrambling. Teo climbed to the deck as Lu shot forward.

"Stop—Teo! I'm not leaving you alone with a raider!"

Vex snapped a hurt look at her. "You think I'm a bad influence?"

"*Yes.*"

"Says the woman who broke a wanted criminal out of the castle."

"I wouldn't have done that had there been another choice," Lu replied. "But *you* have chosen every horrible act you've committed. Do you feel anything beyond selfishness at this point?"

Lu's eyes went wide, telling Vex she felt she'd crossed a line.

He forced a callous smile. "Of course not, Princesa," he said. "I'm a cold-blooded, good-for-nothing outlaw. Now—coal. Furnace."

He hopped up the ladder and slammed the hatch on Lu.

13

BEN SAT BESIDE his father's throne, as still as the statues of the Graces guarding the room in their ornate alcoves, candles and offerings spread at their marble feet.

The receiving room in the palace was a mess of people. Duques and duquesas, condes and condesas—aristocrats from the highest reaches of society as well as those who barely had any property to their name. But the fire yesterday had ignited a passion in everyone, which didn't fit the somber browns and deep blues that coated the walls.

As Ben stared out at the crowd, a slow, dull ache spread through his shoulders. If he didn't move, perhaps people wouldn't say what he feared they would.

Defensors flanked the dais. Jakes stood behind Ben's chair, and Ben found himself wanting to look back at him for reassurance.

Elazar leaned forward on the throne, telling those who

crowded around the dais that he would listen. They all started talking at once.

"The prince was attacked! Who is safe?"

"But the Church condemned the University—it should have burned long ago!"

"We must be pure!" That cry came from monxas dressed in the deep purple habits of nuns from Deza's Grace Isaura Convent. Women joined the convent to proselytize for Grace Isaura's sainted pillar: honesty. "The fire is a sign from the Pious God that we must continue our purification from magic! We must abandon the treaty with Grace Loray and seek to cleanse them, and ourselves!"

Elazar lifted his hands for silence. One swung close to Ben, and he shut his eyes, expecting an impact.

All that came was Elazar's voice.

"I hear your concerns," he said. "Security measures are being undertaken to ensure protection to those of virtue. If you follow the Pious God's teachings, you have nothing to fear. I will address more at the service tonight, where we will honor the holy lives lost in the fire."

Ben cut his father a look. Which lives was Elazar talking about? The eleven protesters, who had started the fire under the guise of the Pious God's will, or the four defensors, who had tried to stop them to protect the prince?

Ben remembered voices chanting that name, Príncipe Herexe, as the crowd looked up at him with fear and hatred.

"I can assure you that the agents I have sent to oversee

the Grace Loray treaty are of the strongest caliber," Elazar continued. "Many of you know General Ibarra from his staunch leadership during the war. I select only the most unyielding souls to do the Pious God's bidding."

Ben's heart thundered. Every word from his father sounded like it would be followed by *"And my son has proven himself impure—tonight, we will watch him burn. . . ."*

It was a trap, he knew—he'd *known*. But he hadn't stopped. He could have, at any point, to save himself what was happening now. But he'd kept working with magic. Why?

When a condesa stepped forward, Ben swore he could feel a pyre building around him.

"My king, I must cleanse myself of a burden," the condesa said, sinking into a curtsy. She whipped toward the crowd and pointed. "The duque of Apolinar has admitted to sympathizing with those corrupted by magic. For our own safety, the Church must cleanse him."

The people closest to the unfortunate duque pulled away. The boy—younger than Ben—put his hands out, horror on his face.

"I did not!" he cried. "I serve the Pious God! I am pure!"

The condesa spun back to Elazar. "My king, I beg you to purify our ranks."

The room met her accusation with enthusiasm. People shoved others forward—*"Here is a heretic!" "I saw this woman tending a garden—there could be evil plants growing on her estate!"*

The room was a building storm.

Ben wasn't shocked. He felt, watching them, the answer to his question: Why had he kept working in magic? Why would he continue?

Because of this. The way Elazar held out his hands and assured everyone that the Church would deal with each accused, as was custom now.

Ben looked up at Jakes, whose face showed the same horror.

"Steady, my prince," Jakes whispered.

"Steady?" Ben's voice shook. "This is unbelievable—"

Jakes dared put a hand on Ben's shoulder. "I cannot believe everyone accused is truly impure. Likely most will repent. Your aristocracy is not this compromised."

Ben's jaw dropped open. He closed it and shifted forward.

That had not been what he'd meant. It was not unbelievable that so many people could throw themselves into these accusations—it was unbelievable that they were taken *seriously*.

Defensors intervened to lead away the accused, gently, as they were still nobles—but no title excluded a soul from corruption.

"It is a great sacrifice to bring up the impurities of one's neighbor," Elazar said. "The Pious God rewards those who stay loyal to him when the way is difficult. Conflict festers in corrupt hearts—they want to be cleansed, even as they sin. In handing over your neighbors, you are servicing both the Pious God and their souls."

"What of Prince Benat?" a priest asked. "His soul is in question."

The room went quiet. Ben's heart beat so fast it purred in his ears.

Jakes moved closer. Ben forced himself to ask—would Jakes leap to protect him from the accusations, or be the one to lead him to Grace Neus Cathedral? Jakes would never think that Ben might fail to repent. That was the divide between them, no matter how tightly Ben held Jakes at night—that Jakes believed in this. In purity. In righteousness.

And Ben was what the crowd feared him to be.

Terror ate up his senses until there was only Elazar, saying:

"I will deal with Benat."

The priest wasn't convinced. "My king, if you would—"

"I am the Eminence," Elazar said, his declaration echoing over the room. If it had been quiet before, it was like death now, everyone remembering to whom they were airing their grievances. "You are lambs in my fold. You have neither the fortitude nor the capacity to understand the decisions your shepherd makes. Do not question me further."

The priest bowed. "Eminence. You are holy and true."

Elazar dismissed him, dismissed the room, by standing and turning his back on the crowd. The defensors resumed picking through the lot, trying to find the accused, but it would be madness—it *was* madness, this waste of fear.

Ben didn't stand. Elazar walked past him, making for the door behind the dais, when Ben, in a soft voice, asked, "Are you trying to kill me?"

Elazar stopped. Jakes heard too, and Ben sat between them, numb.

Elazar looked down at Ben. His gaze was heavy. "As I said, Benat—the sheep cannot understand the shepherd's decisions. Argrid does not do well with sudden change." He paused. "But no. I do not think you will give me a reason to kill you."

Ben nodded, a weight grinding on his heart. His father had gone from believing some magic was tolerable under the Inquisitors, to overseeing dozens of burnings a week for people who had magic, to tasking Ben with healing their country through magic now.

What was true? What was lasting? Ben had been playing this game for years, and he was tired of the rules changing. Tired of his father shifting beliefs on a whim.

There was one thing Ben knew: he was done having his beliefs chosen for him.

The sun licked the horizon when Ben's carriage deposited him outside Grace Neus Cathedral. Citizens from every rank in Deza made a solemn procession into the cathedral, hands pressed together in supplication to the Pious God.

Ahead, Elazar stepped out of his own carriage. Ben couldn't deny the toll this had taken on his father. Elazar's countenance mimicked the bent shoulders and drawn faces of the crowd.

The inside of the cathedral complemented the exterior in grandeur. The ceiling lifted as tall as the building, lacework arches holding stained glass so the setting sun shot through in oranges and pinks and blues. Hundreds of pews were already filled, but defensors led Elazar and Ben up the aisle to the row of honor before the altar.

Elazar left to begin his duties as Eminence while Ben took his seat. Around the altar, statues depicting every Grace stared at him. Grace Neus, who had built this cathedral; Grace Loray; Grace Isaura; Grace Aracely; Grace Biel; and dozens more anointed men and women who, through their selfless, uncorrupted acts, had made the world a holier place.

They were everywhere. In Elazar's office. In the throne room. In the cathedrals. Beacons of the Church, always watching with empty eyes that judged Ben as intensely as the people taking their seats behind him.

He looked at Jakes, under the mezzanine where guards could watch the service as well as their charges. Jakes nodded once, encouraging.

A door next to the altar opened, and monxes came out, carrying tapers. They lit candles beneath each Grace statue, chanting for the Pious God to pass the strength he had given these select servants on to everyone in Argrid.

When the candles were lit, the monxes took seats at the rear of the altar, hands folded against their black robes. Elazar emerged in the vestments of the Eminence: cords around his neck, woven with colors representing every Grace; a tall ivory hat in the shape of the beseeching V; a scarlet and gold robe that pooled around Elazar's feet like ornamented blood.

Ben's knee started to bounce.

Elazar stood at the head of the altar. "Brothers, sisters," he began, his words catching on the walls, a design that made the building resonate. "It is in the wake of tragedy that we hold today's service. Flames that started out of fear burned fifteen souls. Fear is a tool of the Pious God; it is his way for us to distinguish between pure and impure acts. I beseech the Pious God's children to listen to the apprehension in their hearts. Fear will save you from falling into a path that condemns your soul."

Elazar waved for the monxes to press on with the service. Ben sat, paralyzed, while the cathedral filled with murmurs.

His father hadn't condemned the burning. In fact, what he'd said felt as explosive as if he'd told the fanatics to carry on with their dangerous beliefs.

Elazar could have been easing the transition. Such prejudices would not change in a day, as he'd told Ben.

But they wouldn't change at all like this.

Ben looked up at the Grace statues. And stood.

Elazar watched his son with narrow eyes. Conversations halted, the silence rippling out from Ben as though he were a stone plunked into a pool.

His next actions would define who he was. Would he be poor Prince Benat, the shameful, weak man? Or the pupil of the High Inquisitor, his uncle, a heretic?

He already knew.

"Eminence," Ben offered. He faced the crowd, steeling himself when he realized how many people were in here. "Fellow Argridians. I do not intend to contradict the Eminence, our merciful teacher of the Pious God—but the burning of the University was a tragedy that the Church should respond to with outrage."

"Benat," Elazar said, a warning, but he didn't make a further move to stop him.

"Innocent people lost their lives because of a prejudice that the Church should, in its wisdom, condemn. The things I do, I do with the blessing of the Eminence himself. Our current state of suffering is not punishment from the Pious God—it is due to our own ignorance and fear."

Ben faced Elazar. Dread clawed at him, but he kept speaking.

"I ask you, Eminence, to condemn the burning and to reinstate the Inquisitors. Their banishment has surely atoned for any sins of their leader"—though he didn't mention Rodrigu and Paxben by name, Ben had to fight to keep his voice from catching—"and you cannot deny that Argrid has need of their wisdom."

Elazar held his gaze, cold. "Benat, you disgrace me. You do not yet bear the burden of Eminence, so you do yet have the luxury of arbitrary questions. Leave, until you can be contrite and humbled by your position as an instrument in the Pious God's inconceivable plan."

Ben took a stumbling step backward. Elazar's eyes darkened as the crowd gasped. The Eminence King had told his heir to leave Grace Neus Cathedral.

But all Ben heard were words like threatening fingers around his neck.

Obey me without question. Do my bidding and be grateful to be valuable.

A hand took Ben's arm. Jakes. "Come, my prince," he pleaded.

Ben let Jakes pull him away. Elazar addressed the crowd, apologizing for the outburst.

Ordained in blood. Ben remembered his father's words in the crypt. *Ours is a family of tragedy. The Pious God ordained us in blood.*

14

VEX MANAGED NOT to tell Nayeli where they were going as they sailed through the night. Teo acted as a yappy buffer, bless him, and stayed up until past dark asking questions and squealing at fish jumping from the water. When Lu came to take him to one of the bunkrooms and asked after their progress, Nayeli was asleep at the bow.

But now, with the morning sun stark overhead and the eastern shore of Lake Regolith less than half an hour away, Vex knew it was coming.

"We're in the business of fighting Argrid now?" Edda asked from where she and Nayeli were doing inventory of one of their storage areas. "I thought we were avoiding them until we could get enough money to hole up away from fighting anyone or getting caught up in other people's problems."

"I don't know." Vex rubbed his face, straightening his eye patch by reflex. "The general was abducted, but Lu doesn't think it was real—and, honestly, I don't either. Argrid's up to something. They've wanted more and more plants from us, and now one of their highest-ranking generals ups and vanishes? Don't tell me that's not suspect."

"We're still retiring in Port Fausta, right?" Nayeli pleaded.

"Port Fausta? Last week you wanted to refurbish one of those old dormant volcanic tunnels in the northern mountains."

"Too much work. Besides, Port Fausta's where the good alcohol is. I swear on all four gods, if I'm not neck-deep in a tub of wine in a few months because you've decided to go *heroic*—"

"Lu's paying. Magic concoctions," Vex assured her. "You should see what she can do with plants. We'll be swimming in galles, enough to retire early."

Nayeli lit up. "Where are we going? Where do you think he went? We gonna hunt down the Argridian bullies who keep coming after us and see if they know anything?"

Vex fought to keep from wincing. Or locking the pilot-house door and hiding behind the wheel. He was the captain, damn it. He shouldn't be afraid of his own crew.

"I don't think Lu wants to outright accuse Argrid of staging Milo's abduction without proof—"

As if she knew they were talking about her, Lu popped up from belowdecks. Vex watched her note their location—the southeastern shore of Lake Regolith had come into view, New Deza so far behind to the west, all that was visible was blue lake—before she made for the pilothouse.

"How long until we reach the Tuncian syndicate?" Lu asked.

Nayeli shot to her feet. "What?" she asked.

Lu looked at Vex. His sympathy won out—he deserved Nayeli's wrath, not her.

"We need your aunt, Nay," he said. "Her Budwig Beans are our best chance of hearing what might've happened to Ibarra."

Each Budwig plant came with two beans. One could be put in one person's ear, the other in another place or even someone else's ear, and the two beans relayed sounds across the whole island. It was one of the rarest plants in Grace Loray—raiders hid Budwig Beans in other syndicates' territories to spy on them; elite members of Grace Loray's military used them to communicate; and they grew only in the eastern part of the island. Unfortunately for Vex.

Nayeli barreled into the pilothouse and punched him. "You *traitor*! Do you have any idea what it's like when I go back? No, because all you think is *Vex get what Vex need*—"

"Budwig Beans?" Lu ignored Nayeli's ranting and stared at Vex in shock. "That . . . might be useful."

Nayeli stomped out onto the deck, her curses muffled.

But Lu was gaping at him. Vex grinned.

"I know, Princesa, I'm actually helping you! Shocking, isn't it?"

"But I take it, from Nayeli's tone, that the Tuncians aren't friendly?"

Vex gave Lu a confused look, then realized what language Nayeli had been shouting in. "Oh. She was speaking Thuti—a dialect from Tuncay. I thought you'd know that. You look like you have Tuncian blood. But while I'd love to give a history lesson—"

Lu picked up on it faster than he expected. "Was Nayeli part of the Tuncian syndicate?"

"Captain!" Edda cut in, pointing at the shoreline.

Vex swung out a spyglass, but Lu snatched it from him. She surveyed the mouth of the approaching Leto River that was a rippling break in the line of jungle.

Vex ripped the spyglass back from her. "Don't touch my stuff."

"Twelve steamboats," Lu stated. "In a row, unmoving, not flying Council flags. Are they Cansu's boats? She must have guessed you'd go to her."

Vex grumbled. "Nayeli! Edda! I'm open to suggestions."

Nayeli spun away from where she'd been sulking on the bow. "Oh, I have a suggestion for you, asshole," she said in Thuti and made a gesture that Lu had to understand without any translation.

"How hostile is Cansu? Could we negotiate with her?" Lu asked.

Vex shrugged. "Best we reach Nayeli's aunt, use what Budwig Beans she'll give us, and be on our merry way.

Cansu won't be thrilled if she finds out that you're with the Council and trying to save an Argridian."

"It's for her benefit as well," Lu countered. "If Milo isn't found, Argrid will force the Council to blame the raiders—"

"Yeah, she won't care. It'll piss her off that you assume she needs the Council to protect her syndicate." Vex jerked on a lever, slowing the *Meander* to a halt so they could think. "I need to get past her blockade. What if we—"

"The Schilly," Lu said. "Go north. Take the Schilly River. It connects with the Leto farther inland—you can avoid Cansu's raiders that way."

"You're neglecting to mention how the Schilly connects to the Leto," Vex countered.

Lu's brows lifted. "Are you afraid of a little waterfall?"

"A *little* waterfall?" Vex chirped, then heard the cracking of his voice and cleared his throat. "I'm more worried about the Council-run system of platforms and pulleys that lower boats down the falls. You have to pay the Council soldiers, who have free rein to search your boat if, oh, say, a diplomat is missing and an escaped convict is on the loose."

Lu gave the smile she'd given from before they'd escaped the castle. The one Nayeli now wore too, eager and demented.

Oh god, Vex thought. *Did I bring another Nayeli onto my boat?*

"What if I could get you past the falls and the Council soldiers?" Lu asked.

"No Cansu? No soldiers either?" Nayeli hurled herself through the door and looped one arm around Lu. "I like this one *a lot*. Can we keep her?"

But Vex's eye was pinned on Lu. "How, Princesa?"

"You mentioned to the Council that the last time you dealt with Ingvar Pilkvist, it involved a shipment of Aerated Blossoms," Lu said. "Do you still have it?"

Vex considered. "Edda, mind the engine—make sure we have enough fuel to get up to the Schilly. Nay, go get our Blossoms."

"Only three," Lu corrected. "Edda and Teo can pose as a family and take the lift—soldiers won't look twice at something so innocent. You, Nayeli, and I will take another route."

Edda dropped obediently through the hatch as Nayeli pulled back from Lu, aghast. "Are you saying I don't come across as *innocent*?"

Lu laughed, and it stopped any smart-ass comment Vex had been about to make.

"Not even a little," Lu said, smiling.

Nayeli beamed. "Good. I'd hate for that rumor to start."

"We're splitting up?" Vex drummed his fingers on the helm as he plowed the boat northeast, away from the Leto. "I figured you'd use the Blossoms on the boat somehow."

"You thought I could make the whole boat fly?"

"You melted an iron lock. A flying boat isn't that far-fetched."

Lu gave him an incredulous look. "We'll each take a Blossom and jump off the cliff away from the falls, out of the soldiers' sight. The moment we get close to the ground, we'll—"

She stopped, her eyes going to where Vex tapped a loud, incessant rhythm on the helm.

"You're afraid," she guessed.

Vex's hand stilled. "Of falling to my death? Ridiculous, I know."

"You won't die. The timing must be exact, but—"

"You know how long the effects of Aerated Blossoms last, don't you? Only as long as you inhale. *A few seconds.* Which means our margin for death is that long."

Lu smiled. Vex squirmed. He'd been right to be terrified—so far, her plans had a certain perilous twist to them, as though she wasn't aware of how *mortal* some people were.

"It's been a few years, but I've done this before," Lu said. "We'll be fine."

"A few years? Back when you were a killer child? Or whatever the hell the revolutionaries made you into."

The lightness on Lu's face vanished. Vex stepped closer, as if he could chase it down and coax it back out.

Her expression went furious. "If the plan doesn't suit you, find your own way, raider."

Before Vex could say anything else, Lu threw herself down the hatch.

Lu landed in the hall as Nayeli emerged from a bunkroom with three Aerated Blossoms. The spiky balls were no bigger than her palms—an untrained eye would dismiss the plants as sea urchins.

"Now what?" Nayeli asked, but Lu pushed past her.

"Ask your captain. It is what I'm paying him for, after all."

Lu heaved herself into the opposite bunkroom. Teo sat on the cot they'd shared.

"Lu? Is it morning?" He rubbed his eyes.

Lu dropped onto the bed and put her arms around him. He stilled. "Lu?"

Once, when she was small, her parents had taken her to a Church service outside Port Fausta. The other parishioners had dismissed them as a devout family, freeing them to get the layout in order to rescue allies Argrid had imprisoned beneath the main mission building. As Lu's parents had counted the windows and doors, she'd listened to priests beg the Pious God to forgive the congregation for the impure acts they had committed.

"*Hypocrites,*" her mother had called the priests afterward. "*They call free thought impure so they can burn a man for speaking against the Argridian king, but the burning doesn't displease their god?*"

Lu had nodded gravely, folding away words like *impure* until the day she first stumbled back to a safe house with blood on her hands. She learned why the priests didn't beg forgiveness for killing people. Not even the Pious God could cleanse a soul of that stain.

Teo shifted in Lu's arms, reaching up to pat her on the head. "It's all right, Lu."

Tears warmed her eyes. She was so grateful to have Teo with her, an anchor to the life she was meant to lead. Even though he was still a few years shy of how old she'd been when her father had first sent her out to spy on Argridians, she was glad she had brought him on this quest.

How weak she was, to be so selfishly relieved for his presence here.

Lu held Teo and breathed.

❖❖❖

Night fell, the darkness so disorienting that Vex almost forgot their plan as he followed Nayeli and Lu up the tree-lined shore. Dense jungle pressed against the Schilly, the trees hung with moss and vines that wafted in the breeze. The churning, bellowing anger of the Schilly-Leto water-fall drowned out any chirps of wildlife.

Vex met Lu where she hid behind a wide tree trunk. The water from the falls made the humidity worse, and Vex's hands were damp, his eye patch chafing. He peeked around the trunk to get a view of the area where captains anchored to pay the fee before their boats were lowered down the falls—or searched.

Lanterns glowed from the flat wooden buildings on either bank of the river. Steamboats waited along each side in two long lines for the lift to lower them down. The soldiers on guard checked the boats that sailed up to the docking stations.

Vex had braved this route when there was a soldier on duty he could pay off. Back then, only one in four boats was ever pulled over in random searches. Now triple the guards fanned down the walkways, swarming *every* boat.

The higher security didn't sit well with him, in the same way that New Deza's wharf market had seemed off. Something had changed. Was it because of the missing Argridian?

The *Rapid Meander* was third in line. Vex clamped his hand on the tree trunk, knuckles tense.

He felt attention on him and looked at Lu. "Can I help you, Princesa?"

She pulled back, rolling her eyes.

"She doesn't like when you call her that," Nayeli whispered, lounging against the tree.

Vex frowned. "Really?"

"You thought I enjoyed it, raider?" Lu scoffed. "That I flinched out of pleasure?"

"But there you go, calling me raider! It was a give-and-take."

Lu bowed her head to the trunk. "Fine. I won't call you *raider*. You won't—"

"Shhh!"

"Excuse me? I'm trying to—"

"No! Look."

Vex pointed. The *Rapid Meander* had sailed up to a

walkway that stretched beyond the payment station, and guards came up. Edda went to the starboard railing, her hand lifted in greeting. Teo's vague outline could be seen sitting on the table in the pilothouse.

Vex exhaled. Held it. Struggled to breathe.

As soldiers reached Edda, others on a boat behind the *Meander* shouted, "Raiders! Tuncian syndicate!"

A scuffle broke out as soldiers grabbed the crew of the raider boat and wrestled them to the deck. The guards approaching Edda dove for the other boat, helping their comrades pin down the crew and rip into their lower-deck hatch.

Nausea made Vex waver, his knees slipping on the moist undergrowth. Memories overlapped this moment—watching soldiers attack people for merely looking suspicious. Tearing apart their property. Screaming, *Heretics! Sinners! The Pious God condemns you—*

Vex's body went rigid.

Had the bill that the Argridian diplomat lobbied for, the one to eradicate stream raiders, passed? Even if it had, surely the Council wouldn't have implemented anything so soon? Lu would have said something to him, right?

Edda slipped back into the pilothouse and the *Meander* sailed on. From this angle, all Vex could see was the stern bobbing as the current shoved his boat against the barrier that kept it from plummeting over the falls.

Vex couldn't feel a damn thing until the *Rapid Meander*

drifted forward, swallowed up into the lift contraption. The soldiers had let it pass. They'd accepted the galles and the story about Edda and Teo being a family.

Vex gasped, forehead going to the tree trunk. God above, he needed a drink.

"There weren't as many soldiers when I was here last," Lu whispered. Her words made the silence between the three of them more potent, and Vex realized they'd *all* been on edge.

"Yeah." Vex lifted his head, eyeing Lu. "We're in Cansu's territory, for god's sake. Why would they care about a boat of hers that much? It wouldn't be unusual."

At the mention of Cansu, Nayeli stalked off into the trees.

"They're looking for Milo," Lu breathed. "The Argridians would have been insulted if the Council hadn't increased security at checkpoints." She glanced at Vex, then back to the docking stations. "At least the Council can control this."

Vex gestured at the soldiers. "Why'd they go after the Tuncian boat, not ours? The Council doesn't think raiders took him, right? They should be looking into everyone. Equally."

He was trying to get her to say it. *Oh, raider, I forgot to tell you—the Council is actively trying to kill people like you now. Not that that affects our arrangement.*

Lu shook her head, but her brows pinched. "We should go."

She stood and Vex stepped in front of her, rage shooting through him.

"Your Council isn't as holy as you think they are," he snapped. "If raiders did abduct the Argridian, you'd better believe they had damn good reasons for it. They're shunned from society because your precious Council refuses to help them. You remember Pilkvist shouting about the Council stealing money? Well, *they are*. They may not think they did, but the Council ripped away the main source of income from the syndicates when they started Mainland trade. And instead of helping the syndicates fill in that gap, the Council blames them for suffering. I hope raiders did abduct that dumbass Argridian to shed light on the Council's many, *many* flaws."

"By starting the war again?" Lu retorted, a biting whisper. "If this is truly raiders seeking attention for injustices, it proves that they have no love for Grace Loray. They endanger our whole country, and they deny that the Council's changes have helped other people on this island. Other *law-abiding* people. There are jobs now! Jobs in magic, in trade, in sailing. How can the syndicates be so upset as to go to war?"

"None of those jobs went to raiders," Vex said. "None of the Council's support helps anyone too poor to even know where to start. Not that I'm a huge proponent of the syndicates—they *definitely* have their flaws, too—but they aren't wholly bad. And the Council isn't wholly good."

Lu opened her mouth but stopped. Her pause showed confusion on her face. Like maybe he was right.

"If none of this had happened," Vex continued, "if that Argridian was still in New Deza sipping tea and eating fruit tarts, would you have given a thought to raiders?"

Lu's face slackened.

"Honestly," she breathed, "no."

She left before he could respond.

�֍✖֍

Vines lashed at Lu's face as she shot into the jungle.

She had expected the Council to increase security in response to Milo's abduction, as she had told Vex. And it wasn't unusual that the soldiers would target raiders—they were the criminals on Grace Loray, and going after them would appease the Argridians.

The reason Lu didn't think that raiders had abducted Milo was that she distrusted Argrid more. But if she hadn't, she felt the seed of what her assumption would have been— the same seed that had let her dismiss the boat at the falls.

Could Lu afford to weigh ethical arguments with war looming? She hadn't considered morality during the revolution. She had taken definitive action at her parents' behest.

Lu looked back at the docking station, where soldiers still searched the Tuncian boat, its possessions spread across the walkway along the riverbank, the crew bound and silent.

What was she fighting for? Lu was trying to find Milo to discredit Argrid, but she was trying to show raiders that the Council could protect them, too. That was what she wanted, what she had to believe the Council wanted—for the raiders to stop carrying on with their own syndicate governings. For them to submit to Council rule.

But she had never asked herself *why* the syndicates were so opposed to the Council. They were criminals; they were stubbornly set in their ways; they warred with change— the reasons had been varied and flippant. Nothing true, though. Nothing concrete.

Nothing like what Vex had said, that there were gaps in the Council's rule that the syndicates made up for.

Lu hated herself, suddenly, brightly. She was better than this. She was better than assumptions and prejudice.

Such things felt too much like Argrid.

The cliff eventually sputtered into flatlands, but it would take hours to reach them. The quickest route lay where Lu came to a wobbling stop: at the edge of the cliff, looking down into a jungle so thick and dark that she couldn't see the ground. It would be like jumping into . . . nothing.

Vex stopped beside her, Nayeli with them again.

"Don't use the Aerated Blossom until you get as close to the ground as possible," Lu said, glad to have this simple task to refocus her. She had attached each of their Blossoms to a string around their wrists. *Inhale through the hole at the bottom,* she told herself. *The gases within will let you levitate for a span equal to the time of inhalation.*

Nayeli grinned, her teeth a slice of white in the darkness.

Behind her, the lanterns of the lift base glowed, distant enough that it was a blur of yellow. No one would see them.

No one would know if they crashed to the ground, their bodies breaking on impact.

Vex seemed to be thinking that exact thing. He readied the Blossom in his hand, rolling his shoulders back, stretching his neck. "All right. *All right.* We can do this. We can—"

"Of course we can," Nayeli said, turning to Vex. Her foot hit the edge of the cliff. "Don't you worry, we'll be—"

She tripped, flailed, and fell into the darkness.

Vex teetered next to her. "Shit!"

But Nayeli's manic giggles flew up to them before the shadows swallowed her.

"I hope she hits a tree," Vex whined. But he watched the darkness, one ear tipped, waiting to hear either a shout of pain or the crack of bones. But there was nothing.

Vex exhaled, but the tension in his stance didn't ease.

"I find it hard to believe that the infamous Devereux Bell is afraid of heights," Lu said.

Vex snapped a look at her. "If you tell anyone, I'll—"

"You'll do what to me, Vex?" Lu made her voice sultry and pressed closer, trying to distract him like she had in the dungeon and on the dock.

His eye narrowed when he realized what she was doing. "I think I hate you."

"Not without reason," Lu replied, and shoved him.

Vex sank into the air with a curse. Lu gathered her

strength and jumped after him.

The night wind slapped at her as she fell, coaxing tears from her eyes. Her stomach lurched into her neck, bounced into her toes, the air tugging her body into shapes she didn't know it could make. Her heart thundered with adrenaline, and all else faded until there was just the roaring of the falls and the softness of the wind and her body, floating, hovering, unwinding.

She had always loved traveling this way as a child. She'd used avoiding the Argridian soldiers stationed at the lift as an excuse to dive right into the emptiness, and as she fell now, she imagined the broken parts of her lifting into the sky. She imagined coming back together, the best pieces, renewal and rebirth.

Branches scratched her cheeks. Vines snapped under her weight. As the ground came up in a rush, Lu put the Aerated Blossom against her lips and inhaled. The gases filled her lungs, tasting of grime and brackish river water. Her body jerked to a stop so close to the ground that she could reach out and place her palm flat to it.

The gases evaporated and Lu fell to her hands and knees—Blossoms were one of the few plants Lu used, for that reason. They didn't linger.

Someone grabbed her shoulders and yanked her to her feet.

"Why the hell did you wait that long to use the Blossom?" Vex shouted. Here, the falls' noise was deafening.

"You—you were worried for me?"

"Yeah, I—"

Lu's brows rose. Vex appeared to notice his words at the same time she did.

His mouth slanted. "You still owe me any botanical elixir I want."

Nayeli stood nearby, tapping her foot. "Come *on*—I don't like it here." She turned for the Schilly, where they planned to reunite with the *Meander*.

"And if you died," Vex continued, walking beside Lu, "I'd be stuck with Teo. Don't get me wrong, he's a great kid, but I don't much want to add a six-year-old to my crew."

"I get it," Lu said. But she smiled. "It would be a horrible inconvenience to you if I died."

"Glad we understand each other."

The Schilly wove on after the falls, curving around and linking up with the Leto River. The *Rapid Meander* had already docked at the bend, lights dimmed so anyone else would miss it.

Lu hopped aboard, followed by Nayeli and Vex. "Teo?" she whispered as she moved toward the pilothouse. "It's all right—"

A lantern flared to life on the map table.

Lu ripped a knife out of her holster. The woman near the lantern had a pistol on one hip, a sword on the other, and a brand on her wrist. Her short black hair draped around her face, revealing a mark on her neck: four dots, two vertical above two horizontal. A Tuncian tattoo.

"You thought you'd outsmart me in my own territory?" The woman clucked her tongue, golden-tan skin glowing in the lantern's yellow light.

Adrenaline surged into Lu's veins. "Who are you? Where's Teo?"

"Lu." Vex's voice behind her was flat. "This is Cansu Darzi."

Cansu cut a harsh grin. "The boy is safely on his way to Port Mesi-Teab with my raiders. Which is where you were headed, weren't you, Nay? You know Fatemah doesn't like outsiders. But I should have expected as much—you don't give a damn about what we want."

Lu threw an accusatory glare, but in the lantern's jerky light, the expression on Nayeli's face was sorrowful.

Whatever was happening was exactly what Nayeli had feared.

"What's going on? Who's Fatemah?" Lu demanded.

"Fatemah is Nayeli's aunt," Vex said with a sigh. "The woman we were going to see. The Tuncian syndicate's magic expert."

15

WELL, THIS HAD unraveled quickly.

"Did you think we were maybe trying to *avoid* confrontation?" Vex asked Cansu as he steered down the river. He kept his focus on the shadowed bow of the *Meander* and the hunched shape of Lu, probably glaring at him. Nayeli had stayed on deck only as long as it took to announce that she'd oversee the engine in Edda's stead.

Vex could feel the tension radiating off Nayeli. When she exploded this time, it wouldn't be with curses. She'd be quiet and sulking and damn heartbreaking, and Vex clenched his fists on the helm to keep himself from punching Cansu. She'd probably drop him to the deck before he could even land a blow, and Nayeli wouldn't want him to assault her anyway.

"You can't slip in and out of my territory whenever you want." Cansu's voice came from behind him, where she sat on the table. "I don't need you mucking stuff up like you usually do."

"I don't steal from you," Vex hissed. "Nayeli won't let me."

Cansu grabbed onto that. "She doesn't deserve your protection."

"The fact you can say that proves she was right to leave. She's part of you, Cansu. I mean, god, she *jumped off a cliff* to avoid seeing you—there're some strong feelings still."

Nayeli would kill him if she knew he'd said that. No, castrate him, *then* kill him.

Cansu darkened. "It doesn't matter. You shouldn't have come here. I don't need your distractions, not now."

Vex eyed her. "Why not now?"

Cansu shot him a derisive look. "Gods, you were in the Council's dungeon; don't tell me you didn't hear what's going on. They've created a bill to *wipe us out*. One of the Argridian delegates vanished three days ago, and they think we abducted him, of course. You saw the security at the falls? It's that way everywhere—the Council didn't waste any time bowing down to Argrid's call to turn on us. Tell me why the hell you need to see Fatemah. It'd better be important. We've got too much to worry about otherwise."

Vex felt a twinge deep in his gut. He'd suspected that was why things were getting worse, but having her confirm it was almost more than he could handle.

He nodded at Lu. "She hired me to help with something so the Council doesn't—"

Cansu shot off the map table. Vex flinched. *Shit.*

"You aren't stupid enough to bring a Grace Lorayan to my territory. *For help.*"

"Let Fatemah decide who gets help," Vex said. "That was the deal, right? You run the syndicate, Fatemah manages the needy, and Nayeli gets battered by your emotional warfare."

Cansu opened her mouth, so Vex said what he knew would shut her up.

"You aren't the one who has to pick up the pieces every time you hurt Nayeli." He looked back at Cansu. "If you love her like I know you do, you'll let us do our business and leave. *Peacefully.*"

Cansu slumped back against the table. Moments like these clashed with her raider Head guise, making it impossible for Vex to be intimidated by her.

But everyone had weaknesses. The one thing that no matter how deeply buried would send them to their knees.

"Just drive," Cansu mumbled.

Vex faced forward. "With pleasure."

�֍֍֍

As the *Rapid Meander* sped into the night, Lu paced from the bow to the pilothouse and back. Were they Cansu's prisoners now—was Teo? Were they going to see Fatemah? Should they tell Cansu their mission? Surely she would understand the importance of finding Milo.

But every time Lu gathered the gumption to storm into

the pilothouse, she saw Cansu glowering at her with eyes like fire and blood.

Lu paced back to the bow.

After sunrise, the *Rapid Meander* joined up with other boats chugging toward the bustle and hum of Grace Loray's largest southeastern city: Port Mesi-Teab.

Like the other four main ports on Grace Loray, it could trace its origins to an immigrant settlement—in this case, a group of Tuncians had founded the city when they'd settled in Grace Loray centuries ago. It sat at the confluence of the Leto and the Draydis Rivers, just above the southern swamplands. With the sun lifting behind the city, the port's iconic skyline took Lu's breath away: an old Argridian fort of walled gray stone at the divide between the two rivers. The wall that faced up the Leto bore the Church's symbol, a monstrous section of white stones in a curved *V*.

"Fort Chastity," said a voice beside her. Lu flinched but didn't move from where she leaned against the exterior of the pilothouse. Cansu, halfway out the door, folded her arms. "The last thing some Tuncians saw on this island. At least it was a pretty view."

"Why is it still standing?" Lu asked. She had never spent much time in Port Mesi-Teab, but in other cities, citizens had been quick to dismantle or repurpose anything that had been used by Argrid. Seeing the Church's symbol unscathed was rare.

"To remind us," Cansu said. "The Argridians named it *Chastity* because they labeled Tuncians whores for having four gods and not worshipping their one. Every time we see it, we remember where we came from and who we are, and how no one can take that from us."

Vex, at the helm, let out a sharp whistle. "Stand down, Cansu. We're almost there."

Cansu gave Lu a cold smile and ducked back into the pilothouse.

Lu's grandmother—Kari's mother—had been Tuncian. Lu had only vague memories of her—the war had taken Kari's parents early. And with bloodshed and cannon fire a too-regular part of life, Kari hadn't been able to pass down the culture of her history. Family traditions became as rare as sugar—delicious when they had it, but not crucial to their survival, and as the war dragged on, Kari told Lu less and less.

Lu knew general things about Tuncians. The four-dot tattoo some of them wore as homages to their gods; certain recipes Kari made on occasion, a sweet bean pastry for birthdays or a breakfast dish packed with spices that lingered in Lu's nose for days after. But Lu didn't consider herself Tuncian, as much as she didn't think about her Argridian heritage from Tom. She was Grace Lorayan.

Lu's head began to throb. She blamed sleeplessness, and focused on staying alert as the *Meander* followed the Leto along the southern stretch of Port Mesi-Teab.

Dozens of docks stretched around Fort Chastity,

hosting a variety of vessels in the dawn's mist. A few patrol boats were stationed in the widest part of the river, where it forked in two, keeping watch over early-morning extractions as crews lowered diving bells into the water and hauled up plants. Shadows from Fort Chastity darkened the river, and more shadows continued in patchy sections as the fort ended and the haphazard city buildings began.

Smaller tributaries of the Leto snaked into the port just like the rivers that made a spiderweb through New Deza. But as Vex steered the *Meander* into one of them, the difference became clear: where New Deza's rivers were mostly clean, lined by well-kept stones and ducking beneath arched bridges, these waters ran brown, the color growing darker the farther into the city they went. What bridges they passed under were wooden and decrepit, the banks sliding off in wet chunks. People sat along the water regardless, fishing rods dipped into the surface.

Lu had heard of such poverty in New Deza. *If the raiders would submit to Grace Loray's governing,* councilmembers said, *things would improve for them. But Council funds will not support defiant anarchists.*

But was every soul suffering under these conditions a raider who refused to acknowledge the Council's sovereignty? Even so—did it matter? They were citizens. They were *here*.

Lu swallowed the foul air, the throbbing in her head growing more potent.

The *Rapid Meander* wove into Port Mesi-Teab until they saw the tangle of jungle that fought the back wall of the city. Buildings in cramped blocks let the barest hints of sunlight through, trapping bitter air in narrow, dirty streets. When they were so far from the Leto that Lu wasn't sure she could find her way back to it, Vex let the *Meander* drift to a stop against a dock.

Cansu left the pilothouse, followed by Vex. After a beat, Nayeli emerged from belowdecks, but she didn't make eye contact with anyone.

"Your people should be within," Cansu told Vex. Her voice was softer, or tired.

Lu searched the buildings for the one Cansu meant. But the streets were nearly empty, save for a stumbling beggar or two. Faces peeked from windows behind holey curtains; shadows wavered as people watched them from doorways. Silence clouded the boats that drifted past, manned by crews with gaunt, watchful faces.

The jolt of recognition was as unpleasant as the air. This was how every port had been during the war: filled with dread, people hiding in fear of Argridians snatching them up for cleansing.

The boat jerked, followed by the thump of boots hitting the ground. Cansu walked off down a road. For all her worries about escorting them in, she was leaving now?

She hadn't intercepted them for the escort, then. She was saying, *This is my territory.*

Nayeli jumped off the boat without a word, trailing Cansu into the port.

"Nayeli is from Cansu's syndicate," Lu guessed. "She left to join your crew."

Vex gave a grunt that could have been a laugh. "If only it were that simple."

The boat teetered, the mud on the starboard side sucking against Vex's boots. Lu plopped on his right side, and the thud of her next to him sent him rocking back. She grabbed his wrist to steady him and felt a shiver rush up his arm before he jerked away.

"Blind on this side," Vex snapped, waving his hand on the side of his head.

"I didn't mean—"

"Come on," Vex said, irritated. "It isn't far."

He started after Nayeli and Cansu. Lu followed, unable to tolerate the tension in Vex's corded shoulders. She had affronted him—and she hated that she not only realized, but cared.

He turned a corner, and as she hurried after him, she steeled herself to apologize—

But Cansu stood on the road, facing them, holding a sack.

Vex put his hands out. "This isn't necessary."

"It's always necessary for people we don't trust."

"I trust her," Vex returned, and Lu knew shock showed on her face. "She won't tell anyone. Will you, Lu?"

"Tell anyone what?"

Nayeli crossed her arms, sighed softly. "Wear the bag. It's easier."

Lu's mouth dropped open. Wherever they were going, Cansu didn't want her to know how to find it. A secret raider lair, no doubt.

"Teo's there?" Lu demanded. "Where you're taking me. He'll be there?"

Cansu bowed. "Safe as can be, on my honor as the Tuncian raider Head."

Lu's focus went to Vex. "And this place," she said, "is where we need to go."

Vex popped a shoulder. "Fatemah hears everything that happens on this island."

Lu snatched the bag from Cansu. She tugged it over her own head, blocking out what depressing daylight there had been, and held out an arm.

"Let's go."

Fingers clasped one of her elbows, guiding her, and all Lu had to identify their location was the ground beneath her boots. The squishy mud of the road; hard thumping floorboards; squishy mud again. They were leading her in circles, she guessed, to make it harder for her to find her way, but she didn't care. Let her be with Teo; let whatever help the Tuncians could give in finding Milo be given. Let this be *over*.

After at least an hour of trudging through the port, someone—Nayeli?—hissed in warning.

"Soldiers," whispered a voice next to her. Lu started to realize it was Vex holding her elbow, not Cansu. But muffled, gruff orders and the crash of a window made her tip her head, straining to hear more.

"What are they doing?" She reached for the edge of the sack. "I can—"

"Remove that sack and I'll leave you here," Cansu snapped ahead of her.

Beyond their hiding place—an alley, maybe—someone shrieked, "We don't know anything! We aren't involved!"

Another crash of glass breaking. "Bad enough you stink up our cities, but now you raiders stir up trouble with Argrid—do us a favor and get off our island!"

A chorus of cheers followed. Lu swayed, disoriented.

"Who is that?" she whispered. "We have to help—"

"My people will deal with the Grace Lorayans," Cansu said. "We'll have to go a different way."

A battle cry came from a different source, and sure enough, someone cried, "Tuncian raiders!" and the distinct clash and bang of hand-to-hand combat echoed.

Vex pulled Lu away as the chaos behind them intensified, shouts and swords chiming.

"Those couldn't be Grace Lorayans," Lu breathed. "It isn't like this—"

"Like it was at the docking station?" Lu couldn't see Vex,

but she heard the dare in his voice. "Tensions with Grace Lorayans—especially soldiers—are usually high. But no. It isn't always this strained."

His grip on her tightened, and his final words weighed heavy. He was trying to get her to realize something, as he had at the falls.

But she had already realized it. She was on this journey because she had foreseen this outcome from the start: Grace Loray at war again.

She felt the depth of it now. The true divide in where the conflict would originate.

"That's why the place we're going still exists," came Cansu's voice. "Thought we'd be able to shut down the sanctuary after the war, but turns out we traded one tyrant for another."

Lu had no argument. Just that ache in her head that would not go away.

Once again, floorboards thudded under their boots. A staircase led down, a door creaked open, and they stopped.

The sack was yanked off Lu's head and she blinked in hazy light. A yard stretched before her, enclosed by looming buildings on three sides and the wall of the city on the fourth, complete with tangled vines and branches trying to crawl over the top. Hovels filled the area, interspersed with campfires, lines hung with laundry, and stacks of barrels.

And people. Dozens of people, kneeling over those fires or hanging that laundry, men, women, and children. Dirt smudged each face; every outfit was in tatters. Some rested on mats, their bodies quaking with tremors Lu knew too well. Shaking Sickness.

Everyone was Tuncian, as the language Lu heard was not the Grace Loray dialect or Argridian. What had Vex called it? Thuti?

But a voice brought her out of her shock and confusion. "Lu!"

She shot forward, and Cansu didn't stop her. Not that anyone could have—the moment Lu saw Teo racing up a dirt path toward her, she forgot all else. He was grinning, and he didn't look harmed or mistreated.

He locked his arms around Lu's neck, grip clamping and choking, but Lu didn't care as she scooped him up just as strongly.

"Are you all right?" Lu shifted to look at him. "Are you hurt?"

"I'm fine! Edda took real good care of me. She made the raiders get me a type of candy—I don't remember the name—but it was *so* sweet! Like those pastries you got me and Annalisa, remember? Like that! You have to try it! Come on!"

Teo wiggled until she set him down, and he took off again. Edda, coming up the road behind him, caught him, and the two headed back to wherever they had been.

Lu looked at the crowd. Those who had been doing chores stopped, giving her wide berth while they stared.

Lu felt, standing in the middle of them, the full weight of everything she had begun realizing.

Lu had known her country. She had spent the bulk of her life fighting to better it.

But all that fighting hadn't changed anything.

The Council had brought peace to Grace Loray—but the old traps of prejudice and disunity were in place for the island to disintegrate again just as it had under Argrid.

Vex broke free of the crowd. "They aren't the best at welcomes," he told her.

She stretched taller despite the growing pressure to buckle. "What is this place?"

"A place of sanctuary," someone else said. "A place of transition."

The crowd parted for a short, intense woman with graying black hair so long it served almost as a cloak around her knotted dress. She had a tattoo identical to Cansu's, the Tuncian mark of their gods, though hers sat delicately across her round nose. She stopped, looking up with annoyed, dissatisfied eyes that made both those emotions seem like Lu's fault.

"Fatemah," Lu guessed.

Fatemah lifted an eyebrow. "And you are?"

How best to introduce herself? Lu straightened. "A . . . representative of the Council."

Fatemah glowered. She said something in Thuti. Vex responded. Fatemah frowned, said something back to him, and Vex batted his hand at Lu and replied again.

"I'm right here," Lu said. "I already know you speak the Grace Loray dialect."

Fatemah frowned at Lu. "There are *five* languages spoken in Tuncay," she snapped. "How many can you name? I speak the Grace Loray dialect for the same reason all Tuncians do here—because we have no other choice."

Lu slid back a step. "I'm sorry" was all she managed. "I'm sorry I—"

"We do not want the Council's sympathy. Why did you come?" She scowled at Vex. "Why did you bring her here?"

"We need your help," he told Fatemah. "An Argridian diplomat's gone missing. We thought you might be able to hear what happened to him, or his location, or—"

Fatemah pivoted, cutting Lu out of the conversation. But based on the furious pitch in Fatemah's voice and the harsh flush of red to her golden-brown skin, Lu found she was all right with not being the woman's focus. Cansu was nowhere to be seen—if she had heard Vex, likely they'd have two angry people to fend off. But finding Milo would help them by stopping the tensions with Council soldiers. Things would get *better*.

As Lu stayed next to Vex and Fatemah, with the crowd's disdainful eyes on her, she felt more and more like an intruder. Would uncovering Milo's plot and having Vex bring him back to the Council fix the wrongs that made this raider sanctuary necessary?

"Can you assist us or not?" Lu interrupted, panicked about the slow, methodical unwinding of the plan that she had put her faith in.

Fatemah rounded on her. Despite the woman's short stature, she seemed to tower over Lu. "You have no idea what you have risked coming here."

"I do," Lu tried. "If you do not help me find General Ibarra, the Argridians will push the Council to blame raiders for his disappearance."

"The Council has *already* blamed raiders for his disappearance." Fatemah pointed out people as she mentioned them. "Soldiers who were raiding tenement buildings forced those people from their homes. The people there? Soldiers confiscated their boats while looking for the missing Argridian. More are here because this syndicate no longer has the resources to employ them, thanks to the Council's seizing of the Tuncian Mainland trade. The Council is the reason for this place as much as Argrid once was—whatever you think to change by finding that Argridian general, it will not help. You do not understand the problems here. None of the Council does."

Lu faltered, struck breathless as she looked at wide-eyed children and their somber parents. She remembered the soldiers at the falls, and the Grace Lorayans in the streets of Port Mesi-Teab.

"We do not fear the Council," Fatemah said. "We lived

through Argrid's oppression. We lived through five years of the Council telling us to either conform or become destitute. The Council would not have won the war without us. Tuncay worships the God of Chaos and the God of Death, as well as those of Rebirth and of Life. We do not fear—"

Nayeli shoved out of the crowd. "How long are you going to pretend this is working?"

Fatemah responded, but in Thuti, the brush of her hand signifying that she was trying to ignore Nayeli's question.

"What should we do?" Cansu appeared now. The look on her face was a mirror of Fatemah's, but closer to grief than fury. "Become *Grace Lorayan*? It's not as easy for everyone to abandon their culture as it is for you."

"I didn't abandon anything," Nayeli spat. "This *isn't* Tuncay. We *aren't* Tuncian. We don't owe allegiance to the empress, and we've never even seen Tuncay's deserts or its mountains. I can't keep living in between." She spun on Lu. "Tuncians started this sanctuary to protect the people Argrid tried to imprison up at Fort Chastity. They'd even smuggle some people out"—she motioned at the looming wall—"to safe houses away from the port."

Cansu hissed for silence, but Nayeli kept talking.

"They should've shut it down when the war ended, but they still let Tuncians live here—new immigrants, and families who've been here forever too. Gods, it's crazy, right? They're so damn proud that they'd rather be here in squalor, but still call themselves *Tuncians*, than have a better life and be Grace Lorayan."

Cansu wilted. "You're as bad as the Council for thinking it's that simple."

Fatemah stated something in Thuti. Nayeli, for the first time, responded in Thuti, but she dropped her eyes to the ground.

Fatemah reached into her collar and freed a necklace made of stones. They clinked as she worked one loose and tossed it at Nayeli's feet.

"We will help," Fatemah said. "Then you will leave. Don't return. Not anymore."

She left, Cansu and the crowd trailing after her. Nayeli's eyes stayed rooted on the stone.

"Thanks, Nay," Vex said.

She looked up. "Please. Fatemah's predictable. And Cansu? Wave a busty woman in front of her, and she's a goner. It doesn't take much to get them to comply."

Her words were light, but her face was hard. She bent to snatch the stone, and Lu saw a symbol she didn't recognize carved into the surface.

"What does that mean?" Lu asked.

"She's my aunt." Nayeli sniffed. "Rocks have special meaning in Tuncay—you take one from near the home of someone you love and carve this word on it. It says *family*."

Nayeli let it fall out of her hand before she lifted her eyes from Lu to Vex.

"What are you idiots still doing here? Don't let them change their minds."

Before they could say more, Nayeli riffled her hands through her hair and strode down one of the dirt paths.

Lu gawked after her, but Vex cleared his throat.

"This happens every time we visit. Though there's usually more bloodshed."

He started in the opposite direction. Lu followed—after swiping up the stone.

Would Kari have had stones like this if the war hadn't interrupted their lives? Would Lu, if she hadn't been so determined to be Grace Lorayan?

The stone should have felt brittle, a rock beaten by river currents.

Lu slid it into her pocket and hurried after Vex.

16

BEN SAT AT the desk in his front room, crouched over parchment and quill. He wrote until his vision swam and his candle burned low and every muscle in his back cried out for reprieve.

Of the more than fifty varieties of botanical magic native to Grace Loray, Inquisitors found that four were pure enough to use to heal people.

A tray of garlic fish and tomatoes slid onto the desk. "Eat," Jakes prodded.

Ben didn't look up, wringing his brain dry to extract every drop of magic knowledge.

Several texts from Grace Loray claim there are more, but some, like Drooping Fern, have proven too dangerous to use, as their effects inflict harm or encourage the sins of overindulging and intoxication.

The holy ones are: Cleanse Root, Healica, Powersage, and Alova Pipe.

Jakes planted his hands on the tabletop, jolting the candle flame.

"Tell me what you need," he whispered. "Let me help you. Let me in."

Ben closed his eyes. He needed supplies. He needed a new laboratory. Could he still use the Mecht's aid money? He needed plants, too, but he doubted his father would provide more.

But he needed this *now*. Before Elazar swept in and withdrew his orders. Before Ben lost his feeble grip on change and defensors led him to a pyre the same way he had been living all these years: alone and afraid.

Though—that wasn't true. He hadn't been alone.

Jakes's breathing was calm and rhythmic.

Ben kept writing, forcing himself to remember everything Rodrigu had once taught him.

Healica and Alova Pipe used together cured boils. The result was instant when applied to the skin in a paste and imbibed in a liquefied tonic.

Powersage and Healica cured influenza—again applied in both a paste and a tonic, but healing came after two days of repetition.

Jakes grabbed Ben's hand and lifted the quill. Ben rose with it.

"This is what I am." Ben spoke so Jakes couldn't. "A servant of the Pious God, doing the bidding of our Eminence." *Until he decides what I am doing is sin. Until he reveals his true motive, and it was to get me on a pyre all along.*

"I know," Jakes said. "You walk around as though the fate of your people's souls hangs on your actions. It is one of the things that made me fall in love with you—you *care*, in a way few people in Argrid still do. In the way my family did." Jakes's smile was lopsided. "When I see your devotion, I hear my sister's voice, speaking of honor and loyalty to Argrid. You will, one day, be the king Argrid needs. Grace Benat."

Jakes smiled, expecting Ben to be honored. But Ben's heart squeezed.

Would you love me if you knew what I believe?

The question sent him buckling back into the chair. When it came down to Elazar's will or Ben's, which side would Jakes choose? The side of the Pious God—or the side of a heretic?

Ben crouched over, bile crawling up the back of his throat. If he lost everything to create this tonic and show Argrid that magic could be good, he would make the best goddamn healing tonic the world had seen. It would cure everything, even Shaking Sickness, like Elazar wanted.

Where to start, though? Ben hadn't gotten further than breaking down a few plants before the fire three days ago. How to combine them into a healing tonic? How to test it?

The ink on the parchment blurred and the words melted and all he saw were flames spreading out from the candle, taking over his world.

Ben jolted as though he'd been burned. He was an idiot. *The Mecht warrior.* The one his Inquisitor patrol had caught along with the raider crew. He had spared the man's life because he knew things about botanical magic that no one in Argrid did, yet Ben had made no move to interact with him.

Ben shoved himself to his feet and took determined steps around his desk.

Jakes intercepted him. "Where are you going?"

Ben stopped, feigning nonchalance. "Grace Neus."

"Now? Are you—"

"I don't need your help," Ben told him. Begged him.

Stay here. Don't see what I must do. Don't see this side of me. Please, please—

"No, it's fine. I'll ready a carriage," Jakes said, and disappeared.

Ben sank to the edge of the desk. Jakes would follow him into the holding cells. Anything he said to the Mecht, Jakes would hear.

But Elazar had not yet told him to stop working on the potion. He had to do so with caution—before he lost more than he could bear.

Grace Neus Cathedral never closed—the Pious God always welcomed children who needed guidance. When Ben entered, he wasn't surprised to see wayward souls huddled in the pews, monxes and a priest lighting candles for the Graces.

Ben hurried up the side, making his way to the door at the front of the cathedral, one he'd gone through with his Inquisitor patrol dozens of times. The door led to a staircase, guiding Ben and Jakes down to an intersection of halls lined with barred cells.

Here, the color of the cathedral met its opposite. The walls, floor, and ceiling were dark gray stone, with sconces providing intermittent light. During services, this floor echoed with the crooning of the monxa choir and the Eminence's sermons, an intentional design to let any present here listen, meditate, and repent.

"You shouldn't be—" a monxe started to say, coming out of a supply room on their left. His eyes widened when he recognized Ben. "My prince. What can I do for you?"

"I pardoned a Mecht raider," he said. "I need to speak to him."

Behind Ben, Jakes straightened, but he stayed silent.

The monxe's shoulders hardened. "Yes. Follow me."

He started off. Most cells they passed were occupied, and Ben recognized the aristocrats from the gathering yesterday. They either slept on cots or knelt before the carving that decorated the back of each cell—the Church's cupped hands.

The monxe made another turn and stopped before a cell near the end of the hall.

The hangover Ben had had and the chaos of that Inquisitor patrol blurred his memories of the raider. All he remembered was the sun high in the sky, and in the man's blond hair.

When Ben looked inside the cell, he let out an audible groan.

The Mecht wore the same clothing Ben had caught him in, stained now. He stooped on his knees, his arms tied at the base of his spine to chains that snaked up the walls, his head drooped, hair matted. He grunted as though it took physical effort to hold himself upright.

"The prince wishes to have a word with you," the monxe informed the raider as he unlocked the cell. "The Pious God watches your every move."

The Mecht snorted, but the noise was hard to catch. He lifted his head, and Ben saw why: monxes had fastened an iron mask over his mouth and nose.

Ben had seen raiders confined, the more reactive ones restrained. But this one wasn't even allowed to *breathe* freely.

It was Ben's fault the man was chained like this. His fault that the Mecht had been transformed from a sun to a flickering candle flame.

"He's safe," the monxe told Ben. "This is to remind him of the restraint he must show as a child of the Pious God."

"Leave us," Ben rasped. The monxe bowed and left. Without him, it was quiet, and Jakes stayed so silent that Ben looked at him to make sure he was still there.

Jakes's attention was on a cell across the way, where a man lay on a tattered pallet. His body shook, tremors that made his limbs twitch, but otherwise, he appeared unconscious.

Shaking Sickness.

"Are you sure you wish to be down here?" Jakes asked, his voice brittle. "How will this help you make the tonic?"

In response, Ben entered the Mecht's cell. The man's eyes narrowed in either a glare or a squint—it was hard to tell.

"Can you speak?" Ben asked. "Have you recanted?"

The look he gave Ben was now definitely a glare. The fury in his bloodshot eyes was so strong, the blue depths darkened.

"I'll take that as a no," Ben said. He lowered himself to the floor, level with the Mecht. Pious God above, Ben had forgotten how big the man was, his size intimidating even while restrained.

The Mecht jolted at Ben's movement, his shirt shifting across his chest. Light from tapers in the hall caught briefly on his sternum, showing red welts that made Ben lean closer.

"What happened?" Ben dared to grab the edge of the Mecht's shirt. Their close proximity made him flush with the heat that radiated out of the man's skin. "Did the monxes do this? If they're—"

"Your people cannot hurt me," the Mecht said. "In the Mechtlands, we are taught to worship Visjorn: bear spirit, rampaging and brutal, eternally hungry. I do not fear your petty god of words and obedience."

Ben froze, his fingers pinching the Mecht's shirt. The Mecht's words and the scar on his chest were what stopped him: four swirling lines branched out of a circle. It looked like a brand, but the lines were jagged and unsteady, as if someone had painted the wound on by hand.

"It's an emblem," Ben said. His eyes lifted to the Mecht's. "A clan mark, I'd guess."

The Mecht didn't respond, but his words and attitude gave Ben hope.

"There are things I want to know." Ben released his shirt. "The Eye of the Sun is—"

A deep chuckle resonated against the Mecht's mask. When he spoke, it was in a language Ben didn't understand, one of the dozens of tongues of the Mechtlands.

"Excuse me?" Ben pressed.

"I say *Argridian prince is* . . ." The Mecht paused, the corners of his eyes wrinkling. "*Argridian prince is* . . . like dumb, only worse. Only you do not know you are."

"I'm not asking you to tell me your secrets," Ben assured him. "I want . . ."

What *did* he want?

The Mecht shrugged his torn shirt up his shoulder, covering his mark as best he could. The temperature of the cell ramped higher and sweat trickled down Ben's spine.

"Your magic is permanent," Ben whispered.

The Mecht tipped his head in confusion.

Ben risked a glance back. Jakes's focus was on the sick man across the hall. For a moment, they had privacy.

"I don't care about Eye of the Sun itself," Ben whispered.

"What I care about is that it's permanent. There aren't any other plants with effects that last that long. How did you do it?"

"They do not give Eye of the Sun to those who will talk," the Mecht countered, and Ben got the impression that his lips were sealed as unbreakably as his iron muzzle.

"How many of your people have died in Argrid?" Ben asked. The Mecht looked away. "All because this country fears magic so much they'd rather kill those who use it than understand it. I can make them understand. But I need you to help me."

The Mecht didn't look at him. Ben tried another tactic.

"It can't be any of the traditional methods. Not a paste, a tonic. Not inhaled."

The Mecht didn't react. Ben's eyes fell to the parts of the mark he could see. It almost looked like a burn Ben had received at a feast as a child. Melted sugar had sat in a pot for people to dip fruit into, and when he'd gotten some, a strand of the molten liquid had squirmed across his arm. For days after, he'd had a nasty red mark on his skin, like the Mecht's scar.

"A syrup?" Ben said aloud. Thicker than a tonic, more condensed.

The Mecht looked up, his eyes unreadable.

Rodrigu had dissolved Healica pods in boiling water, and other plants were dissolved to make tonics, but Ben had never heard of a plant reduced beyond that stage. And he had seen an Eye of the Sun flower once, in a shipment long ago—it had no buds for nectar, no part of it that contained a naturally occurring syrup.

Ben rocked forward, so close to the Mecht that if the muzzle was removed, the man would only need to sigh to singe Ben's face. But Ben reached forward, and before he realized what he'd done, he laid a finger on the Mecht's scar.

The flames that had burned up Rodrigu and Paxben hadn't been this hot. This heat was frantic, and Ben launched to his feet, staring at his hand as if he expected it to be on fire.

The Mecht looked up at him, eyes wide with fear.

"They branded you with the liquid," Ben guessed. But that wouldn't work with healing plants. He could reduce them to a thick liquid and heat them hot enough to scar, but he had helped study an Eye of the Sun flower—it let off its own natural heat. That was likely what made it brand the skin.

Ben looked back. Jakes had his back to them, still watching the sick man. Hadn't he seen someone with Shaking Sickness before?

Then Ben remembered—Jakes's sister and her children had died of it.

The silence from Jakes was more potent suddenly. He was too stricken even to hum that song.

Ben's limbs flooded with anxiety—they needed to leave.

Ben dropped in front of the Mecht again. "Did they make you drink it? How did you ingest it? You *had* to have taken it. There has to be more."

If Ben could make healing plants permanent, like Eye of the Sun was permanent, he could show Argridians that they didn't need to fear magic. That good could come from it. He could break his country's dependency on the Church, and Elazar, and—

The Mecht hissed in his own language, an unmistakable curse.

Ben reached behind the man's head.

Jakes jolted into the cell. "My prince—"

But Ben was already unhooking the muzzle. If the Mecht had ingested the concoction that had burned his chest, he'd have scars in his mouth too.

The muzzle fell. The Mecht's upper lip curled. "Dumb prince," he rumbled, and blew out.

Ben jerked to the side—but no fire came, only a long string of smoke. He whirled back to see the Mecht coughing. The man leaned to the side, his chains keeping him from lying flat out, and he hung there with his arms bent behind his back, his whole body shuddering.

Jakes grabbed Ben by the waist and hauled him up, but Ben planted his feet.

"They aren't feeding him," Ben stated.

"With good reason," Jakes said. "The Devil's grip on him is too strong."

Ben shrugged Jakes off and grabbed the Mecht's chin. Those furious blue eyes found his, his anger intensified now that his whole face was free.

Ben lifted the fingers of his free hand. The Mecht's jaw was warm in his palm, heat spreading into Ben's body and planting urgency in his gut. Neither of them moved. A spell of shock linked them—Ben, that the Mecht hadn't shoved him off yet; and the Mecht, maybe that Ben was being so gentle.

Forcing himself out of the spell, Ben parted the Mecht's chapped lips.

The Mecht jerked away. Jakes mistook the movement for attack and slammed into the raider, who bashed his head against the wall. He cried out, body wilting, but the chains kept him upright, unable to rest, unable to lie down.

Ben had felt the rough flesh on the inside of the Mecht's mouth, against his teeth.

His lips were scarred.

"Monxe!" Ben shouted.

The monxe appeared, hands clasped against his robes.

"Give this man food and water," Ben ordered. "Unchain him. We don't—"

He almost said, *We don't murder people here.*

But it was a lie. One he'd helped form, obeying the Church without question, because what could he do to stop them? He'd been part of the problem for years.

He'd been as much a murderer as Elazar.

The Mechts had created a syrup from Eye of the Sun. The exact method of preparation was a mystery, and who knew what they combined the flower with to achieve the desired state? The healing magic would likely be different anyway, another combination of plants. But the information was a start—and with it, Ben would free his country.

Ben marched out of the Mecht's cell. Jakes followed, waiting until they'd taken the first two steps up the stairwell before he grabbed Ben's arm.

"Don't you *ever* do something like that again," he barked. "I'm used to you being reckless, but that was a new level of risk that I'm not willing to let you take."

Ben shoved back. "I'm willing to do what I have to. If you can't, I'll find a guard who—"

He stopped, staring, because he never thought he'd say something like this.

Jakes's face went cold. "Yes, my prince," he said. "I will not question you again."

"Jakes—"

"*No.* I'll be whoever you need me to be, if it means keeping you safe."

Ben put his hand on Jakes's cheek.

"I love you," Ben told Jakes in the stairwell of Grace Neus Cathedral, with condemned souls below and righteous parishioners above. "When it breached propriety, a prince and his guard; when it went against the pillar of chastity. *I loved you.* That was always true."

Jakes linked his fingers around Ben's wrist. "What—"

But Ben wanted this moment to stay pure when, one day, Jakes would realize that the rest of Argrid was right about him.

Prince Benat is a heretic, they said. *He is irredeemable.*

Ben started up the stairs, climbing for the light.

17

LU FOLLOWED VEX into the Tuncian refuge. They saw tents of taut animal hide and small cottages of stone or weather-beaten wood—some temporary structures, some permanent.

As they passed children rolling a ball between them, Lu asked, "What do they do here, exactly?" It came as a whisper, weighed down by the dozens of other questions waiting on the cusp of this one.

"If I tell you, you can't get all Council-righteous on me again," Vex said.

Lu hesitated, considering if she would, but he took her silence as agreement.

"Fatemah helps anyone with Tuncian lineage," Vex said. "New immigrants camp out until they can get set up with houses and jobs, and any Tuncians already living on Grace Loray can hide here if they're being threatened or need a place to stay during a rough time. Which has been a lot, lately." He motioned to a family, a mother tending her child's scraped knee outside a tent.

"They're forced to join Cansu's syndicate, then," Lu guessed. "They become criminals."

Vex's jaw spasmed. "They aren't criminals. They're people."

"They join the syndicate, though. They steal plants from the Council's rivers and sell them under Cansu's banner instead of Grace Loray's. They have another option! That is what I find so frustrating. They don't have to be criminals, or—"

"They're *people*, Lu." Vex rounded on her. "Sure, some join Cansu's syndicate as raiders, but most want a good, honest life, and that's what Fatemah helps them get. Because as soon as they land here, the Council writes them off—or, worse, targets them."

Lu shook her head. "Many Tuncians have become Grace Lorayan and aided in the country's progress. They help build a system that—"

"Yeah, the lucky ones. The ones who have connections, or find someone willing to give a raider or an immigrant a chance. But there's no system set up to help people actually *become* Grace Lorayan—you know that, right? The Council won the war and expected people to instantly get jobs and steady lives, and when people couldn't, they got blamed for their problems. Which is why there are so many raiders—and why they're all really pissed that the Council took away their source of income and scream at them for not being *productive members of society.*"

Lu willed an argument to form. There were jobs now— for people who sought them out. There were proper lives—for people who worked to get them. But for those who arrived on Grace Loray's shores, like that Mecht immigrant ship she'd seen in the market days ago, with nothing but hope? And for those who had been in poverty under Argrid's rule, with no way to change their situations once the Council had taken control?

Whole groups of Grace Loray's citizens were destined for failure.

The Council dismissed raiders and immigrants alike as creating their own problems. But if the Council wanted their country to function and operate for everyone, they needed to accommodate everyone—and start taking responsibility for everyone as well.

Lu watched herself grab Vex's arm as if her mind had risen from her body.

"I'm sorry," she said, fast and aching, as though apologizing to him would mend these wounds. "It should have worked for everyone. I'm sorry."

Vex's eyebrows rose. "It's not your fault," he said, unsure why she apologized.

It is. "Why did you bring me here if this place exists because of the Council's shortcomings?" Lu asked.

Vex cut her a grin. He didn't respond until he stopped outside a shack on the eastern edge of the sanctuary. Smoke floated through a hole in the top, sending out the herbal tang of cooking plants.

"Are you saying I should do a worse job of helping you?" Vex tried for amusement.

Lu didn't encourage him. "I want to understand this."

Vex's smile fell. He leaned toward her, his body pressing close. Lu jolted, but Vex grabbed the door behind her and drew it open, the smirk on his face saying he'd intended to unsettle her, just as she had done to him on the falls.

It worked. Warmth rushed over Lu's body and her mind went blank, but Vex smiled wider.

"After you." He beckoned her on. Lu ducked inside with a glare.

The shack could have fit on the deck of the *Meander*. Rugs of woven dyed leather covered the floor, while drying plant clusters hung from the ceiling, filling the space with the earthy musk Lu had secluded herself in for years.

She felt, for a brief moment, home.

Lu knew magic. Everything else could be in chaos, but she would endure, because she knew that speed-giving Incris negated that bundle of immobilizing Lazonade, and that Awacia countered that Drooping Fern bunch, and—

Cansu rose from the carpets. "We'll help, but you aren't needed here."

Fatemah sat by a small fire in the center of the shack,

stirring a pot over the flames. She didn't pay Lu or Vex any attention, letting Cansu play guard.

"What do you mean, *you're* going to help?" Vex asked. "All we need is Fatemah."

"My syndicate, my plants. I don't trust that whatever you're doing won't hurt my people in some way."

The way Cansu said *my people* made Lu's heart twist with the same discomfort that had been building for hours.

"I can help." Lu gestured to Fatemah. "I've studied every plant on this island. You're using Budwig, yes? I'm guessing you have beans scattered across the island and have the corresponding beans here. I can listen through some of them—"

Fatemah gave her an incredulous look. She lifted a bean, but when Lu reached for it, she fed it to the pot in front of her. Lu leaned over it, noting the brew, a murky maroon color the same as the bean, with a biting spiced scent that burned her nose.

"You're dissolving it?" Lu frowned and knelt on the floor. "I thought the beans of the Budwig plant were placed in the ears, allowing people to hear each other over great distances."

Cansu chuckled. "Did you memorize *Botanical Wonders*?"

Instinctively Lu reached to her side, where her satchel usually was. But she had left it and her book on the *Meander*.

Lu had experimented only with the higher concentrations of plants that worked in liquid form. To cook Budwigs, or use any plant in a different state . . .

She sat up taller. "Clearly you have not read it, or you would know that you are wasting rare magic on a preparation that was never outlined in the book."

"The original settlers of Grace Loray wrote that book more than two centuries ago," said Fatemah. "What makes you think they knew everything about magic? What makes you believe that you, a Grace Lorayan, too bothered by war and trying to control the world, would know the secrets of this island?"

Lu drew back. "Excuse me?"

Vex sat next to her. "Be nice, Fatemah."

"You're wrong," Cansu said. "What she's trying to tell you is that you're wrong. No one in any syndicate knows more about magic than Fatemah."

A rebuttal rose in Lu's throat, but she couldn't let it past her lips.

She *was* wrong—or had been, with so many of her assumptions about raiders and immigrants, and admitting that much made her queasy.

She steadied on the floor, fingers splayed on the carpet. Was she wrong about botanical magic too? She had made it her purpose after the war to learn as much as she could. It had been all she wanted, to find something that connected her in a pure way to this island. Something *safe*.

Fatemah looked at Lu through the billowing smoke.

"We are helping you because you are Tuncian, as much as

you may have forgotten. Our gods have not forgotten you," Fatemah said. Lu's eyes widened. They had recognized her lineage. "And because one of our own has asked it."

"I'm not doing this for Nayeli," Cansu muttered. There was a deeper tension in the way Cansu reacted, something different from the familial betrayal Fatemah exuded.

"The knowledge you gain here is yours to do with what you will," Fatemah said. "But if the Council learns of this place from you, you will die."

She said it so straightforwardly that Lu had no choice but to bow. "I will use this honorably. You have my word."

Fatemah nodded, whether in acceptance of Lu's promise or because she knew the Tuncians would be able to kill her otherwise, Lu couldn't guess.

"Cansu," Fatemah said, and sat back on her heels.

Cansu took the spoon from Fatemah and ladled a scoop of the now-syrupy Budwig. She pinned Lu with a heavy stare. "What's the name of the Argridian?"

"I can do this," Lu said. "I know you have no love for Argrid, but you don't need to be involved beyond this. Vex will be the one to bring back Milo and prove that raiders didn't abduct him. Tell me what to—"

"Don't think we need you," Cansu barked. "I'll get you what information you need, and you'll leave. This doesn't change anything between the Council and us. Now tell me who I'm looking for, or I'll throw you out no matter what Nayeli says."

Lu gave in. "Milo Ibarra."

"Where was he last seen?"

"New Deza. The castle."

Cansu nodded, took a deep breath, and let it out long and loud. Another. On a final inhale, she brought the spoon to her lips and gulped a mouthful of the dissolved Budwig.

Lu rocked toward her as Cansu moaned, the liquid no doubt searing her throat. But Fatemah intervened, batting away Lu's attempts to help. The motion sent an aroma wafting off her—coconut and spices and a distinct memory of Lu curled up on her mother's lap.

"She's done this before," Fatemah said. "We have Budwigs in many locations around Grace Loray. With these beans dissolved and concentrated, the effects of their counter beans are enhanced. This will allow her to hear through all the Budwig plants at once. It takes a great deal of concentration to focus through the sounds each Budwig picks up—so if you don't mind."

Fatemah jerked her head toward the door. Vex was already peeling himself off the rugs.

"Thanks, Fatemah," he said, taking Lu's arm. "Let us know when she hears something."

Vex dragged Lu out of the shack and grinned.

"You're welcome," he declared, hands out as if he might bow. "I told you I'd help."

"Cansu—she can hear through every Budwig they've placed on the island?" *Can she listen for news from New Deza?*

was what Lu wanted to ask. She had managed not to let herself linger on the horrors her parents might be dealing with—the furious Argridians who would be demanding justice for Milo and punishment for the escaped Devereux Bell; searching for Milo, both through the Council and her parents' loyal spies; and dragging out treaty negotiations.

Though it appeared that delaying the treaty finalization and Milo's bill of eliminating stream raiders was not preventing soldiers from taking steps against raiders already.

Kari, at least, would be as overwhelmed by this sanctuary as Lu. She would feel the familiarity. The connection. The guilt.

Lu became painfully aware of the heat in her eyes.

"I didn't know about any of this," she murmured.

Vex shrugged. "Don't be too hard on yourself."

"Oh, no, I quite deserve this guilt. What I can't figure out is why you feel none. Have you helped them? Why have you done nothing? If you knew how lacking the Council was in helping immigrants and raiders, why not rally to change things?"

Vex gaped at her, his face dropping muscle by muscle into a resolute stare. "This isn't my fight," he stated. "And I have tried, so don't act like I'm some monster. I'd do anything they asked of me, but all they've asked is that I keep this place and what they do here a secret so the Council doesn't mess it up."

Lu opened her mouth.

For five years, her passionate belief in Grace Loray's Council had been her guiding light. But the Council was so much less effective than she had believed, and she was powerless to change it. One mention of this secret lair, and soldiers would swarm in to dismantle it—before or after the Council put measures in place to compensate for the help Fatemah offered here?

Lu knew the answer. *Immigrants? Hiding away here? They're raiders! Arrest them!*

And the things Fatemah did with the Budwig Beans. What other knowledge of plants did she have? How much would people pay for her secrets? What could be accomplished—what diseases could be cured?

Lu all but dropped to her knees right there.

Had the cure for Shaking Sickness been within Lu's grasp the whole time? If she had broken down plants, liquefied them even though it was never mentioned in *Botanical Wonders of the Grace Loray Colony*, could she have saved Annalisa? Could she have even saved Annalisa and Teo's mother, Bianca, two years ago?

Lu had always believed the Council's purpose was to spread equality on an island that had suffered too long under Argrid's cruelty. But who benefited from their justice? Not the people who used the Tuncian refuge, and not, she suspected, any other immigrant group. Not the raiders who, though criminals, did not deserve to be treated as subhuman.

The system Lu had bled to put into place was not the system this island needed.

"We aren't enough" was all Lu could think to say.

Vex lifted one hand as if to cup her shoulder. "Fatemah and Cansu don't expect—"

She pushed around him, arms folded, and stalked off down one of the winding pathways.

Lu was a daughter of the revolution. She'd done unspeakable things to help create a country built on fairness and loyalty, hard work and justice. But she had looked at the future through fogged lenses, expecting the benefits of a new country to be so *obvious* that she had dismissed anyone else's feelings. Who wouldn't want a fresh start? Who wouldn't want to help build something as grand and full of potential as the Council? These raiders who abused her system were wrong, so why should the Council heed them?

But no. *Lu* was wrong. She had been wrong all along.

She wandered until she found herself in a clearing, a bonfire keeping the shadows of night away from a circle of tents and shacks. Tuncians filled the area, and Lu noticed now the brands on several of their wrists, the *R* behind Argrid's crossed *V*. Edda helped Teo roast food in the fire while Nayeli, seated in the shadow of a tent, sorted plants in her lap.

"Fatemah show you the *magic*?" Nayeli fluttered her fingers as Lu knelt beside her.

Lu nodded. Yes, the magic. And too many other things.

She scrubbed a hand down her face, not yet strong enough to talk of it. She asked an easy question. "Is Cansu angry only because you disagree about the sanctuary? Something else happened to keep you out of her syndicate."

Nayeli grinned but didn't give anything away.

A mystery as simple as the tortured past between Nayeli and Cansu was comforting. Lu tipped her head. "You love her still."

Nayeli's eyes went wide, and a warm red blush tinted her cheeks, but she shook off her surprise with a laugh.

"You're too smart. I might not like that eventually."

"It makes sense now, why she helped us," Lu continued. "It was for you."

"No," Nayeli countered, too forcefully. "It'd be more likely for you and Vex to end up in bed together. Er, cot, as it were. The *Meander* doesn't have beds. And they are *very* squeaky, so Gods, if you do decide to roll around with him, do us all a favor and fornicate somewhere less—"

Lu blanched. "Do you say everything that comes into your mind?"

"A lot of people have told me I should think before speaking." Nayeli considered. A look of abject horror crossed her face. "Damn. I'd never get to say anything fun again."

"Lu!"

The panic in the voice yanked Lu to her feet. Vex sprinted into the clearing, his head whipping back and forth until he spotted her and dove her way.

Behind him, up the path he'd come, Cansu stormed out.

"Raiders, to me!" she bellowed, just as Vex reached Lu and said, "She found Ibarra. He's—it's bad, Lu—"

More people and raiders hurried in from side roads, squeezing between shacks to gather around the bonfire at Cansu's command. The violent orange of the flames thrashed as Cansu lifted a fist into the air, punching her words.

"Too long have we lived in squalor, waiting for the Council to make good on a promise they never intended to keep. Too long have we let them treat us like vermin in their sewers—now we prepare to fight back!"

Lu's blood felt as though it would burst out of her veins. "What happened?" She whirled on Vex. "What—"

But Cansu stalked toward them. "The Council turned on us when it was only a hunch that raiders abducted the Argridian. You said so yourself—the moment they find out that raiders *did* abduct him, they'll declare all-out war against us."

Lu staggered back, lungs emptying of air. A hand was on her back. Vex?

"Lu," he said. "I'm sorry—"

"The Mecht syndicate has him," Cansu declared viciously. "Pilkvist's raiders abducted the Argridian general."

18

EVERYTHING RUSHED INTO Lu at once, her mind scrambling for sense amid the senseless.

Three days ago, she had freed the most notorious raider on Grace Loray from prison. She had defied her parents and no doubt brought turmoil to the Council. She had dragged Teo into it as well, not even half a day after his sister's death.

Before that, a memory tugged at her.

Plants used in unusual methods. Drooping Fern, in a pot of tea . . .

She had been so certain Milo, and Argrid, had staged this. She had based every action on her gut feeling that Drooping Fern could not work in that preparation—but she had watched Fatemah boil Budwig to increase its potency, a plant Lu never would have fathomed preparing like that.

Lu lifted trembling fingers to her forehead.

She had been wrong in how she viewed immigrants and raiders. She had been wrong about the extent of Grace Loray's botanical magic, and how it could be taken further, enhanced.

Had she been wrong about Milo's abduction?

A hand tightened on her shoulder, and she realized the only thing keeping her from collapsing was Vex's gentle, constant grip. He met her eyes with utter sympathy.

She must have looked wretched, to warrant such a reaction from him.

"The Council will see this as an act of war!" Cansu shouted at the gathered crowd of Tuncians, raiders and families alike. "They were already planning to use our blood to pay for peace with Argrid. We've let them play god over us for too long. They wouldn't have even won the revolution if it weren't for the help of the raider syndicates. This island belongs to us!"

Cheers sounded from every direction. Some of the fists thrown into the air showed raider brands; some had that and the Tuncian tattoo. But those distinctions didn't matter as they cried for battle—they were Tuncian, they were Grace Lorayan, they were Argridian. Lu shook her head, desperation clawing inside her to stop this, stop the chants, *stop the war*—

"You can't!" Lu implored. The fire heaved hot and bright, stoking her frenzy. "My mother is a Senior on the Council—she will hear your grievances! She was the one who brokered an alliance with the raiders during the revolution. She can make the Council see reason!"

"They'll only care about Pilkvist breaking that treaty they were trying to sign," Cansu shot back. "They don't see the syndicates as separate entities. They'll come after every raider, and I'll be damned if we don't strike first. We've let them make a mess of this island, ignoring our needs, trying to make Grace Loray into something it isn't. This island is an island of raiders! We've never needed a government—we control our own lives!"

Lu wanted to protest, but she knew the truth. If the Mecht raider syndicate had abducted an Argridian diplomat, the Council would go to war to solidify their control of the island and enact justice for Milo. They had taken steps in that direction anyway, and without proof.

Lu's plan to stop that had been to bring back evidence that Argrid had staged Milo's abduction. But raiders *had* abducted Milo. Grace Loray was tearing itself apart, and even if Argrid hadn't planned it, they could take advantage of this conflict by swooping in and retaking a weakened island.

The world throbbed and shifted, and Lu couldn't steady herself long enough to think past her horror.

It's happening again.

Someone moved next to her—Nayeli.

"You don't want to fight the Council, Cansu," she shouted. "What's your endgame? An island ruled by warring raider syndicates? That's the life you want?"

"We want *freedom*," Cansu shot back. "We want to walk our streets without fear of arrest. We want opportunities and safety. Argrid sure as hell didn't give us that; the Council hasn't either. The only way to change this island's fate for the better is if *we* guide it!"

More chanting rose from the crowd. Lu's focus snapped from person to person, her heart in her throat—

Teo stood beside her, looking up with round, scared eyes.

A voice plowed through Lu's mind, and she stumbled a step toward Cansu.

"You've done so well on missions," her father had said. *"But you need to stay safe if things get dangerous. This is war, Lulu-bean— you must be ready."*

She had managed to keep her rationale the first time she had had to kill someone, and the second—it had been self-defense, she had reasoned. Men who turned violent when they figured out that she was listening to them.

But the third time, Tom had kissed her forehead before they left the safe house, heading to a part of the jungle deep in Argrid territory.

"This one is . . . different. I wouldn't ask it if it wasn't necessary."

"Can't Mama help you?" Lu had pleaded. *"I don't want to do this—"*

"Kari doesn't know about this enemy. It will be so helpful to her, to the war. This is why you're my Lulu-bean—because you can keep a

secret so well, it's as if you took a magic plant that sealed your lips. Now, just a quick trip. You won't see a thing, I promise."

"Lu?" Vex brushed her arm. "What—"

War had destroyed any chance she might've had for a childhood. Everything else, Lu's worries and guilt and her shifting mind-set, splintered around a penetrating desire not to let Teo live the kind of life that war had forced on her.

Lu shoved Cansu.

The raider Head stumbled back. A gasp ripped through the crowd, and chanting paused, everyone gaping at the girl who had dared assault the Tuncian raider Head.

But Lu was beyond herself.

"You will not go to war," she declared. "Call off your attack. *You will not start a war.*"

Cansu flew up and slammed her forearm into Lu's chest. "Don't you *ever* touch me."

"Lu!" Teo's voice pitched with fear. "Stop! Please stop!"

Reality cracked over her and Lu panted, gulping air that sliced her insides to pieces. Every face she saw showed a mix she'd seen too many times. Wariness, confusion, disgust.

"Lu?" Vex put a hand on her shoulder. "Hey, look at me—"

She shoved him away and ran away from the clearing, hands over her temples.

She didn't stop until she came to the rough stone wall of the port. There, she fell to her knees, the chirps of the jungle rising over the barrier.

This journey had been a mistake. Freeing Vex had been not only insane, but unforgivable. She needed to get Teo back to New Deza and pick up the fragments of everything she'd broken—and end this new turmoil as well. What had she expected? Only destruction followed when she gave in to the monster she used to be, the one who fought for causes and never questioned what she was helping to achieve.

Leaves crunched as someone sat beside her.

"Not now, Vex," Lu said. "Let me—"

"It was a damn fool thing you did" came Edda's voice. "But I can't say I haven't wanted to push Cansu around a few times myself."

Lu looked at her, squinting. "You weren't in the clearing."

She had been, though. Lu had seen Edda across the fire before—

Before Cansu declared that the Mecht syndicate had abducted Milo.

Edda shrugged. "Wasn't sure how Cansu'd feel about Mechts after that news about Pilkvist, so I pulled back. She seems kind of grateful, though, don't she?" She looked pointedly at Lu. "But I don't think I'm the only one who left that clearing out of fear of what I am. Wanna tell me what's going on? You've been at war with yourself since you set foot on our boat."

War. The word made it impossible for Lu to respond.

Edda must've seen the agony on her face.

"I killed my husband," she said, candid. It shocked Lu out of her own pain.

"What?"

Edda nodded. "It was self-defense. He was a monster. He'd come after me and others one too many times, and I . . ." She shrugged. "In the Mechtlands, they teach us as kids to embrace that kind of brutality in ourselves—they call it the Visjorn, spirit of the bear. But once you *do* something like that, it changes you. And I ran from it for years. I did everything I could to pretend I wasn't someone who would've been that vicious. But you know what? *I was.* I wish I could say I regretted it, or that there'd been another way. But I don't, and there wasn't, and it got to a point where I realized I couldn't live with some fantasy of goodness, not with blood on my hands.

"Point is, whatever you fear so much about yourself, it's part of you. You can either keep fighting or change your expectations, but whatever you decide, you gotta commit. This back-and-forth is what'll get people hurt, and it's my job to keep this crew safe. Which means I won't tolerate people who might jeopardize that safety."

Edda looked at Lu with a conviction developed after years of painstaking construction.

"Didn't you hear what Cansu said?" Lu's heart ached. "The Council won't care about one syndicate or another—they'll attack all the raiders, and even if Argrid didn't plan for this, it'll destroy us all the same. We'll go back to being the worst versions of ourselves. I can't—"

"Bullshit," Edda interrupted. "Look around, girlie. War may be lapping at our shores, but it ain't here yet, is it? And *you* know the difference between syndicates now. You got the ear of the Council, so tell 'em until they listen, or until war does come, but don't you sit here and speculate about *might* and *maybe*. It's a waste of energy."

Edda stood.

"It wasn't always defense," Lu whispered.

Edda paused. But Lu couldn't meet her eyes.

She choked. "Have you . . ."

Murdered someone? Have you fired a pistol into the darkness and heard a body drop? Have you fallen asleep to your father's lullabies so you didn't hear dying gurgles in your memory?

Have you done terrible things, then realized they were pointless?

Lu regretted saying anything. She barely knew this woman and didn't trust her captain. Yet Lu had opened a door, a crack she had never opened with anyone.

"You forgive yourself for what you've done," Edda told her. "You admit your mistakes. You learn from them. And you improve."

She stalked off, leaving Lu on the ground with advice she didn't know what to do with.

Forgive herself. A simple idea, one she had never deserved, not after the lives she'd ended, the men she'd killed without allowing them a chance to fight.

All to build a government that understood the people on this island as little as Argrid had.

Lu looked up, watching shadows move against the buildings.

Forgiving herself might have been too big a task for this night, but there were other things she could fix. Teo, for one—where to begin apologizing to him?

But first—Edda was right. War had not yet come, and Cansu had to see reason. Her concerns were valid, but civil war must *not* tear Grace Loray apart. They wouldn't recover from another bloody conflict, and Argrid must not have an opportunity to dive in again.

Lu would talk to Cansu and convince her of that. They could even meet with the Mecht raiders and discuss their concerns too, determine why they had taken Milo. Lu would listen to Cansu, and Pilkvist, and all the raiders on this island, and anyone else who needed to be heard.

She would insist on the same from the Council. She would refuse to relent until they admitted that their priorities were not what Grace Loray needed; that raiders, and immigrants, deserved better than prejudices. Kari, at least, would listen, and support her.

She had to try. She had to fight for a peaceful resolution.

Lu headed into the sanctuary. The clearing was empty by the time she reached it, the bonfire burned down to embers. Had everyone left to make good on Cansu's orders?

Or had they retired for the night, leaving the task of war for morning hours?

Lu roamed the pathways, looking for Vex or Nayeli or anyone who could direct her to Cansu. She ended up outside the shack where Fatemah had dissolved the Budwig Beans, light flashing along the bottom of the door. Lu lifted her fist to knock when muffled whispers filtered out.

Through one of the cracks between the shack's weather-beaten planks, Lu caught sight of Nayeli seated on the rug next to Vex. He said something in Thuti, and Nayeli responded.

Vex bent forward, elbows on his knees. "Is that what they wanted me to do?" he asked in the Grace Loray dialect.

Nayeli shrugged. "You think it was staged?"

Vex stared at the dusty rug under him. "Pilkvist's smart enough to know the repercussions of taking Ibarra on a whim. War is the only outcome, whether it's started by Cansu or someone else. I always knew I couldn't be the only raider on this island in Argrid's pocket." He shook his head, his voice warbling. "I got a bad feeling, Nay. A really bad feeling."

He kept talking, but Lu didn't hear. The blood pounded in her ears, a deafening rush.

In Argrid's pocket.

Vex was working with the Argridians.

❖❖❖

"I should be insulted. They've been using the Mechts too? Here I thought I was special." Vex looked at Nayeli, trying for humor, but he fell flat. She was an unstoppable force of joy most of the time, but when she was serious, god—he knew anything that came out of her mouth was true.

Nayeli put her hand on his knee. He hadn't realized he'd been bouncing it.

"I'd say anything to get us to leave Port Mesi-Teab," she said. "But we need to go find your Argridian contacts and figure out what's going on before Cansu gets a bunch of Tuncians killed. It's time we stopped running from Argrid and made them answer for what they've done."

Vex smirked. "What? Even if it means you won't be— what'd you say—*neck-deep in a pool of wine* in a few months?"

"A tub of wine." She sighed. "Despite what Cansu thinks, I'm not heartless. And"—she paused, her eyes dropping from his—"you never wanted to hole up somewhere like I did. You wouldn't have been content to retreat and let chaos keep churning."

Vex had never asked himself what he wanted. He, Nayeli, and Edda had planned on retiring for months—but that was back when Vex thought Argrid had just been after him. The moment he'd suspected a bigger scheme, he'd let Lu's righteousness infect him like a plague.

His shoulders went slack. "We should make each other's life decisions from now on. I'll put you back together with Cansu, and you can make me some kind of hero."

Nayeli yanked her hand off his knee. "Asshole."

"You love me."

Outside the shack, the thud of a footfall made them both shut up. But when Vex stood and opened the door, the road was empty.

Nayeli came up behind and gave him a shove. "Find Lu. You need to explain your real connections to this."

Vex groaned, long and loud and more than a little childish. "Yes, Mother."

She slapped the back of his head. He relented, plunging into the night.

Vex ran into Edda outside the lodging his crew used when they came here. She sat on the ground, watching nearby Tuncians take turns throwing knives—either a game or, after Cansu's announcement, practice for what was to come.

Vex shivered. Yeah, he needed to stop this.

He kicked Edda's boot. "You seen Lu?"

She nodded at a tent across the way. "Saw her going to talk to Teo."

Vex ducked inside. It was dark when the tent flap closed behind him, so he held it open to let in light from the torches outside.

"Lu?" he whispered. "You in here? I need to—"

A gust of wind carried through the open flap, but where it should've fluffed the other walls, it hissed through a split in the back. Vex squinted.

And started to panic.

"Lu? Teo?" He moved the flap wider to let light into the whole tent. The slice in the rear of the fabric was tall enough for a body slip through, and the bed in the far corner was mussed but empty.

Vex burst through the cut. He was on a narrow path that ran between other buildings, one that wouldn't be visible from the main road.

By the time Vex got back to Edda, Nayeli had joined her. He was shaking too much to be grateful that they both looked up at him—he knew they'd jump into action with only a word. But all he could think about was that footfall outside the shack when he'd been speaking with Nayeli. About *Argrid*.

He grimaced. "I think they're gone."

19

RAIDERS HAD ABDUCTED Milo. And Vex, all this time, was working with Argrid.

Lu's terror slammed up against the pieces of information she didn't yet know—what was the extent of Vex's involvement? Did he follow Argrid out of loyalty, or was he a pawn? Had his arrest days ago been part of some scheme after all? But *why*?

Lu could stay with him and his crew until she pieced together more. Vex didn't know she had heard him. . . .

And she would have stayed, if not for the boy holding her hand. She had tolerated Teo here because she'd thought, in some questionable part of her mind, that she had control over this journey.

Now she knew she was had no control at all.

She had to get Teo back to New Deza. She would slip into the castle and speak to her parents before news of her return spread—Kari and Tom would be able to understand the convoluted events, the brewing tension with Cansu's syndicate, the definitive threat from Pilkvist's. More, they would be able to forgive her for running off with Devereux Bell.

Lu had no right to feel betrayed. Vex and his crew had never promised to be anything but what they were—raiders. Criminals.

She wheezed on a sudden thought: If Vex was connected to Argrid, could Pilkvist be as well? Could Milo's abduction still have been staged? A syndicate working with Argrid to cripple Grace Loray meant threats would come at the Council from two fronts: within and without.

Cansu had rallied her syndicate to attack on the belief that the Council's own manpower was weak. And it was. The revolutionaries had needed the support of raider syndicates to overthrow Argrid in the first place—so if both Argrid *and* raiders were to attack the Council?

Everything would crumble.

The threat was too big for her to handle—prejudices, fears, collusion, hatred, war. A self-indulgent desperation sent a whimper scratching at Lu's throat. She wanted her parents. She needed to tell Kari and Tom everything she had learned, and they would take the information and work their wonders to smooth it away. Just like they had when she was a child.

They would make it better. They always knew what to do.

Lu stopped between two quiet shacks and knelt before Teo, rubbing her thumbs over his wrists. "I'm sorry I scared you earlier. I should not have behaved like that."

He smiled in the twilight. "You're sad. People do lots of things when they're sad."

Lu put her hand on his cheek. She didn't deserve his smile.

"We have to—" Oh, he'd hate leaving Vex and his crew, and Lu couldn't tell him the truth of it. "We have to play a game now. We have to get to the *Rapid Meander* without anyone catching us. Can you do that?"

Teo lit up. "Oh, *yes*."

He grabbed her hand and shot forward, yanking her arm so hard her shoulder popped. Lu pushed to catch up, correcting their path before he led them in the wrong direction.

They raced between shacks, dodging the noise of the Tuncians, until they came to the edge of the sanctuary. The door Lu had arrived through stood in the wall of one of the looming tenement buildings, plain and nondescript. Would there be guards be on the other side?

Lu's hand went to her weapons holster. She yanked it down and led Teo to the door.

It opened easily enough, revealing a staircase leading up. As soon as they entered the stairwell and shut the door behind them, darkness enveloped them.

Teo's grip tightened. "Lu?"

"Yes?"

"Thank you for bringing me." He sighed. "Mama and Anna would have liked it. Being a raider, I mean."

No, Lu almost said, the word a kick in her throat. *Bianca and Anna wouldn't have liked this. It's dangerous and too much like how we used to live. They didn't deserve it. Neither do you.*

Lu squeezed Teo's hand, her heart fracturing. "I know" was all she managed.

She led Teo up the stairwell, one hand on the humidity-slick wall. All was silent apart from the creaking of the building at night and the occasional distant snore.

They reached another door, this one leading to a hall. A few moments of wandering up and down shadowy door-lined hallways ended when Lu reached a pair of doors set in an alcove, cleaner air filtering through.

Lu took a knob in her hand, but paused.

She had been blind when they came here, and Cansu had disoriented her even further. How would she find the *Rapid Meander*? What if Vex had moved it? What if, while hauling Teo around Port Mesi-Teab to find it, she stumbled into a situation more dangerous than lurking in shadowed tenement halls?

"Lu?" Teo tugged on her. "What now?"

Anxiety gripped Lu. Any moment, Vex could come looking for her. Edda could find Teo missing.

Ignoring the scream of objection from her better self, she bent closer to Teo.

"You see this corner, right in here by the door?" She

pointed to the double door's alcove. "Stay here. I'm going to chart our path."

Teo crossed his arms. "I can come. I'm supposed to find the boat too!"

"You will, but I need you to stay here and keep watch. If you see anything, shout—and keep on shouting until I get back to you."

If not the *Meander*, surely Lu would find a transportation option within shouting range of this building.

"I thought the game was to be quiet?"

Lu winced. "That was before we got out. This is different." She pointed at the floor. "Sit here and wait for me to come back. I won't be long, I promise."

Teo nodded. "I'll be good. You can trust me."

He dropped, curled into a ball, and stared straight at the door.

Lu moved before she could rethink leaving him alone in this decrepit tenement building, where anyone could come out and see a defenseless little boy. What were her options? She had no idea what prowlers populated Port Mesi-Teab.

Lu swallowed her objections and utter self-hatred and pushed her way outside.

Night had lifted some of the dense humidity, making it easier to breathe. Lu heard raucous shouting on the left along with the whining of a stringed instrument—a tavern. She headed to the right, trying to smell her way to a river.

But every road stank the same, the musk of mold and the rancidness of festering waste.

Lu strained to hear any noise from behind, either Teo screaming or voices in search of them—but each step she took weighed on her. She cut down a road, slinking through shadows to avoid men heading in the opposite direction, and paused to think under a holey awning.

A river couldn't be this difficult to find. Had she gone far enough west? Should she—

"I know your type."

Lu's heart shot into her throat. Cansu leaned against the doorway of a closed butchery, her body wrapped in shadows.

"Self-absorbed Grace Lorayans who'll sell out raiders for half a galle," Cansu continued. "You're off to warn the Council about our uprising, aren't you? Fatemah told you—you won't survive betraying us."

Lu pushed past as if she didn't find Cansu a threat. "I won't betray you. This has nothing to do with the Tuncians."

She turned a corner, Cansu just behind her—and finally, a river appeared between the buildings. The other bank of the waterway showed the city suffused in the late hour's blue-black hue with silhouetted people shuffling down the roads.

Lu looked downriver, then up. The light from the half-crescent moon might have been weak, but it lit enough that she could see a boat tethered a few paces down, on the opposite bank. The *Meander*? She doubted her luck was that good.

Something metal poked her rib cage. A knife.

Molten terror swept down Lu's spine. "You won't kill me here," she tried.

"I'm a raider Head. I've killed people all over these rivers. I'm not about to let some Grace Lorayan brat warn the Council that—"

"You've killed people all over these rivers," Lu repeated. She looked over her shoulder with a grim smile. "So have I."

She rammed her elbow back. Cansu dodged, thrown off enough that Lu had time to spin, sweep Cansu's legs, and send the raider Head crashing to the muddy road. Lu took off up the riverbank. The walkway was narrow—buildings pressed so close on her left that she kept a hand on the scratchy wood to steady herself, the stones of the shore disintegrating under her boots to the right. A thumping carried from behind—Cansu pursuing.

Lu ran faster as she came upon the moored boat. She eyed the distance across the river to it—she would have to swim. The thought of sinking into the polluted, oily water made her stomach spasm, but she drew a breath—

And tripped, catching herself on the windowpane of a building. Behind her, Cansu struggled up the walkway, but Lu ignored her to get a look at what had felled her.

A log. She slid her fingers under it. The bark didn't crumble in her hands—it might hold her weight across the river.

But all her plans clattered away as the log . . . moved.

The rough wood squirmed against her palm. Lu jolted upright, her foot hitting the edge of the slick riverbank, sending her crashing back to the ground. Shadows listed as the log rose, swung around—and looked at her, two glassy eyes blinking over a jagged snout.

A crocodile.

Lu didn't move. Didn't breathe. Her eyes stayed on the croc's, every nerve strung too taut to function.

Crocodiles populated the southern swamplands. But outside of that, they were rare—so rare that seeing one here petrified her.

"Whoa there!" a voice bellowed. Not Cansu.

The steamboat on the other side of the river had sailed over, its engine rattling. The dark hull, battered with lack of upkeep, stopped so close Lu could have touched it.

It wasn't the *Meander*.

Lanterns sprang to life on the deck. One of the men aboard looped a cord around the croc's neck, pinning it at the end of a long rod.

"Well now, what did my pet catch me tonight?" he drawled.

Lu didn't need to look at him to know who he was. These raiders were the only ones who would have animals from Backswamp: raiders from the Mecht syndicate.

Downstream, Lu heard nothing. She risked a glance—the walkway was empty.

Cansu had left her to fend off these men alone.

Mud soaked into Lu's backside as she stared into the crocodile's eyes. The leash around its neck wasn't comforting—one move, and it could snap its jaw around her ankle. Haul her deep into the river. Thrash her around the bottom, over and over until her lungs filled with water. Teo would be left alone until Vex found him, or Cansu, most likely.

Lu transferred her gaze from the croc to the Mecht raider. He smiled, his sweaty cheeks pale in his boat's lantern light.

"Look what we got here." He kicked one leg up to lean on the railing, chewing as he sneered at her. "Heard a tip that Bell'd been spotted in this area. Yer not what I was hoping for, but you'll be useful. Now, where's that captain of yours?"

They wanted Vex? How did they know she was with him?

"He's not my captain," Lu said. But—damn it, what cover would be best? Would it work to have them believe she was his prisoner, or his crew member, or an errant bystander?

The Mecht tugged on the leash, and the croc clicked its jaw in a threat that made Lu jolt.

"I was looking for him," Lu tried, her voice high and fast. "I thought your boat was his."

"Uh-huh," the Mecht repeated. "See, I'm not so sure about that."

He didn't tug this time—he let the rod go limp. The croc dove at her, its massive jaw opening. Part of Lu knew it would be a trick again, a hiss and a snap only to scare her.

She couldn't process the feeling of teeth in her leg.

She watched, muscle and flesh tearing as the croc clamped its jaw into the meat of her left calf. The sensation came to her slowly, her mind removed so the pain traveled up her leg, creeping through her belly, until it ruptured out of her mouth in a scream.

Like a dozen weighted daggers slicing into her leg. Like the force of a hundred bullets exploding into her nerves all at once.

Lu gagged, a broken shriek filtering through her clamped lips.

The Mecht tightened the leash, keeping his pet close enough so the croc held Lu's shin like a clamp. Blood leaked down the creature's teeth, dribbling onto the mud as the croc dug its claws into the bank, readying, *needing* to drag her into the river.

Lu fought the desire to arch back, to fight. Her needs were as strong as the croc's, frenzied and feral, and all she wanted was to grab one of her knives and impale the creature between its eyes. But even the movement of breathing tore its teeth deeper into her leg.

"Now, I ask again," the Mecht said, "where is Devereux Bell?"

"Burn in hell," Lu rasped, sweat pouring down her face.

The Mecht smirked. "I intend to. But I'll bring you with me."

He waved at some of his crew, who leaped off the boat and landed next to Lu. The captain clicked his tongue twice and the croc opened its jaw, breaking free of her leg. The teeth ripping out of her flesh were almost more painful than the bite—Lu bit down on her tongue to keep from screaming again.

Don't draw attention. Teo probably already heard.

She was so distracted by pain and the certainty that Teo would show up at any moment that Lu forgot the men until they grabbed her arms. They lifted her awkwardly, sending all her weight rushing onto her injured leg. She moaned, hands in quivering fists.

The crew tossed her aboard. The captain crouched before her on the deck as his men clambered back onto the boat and the engine revved, steam chugging into the sky.

Now that Lu was closer, she saw the bloodshot veins around the captain's pupils, the bruised quality under his eyes of someone on a Narcotium Creeper high.

"Think Vex'll come to save you?" he drawled.

Lu panted. "I don't need him to save me."

The Mecht dug at one of the tooth punctures his croc had made in her leg, finger crooking into her muscle.

Stars swam over Lu's vision. All she could see was blackness, throbbing and hot, and she dropped to the side,

retching on the deck as that blackness became too powerful, too enticing.

"You better hope he comes after you," the Mecht said,
rising to tower over her. "If he doesn't, you'll get to see
more southern stream raider hospitality."

Don't faint. Lu braced herself on the deck, spitting vomit
on the boards. *Observe. Plan. Act.*

But each blink sent her vision spiraling further, her body
drifting in a current of debilitating pain. Pain as she had
endured once before.

The memory of it made her erratic pulse hum.

She had known men like these, but Argridian soldiers. A
night like this, only five years ago. The rebel headquarters
instead of a steamboat. Tied to a chair instead of sprawled
on a deck.

Then, the clanking of vials. A voice. "Drug her."

Lu heard it so distinctly from her memory that when she
saw the captain's lips move, she shook her head, not understanding him until he added:

"Lazonade. It'll keep her nice and quiet till we get back."

*Lazonade. Rare, coin-shaped green leaves. Made into a paste. Rubbed
on the skin.*

*Causes immobilization. The taker retains consciousness. Counter-
acted by the speed-giving plant Incris.*

Despair pulled every sense toward a collective unraveling.

Lu shoved onto her hands and hurled her body at the
railing with enough momentum that she started to go

overboard, but the Mecht's crocodile barred her escape—it snapped up against the boat, water spurting from the river, bloodied teeth flashing at her head.

Lu dropped backward, her mangled leg tearing on a crate next to the railing.

She was unconscious before she hit the deck.

❖❖❖

Vex and his crew didn't find Lu or Teo in the sanctuary, and none of the Tuncians had seen them. Which left the surrounding city. Or the jungle.

So, anywhere.

Vex wanted nothing more than to keep stomping around the sanctuary's streets like a madman, but he made himself stop. He needed to think like Lu. Where would a politician-assassin-botanical-magic-expert go when she thought she'd been betrayed?

Well, *thought* wasn't the right word.

He'd known from the beginning that she'd be pissed when she found out he had Argridian connections. But damn the Pious God above, he hadn't kidnapped Milo Ibarra, and he'd been *running away from Argrid* when he'd ended up in jail, which he'd have told her if she'd stayed instead of racing off. Stubborn, infuriating—

Wait. Was it so terrible that she was gone? He didn't need her. He could do what Nayeli'd suggested—find his Argridian contacts, see if Argrid had some plot afoot to retake Grace Loray and if he could stop it.

But Lu's payment tempted him. Taunted him. Any magic concoction he wanted.

A shiver vibrated up Vex's spine. Unable to come up with any brilliant revelations about where Lu had gone, he shouted at the ground. Which wasn't helpful and didn't make him feel better.

Movement came at him from two directions—his crew emerging from a path beside him, and a shadow in front of him that he whipped his head toward.

A door opened in one of the tenement buildings. Cansu shot out, dragging something—someone?—behind her. The look on her face was so wrong that Vex had to blink twice.

Regret?

"What the—" Vex's attention shifted behind her. Teo.

Lu wasn't with them. Didn't come stumbling out after them.

Nayeli and Edda joined him. Vex was pretty damn sure his chest was about to combust.

"Found him sitting by the door," Cansu explained, depositing Teo in front of them.

"Where's Lu?" Teo asked, hands in fists. "I heard her—I think I heard her—"

He eyed Cansu, wary. Afraid.

"What did you *do*?" Nayeli rose to the offense. Edda went to Teo and picked him up, and Teo seemed to relax, though he didn't look away from Cansu.

"I caught her running," Cansu snapped. "She was gonna turn on us. I . . . might have attacked her." Her words got less aggressive. "Some Mechts showed up. Looking for *you*, Vex."

Vex curled his hands into fists, mimicking Teo.

"They caught her but didn't see me." Cansu rubbed a hand through her hair. She wouldn't meet anyone's eyes. "They had a croc and let it get hold of her leg. Thought she'd tell 'em everything, where to find you, so I was ready to raise all kinds of hell." Cansu finally looked up. "But she didn't say a damn thing. They took her anyway."

Vex felt a hundred different things, every one of them brand-new.

Lu might have left out of fear of his betrayal, but she wasn't vindictive. He might be able to convince her that he wasn't the heartless criminal she thought he was.

But for years, he had been heartless. Ignoring injustices. Living only for himself.

Vex cared suddenly that Lu knew he was a good person. That she didn't hate him.

With that need, or maybe because of it, he was overcome with mind-numbing fury.

Vex pointed at Cansu. "You're going to help us."

She balked. "Excuse me?"

"Look, this is partly your fault too, all right? Lu wouldn't have run if you hadn't threatened war." Well, she likely would've run when she found out about Vex's Argridian involvement, but still. "You think you can make Grace Loray a lawless island of syndicates? Argrid'll be burning people again so fast. That's why they got a hold last time—because no one syndicate is enough to stop them. Lu was right. There's another way."

Cansu folded her arms, livid, but controlled. "What way is that?"

"Rescue Lu. Find Ibarra, like she wanted." Vex was shaking—he'd never felt this before. Something like *valiant*. "Take 'em both back to the Council and sort out this whole mess. *Peacefully.* The Council will have to recognize you as separate from the Mecht syndicate if you return Ibarra, and they'll be willing to listen. You don't want war, Cansu. No one does."

"Peace is always better," Edda added. Of all his crew, Vex was glad she'd spoken up—it was impossible to argue with her when she felt strongly about something. "War may sound like a noble cause, but watching your family get slaughtered ain't noble. Better to wound your ego with compromise than feed your own pride with blood."

Cansu's nose twitched. She looked close to agreeing, so Vex didn't let her think long. He looked at Nayeli, who nodded, and they made for the nearest shack to start planning how to get Lu back. Edda fell in beside him with Teo.

The Mechts were still looking for Vex. If they were

Argridian lackeys now, they were probably hunting anyone trying to escape Argrid's service. It wouldn't have been hard for them to hear about Lu being on his crew and take her to draw him out.

Oh, it'd draw him out, all right. If he'd needed a push to commit to taking a stand against Argrid and the hell they unleashed, this was it.

No one fucked with his crew. *No one.*

20

THE DAY AFTER visiting the Mecht in Grace Neus Cathedral, Ben was in a stupor.

On the edge of his awareness, he felt Jakes move around his apartments. Sometimes he heard silence; sometimes Jakes's distant, exhausted voice. Ben knew nothing but the plants on his desk, the notes in his ledgers, the mortars and pestles and *possibility*.

He had plants from the chest he'd salvaged from the University—not many, but enough. He was, surprisingly, able to access aid money from the Mechts, which let him have what he needed.

Still Elazar did not come to stop him.

Ben lit a candle under an iron bowl and saw the Mecht's blue eyes, churning like the sea. He ground up Healica and Alova Pipe and saw the Mecht doubled over on the floor, fighting for consciousness.

Ben would one day rule a country that captured people and called their resistance evil. A country that had never needed a strong military because faith fostered obedience in each Argridian, in their soul and their being. And when people resisted, the Church killed them.

He put the pestle to the Cleanse Root and broke it down.

A lifetime later, he fell into the chair at his desk. Soot and sweat stained the rolled edges of his sleeves as he steepled his fingers against his lips and stared at the glass jar perched on the edge of his desk.

Healica. Alova Pipe. Cleanse Root. The three healing plants he'd had in that chest. He'd followed the methods Rodrigu had taught him but taken them further, grinding and dissolving and cooking so all that remained was the essence of the plants' magic.

Ben felt as though he'd look up and see Paxben leaning over his desk, offering comments or turning to ask his father a question. And Rodrigu would slap Ben on the shoulder and say how such ingenuity was the sort of thinking that the Inquisitors valued.

He'd done it. Maybe. Whatever he had, there was enough to test on one person, two if he limited the doses to sips.

Ben leaned back in his chair, his hope venting on further complications. How would he test it? He had no true allies. Some of Rodrigu's contacts might be alive, but how would

Ben find them if they'd evaded the Church this long?

No—Ben had to do this on his own. If he went back to the holding cells under Grace Neus, he could test the potion on that man he'd seen with Shaking Sickness. It wouldn't hurt him—at worst, it just wouldn't work. Best case, it'd cure him, and Ben could go around Argrid, giving ill people *permanent* health, explaining as he went that it was because of magic, not the Pious God.

He stood, stoppering the glass jar, and was halfway to the door when Jakes opened it.

Tension had been coiled around Ben and Jakes since the moment in the cathedral's stairwell. The feeling was palpable now when Jakes saw the jar in Ben's hand.

"You finished it? A healing potion?"

Ben's body went numb. "I need to test it," he said, a truth, finally. "Though I'm not sure—"

Something in Jakes's expression changed. A crack formed.

"I know how you can make this work," Jakes whispered. "I know who you need to heal."

"What?"

"Trust me." He smiled. Ben agreed without question, swept up by the joy on Jakes's face, by the hope in the jar in his hand.

This was it. The beginning he'd waited for. The start of a new, stronger Argrid.

If Jakes saw what he could do, maybe they could change Argrid side by side.

The two of them raced outside into the still-breaking dawn. Ben had spent a full day ensconced in his room. He had barely felt the time pass—and he was so caught up in rethinking his development of the tonic that he didn't realize where they were going until their carriage stopped.

He stared up at the tall gray building. "Grace Neus?"

"Trust me," Jakes said again, opened the door, and leaped out.

Ben followed. The cathedral was busier now, monxes and monxas fluttering around, cleaning. More visitors sat in the pews, conversations filling the air.

Jakes led him up the side aisle, toward the staircase they had gone down one night ago. This was where Ben had intended to go to test his potion. Why would Jakes bring him here, too? He could have remembered the Shaking Sickness prisoner as Ben had.

But why did Ben's stomach twist?

On the lower floor, Jakes shot forward. They walked past cells with people on their knees, others thrashing and weeping on their cots. Monxes stood in one cell, praying over someone who screamed their innocence.

The injustices had been easier to ignore at night.

They reached the Mecht's cell. True to Ben's command, the monxes had unchained and unmuzzled him, and he was now sprawled on the floor with his back to the wall. He didn't stir at their passing, his eyes closed.

Ben touched the jar at his hip and left a silent promise at his cell that it would be over soon. No more pain. No more ignorance. Only understanding.

The Shaking Sickness patient thrashed in the cell across from the Mecht's. Outside, a man stood, watching the prisoner writhe.

Ben's brain tripped when he saw the man, but Jakes walked forward, beaming as though he'd expected this visitor to be here.

Ben shook his head. He couldn't comprehend what was happening.

Elazar, in Grace Neus Cathedral's holding cells. Elazar, *smiling*.

And Jakes, saying, "He's done. The prince is ready to join our holy crusade, Eminence."

21

LU AWOKE TO the odor of vomit and mold. A moment after that, her other senses came to, muscles stretching and throbbing. Relief swept over her—she could still feel her body, which meant the Mecht raiders had not used Lazonade, as they had threatened.

Her gratitude evaporated when the wound on her leg screamed with pain.

She bolted upright with a hiss. At some point in her delirium, she'd been given a strip of stained fabric to stop the bleeding, but it surely had doubled her risk of infection. Though being in the cargo hold of a ship where cleanliness was an afterthought had guaranteed one.

Lu left a hand on her knee, as close as she dared get to the teeth marks for now, and surveyed the room. Ropes tied boxes and barrels to the walls, and a single iron door led, presumably, to the rest of the lower deck. The Mechts had taken her weapons, and from the shouts of activity above-decks and the vibrations in the floor, she knew they were moving.

But Teo is safe. He could have run back to the sanctuary—or Cansu could have him.

Lu swallowed and steeled herself. Fear for Teo would do nothing but hinder her. He was smart—and Cansu couldn't be heartless enough to harm a child. He would be fine, and Lu would break out of this ship and be back with him by nightfall.

But . . . *should* she escape? She was in the custody of the raider syndicate that had taken Milo—whether to protest the Council's unfair treatment or because Argrid had convinced them to stage the abduction. If Lu stayed, she could find out if Argrid had masterminded this to weaken Grace Loray or if the Mechts were stoking only a civil war.

Appalling that Lu even thought the phrase *only a civil war.*

Vex was a factor now, though. Vex, whose motives were a mystery, and who had lied from the beginning. If Vex was a pawn of Argrid's and he decided Lu's actions didn't work in his favor, Teo could become a hostage.

Lu couldn't tell if her reasoning was rational or if it came from the terrified place in her chest that refused to be at anyone's mercy. This situation had spiraled so far out of her control that if she thought too long about it, she found it impossible to breathe.

Return to the sanctuary. Get Teo. Then take the information I've gathered and let my parents form a plan.

Lu grabbed the nearest crate and shoved herself upward, standing on her uninjured leg. Dizziness rocked her, but she hobbled a step and opened the first crate.

"I've gotten out of worse situations than this. Like the fourth mission I went on—the one in Port Fausta," she said, talking to combat the agony. Inside the crate, dozens of wrapped bundles sat like treats at the bakery where she'd bought pastries for Annalisa and Teo. "*That* one was bad. Every person in that tavern was an Argridian soldier."

Lu lifted a package and unraveled it. Rations, dried meat. She returned the lid and moved to the next crate. Clean bandages, or at least clean fabric. She took one and bent to rewrap her leg, her vision spiraling as she peeled the old bandage out of the deep, maroon-black wounds.

"One little girl was out of place in that tavern." Lu steadied herself on a breath. "I escaped by sliding out of that garbage shoot. It was the first time I got shot."

Lu teetered, landed on her injured leg, and nausea ripped through her, a gray veil flickering over her eyes.

"I think I'd rather be shot," she hissed, and tore open the next crate.

Inside lay vials of plants. Lu grabbed one, her body going numb in a swell of hope. A healing plant? She shook the vial, eyeing the green leaves. Bright Mint?

That the Mechts had Bright Mint, known for its ability to increase mental alertness, was not unusual; they could have purchased it at any market. More unsettling was the fact that the entire crate contained vials of it, a plant found in northern Lake Regolith—*not* the Mecht syndicate's territory. They could have traded for it, but what would the Mechts need with so much Bright Mint? It wasn't particularly lucrative on any market.

Lu hobbled to the next crate, finding rows of bundled Narcotium Creeper. Ah, now this could be useful. She could find the boat's wine or water supply, clean her leg as well as she could, and dump in the Narcotium Creeper. In high concentration, its juices caused hallucinations, and in smaller doses induced relaxation. Either way, it would be a matter of waiting for the crew to drink and letting the plant take effect so she could escape.

But the captain had been chewing on Narcotium Creeper, as the Mechts were well known for—no doubt most of the crew had the same addiction and tolerance. Lu would have to put a great many leaves into the water supply to make any difference. But what other option did she have?

Lu grabbed bundles of Narcotium Creeper and surveyed the room. Three barrels sat in the front corner, but as Lu moved, the ship lurched, grinding to a halt. She dropped, landing on her forearms while her mangled leg smashed into the floor. Sparks of pain shot up her body.

Abovedecks, feet stomped, the thundering of more raiders than had been on the boat earlier.

Lu clawed across the floor and up the barrels. She shoved

her fingers under the lid of one, splinters breaking off in her nails as footsteps descended the ladder.

It was like the tavern in Port Fausta all over again. Only this time, the hatch that had released her into the night would not prove so helpful.

The door opened. Lu dropped, hanging limp off the closed barrel, the Narcotium Creeper falling unused to the floor.

In the doorway stood Ingvar Pilkvist. His chest was bare beneath a crocodile-skin vest, pistols strapped across his torso, a machete at his waist. Wooden toggles swung in his long white hair, and his blue eyes might have been kind if not for the way he watched her, hands on his hips, lips peeled in a smile.

If the Head of the Mecht syndicate had taken it upon himself to come see her, this was as deadly as Lu had feared. And she had no other plan.

For now.

The Mecht raider syndicate had claimed the southern third of Grace Loray as their territory, so it followed that one of their bases would be deep in an area that even the legal magic extractors preferred not to visit: Backswamp.

The swamp ran the full length of Grace Loray's southern shore, a waterlogged tangle of cypresses, willows, mangroves, and other trees that clawed their roots into the slimy waters. The branches formed a continuous roof that thickened the humidity, and the bloated rivers had congealed into one unbroken body. Crocodiles and snakes thicker than a man's thigh glided between dilapidated bungalows owned by the most resilient residents, and darkness ruled, a world where the sun couldn't reach.

Hours later, Lu and her captors arrived at their destination. Stilts held a building—if it could be called that—over the water, each leg straining under the wear of river sludge and the weight of the home. The walls, roof, and floor were planks of wood that had endured far too long in Backswamp's soggy climate. The docks that floated around the bungalow drooped in the water, jostling under raiders as they unloaded their cargo. More bungalows stood beyond; one released fiddle music into the air, the other held stumbling, drunk raiders on a long deck. A community of outlaws.

Lu saw it through new eyes. Outlaws—or Mechts with no other options? This area looked as poor as Port Mesi-Teab, but it was harder to milk empathy from this situation when a raider threw her over his shoulder and hauled her off the boat.

Pilkvist disembarked and led his group into the main structure. The raider who had Lu slung over his shoulder had to balance her to climb the ladder. Remarkably, it didn't break, and neither did the bungalow as they entered and the raider deposited Lu on the floor.

Furs draped from the ceiling. Carvings of animals

decorated the furniture; one piece in particular, a massive oak chair, had an intricate relief of a white bear on the back, its jaw spread and its lips curled in a vicious, hungry snarl. A table held steins and platters of shredded meat and fish. All links to the Mechtlands, a country these people had long since left or never even seen.

Pilkvist dropped into a chair at the table. One of the half dozen raiders who had accompanied him burst forward and grabbed a carafe and stein, pouring a shaky amber stream of ale before backing away like a browbeaten servant.

Lu propped herself up, her leg stretched before her, blood leaking through the bandage. Sweat soaked her clothes, her hair sticking to her neck and face as she fought to subdue her labored breaths.

Pilkvist took a sip. "We got news that a lady had run off with Devereux Bell. First I thought it was a con of his, but now that I see you—" He made a great show of taking her in, which intensified Lu's glare. "Yes," Pilkvist said with a smirk. "He'll come for you."

His eyes fell to her leg, and he snapped something in another language—the Mechtlands had almost as many languages as they did clans. The raider who poured his ale made for a chest in the corner, his arms shaking.

He withdrew a vial of orange paste and tossed it into Lu's lap. Healica.

"Can't have you dying before he comes." Pilkvist stood,

straightening his vest. "Now, it'd make this a lot easier if you—"

He cocked his head. It took Lu a beat longer to hear the squeal of ladder rungs.

Then, a knock on the door.

Pilkvist lifted an eyebrow at Lu as he waved to one of his men to answer. "It would appear someone followed us. Good work, child."

But when the door opened, it was not Vex, as both Pilkvist and Lu had expected.

Cansu strode into the room as though this were her own syndicate. Three of her raiders trailed her, every limb strapped with weapons.

The anticipatory joy on Pilkvist's face disappeared. Lu kept her own face expressionless.

Cansu. Not Vex?

And why had Lu assumed, for that breath between the pause and the knock, that Vex had come for her?

"Pilkvist," Cansu said, her grip on two pistols tucked into her waistband.

Pilkvist faced her, not bothering to return her unspoken threat. The machete as long as his thigh said enough, its handle glinting bronze at his waist. "Don't tell me you're here for *her*." He nodded at Lu. "When did the Tuncian syndicate start giving a shit about an unaligned crew? This isn't your business, Darzi. Get the hell out of my territory."

"I'm not here for the girl. I'm here about that Argridian you got stowed away."

Lu shot Cansu a tight frown. But Cansu wouldn't look at her, and Lu couldn't tell if it was so Cansu wouldn't give something away or because she truly had come to discuss Milo.

An uneasy feeling gnawed at Lu the longer Cansu stood there, her raiders eyeing the Mecht raiders, the whole room taut with pressure.

Pilkvist bellowed a laugh. "An Argridian? *Here?* You're out of your damn mind."

"I'm not the one whose entire syndicate is strung out on their own product half the time. So, no, I'm not out of my mind."

Pilkvist's pale face went red, his lips wrinkling. But Cansu kept talking, pacing around the room with ease. She lifted a stein, examining the carvings.

"I should thank you," she said, thumb running over the metal rim of the cup. "Someone needed to send a message to the Council. It's about time we reminded them who helped them get the power they've been abusing. If not for us, Argrid would have kept control of the revolutionaries' headquarters, and the war would've ended quite differently."

Pilkvist hooked his thumbs in his belt loops. "Well, we may've had our differences in the past, Darzi, but yer finally starting to sound all right."

Cansu set down the stein. "So you did take the Argridian?"

Pilkvist smiled. Lu didn't let herself breathe.

Cansu returned his smile with a harsh one. "You planning on attacking? I want in."

"Attack?" Pilkvist chuckled. "I'm not getting my hands *that* dirty. My job's done. Now I get to sit back and watch the Council collapse and reap the rewards."

Cansu's facade faltered, a ripple on the surface of a lake. "What?"

"I got someone else doing the hard work. Someone who wants the Council gone as much as we do. Give it about a week, Darzi. Maybe two. You'll see."

All the blood in Lu's head drained out, making her teeter, dizzy.

Pilkvist couldn't mean—he *didn't* mean—

Was Argrid coming?

Cansu blanched. "I've been hearing of Council soldiers all over this island, arresting my people *and* your people because you're taking orders from *someone else*—"

"You got no right judging me." Pilkvist cut her off. For the first time, he looked sincere. "Nothing's wrong in Tuncay, so when people come here, they aren't running from anything. But the Mechtlands? My whole syndicate is made up of people who came to escape *death*. When Grace Loray's revolution ended, we thought it'd mean freedom. Little did we know that freedom was only for certain folks on this island. I'm tired of Mechts getting treated like mindless barbarians. I'm tired of the Council stripping away my ability to help my own people. Argrid gave me the means to change things. You bet your self-righteous ass I'm gonna."

"Argrid," Cansu spat the name. "You're in bed with them now? And they're coming here? What the hell have you gotten yourself—"

"They've changed," Pilkvist said. "Argrid knows what they did wasn't right. They even agreed to change New Deza back to Port Visjorn. And they promised to—"

He kept talking. Saying things that made Lu's heart fracture.

Pilkvist had, in a way, done this to shake awareness into the Council after all. Lu had known of the clan wars in the Mechtlands, but had always written them off as the natural state of things—but it wasn't *natural*. The Council should have analyzed it more closely, like everything they dismissed because they didn't see immigrants or raiders as people. No one saw them as Grace Lorayan.

Now Argrid had taken advantage of the disunity on Grace Loray. They wanted the Council at odds with their only possible allies—the raiders—so Argrid could finish the cleansing they'd started decades ago.

Argrid's attack was coming. In—what had Pilkvist said?—one week, two at most.

Lu looked at Cansu, who stared sadly back at her. In that sadness Lu saw her realize that the uprising she had wanted was becoming infinitely more complex.

"Pilkvist," Lu said. She snapped her eyes from Cansu to the Mecht raider Head, who gave her a startled look as though he had forgotten Lu was here. "Argrid spent decades trying to cleanse this island of people like you. What makes you think they'll give you anything now? Are they really a better ally than the Council?"

Once, she might've posed the question as an attack. Now she wanted an answer that would help her understand why he had chosen this route.

But she knew. The Council had promised fairness and equality but delivered threats and blame. Argrid had killed raiders, but they had never made promises. Now that they had—who would Lu have trusted? Someone who had already proven to be a liar, or someone who claimed to have learned from their past mistakes?

Pilkvist ignored her with a wave of his hand, and Lu knew she deserved the dismissal. "Take her to a cell. We have Vex to clean up." He turned to Cansu. "You don't know where he is, do you?"

Lu snatched the vial of Healica before hands lifted her. She buckled, biting back a whimper, and Cansu's eyes met hers once more.

"Haven't seen Bell in weeks," Cansu said.

What? Lu kept the confusion off her face as raiders forced her to the back of the room.

Down a short hall, the Mecht raiders took her to a room

full of crude iron bars that formed four narrow pens. A prisoner sat in the cell across from the one where the raiders tossed Lu, a patched cloak draped around their body. Even during the revolution, Milo had worn the attire of his station: bruised and beaten, holding a dented scabbard, he'd donned tattered silken shirts and fine breeches. Whoever that was could not be Milo.

But he wouldn't be in a cell, would he? He wasn't a prisoner. Who even knew where he was now? The Mechts likely had any number of places to hide him, or he could have been gone too, on his way back to Argrid.

Though if war was coming for Grace Loray, Milo would stay to see it through.

The raiders holding Lu confirmed that the other prisoner was not Milo. "Who's that?" one asked.

Another gave an uncertain grunt. "Must've caught some idiot try'na poach in our territory."

"Dumbass." The first raider laughed and they left, closing the main door behind them.

Lu lost her feeble grip on self-control. Sweat broke out down her spine, made her palms slick, but she forbade herself to think about all that had happened. She dropped to the floor and opened the Healica, removing her bandage to scrub the cream into her wounds. Each touch burned, but Lu forced the medicinal magic in, a silent scream parting her lips.

When she finished, the worst of her wounds mended

under the Healica. Another application of the plant, and her injuries would be gone.

"Poor dear," the other prisoner croaked. "Did he hurt you?"

An old woman, by the wear in her voice, and that made Lu hate Pilkvist more.

Lu coiled her fingers around the bars. "I'm fine now. Are you?" She held up the Healica.

The woman shook her head, cloak rippling.

"Thank you, dear," she cooed. "But the last time you offered me medicine, you said it might be poisoned, so forgive me for not trusting you."

Lu stared. *"Vex?"*

22

IT'D BEEN EASY to slip into Pilkvist's prison while Cansu kept them distracted. The high of the con made Vex giddy—and unprepared for his reaction when he saw Lu get tossed into the cell across from him.

Relief socked him in the stomach so hard he couldn't breathe. He might've hugged her, but two sets of cell bars stopped him from making an ass of himself.

When she figured out who he was, Vex threw back the hood of his cloak with a roguish grin.

"Surprised, dear?" he asked in a parody of an old crone.

Lu used the bars to climb to her feet. "How—" Realization dawned. "Cansu. I thought—"

"That she'd come to ally with Pilkvist?" Vex stood. "She did. Or might have, if Pilkvist wasn't in cahoots with Argrid. But I'm guessing by the greenish tint to your face that either this turned out to be an Argridian plot or they gave you some bad river-snake jerky."

Lu didn't react to any of that. "Where is Teo?"

"With some of Cansu's raiders on the *Meander*."

She pushed all emotion off her face, as if showing it might give him some leverage over her. "What's the plan?"

Vex tugged on the bars. "I don't suppose you have Sweet Peat handy?"

Lu gave him a stare so furious that he didn't have to look at her to feel it.

"You don't have an escape plan? Cansu will leave us here?"

Vex drew his shoulders back. "Hey, I made Cansu tear off into the night the moment she told us what'd happened. I was only supposed to make sure you weren't *dead*. And you aren't. So I succeeded. The rescue party should be showing up soon."

"Why would you have cared if I was dead? Oh yes—you wouldn't get those elixirs I promised. But I think you have more at risk than what you have led me to believe."

Vex narrowed his eye at her. "Why do you do that?"

"Do what?"

"Your voice." He pointed at Lu's head. "It gets formal. Usually when you're trying to intimidate me."

"The bigger issue at hand is that I heard you talking with Nayeli."

"Ahh." Vex nodded to cover his wince. "I figured."

"You lied to me." Lu pressed as close to the bars as she could. Two paces separated their cells, and Vex was glad for that cushion of safety. "You led me to believe you had nothing to do with Ibarra's disappearance—"

"We're back to *Ibarra* now, are we? What is your relationship with him?"

"—when you had connections to Argrid all along!" Lu deflated. "I expected you to turn on me. You're a raider. But I was a fool, because I thought even a raider would not endanger a *child*. Teo worships you, and if for no other reason than that, you should have told me—"

Now Vex was the one to press against his cell's bars. "I'm getting tired of you accusing me of endangering that kid. I've done nothing but keep him safe since we started this misguided romp, while *you're* the one who left him alone as you were trying to run away. Cansu was certain you were going to sic the Council on us . . . until you refused to tell the Mechts where I was. Which I find confusing— someone who hates me as much as you claim to wouldn't protect me like that."

"I wasn't protecting you—I was protecting the Tuncians! You've been—"

Voices carried from the hall, drawing closer.

"This isn't over," Lu hissed.

Vex hefted his cloak back up and slumped into the wall. But he smiled, stupidly.

If the Mechts had tortured Lu, there was no way she'd tear into him with her usual level of passion. She was fine.

Well, she was fantastically pissed at him, but fine.

The door opened. Two people stumbled in, shoved forward by Pilkvist's men. Vex kept as still as possible until the raiders locked the new prisoners in the remaining two cells and left.

"Your plan was to get Nayeli and Edda captured too?" Lu asked. "Brilliant. How long until Pilkvist realizes it isn't a coincidence that he was able to collect your whole crew?"

Vex threw off the cloak again. "Look, I understand you're upset. I've been lying to you. But I swear on whatever you hold most holy that I am not, despite your low opinion of me, acting out of selfishness. And I'll explain it—but goddamn it, can we get out of this hellhole first? It smells like a crocodile's ass in here."

"Gladly."

Both Lu and Vex faced the cell where Nayeli stood, smiling.

"Lu!" she exclaimed. "You're not dead!"

Nayeli crouched, prying at the laces of her boots. "They check your shoes, if they're smart, for hatches and whatnot—but they never check the laces."

She unraveled the first one, revealing the long stalk of a plant wrapped around the lace.

"You hid *explosive* Hemlight in your shoes?" Lu balked.

"Of course."

Vex braced for Lu to tell her how stupid that was. But she laughed.

"You're mad," Lu gasped.

Nayeli winked at her. "You stood up to Cansu. And I've done riskier things for dumber reasons."

When she finished unraveling the laces, eight strands of Hemlight lay on the floor of her cell.

"Edda?" Vex asked.

"On it." Edda reached into one of her pockets and came up with a key ring. "Lifted it off the raiders as they were leaving."

Edda pushed out of her cell and let out Nayeli, who went to the door, testing the handle as Edda freed Vex and Lu.

Vex swept out of his cell, arms spread. "What'd I tell you? A rescue—"

Lu punched him in the stomach. Vex doubled over, a cough breaking apart the curse he managed to squeak out. He cradled his gut and squinted up at Edda for help.

But Edda shrugged. "You deserved that."

Muscle by muscle, Vex managed to stand upright. "This feels familiar," he panted.

"At least it wasn't your nose this time," Lu said.

"Fair point."

Nayeli looked over her shoulder. "There's no lock on this side. We'll have to blow it."

Vex's eye went to Lu, who was testing her injured leg.

The Healica had worked wonders, but she'd still be weak from wounds that deep.

"Follow us," Edda told her. "If you can't make it, we'll carry you."

Lu's grimace revealed that she was less than thrilled with that idea. But Nayeli batted everyone back, took aim, and launched Hemlight at the door. An explosion ruptured the wood, sending smoke and splinters into the air.

⁕⁕⁕

Lu lifted her arm to shield her eyes. The dust hadn't yet settled when Nayeli ripped open the door and ran out, wavering for a beat as the others scrambled after her.

Four closed doors lined the hall. Left would lead them to the main front chamber; to the right, the hall ended in a door with vines snaking under the threshold.

Lu started for that one, but Nayeli held her back.

"They'll expect us to take the quickest route outside," she said as the door that led to the main room rattled, voices rising from the other side.

"Hey!" one of the raiders shouted. "The keys are missin'!"

Edda huffed a laugh and shoved open the door to a room across from the prison cells. The rest of them slipped inside and shut the door as raiders kicked into the hallway.

The new room was dark, a lone window showing the dismal swamp beyond. Boxes were stacked along the walls and a table filled the center. Edda pressed her ear to the door's seam while Nayeli recounted their escape options, but Lu hobbled away, her eyes on a mortar and pestle on the table. Next to it sat a bell jar like the one she'd used to capture the Drooping Fern smoke, along with a cup holding scalpels and knives. At the back of the room, more boxes sat open, revealing plants like she had seen on the steamboat: Drooping Fern, Healica, Variegated Holly, Alova Pipe, and—

"Cleanse Root." Lu grabbed the vial, gaping at the rare plant. "What—"

She surveyed the room again. The variety of plants; the equipment.

"This is a laboratory," she said.

Vex frowned. "So?"

"Raiders don't combine botanical magic. At least, they've never been known to—they sell the raw materials. Mixing plants into tonics or breaking them down takes finesse that most raiders don't waste time on, or they would rather use individual plants for their singular effects."

She expected Vex to make a flippant remark, but he jutted his chin at the crate. "What's it mean that the raiders have a setup like this?"

"They could be trying to make any number of things. Why, though, I couldn't—"

But she remembered the raider Pilkvist had treated like

a servant. The tremors he'd shown. Her hand tightened on the Cleanse Root. "One of Pilkvist's men has Shaking Sickness. Maybe . . ."

Not all these plants were meant for healing, though. Most of them weren't even from Mecht territory; they would have had to trade with the Tuncians to get this much Healica, and with the northeastern Grozdan syndicate to get the Alova Pipe. The syndicates didn't get along enough to have regular trade set up between them. It was why uniting them all during the revolution had been such a challenge—they hated each other.

Likely Pilkvist had stolen these plants, then. But why so many?

Lu paused. This room had dozens of crates, all likely containing plants. And the equipment on the tables—jars, mortars, pestles, clamps—a raider would need only empty vials to store the magic plants before selling them here or shipping them to the Mainland.

The Mecht syndicate was equipped for mass production of prepared magic. What were they trying to make? Why would they need such a variety? Were they delving into prepared magics to compensate for the Council taking over the Mainland trade?

The door squealed as Edda pulled it open. "They're gone! Move, now!"

Nayeli sprinted out behind Edda, and Lu slid the Cleanse

Root and a few other vials into her pocket before shuffling forward. Every step made her wince, faltering.

Vex started out the door, cursed, and swung back to her.

"I'm fine." Lu brushed him away, but he looped her arm around his neck.

"Shut up and let me help or I'll start calling you Princesa again."

Lu complied, and they followed Nayeli and Edda.

Nayeli was right—the raiders assumed their prisoners had used the back door. While Pilkvist's men scoured the rear of the bungalow, Lu, Vex, Edda, and Nayeli slipped into the empty front room. Where Cansu had gone, Lu couldn't guess.

Edda grabbed a sword from a rack; Nayeli found a pistol on a table. Vex armed himself with a knife from the dining set and handed one to Lu. She slipped it into her belt, her mind still stuck on the laboratory.

It could have been as simple as Pilkvist trying to find a new way to make money for his syndicate after the Council had taken their usual method of income.

But simplicity felt too convenient. Not in the syndicate that had staged the abduction of Milo Ibarra. The one that was allied with Argrid.

Was Pilkvist stocking up on magic in preparation for Argrid's takeover? What were they planning to make in their laboratory?

Though threads were missing, a patchy tapestry formed in Lu's mind.

The humidity of the swamp was stronger outside, the air slimy. Lu followed Nayeli down the ladder, putting as little weight as she could on her injured leg. They reached the bottom and hit the bobbing, drooping planks that connected the docks in front of the bungalow, and trouble found them.

A shot sounded. Mecht raiders approached, their steamboats chugging through the swamp water. Lu and the rest ducked, clambering down the dock, but the rhythm of their steps thrust the wood up with each footfall. Lu, already unsteady, grabbed the hull of a moored boat to keep herself from falling.

"Down there!" a raider shouted, and another shot ricocheted in the dark. Footsteps pattered through the bungalow, and the doorway filled with people fighting to get down the ladder at once.

Raiders were behind them now, even more were on boats to their right. Neither the *Rapid Meander* nor any of Cansu's boats could be seen.

Vex dropped to the hull beside Lu and wound his arm around her again. He shuddered, a brief, sharp spasm, and helped her up.

More shots came, the dock rocking dangerously as Pilkvist's raiders stomped down it. Ahead, Edda and Nayeli ran as though the end of the dock weren't approaching, as though they planned to leap into the crocodile-infested swamp waters.

"Stop!" Lu's voice broke. "Edda! Nayeli! No!"

A boat barreled out of the swampy darkness—the *Meander*, its smokestack belching steam, water sloshing against it in feathered waves. Cansu steered while her raiders fired cover shots at Pilkvist's men.

Edda, already airborne, crashed to the *Rapid Meander*'s deck. Behind her, Nayeli leaped, twisting backward to give Lu a smiling wave.

The surprise of it made Lu forget her footing. The unstable dock slammed up as she stepped down, jamming her injured leg. Pain lanced into her half-healed wounds, ripping her from Vex's arms, and she hit the wood.

Vex didn't see Lu fall until his legs slipped out from under him too. He dropped onto her, and as their weight pressed into the left side of the dock, the raiders jostled it again—and the two of them tumbled into the murky water.

The chaos above instantly muted. There were no gunshots, no shouting, just the hum of Lu's heart in her ears. She forced her eyes open, fighting past the water's burn, but she saw hazy light through the sheet of filth on the surface. Silhouettes and shadows rippled as the water wrapped its greasy limbs around her and danced her deeper.

A hand found her wrist. Lu grabbed onto Vex. In the murkiness she saw him put a finger to his lips and point up as darkness filled in the weak light.

They had drifted under the dock.

Vex released her hand and kicked into a swim down the same path they'd taken on the dock. Lu followed faster without weight on her leg, but her lungs started to itch. She needed air.

The dock's shadow lifted in hazy light. They were halfway to the *Rapid Meander*'s hull when another shadow slithered overhead. The jolt of it made Lu realize there hadn't been a single shot fired into the water even though they'd made easy targets.

Now Lu knew why the raiders had saved their bullets.

She stopped, her body buoyant—there was nothing but her, her heartbeat, and her eyes lifting to the surface.

The shadow slithered back, stopping above them.

Panic crept over her, limb by limb. Lu looked ahead. Vex hadn't noticed and was still swimming, forming bubbles the crocodile lapped up like wine.

She called Vex's name, daring to release air bubbles of her own, but there was no noise here. Just sight, and feel, the water thick and warm, her body weightless and useless.

The crocodile writhed in anticipation and plunged through the water, a slick, unstoppable bullet.

Seconds before it reached Vex, its jaw opened. Lu moved.

She tore through the water, flailing as much to swim as to draw the croc's attention. It whipped its head to her, sizing her up. Competition? Or food?

Lu scratched at her leg wounds—opening them, letting blood gather around her in murky clouds as her lungs throbbed beyond the point of desperation for air.

Food, she willed.

The croc snapped around, the force bashing water into Vex's still-swimming legs.

Vex curved back. His eye widened. His mouth opened.

The beast clawed for Lu.

She was ready, though. She gripped the knife, the one she'd stuck in her belt.

The croc's mouth opened, but Lu grabbed the top of its jaw. The beast shook its head and veered to dislodge her, but she twisted, trying not to slip into the croc's mouth or lose her grip on the knife.

She slammed the blade into the more pliable area under the croc's neck. The crocodile bucked away, its mouth snapping open and shut as it fought to escape the metal embedded in its chin.

Lu wasted no time. She kicked, scrambling through the water to put as much space between herself and the croc as possible. The swamp waters started to blur in front of her, darkness playing at the edge of Lu's vision—she had gone too long without air.

Something twisted around her waist, and Lu thrashed in terror, but to what end? If the croc had her, she was beyond saving.

She looked up to see Vex, and the joy of it hit her in a

refreshing wave. But her need for air was more important, and she swam, her arms tangling with Vex's as they fought to reach the surface. They broke free with a collective gasp, grime spraying around them, chunks of green sludge sticking to their faces.

No sooner had they inhaled than a shot rang out, a bullet funneling the water next to Lu.

"This is your warning, Bell!" came Pilkvist's voice. "There's a price on your head!"

Lu smacked into the hull of a boat before hands scooped her up and dumped her on deck. Vex dropped down next to her while more shots blasted off the *Meander*. The engine roared and the boat launched away from the Pilkvist's dock, Cansu at the helm, her raiders, Edda, and Nayeli firing their weapons like mad.

Lu braced a hand on the deck and pushed upright, terror stricken until she saw Vex, folded over his knees, taking shaky breaths into the hollow his legs made.

He was all right.

A knot in her chest unwound, letting her breathe.

Vex looked up at her, water dripping from the coiled ends of his hair. "Thank you."

His genuine gratitude would have been shocking enough—but he had lost his eye patch in the water.

Scars burrowed through his right eye socket in an almost perfect X, uneven but long healed, a wound he must have received when he was much too young.

Lu's lips parted. When her gaze shifted back to Vex's other eye, she saw that he was struck with the same panic that had gripped her when the Mechts had threatened to drug her.

The horror of nightmares playing out.

Vex gasped once, a broken sigh, before he sprang up, threw himself at the hatch, and dropped belowdecks.

23

THE MOMENT LU stepped belowdecks, Teo hurtled out of the engine room and attached himself to her waist. He didn't let go until they both lay on a cot in one of the *Meander*'s bunkrooms, Lu rubbing his back and humming the revolution song.

Lu knew she needed to rest, if only to get Teo to sleep after all the turmoil. Though a voice in her mind still whispered her unworthiness—especially after she had left him in Port Mesi-Teab—she couldn't deny the peace she felt lying there with him.

A few hours later, Nayeli stumbled into the room and heaved herself onto the bunk above Lu. She flopped an arm over the edge, pointing down at her.

"I hope you know how lucky you are that I stayed up all night just to save you. The list of things that can keep me up is like Edda's stature: short."

In the bunk across from them, Edda chirped in her sleep.

"Thank you," Lu returned, whispering so as not to wake Teo. She doubted much could wake him now, though—they were exhausted. "Pilkvist hasn't come after us?"

Nayeli slid over the edge of the bunk, looking at Lu upside down, her hair draping in a curly sheet. "If he does, we've got Cansu and her raiders for protection. We'll be fine."

Lu watched for emotion when Nayeli spoke of Cansu, but the bunkroom's dim light let things go hidden. "Have you spoken with her?"

"Have you spoken with Vex?"

Lu shifted Teo, pulling the blankets around him. "I'm not sure what you mean."

"He's in the pilothouse. I'm not good at leading by example, but you should talk to him. He did just save your ass."

She disappeared back into her bunk.

The *Meander*'s engine whirred, the noise echoing through the walls.

Lu lay still for one long breath before she slipped her arm out from under Teo, crawled around him, and stood. Her leg had completely mended, thanks to another bottle of Healica, this one from the satchel she once again had. She took it from the wall hook where she'd left it and slung it over her shoulder.

She was level with Nayeli's bunk now. Nayeli grinned at her.

"When this is over," Lu whispered, "if we're still alive, I'd like you to take me back to the sanctuary. Tuncay is a part of who I am." She shrugged toward the outside. "I want to know what it means to be Tuncian on Grace Loray."

Nayeli's face was unreadable. "That's why, actually."

"Why what?"

"Why Cansu and I . . . aren't. Why Fatemah threw the family stone at me. I wanted the island to know about the Tuncians and that sanctuary, and Cansu and Fatemah wanted it to stay hidden. I thought maybe if the Council was aware of how things actually were, they'd do something about it."

Lu didn't move, overcome by the feeling of honor that Nayeli would tell her this. "I fought for this island so it would have a voice," she whispered. "I'll keep fighting for that. If you would like an ally, that is."

A smile crawled across Nayeli's face. She spoke in Thuti, then translated, "I called you a sentimental fool."

"Could you teach me?"

"To speak Thuti? Sure." She winked. "If you control something first, it isn't as scary."

"I don't want to control it. I want to understand it."

"Same idea, better approach." Nayeli yawned and rolled over, ending the conversation.

Taking advice from Nayeli felt about as stable as the dock at Pilkvist's, but as Lu left the bunkroom and climbed the ladder, she chewed over her words.

Lu had fought for control every moment since the revolution ended, so war would never again occur. But this mission had made her realize what little control she'd had in the first place.

The Mecht syndicate had allied with Argrid, and were, for unknown reasons, stockpiling plants. Lu hadn't seen Milo at Pilkvist's. But where to find him now that their only lead had ended in a run for their lives? Was finding him still the best course of action to convince the Council of Argrid's plot? Add to that the matter of Vex's still-unexplained connections to Argrid, and Pilkvist's revelation that more Argridians were coming—*Give it about a week, Darzi. Maybe two*—and Lu felt as though she'd gone from being hunter to prey.

Worse, she had no proof of anything she'd seen. Her testimony might be enough, yet if Argrid's goal was to incite unrest on Grace Loray, the delegates could twist anything she said to buy time for their bigger plan to unfold. Lu needed something that would undeniably prove that Argrid was behind these latest conflicts and that only the Mechts were working with them, not all raiders. But how?

They were still in Backswamp when Lu emerged on deck. The air glowed a sickly green, as though poisoned by swamp grime, the moisture determined and thick. The canopy made it impossible to tell if it was night or day, yet enough light seeped through that Lu could see the deck, the pilothouse, and the closest trees beyond the boat.

The *Meander* drifted around great coils of cypresses, their roots arching in the water. Steam trickled through the smokestack—Edda had cut back the engine as much as possible to avoid drawing attention.

Vex alone was on deck, slumped against the helm, bumping it right and left with his elbows as needed. His eye was on the bow as though he drove with only the barest reaches of his instinct, letting thoughts cloud his mind.

He'd retrieved another eye patch, the black cup shielding his scar.

Lu stepped into the pilothouse and leaned against the table. Words gathered on her tongue, but she could only watch Vex in silence, her mind recalling the dread she'd felt when the crocodile had pierced through the water for him, as well as her certainty that he'd come for her at Pilkvist's, and the disappointment when it had been Cansu at the door.

She shouldn't let emotion blur her distrust of him. He was a liar and a scoundrel and a criminal.

But he was also caring. Brave. And, in spite of everything, true.

"No comments?" Vex asked when her silence stretched long. "After our interlude in Pilkvist's prison, I'd have thought you've been hoarding all kinds of nasty things to say to me."

"I felt I should first give you the opportunity to explain."

"You're giving me an out? Do I detect *sympathy*? I didn't

take you for someone who would stifle her opinions because of a scar. If I'd known you'd be that easy to manipulate, I'd have shown it to you days ago."

But his voice was too forceful, the pitch of a man who would never willingly remove that eye patch.

"You came after me," Lu said, launching herself off the table to stand next to the helm so Vex couldn't ignore her. "You risked your crew for me. You've kept Teo safe through everything that's happened. I've decided I owe you one chance to tell me the truth. Take it or don't, Devereux, but don't you dare dismiss this as pity. I am not that small."

Vex's jaw bulged, tendons in his neck rising to the surface. Lu had never seen him so close to unraveling. While she might have used it against him at one point, she found herself strangely unable to do so.

"Fine," Lu whispered. "Keep your secrets. All I ask is that you let Teo and me off at the next port. I'll give you the payment due. Consider your services no longer required."

She turned, heart sinking.

"Argridian agents started harassing me," Vex said.

Lu stopped, her back to him, her body framed by the pilothouse's door.

"They made me sell them plants," he continued. "Random things, harmless. They thought I'd do their bidding because I'm unaligned. I have no allies, no loyalties."

Lu faced him. Vex didn't look at her, but the muscles in his neck relaxed.

"They kept wanting more, and I got tired of . . ." He stopped, his eye finally meeting Lu's. "I let myself get arrested so I wouldn't have to be their puppet. I figured if I were in jail, they'd have one less tool on this island. But I wasn't even the worst tool, was I? The Mechts did their bidding instead. And here we are." Vex spread his hands.

Lu bundled her arms. "Who hired you? Argridians, but who precisely? Milo Ibarra?"

Vex didn't say anything, and Lu's frustration reached its end.

"If you knew this, why did you go along with my plan?"

Her demand echoed off her own ears. The moment she had seen Fatemah's magic, Lu should have known Vex wouldn't need her payment of plant tonics. He should have insisted on something he *did* need instead, or left her once she got him out of the castle.

He had kept her for a reason. He was getting something else out of this.

Lu reached to her satchel for the spare weapons. Knives, Variegated Holly leaves, Drooping Fern, poisons . . .

Vex flipped a switch on the wall. The *Rapid Meander* stopped and he faced her, his hands out in surrender.

"Lu, wait—I didn't mean—"

Lu whipped her hand out, keeping him from coming too close. "Was it part of Milo's plan, for you to help me? *Why?* Oh no. . . ."

Milo had made it look as if stream raiders had abducted

him. And she had run off with a raider. If they distorted the details, the Argridians could pin both disappearances on raider abductions and start their war with the full backing of the Council.

Kari would fight it as much as she could, but if an Argridian armada was coming in less than two weeks, it might have been too late to stop anything.

Lu's hand went to her forehead, and she fell against the wall, head spinning.

"How many galles are they paying you?" she panted.

Vex frowned. "What? No one paid me to—"

"Then *why*? What is going on?"

Lu's question ended in a broken plea. She would have hated herself if her desperation hadn't made Vex bite his lips together as though her pain hurt him, too.

He closed his eye. When he looked at her again, she felt she could ask him to bare his soul, and he would.

"Your book," he said. "In the market. You had a book with a bullet hole in the cover."

Lu's fingers went to her satchel. *Botanical Wonders of the Grace Loray Colony* was within. Alongside its bulk she felt another, smaller protrusion—not a weapon, not a vial of plants. Her mind went blank for a moment before she remembered the stone that Fatemah had cast at Nayeli. *Family,* Nayeli had said.

"What of it?" Lu pressed, but her fingers stayed on the stone.

He lifted one hand to massage the back of his neck. "I heard a story about the night the revolution ended." He judged her reaction as he talked. "About a girl the Argridian army found when they took the revolutionaries' headquarters."

Lu couldn't react. Couldn't feel a damn thing.

"They . . . tortured her, to get her to tell them where the rest of the rebels were hiding," Vex continued. "She didn't break, not even to tell them her name. The revolutionaries took the headquarters back that same night with the help of the stream raider syndicates and forced the Argridians to a negotiation. But the girl disappeared."

Backswamp's noises amplified in the stillness. Crickets chirped. Frogs croaked. A whistling wind made the branches shudder.

"Why does this matter?" Lu asked, but she barely heard herself.

Vex's hand fell off his neck and Lu realized he was trying to reach for her. She backed up, but her spine smacked the wall. The pilothouse's door was on her right—

Vex stepped away before she had to flee.

"During the raid," Vex said, hands in his pockets, "the Argridians tried to kill the girl. Shot at her, and a book stopped it. It had to be you. How many people carry around books with bullet holes in the covers?"

"How do you . . ." Lu slowly lost control. "How do you know that?"

"This matters," Vex didn't break for her question, "because of the way they tortured you that night. You don't have Shaking Sickness. At least, I don't think you do. I haven't seen you . . . show signs of it. Do you? Have it?"

"What? No, of course not."

Vex smiled, relieved. "You don't have Shaking Sickness," he repeated, savoring the words. "You survived the things the Argridians did to you. You survived the . . ." A shiver made him twitch. "You survived the methods the Argridian king uses to torture people."

Now Lu's confusion won. "The Argridian king?"

"That's who sent his spies after me to give him Grace Loray's magic," Vex said. "That's who's been experimenting with it for years. Elazar Gallego. The king of Argrid."

24

"HE'S DONE," JAKES said. "The prince is ready to join our holy crusade, Eminence."

A smile lit Elazar's face. It was the most relieved Ben had ever seen his father.

Elazar rushed forward, enveloping his son in a fierce hug. The touch struck horror through Ben, scars crying out from memories of the other times his father had touched him. His body didn't know what to do with this show of affection.

Neither, it seemed, did Elazar. He jerked back a second later, fingers digging into Ben's shoulders. "Benat—you finished the potion?"

In the basement of Grace Neus Cathedral, it sounded like a prayer.

Ben's gut cramped, driving him back a step. He should have planned for this. But here he stood, dumbstruck, a jar of healing potion in his pocket and no idea how to go about this interaction, so he had the power to change Argrid without Elazar manipulating anything good that might happen.

"It's not ready," Ben tried. "I haven't tested it—"

"Let's remedy that. You, there! Unlock this cell," Elazar called, and a monxe flurried down the hall, keys jangling.

Details filtered to Ben. The Shaking Sickness patient—another Mecht, though his body was so thin that he looked nothing like the typical well-muscled people of his land—lay on a pallet, his eyes half open. Bruises and cuts and scars covered his skin, and one leg was contorted so much it might be broken.

Jakes pressed closer to Ben, a hand going to the small of his back.

"He's here. He's ready."

"I know who you need to heal."

"Trust me."

Was Jakes on Elazar's side in all this?

Ben's heart screamed, begging his mind to stop piecing through everything Jakes had said. He didn't know what was happening, but he knew he needed to be clearheaded for this.

The monxe bowed and moved beside the open cell. Elazar swept in and stood over the prisoner, looking from his convulsing body to Ben.

"How do you administer it? Drinking, I assume?"

Ben eyed the monxe, who waited, solemn and unafraid. Why was he not begging for forgiveness from the Pious God? Ben had seen Church servants shudder at the mere mention of magic—and now, when Ben was about to use magic *in Grace Neus*, this monxe didn't care?

Ben stepped forward. He removed the jar from his pocket and prayed for the first time in years—that the potion wouldn't be effective. That he'd have time to work on it more, to develop it for *himself*, not for Elazar.

"He has to drink it, yes." Ben cleared his throat and knelt next to the prisoner. The disease had gripped the man almost to the point of death; he didn't moan when Ben cradled his neck, tipping his head to open his mouth.

Ben uncorked the jar, feeling the monxe's eyes from the doorway. Jakes, a defensor of the Church, stared at him from the hall. And Elazar, the Eminence, stood over him, while Ben held condemnable magic in his hand.

He'd gotten here, to this irredeemable place, because Elazar had pushed him to it; because Ben hadn't had the foresight to escape it; because he *wanted* this. He wanted to offer a real, true cure to someone suffering.

If they killed him for this, at least Ben could die with that satisfaction.

He stilled his galloping heart with a deep breath, put the vial to the man's lips, and poured all of the liquid into his mouth.

Ben waited, and watched, and swore he could already

hear a crowd chanting his name. Príncipe Herexe.

Slowly, the prisoner's skin knit back together. The cuts and scrapes on his body sealed; bruises faded; his broken limb straightened. Even his scars smoothed over, and had he not been unconscious and covered in prison grime, he would have looked the picture of health.

Ben's throat closed, and he fought choking, fought to breathe. *No, no—*

"Did it heal his Shaking Sickness?" Elazar demanded.

As if in response, the prisoner arched his back, limbs snapping onto the stones in a tremor.

The healing tonic had cured everything—except Shaking Sickness.

Ben let out a broken gasp. It hadn't worked. He had time. He could—

Elazar drew a dagger from his hip and raked it across the unconscious prisoner's arm.

Blood spilled over the stones and wrenched Ben back to himself.

He flew to his feet. "Father, *stop—*"

The plea came of its own accord, one he'd quit making years ago, when he'd learned that only things like *I admit my sins*, and *I wish to be the Pious God's servant*, stopped his father.

Jakes wasn't moving to help. He and Elazar stared at the prisoner as blood trailed down his arm onto the floor. The monxe watched too, and Ben's terror returned full force.

"It isn't permanent." Elazar swung on Ben. The prisoner

bled and the monxe pressed a bandage to his arm and Ben's whole world contracted to the solitary action of Elazar's fingers curling into a fist. "This potion is useless to me. It doesn't cure Shaking Sickness. It isn't permanent. You have been wasting my time, Benat."

"Wasting time? Why would you do this here, in Grace Neus Cathedral? The Pious God will condemn us!" He played the part of devout son, the one who was safe and unbruised and *alive*.

Elazar ran a hand down his face. He looked tired. "I couldn't tell you for your own safety. The work you have done was for a greater goal."

In the hall, Jakes moved to the alternating calm and intensity as he hummed the song his sister had written. Ben couldn't look at him. Wouldn't.

"Before you were born, your uncle and I shared a dream," Elazar continued. "Our military struggled against Grace Loray, so we believed the secret to bringing the islanders into the Church lay in finding a holy use for their magic. But Rodrigu's intentions . . . changed. He began to believe that *all* magic could be good, while I adhered to the belief taught by our Pious God—that the Devil corrupts most magic, and common people are unfit to use it.

"But the Pious God has a plan for magic after all." Elazar leaned closer with a bright smile. "We will use magic to overpower sinners and cleanse our country of the sickness and poverty they bring. Which is why your potion is so necessary—the experiments already undertaken to try to enhance magic have proven ineffective."

Ben barely heard his father over the grating of his own breath. Elazar believed magic could be *good*. Only recently had Ben heard his father speak in favor of magic. Before that, it had been *evil* and *sin* and *stay pure* ever since the Inquisitors fell.

Ben held strong. "Experiments?" he questioned.

"Over the years, I have enlisted the services of others like you, who can piece together magic in holy ways with the blessing of the Pious God. They have been attempting to make the effects of botanical magic permanent. Imagine, Benat—to be inhumanly strong *forever*. To be able to heal yourself no matter the injury or illness. To have unmatched speed. No evil could stand up to that!"

"All this time," Ben said, gagging, "you've had people experimenting with magic. After you disbanded the Inquisitors?"

"Rodrigu had corrupted their work. The work I oversaw was pure. But the Pious God has let me see that I am not the one destined to create permanent magic. The experiments I oversaw involved giving subjects larger and larger amounts of plants—but when anyone consumes too much magic, the long-term results are, though delayed, unfortunate."

Ben followed his father's gesture to the prisoner.

"Shaking Sickness," Ben guessed. "You caused it—"

"Certainly not. It is not uncommon for raiders to

overdose on evil. This is further proof that the Pious God condemns it—he chooses when and where to strike them for their sins. But the Pious God blesses those who suffer from Shaking Sickness due to our tests. In the name of purity, to undo the Devil's hold on the world, we must make sacrifices."

The stones under Ben's feet turned to liquid.

Ben mattered little to his father, and he'd often wondered, when he'd been childish enough to hope, if Elazar was capable of seeing *anyone* as a person rather than a tool to be used. But Elazar had been forcing so much magic into people that their bodies shook apart, and he'd been doing it while he condemned others for using magic.

No one was off-limits to him. No one mattered.

Ben stumbled out of the cell, needing air, needing light. But the only things down here were darkness and lies in every brick and stone.

Jakes reached for him. Ben tripped and grabbed the bars of the cell across the hall. Inside, the Mecht stood, close enough for that familiar heat to wash over Ben.

"Our enemies must not know of our work," Elazar continued, "and for the purity of your mind to remain intact, I could not risk letting you know the truth. The result, while not what I asked, is still promising—you have created a potion that can heal even old wounds. I have had people working to unlock the secrets of botanical magic for decades. I have had the most devout monxes try to save

Mecht warriors who might help our cause, but their minds are given over to barbarism. Yet you alone created this enhanced healing potion in mere weeks. With it, they will never defeat us again."

"Who—" Ben caught his broken timbre and pulled it level. "Who won't defeat us?"

"Those, like Rodrigu, who believe the world does not need to live in purity and penance," Elazar responded. His voice put him closer. He'd followed Ben out of the cell. "Those who would see raiders allowed to sell whatever magic they want. Those who would let people live lives filled with excess, debauchery, and corruption. As long as they endure on Grace Loray, the Pious God keeps Argrid trapped in plagues and destitution as punishment for letting Grace Loray's evil infect the world. No more, Benat. No more."

People like me, then? Ben almost said. But he'd been lying for years, and beyond the pain, the betrayal, that survival kicked in.

His father wanted to make all magic permanent. He wanted potions to enhance speed, strength, healing, and more.

"Missionaries are only as successful as the armies behind them," Elazar had once said.

"You want to create an army," Ben guessed.

"Yes—the most unstoppable defensors the world has

seen, who will erase the evil that has cursed us. We will use them to retake and purify Grace Loray; we will use them to purge Argrid; we will use them to ensure the Pious God's teachings are never rejected. You're closer than anyone has ever gotten to a solution, and we will need more than healing—potions for stamina, for defense. The Pious God wills it, and I believe that you are the one he has given us to uncover this destiny.

"I trust you to continue your work." Elazar laid a hand on his shoulder. Ben winced. "Defensor Rayen has kept me updated on your progress, and he assures me that your intentions align with the Pious God's. Together, we can bring the evil of the world to its knees."

Defensor Rayen has kept me updated on your progress.

The words were hands on Ben's back, shoving him.

Ben had asked Jakes if he had heard anything about this task when Elazar first gave it to him. Jakes had been next to Ben the whole time, watching and taking note—and reporting every move Ben had made back to the king. He had feigned ignorance as Ben had worried and hesitated and fought to hide anything that might displease his father.

And all this time, Jakes had been Elazar's spy.

How much had Jakes told? How many of Ben's secrets did Elazar know?

Hold on, Ben pleaded with himself. *Hold on, don't fall apart yet—*

Ben opened his eyes. The Mecht's face changed—his blue eyes were narrow, calculating.

"I'd need more supplies," Ben said, emotionless. "More plants."

Elazar squeezed his shoulder. "I already have a trip to Grace Loray planned—the delegates there have met with success. Your potion will augment that."

Ben almost asked, *How will my potion help treaty negotiations?* But his father hadn't mentioned the treaty.

No, Ben thought. *What have you done to Grace Loray?*

He blew out a breath and faced his father. "I'll also need a laboratory. A true one, safe from attack. And no more lies. I serve the Pious God, and you will involve me in his plans."

Elazar smiled. All Ben saw in that smile was insanity. "We are defensors, and we will cleanse this world anew for the Pious God. Let us leave now."

Elazar took his arm to steer him back up the hall. His control frayed with every affectionate swipe of Elazar's hand, so as Jakes touched Ben's arm too, Ben brushed him off. There were only so many lies he could tell without disintegrating.

"Praise the Pious God," Ben murmured to his father.

Sweet Peat

Availability: moderately common
Location: peat deposits in Backswamp
Appearance: vibrant sapphire flower
Method: ingested
Use: dissolution of internal organs

25

LU HAD NEVER told anyone what had happened the night the war ended. Not her parents; not even Annalisa, who had stayed hidden in the upstairs room while the Argridian soldiers assumed only one girl had been hiding under the narrow bed.

The Argridians killed everyone else in the cabin deep in the jungle outside the northern Port Camden. Few revolutionaries had been there at the time—most, including Lu's parents, had left to seize an Argridian storehouse. But that tip had been a trick to empty the headquarters and make it easier for the Argridian army to capture it and the revolutionary secrets contained within.

As darkness fell, soldiers stormed the building, yanking Annalisa and Lu from their sleep. Lu shoved Annalisa under the bed first, closest to the wall. There they listened to the crash of swords and the pop of rifles, Annalisa weeping against Lu's back, Lu watching the floor from beneath the fluttering of the bed's lace-edged quilt.

As booted feet stomped into the room, Annalisa muffled a sob, but not enough—soldiers, driven by bloodlust, yanked Lu out from under the bed, threw her across the room, and shot at her.

Until a commander entered, furious that the documents they had found were only common maps of the island. They needed information; they needed to know the locations of the other headquarters, plans for attacks, or the names of spies hidden within the Argridian ranks.

"Keep her alive," he'd said. *"She's our only hope for this mission's success."*

The soldiers' desperation had shown in their bloodshot eyes and the commander's ragged voice as a small group of them took Lu into the main room. The war had not been kind to Argrid over the past months—this was their chance to turn the tide.

To keep her awake, the Argridians gave her far more Awacia than anyone should take. When none of their methods made her talk, they gave her Croxy, a rage-inducing plant, and let her thrash and scream and pray her heart didn't rupture.

When that did nothing, they gave her a single dose of Lazonade so she couldn't fight back, couldn't speak. She could only watch, a prisoner in her own body, and by that time the commander didn't care what information they got from her. He only wanted her to suffer, because a child had made him look a fool in front of his men.

Lu came back, her body pinned to the wall of the *Rapid Meander*, the croaking of frogs reminding her that they were far from that overrun, hellish headquarters. But her eyes stayed on Vex, the whole of the pilothouse between them.

His lips parted. "Adeluna," he said, an offering.

She sank to the floor, knees to her chest, hands flat on the wood.

Lu had never told anyone what the Argridians did to her. Tom and Kari found her, the effects of Lazonade keeping her immobile, and Tom took her into his arms while Kari made quick work of the Argridian soldiers they had caught. The rest had fled and would join their fellows in surrender by morning. But voices carried from the room where the revolutionaries held the prisoners—

"They surrendered, Kari! You can't kill them!"

"Trust me" came her mother's iron response. *"I won't."*

Lu only spoke hours later. She asked for the book that had saved her life, and read it cover to cover.

The Lazonade wore off, but the Awacia, the Croxy— those she felt for days after. A constant need to move and go and *escape* that she had attributed to the high doses of magic the Argridians had given her. She took the counter plants to purge her system, as outlined in *Botanical Wonders*: Drooping Fern, to combat the Awacia; Narcotium Creeper, for the Croxy.

Now a raider sat across from her, knowing what would destroy her. All he had to do was threaten her with Lazonade as the Mechts had.

Tears crested on Lu's rising tide of self-hatred, that she could be so easily undone.

"How do you know this?" She regained herself. "What does it have to do with Argrid? With Milo?"

❊❊❊

What did it have to do with Argrid?

Everything.

Vex slid to the ground across from Lu. He couldn't stand while he told her this.

"I made it my business to learn every move Argrid made," he started. "Especially when it involved torturing people with botanical magic."

Vex flexed one of his hands. Dread filled his whole body, but he forced himself to move before he could reconsider:

He lifted his hand and held it straight out. God, he was always so careful, keeping tight control on every damn muscle in every damn limb. But he let go, and his arm started to shake, convulsions that ricocheted to his neck, down his torso.

He looked from his hand to Lu. She stared, recognition clear on her face.

"You have Shaking Sickness," she breathed.

"I found myself a victim of the Argridian king's torture,

same as you," Vex said, curling his hand to his chest. But he'd set off a chain of shaking with that demonstration, and shudders came, wave after wave. He'd learned to hide it, working against each one with precision, a flex of his jaw, a shift of his shoulders. "I was about as young, too, and strong. I became a subject in Elazar's experiments."

Lu's mouth opened.

"He has his soldiers force magic on people." Vex kept talking, eye on the floor. "Vials of plants, clouds of fumes, everything, so much that by the end you can't remember what you were given. They tell you that it's for the Pious God. That it's to find holiness in impurity."

Vex met Lu's eyes again, though it killed him, as though he'd flayed himself raw and her gaze was salt water.

"Afterward, they give most subjects the memory-erasing plant Menesia. Make them forget it happened at all," he said. "But I got branded and shoved back out into the world, knowing what would kill me."

"Kill you?" Lu asked.

Vex paused, letting her think it through.

"That was what gave you Shaking Sickness," Lu panted, rising onto her knees. "The magic."

"Elazar lets a few people go without Menesia," Vex continued, worrying at the mark on his right hand. "And either blackmails them with their own impending death or threatens to give their families Shaking Sickness if they don't do what he says. They look for the cure on their own, but listen when his lackeys come calling in case Elazar finds the cure first."

Vex stopped. So much was left in him, and he felt too close to vomiting everything here in the pilothouse. Besides, he had to know what Lu's reaction would be. She'd seen his scar on the deck and given him that surge of sympathy, and goddamn it, he would *not* spend the rest of whatever time they had together with her treating him like he was weak and damaged.

If she changed, started treating him all, well, *nice*, he'd drop her off at the next port like she wanted. He didn't need her on his crew.

Why had he told her? He knew she'd already given in to pity once. What did he want to happen here?

His breath locked in his lungs, Vex waited, and hoped.

❊❊❊

The *Rapid Meander* bobbed in the current of the swamp. But Lu felt unsteady beyond that, her body a buoy in a sea of information.

Annalisa and her mother, Bianca, had been immigrants from Argrid. The two of them had died from Shaking Sickness while Teo, born in Grace Loray, had never exhibited any signs of the illness.

The cause of the disease had always been untraceable and incurable by healing plants. The symptoms showed up intermittently and unpredictably. The victims or their healers could never pin down a cause—because most people couldn't recall Elazar's men testing on them.

Lu saw Annalisa, strapped to her filthy infirmary bed.

She saw Elazar, a faceless king from a murderous land, raking a knife across her throat.

"What does Elazar want?" Lu asked.

Vex cocked a sad smile. "He claims the Church is trying to find purity in our evil magic. He wants to make the effects of useful botanical plants permanent so he can have an unstoppable military to back the Church. His soldiers wouldn't have to find more plants or retake doses—they'd be perfectly strong, heal instantly, fight without tiring, and so on."

Lu buckled, bracing herself on the floor. "That was why the Mechts had stockpiles of plants," she said. "To support Elazar."

Argrid's king had made the Mecht raiders abduct a diplomat to bring civil war and instability to Grace Loray. He wanted to weaken the island enough to retake it—but Argrid's military remained small, even with a raider syndicate on their side. If the Council allied with the other three syndicates, as Lu hoped they would, Argrid would still be unable to hold the island.

That was why Lu had wanted to warn her parents—if the Council put aside their prejudices and harnessed the support of the Tuncian, Grozdan, and Emerdon raider syndicates, the united force would be enough to prevent an Argridian takeover.

But Elazar had foreseen that, too. He had guaranteed that the Council would be rife with hatred for raiders, and he had something else to tip the balance. Not just magic—the Council and raiders could counter that with their own—but permanent magic.

Once Elazar made magic permanent, he could dominate Grace Loray with an army of undefeatable, tireless killing machines. He was already on his way, according to Pilkvist. Which meant either he had found the way to make magic permanent, or he was close.

Lu refocused on another detail.

"Fatemah wasn't able to cure Shaking Sickness?" she asked. "She has a knowledge of—"

"Healing plants don't work," Vex said. "Fatemah even tried a syrup of Cleanse Root."

Lu frowned. "No. I meant, she hasn't—"

Her eyes widened.

Fatemah hadn't realized what would cure it. The whole island treated this condition as a *disease*. Lu had approached it as such too, because what else would it be?

"It isn't a disease," Lu mumbled, half to herself.

Shaking Sickness was a side effect of too much magic in a person's body—and the most effective way to purge someone's system? Taking the plants that neutralized the ones they had ingested. Even if it had been years since they had been tortured.

Lu had—unknowingly—cured herself of Shaking

Sickness. At the time, she had taken the counter plants as prescribed by *Botanical Wonders of the Grace Loray Colony* because she had wanted to clean herself from the inside out. That had been mere days after the Argridians had tortured her, and the effects might not have needed to be as strong. But for anyone like Annalisa or Vex, who had been tortured an indeterminate amount of time ago . . .

Lu remembered Fatemah dissolving the Budwig Beans to concentrate them and increase their potency, a form never conceived of by the authors of *Botanical Wonders*.

And Lu knew the cure. She knew the cure for Shaking Sickness.

"You know," Vex guessed, rolling forward onto his hands and knees. "You know what you did to keep yourself from getting Shaking Sickness, don't you?"

She almost told him. But she bit down the explanation.

Vex was still working with Argrid.

Lu flew to her feet, resolve stomping out her sympathy. "You will drop Teo and me off at the next port," she repeated from a lifetime ago. "We are done."

They would return to the Council. Lu would alert her parents—without Vex.

Vex scrambled up as well. Surprise crossed his face, a shocked pleasure. She realized he'd been waiting for a reaction like her sympathy when she'd first seen his scar. But she hadn't changed her demeanor toward him, and the relief on his face was undeniable.

"I'm not working for Argrid," he promised, breathy and grateful. He cleared his throat, sobering. "I didn't bring you along on this for Elazar, Lu—please—"

He grabbed her arm as she made to leave the pilothouse. She whipped her head back, glaring, and Vex released her.

"Lu, I lied to you. While a lot of it was because *I don't want to die*, everything I've done since I got out of the Church's prison has been to fight Argrid. They said they'd give Shaking Sickness to everyone I cared about if I didn't do what they asked. But you have no idea how much I hate that country. What they did to me. What they *took* from me. If you believe nothing else, believe that I will do anything to see Elazar brought down."

Lu curled her fingers into fists, her body half turned away from him.

"You think," she started, "that I would help you with that?"

"You figured out the cure. You have the ear of Grace Loray's Council. And you are quite self-sacrificing when it comes to protecting this island." Lightness returned to Vex's face, and he took a step toward her. "I was content to run from Argrid, but . . . this whole mission. *You*. It's made me realize I can't keep running. So, yeah. I'm asking for your help."

Lu's fists relaxed. "You should have told me all this," she said. "From the beginning."

He shrugged. "I'm not one to confess my secrets to

crazed women who use manipulation to ensnare me in their own plots."

Lu squared herself in front of Vex. "Can we at least agree now to trust each other?"

His smile went sly. "Does this mean you're staying?"

The swamp air felt soggy in Lu's lungs.

"Staying to get in my way, you mean."

Cansu stood on the deck. Nayeli was behind her, and Edda—Lu had been so focused on Vex that she hadn't noticed them come up. How much had they heard? Her gut sank, but she faced Cansu.

"You're not still planning to attack the Council?"

Cansu looked away, and Lu latched onto her uncertainty with the ferocity of that crocodile coming after them.

"Say you do go to war with the Council," Lu said. "The Tuncian syndicate attacks, and the Council finds out that the Mecht syndicate is allied with Argrid. Those two betrayals—*two* raider syndicates turned against them—will destroy any trust that might have existed between the Council and the syndicates, which is exactly what Argrid wants. Argrid will come, and while the Council is busy fighting all raiders, Argrid will destroy us with our own magic. That is the only outcome, Cansu." Lu paused. "You know that after talking with Pilkvist. I saw you realize it."

Cansu frowned. "I wanted this island to be *ours*. Free from oppressors. I don't always get along with the other syndicates, but I thought they all wanted that freedom, too." She paused. "But if Pilkvist sold us out to Argrid . . . and they're coming in less than two weeks—"

"Two *weeks*?" Vex gagged. "Elazar's heading here now?"

"Someone is." Cansu shrugged. "Elazar, or another Argridian royal, or their whole damn fleet. Point is, the Mechts are giving our magic to Argrid. Whatever Elazar's doing, his plan is already in motion, and I can't . . ."

Nayeli pushed forward. "You can't what?" she whispered, somehow still demanding.

Cansu kept her gaze on Lu. Calculations swam across her face, and Lu could tell she was weighing the strength of her raiders against the Mecht syndicate, the Council, and an Argridian army augmented by magic.

"I can't fight them all," she admitted.

Nayeli put her hand to her lips and stepped back, a falter that peeled away her hardness. Her face was that of someone who had been starving for years and found nourishment.

"You don't want a war," Cansu told Lu. "But it might be too late to stop it."

Lu's heart sank. She had been coming to that realization too.

The enormity of it loomed before her.

"What do we do?" Lu asked, half to herself. She had planned to make Milo atone, to make him prove that the fear Argrid had stoked between the Council and raiders was fake. Now that seemed useless. Even if all the factions on

Grace Loray unified, would Argrid still be able to conquer them with magic? What would move the Council to action instead of debating blame and prejudices as tragedy lapped at their doorstep?

Again, her chest tugged with desire—she needed to talk to her parents. They would be able to help her piece together an effective plan.

"It isn't too late," Edda offered. "No matter who's coming, Argrid isn't here yet. I didn't think the great Cansu was one to drop without throwing a punch."

Cansu looked at Edda, amused. "I may not have the manpower to take down Pilkvist, but some of my raiders have mixed Tuncian and Mecht ancestries—they can pass enough as Mecht and buy their ways onto his crews to watch for shipments of plants or contact with Argrid. They can stop Pilkvist from doing whatever he's supposed to be doing."

"You want to discredit him with his Argridian contacts," Nayeli expanded. "They'll turn on him, and it'll cut off whatever Elazar was using Pilkvist for."

Cansu nodded.

"I'll do it," Nayeli said, bouncing. "I'll buy my way onto one of his crews."

"You were in Pilkvist's prison," Lu countered. "His raiders could recognize you. And you don't look the least bit Mecht."

Nayeli gave her a furious glare.

Edda cut in. "She's right, Nay. But I certainly look Mecht enough. I'll do it."

Lu shook her head. "They could recognize you too—"

"If they do, let 'em try to do something. I'll love getting to knock around the people who sullied my country by allying with Argrid."

Nayeli giggled wickedly.

Cansu's raiders—and Edda—could discredit the Mechts and make them useless to Argrid. The plan would take out the Mecht syndicate; the remaining threats would be the Council's hatred of the raiders and Elazar's magic.

"Those on Pilkvist's crews can keep alert for news of Milo," Lu pressed.

Cansu frowned. "You wanna find that Argridian?"

"Stopping the Mecht syndicate won't defeat Argrid, not if they have magic to supplement their army. We'll need more than just Council soldiers—we'll need a wholly unified Grace Lorayan army, like what stopped Argrid the first time. We have at most two weeks to convince the Council that they can trust the other raider syndicates. Milo's disappearance is what riled the Council in the first place; ultimately proving that the abduction was a lie will reveal that Argrid was manipulating the Council."

"There's no time," Vex started, leaning on the wall of the pilothouse. "We have two weeks *if we're lucky*. What if we find Ibarra and Elazar shows up the next day? If we have any hope of winning this, we need the Council on our side *now*. Otherwise, it's just . . . us."

"Then we bring the Council here." Lu squared herself. "My mother is a Senior Councilmember. Kari Andreu. If I return to New Deza and tell her what has happened, she will listen. She may be able to convince other councilmembers to send soldiers, or envoys, or *someone* who can bear witness now, so there is no delay. Though I fear the Council will not be swayed if there is no proof—which is why finding Milo Ibarra is still so urgent. He will confirm what I tell my mother."

Cansu grinned. "Wait, your mother is Kari the Wave? You make so much more sense now."

A swell of pride made Lu soften. "Do we agree, then? Your raiders will infiltrate Pilkvist's crews and wait for information on Argrid and Ibarra, and I will return to New Deza to get what I can from the Council."

"With us," Vex added. Lu looked at him, surprised, but he smiled. "How do you think you're gonna get to New Deza? We'll take you."

Edda darkened. "I don't like the idea of you going somewhere without me for protection. Who knows how the situation in New Deza might change? How many days can you spare? Give me some time on Pilkvist's crew. Three days. Maybe four. Let me see what news I can get before you go traipsing off into danger."

"Can we wait that long?" Vex pressed.

Lu thought. "Cansu—can you have one of your raiders run a letter to my mother while we're here? As soon as possible. One raider will surely travel faster than we could, anyway—but I will get to New Deza as quickly as Edda allows."

Cansu waved her hand in agreement and made for the hatch. "Consider it done. I'll get my raiders on their parts now."

She paused, and her attention went for one soft moment to Nayeli.

Were those tears in Nayeli's eyes or just a shadow? But she was smiling, the only one on deck who looked happy.

Cansu briefly returned her smile and disappeared into the hatch.

When Cansu was gone, Vex turned to Edda. "You think you can find Ibarra in three days? I still don't like waiting here."

He bounced on his feet, driven to movement by the same anxiety Lu felt wrapping around her lungs.

"The time would be good, actually," Lu said for Edda. "Edda will have access to a lot of botanical magic. She can get me what plants I need to start working on your cure."

Nayeli grinned. "Aw, Lu doesn't want you to die!"

"I'm not that sick yet," Vex said. "Besides, seeing Argrid

defeated will do me more good than any cure."

"The cure will help others across Grace Loray, too, though," Edda added. "It'll undo a lot of the pain Argrid has inflicted. It isn't just about you, dear Captain. Lu's thinking about the bigger problems, like she always does."

Lu's blush deepened in shame. Edda's words were true—but in the moment, Lu had been concerned only with saving Vex. The simplicity of being able to help him felt so much better, so much less immense, than all their other plans.

Of course the cure for Shaking Sickness would bring healing to others on Grace Loray. Of course it would contradict more of Argrid's influence. Lu should have realized that. Selfishly, she had wanted to do something small and easy and pure, for once in her life.

"I can start working now," Lu said, pushing through. "I'll need plants, though, and a work space to make the tonics. Do you know what plants the Church gave you?" she asked Vex.

"Does it matter?"

"Very much."

He rolled his eye. "Of course it does."

"There are plants that can help with remembering. Bright Mint, for instance." Lu's mind started flying through possibilities, various plants and what supplies she would need.

She could cure Vex. She *wanted* to cure him, and as soon

as she let herself admit that desire, it filled every hollow part of her body.

She would not have to watch another person she cared about die of Shaking Sickness.

Vex grinned. Lu realized she had muttered the last part aloud.

Her eyes widened and she yanked her hand off his arm. He pointed at her, grinning. "You care about me?" he sang. "Oh, I knew this would happen. I'm not sure I have the energy for an errant love affair, so cure me first; *then* we can talk about—"

"I'll be belowdecks," Lu snapped, but her statement made him—and Nayeli, and even Edda—hoot with laughter. "No! I meant— Oh, you're impossible."

Lu swung for the hatch, but compared to the utter misery that had choked her earlier, this happiness felt far too good to let go of.

Her lips rose in a slow smile. "Even if I did mean for you to follow me belowdecks, Devereux, I doubt you would know the first thing about pleasing a woman of my class."

She dropped down the hatch amid jeers and a groan of defeat from Vex. The noises muffled in the hall, and Lu paused, willing this to be all she focused on. This respite let her pretend that laughter was the only thing ahead and behind. That war was not brewing. That she had not decided to press on in search of Milo Ibarra.

But now, when Milo was brought to the Council, an

unaligned criminal would not be the one returning him—a whole syndicate would. It would not merely prove the raiders' innocence; it would set the course for a unified country of the Council and raiders. It would create a nation of acceptance.

Lu's eyes lifted to the hatch. She smiled and headed for the room where Teo slept.

26

THE SHIPS ELAZAR chose to take were galleons in the older style, with masts and sails. Elazar's ship, Ben's, plus three war brigantines made a small armada as they left Deza, gliding into the Ovidic Ocean. The sails would take about a week longer to reach Grace Loray, and these ships were typically used for ceremonial purposes, so it was unsurprising that Elazar told Ben, *"It isn't for speed, Benat—we sail these ships to remind the islanders of the time we walked hand in hand with them on Grace Loray's shores."*

Before the war. Before the Church seized control of the island and started its mission to purify it. Lifetimes ago.

Ben's ship was the *Astuto*. Cunning. Elazar's, the *Desapiadado*. Ruthless.

Ben stood on the forecastle deck of the *Astuto*, elbows on the railing, head lifted to let the ocean breeze pick through his hair. They'd filled the past hours with packing, planning, and tying off loose ends in Deza. Ben had been grateful for every task, mundane things to keep him busy.

Now everything was still.

"We're to meet your father's suppliers off the southern coast of Grace Loray." Jakes's voice didn't make him turn. "They will have more plants for your tonics."

"Who are these suppliers?"

"He didn't say."

The ship reeled. Ben pulled in a lungful of salty air, willing his face to stay stoic as he gazed at the blue horizon. "I haven't given you your assignment for the voyage," he told Jakes.

"Ben—"

"You take liberties, Defensor."

"Don't do that." Jakes grabbed Ben's arm and forced him to turn. "I told your father what he asked me to report, but my heart was always yours first. I obeyed him because he is my king, and his vision will bring about the change the world needs. The change my family believed in before they died." Jakes drew in a breath, his voice quaking when Ben looked away. "It's what you want, too, Ben—I didn't do anything that you don't also—"

"You told me you joined the defensors to serve the Pious God," Ben said. He could dismiss his nausea as seasickness, not his own repulsion at himself. "It should please you to know that the task I have for you now came to me from the Pious God himself. It is your holy, ordained mission."

Jakes stayed quiet. He kept his hand around Ben's arm, and Ben didn't push him away.

"You served quite effectively as my father's spy. That role will continue—Defensor Rayen, you will now be an intermediary between my father and myself. I will send for you when I have need to transport messages to the king."

"You can't be—"

"After this voyage, you may choose any post you like—as long as it is not in my household."

"Ben—"

Ben glared at him, the first time he had looked at Jakes with anything other than adoration. It didn't destroy him as he'd expected—he was too furious for that.

Jakes pulled on his arm, trying to draw him closer. Ben shoved him away.

"Do not expect to entertain the same freedoms you have previously enjoyed," Ben stated. "You have proven fit for one position while in my employ, and that is to spread information to others. The Pious God rewards those who exercise abstinence, and we became far too practiced at sin, Defensor. This is punishment for our meaningless indulgences."

He choked on his words.

It wasn't meaningless. Not to me.

Ben stalked away. The moment his eyes left Jakes, his fury fizzled out. In its place came aching, destructive sorrow.

He'd been a fool to think . . . to *feel*. . . .

And Elazar had used that. He'd taken advantage of Ben, a violation that crawled up from the recesses of Ben's soul and dragged disgust along every nerve.

Ben reeled down the stairs to the *Astuto*'s main deck, scrambling across the wood for the center hatch. He dropped below, dove behind a pillar in the second-deck hall, and retched up everything he'd managed to eat since his entire world had overturned.

He hadn't had time to feel any of this. They had moved from Grace Neus holding cells to the palace to the docks, Jakes with him, Elazar leaving to oversee his own preparations. Now it crashed into Ben, every memory of Jakes warping so he saw Elazar there too, sneering at his son, who could be manipulated by a pretty face, a soft touch.

All those days of Ben letting himself hope. All those moments thinking he could save Argrid and not live a lie. But the future that awaited him was in scheming, making sacrifices of himself for small, weak victories over Elazar.

He had to be hard. He had to not feel. He had to be his father's son.

"My prince?"

It was a different defensor. Jakes hadn't followed him.

Ben dropped against the pillar, pinching the bridge of his nose. "Yes?"

"All is prepared as you asked."

Ben wiped his mouth on his sleeve. Wanting to retch again. Wanting to dissolve.

He straightened his blue tunic and nodded for the defensor to show him the way.

They'd set up his laboratory on the *Astuto*'s middle deck. The room was long and narrow, with two portholes giving light alongside encased lanterns. A table lined the back wall; cupboards were locked and stocked with vials, jars, extra necessities, bought with the last of the Mecht's aid money. A crate held the plants his father had ordered for him.

Ben's final request was here as well. The true request—everything else had been to cover this one foolish hope.

In the middle of the room, the Mecht warrior sat on a chair, chains across his chest with his wrists shackled to the rear legs. A muzzle again covered his mouth, and two defensors, pistols drawn as though the man might break loose on a whim, flanked him.

"Give me the keys to his bindings, and you are dismissed," Ben told the guards.

One of the defensors gave a look of horror. "My prince, I do not advise releasing—"

"How else am I to uncover the secrets of his magic?"

"Then we will stay. For your protection."

"I hardly think so." Ben stepped up to the Mecht. "Is he dangerous? Yes. But we are on a wooden ship, so unless he's suicidal, I do not believe he would risk open flames. Anyway, this man is in the beginning stages of recanting. He will not displease the Pious God. Will you?"

Ben looked at him. The Mecht's eyebrows drew together.

"See? I'll be quite safe, Defensor," Ben said as though the Mecht had agreed. "I would not subject anyone to the work I do. I do not ask you to stay. The Pious God has tasked me alone with this mission. If I require your assistance, I will give the order."

The defensors bowed and handed Ben the keys. As the door closed behind them, Ben undid the Mecht's muzzle.

"You could have made things difficult for me," Ben told him. "Thank you."

The Mecht gave him a disdainful look.

Ben leaned against the table, eyes on the keys that he bounced in his hand. The temperature of the room increased, or perhaps it was Ben's expectation, thinking the Mecht infected the air around him with heat.

"What do you want?" the Mecht finally asked. "I have not accepted recanting."

"You haven't recanted. You don't 'accept recanting.'"

The Mecht snorted as though to say, *You want to talk about grammar?*

Ben smiled, but it was a frail expression. He closed his fingers around the keys.

"My father wishes me to create permanent tonics, as the Mechts have created with Eye of the Sun," Ben said.

The Mecht's blue eyes narrowed, their color intensifying. Ben had never seen that in anyone else, eyes that changed with a person's mood.

"I. Will. Not. Help. You." The Mecht spoke each word with lethal precision. "Your priests think to break me with torture. It did not work. You will not work either."

Blood drained from Ben's head. "They tortured you? How?"

The Mecht fell silent.

Ben shoved away from the table. "It doesn't matter." *It does it does it does.* "My father wants these tonics. The Church backs him. Argrid will rejoice in a weapon ordained by the Pious God to wipe out our enemies and reclaim Argrid's glory."

As Ben spoke, the Mecht's breathing escalated, smoke streaming from his nose. Ben doubted his certainty that the Mecht wouldn't unleash his hellfire on a wooden ship.

Ben shifted around the chair and unlocked the Mecht's bindings, speaking as he worked. "I don't want to know how to make magic permanent. But my father will expect results, and I'm smart enough that I would, one day, figure it out. You know how to make magic permanent—so I need you to stop me. If I get too close, redirect me. Don't tell me why. I need to make it look convincing, as if I'm trying, until I can . . ."

There his great plan ended. He could go back to his one feeble idea, to make the healing potion and give it to the Argridian people, explaining that it was magic, and not the Church, that healed them. But he didn't have enough support, not with Elazar watching so closely. One Heretic

Prince could not bring down his father and the Church, and convince a devout country to change their ways. Elazar would have him burned the moment Ben started to contradict him.

Ben needed time—and this would buy him some.

The Mecht rose from the chair, rubbing his wrists. He still wore his old clothes, tattered and stained, but he smelled more like fire than like he'd spent weeks in a cell. Ben stood behind his chair, and the Mecht turned, his expression hard.

"I can't trust anyone in my whole goddamn country," Ben said. "Which is why you're here. You hate me, and I trust that more than I trust the people around me who claim to serve the Pious God."

The Mecht allowed himself one beat of surprise before his anger returned, stronger. A single flame licked his lips. "This is a trick."

"I understand you have no reason to believe otherwise. But it isn't. Help me, and I can ensure you won't return to a Church holding cell. I can make a case to spare the rest of your crew."

The Mecht shrugged. "Kill them. Free them. I do not care. I bought passage on that ship with service, not loyalty. I joined when they traded off the Mechtland southern coast."

Ben remembered then—the captain of the Mecht ship, telling the defensors in Deza that this man was not part of their crew, and the Church could have him.

"Then I know that you intended to get off that ship a free man," Ben said. "You'll need to recant. Make it look like you're a servant of the Pious God now, so you can move about freely."

The Mecht took a large step back. "A trick. I knew it."

"Not a trick. A *lie*. To survive."

"I would rather die with truth than survive with lies."

Ben's exhaustion had been keeping him in a state of thoughtless movement. But here this man clung to integrity like Ben was some self-righteous monxe chanting empty prayers.

He would have shouted if defensors hadn't been nearby. The best he could do was grab an empty vial and hurl it to the floor, where it shattered, glass spraying against his boots.

Predictably, it didn't make him feel any better.

"Someone will have heard that," Ben said. "Defensors will be here soon, and they'll haul you away to a cell in this ship, then one back in Argrid—or they just might kill you, and this country will keep hurting people because you couldn't say one goddamn lie. I expected more from a fearsome Mechtland barbarian. Didn't realize I'd get a coward."

"We are *not* barbarians," the Mecht shot back. "My country may be dangerous, people dying in the streets, starving, blood flowing—but we know our enemy, and our enemy knows us. Here, you have no honor. It is secrets. It is lies. I will not be Argridian."

"You aren't in the Mechtlands. You can't wage battles here like you do there."

A knock at the door. "My prince? Are you all right?"

Ben kept his gaze on the Mecht. "Am I?"

The Mecht's hands balled.

"I don't ask you to trust me," Ben said, "or like me. I . . ."

His words fell. God, what was he asking? For the impossible.

The Mecht said nothing. Ben's shoulders went slack as he neared the door, one hand out to the knob, already reciting what he would have to say.

The prisoner is not fit to recant. You were right, Defensor. Take him away.

"All right," the Mecht said.

Ben stopped, fingers around the doorknob.

"All right," the Mecht repeated when Ben looked back. "I play by Argrid's rules. But you are *not* my prince, and I am *not* your subject. And we wage war by my rules when the time comes."

Ben forced his face blank as he opened the door. A defensor had his fist raised to knock again, a pistol in his other hand. More were behind him—Jakes, too.

"Apologies, defensors," Ben said. "My new assistant dropped a vial. Days in a cell can do that to a man, I understand. But, Pious God willing, he will soon be strong again."

The defensors looked at a loss. One stammered, "I— what happened, my prince?"

"The prisoner has chosen to recant." Ben kicked the door open wider, revealing the Mecht, who had his arms folded, face pinched in a scowl.

Goddamn it, was Ben the only one who could play off a lie?

"Haven't you chosen to recant?" Ben pressed him.

"This is madness!" Jakes croaked. "He tried to kill you, my prince."

The title made Jakes remember himself. His face disintegrated into the expressions Ben hadn't seen when he'd left Jakes on the forecastle deck: Hurt. Anger. Longing.

Ben ached anew—his father hadn't made Jakes feel that pain.

"Defensor Rayen, take note." The lack of emotion in Ben's voice shocked even him. "My father will wish to know that I am ensuring the Pious God's work is completed. My new assistant is eager to help fill the world with the purity that saved his soul." He looked at the Mecht. "Tell the defensors—"

He didn't know the Mecht's name.

"Gunnar," the Mecht filled in for him. "I, Gunnar Landvik, serve—" The muscles in his jaw swelled. "I serve the Pious God."

27

THE VILLAGE WHERE Lu and Vex decided to dock the *Meander* could barely be called civilization, the waters of Backswamp liquefying the whole area. Every building teetered on stilts, people shuffling between them on sagging, moss-covered bridges. Unsteady docks bobbed under the weight of people in knitted cloaks or crocodile-skin vests, tethering their boats and unloading cargo over the mildew-infested waters.

The remoteness of the village made it easy to forget that in the bigger cities, Council soldiers were still arresting raiders, driven by the Argridian delegates demanding justice for Milo's abduction. Grace Loray was already near civil war—so said the scouts Cansu sent out.

None of the Council knew that Argrid had caused this conflict and was coming to break Grace Loray when it was at its weakest.

Lu stared out the porthole of the *Rapid Meander*, *Botanical Wonders* open against her chest, teeth catching her cheek. In the vials she'd snatched from Pilkvist, she had ended up with two of Drooping Fern, one of Alova Pipe, and one of Cleanse Root. Drooping Fern would be useful if Vex had ingested Awacia. She couldn't imagine the Church *hadn't* given him that plant, to keep him awake. Alova Pipe was not, as far as she knew, a counter to any plant, and it had no use beyond being a skin protectant. Cleanse Root had many uses—if Vex had an actual disease.

Lu closed *Botanical Wonders*, her finger trailing over the bullet hole in the cover.

Two raps came from the door to the bunkroom. Lu opened it to find Vex, his hands cupped to hide something in his palms, one side of his mouth skewed up.

He broke apart his hands, revealing a vial.

"Bright Mint!" said Lu. "You found it!"

"Edda did." He extended the vial and Lu took it, analyzing the segment of bushy green plant within. "The crew she's on did a job to get some."

Lu winced. "She's all right? The Mechts haven't recognized her?"

Vex let loose a rakish smile. "Give us more credit than that."

Raiders lived for this, he'd said. Danger. Excitement. Generally causing mayhem.

One of Cansu's raiders had left the night they'd made their plans, bound for New Deza and Kari with a letter Lu penned. A day later, five of Cansu's raiders—who had a blend of Tuncian and Mecht in their ancestries, with fairer hair and lighter skin to pass as Mecht—and Edda had managed to get into various Mecht crews.

Once Kari read of the Mecht syndicate's involvement with Argrid, Elazar's planned magic abuse, and the Argridian armada's approach, she would take action, and Lu would arrive in a few days to further press for help—hopefully with Milo Ibarra in tow.

With the pieces in motion, Cansu had returned to Port Mesi-Teab to listen for news of Argrid's approach through the Budwig Beans that Fatemah had planted around the island. Vex had suggested staying in Backswamp, where their spies on the Mecht crews could run reports to them— one managed to sink three of Pilkvist's boats and make it look like an accident; another had destroyed a half dozen crates of his plants—and Vex, using a Budwig Bean left by Cansu, relayed it all to Port Mesi-Teab.

Small progress, but enough? Doubtful—seeing as it was one week before Argrid would arrive, if Pilkvist's two-week deadline was correct.

Lu pushed down her worry. She had to believe that her parents would come through. Her mother, Kari the Wave, one of the most feared leaders of the revolution, would find a way to use Lu's information, and Tom was just as resourceful and wise.

But Lu had spent the past five years watching the Council argue over simple things. She wasn't sure they would take her information as proof. Yet Cansu's raider-spies on Pilkvist's crews hadn't found any news of Milo, no correspondence between Pilkvist and Argrid. There was nothing concrete to send to New Deza to supplement her letter.

Lu's dread carved a permanent hole in her chest.

She moved around Vex now, heading for the engine room and the laboratory they had improvised with supplies gathered from the village. The heat of the room had become familiar, as calming to her as the book in her arms.

She busied herself with the beakers on the table beside the furnace as Vex dropped onto Edda's cot.

He leaned against the wall with his arms folded behind his head. "I should've added a kid to my crew years ago. Haven't had this many days of peace . . . ever."

Lu cut him a threatening look. "Teo would be overjoyed to hear you say that."

"It isn't me you have to worry about. That kid's got Nayeli completely under his spell. He already bewitched Edda, too. I think we might be stuck with him."

Vex gestured to the deck, where Nayeli and Teo posed as a traveling brother and sister. Lu had to admit that this way, though it put Teo on display, had proven safest so far.

No one in the secluded village had given them trouble.

Lu broke down the Bright Mint. She had already prepared the Drooping Fern—a bell jar filled with the
knockout smoke waited in the middle of the table, the glass
supported to keep it from falling over. Lu held her breath
and, as fast as she could, slid a plate of Bright Mint paste
into the Drooping Fern smoke.

The combination should result in slumber and enhanced
mental function in a dream state, thanks to the Bright
Mint, which might enable Vex's mind to remember what
the Church had poisoned him with.

After a few minutes, Lu slid the plate of Bright Mint
paste back out, cradling it in her palms. Vex had crouched
forward, elbows on his knees.

His focus leaped from the floor to her with a forced
smile. "Ready?"

Lu didn't approach him. Giving magic tonics to Annalisa had been easier, as she had had no fear of botanical
magic. But Lu briefly imagined the situation in reverse,
with herself seated on the cot and Vex readying to give her
a concoction.

"We don't have to do this," Lu whispered.

The smallness of the engine room let Vex take her wrist
without having to leave the cot, and he tugged her toward
him, planting her between his knees.

"Yes, we do," he said.

He didn't let go of her wrist. His knees pressed on either

side of her legs, and the closeness of him made Lu incapable of moving anyway.

She stared at him, his eye on the Drooping Fern–infused Bright Mint.

"Try to focus on what you want to know," she said, her voice weak.

She realized what she was asking: that he relive what the Church had done. Her heart galloped, a cold sweat warring with the engine room's heat.

This was madness. There had to be another less intrusive way.

But when she looked at Vex, he grinned.

"You're cute when you're worried," he said.

The muscles in her shoulders relaxed. "You aren't?"

"Cute? Always."

"Worried."

A shudder worked down the corded muscles in his neck, a flinch that he fought to cover by shaking his head. But he didn't say anything. Maybe couldn't.

Lu forced a smile despite her nerves. "Let's recount. The fearsome Devereux Bell is afraid of heights, as well as—"

His eye brightened. "You were never supposed to talk about that."

"I'm not the best at following orders."

"You hide it so well."

She used a spoon to gather the Bright Mint concoction

and, as she spoke, pressed it to his lips. "I hide many things, Devereux."

He ate the paste and lifted his eyebrow. "That sounds like a challenge."

Only the slightest tremor told her he was afraid—or it might have been from Shaking Sickness.

She was noticing it in him more. A spasm here, a shiver there. Had he always exhibited signs of the illness, or was she more aware of his body now?

"Oh, not a challenge—a proposition." Lu set the empty plate and spoon on the table behind her. "I make you a onetime offer to have me here and now."

The Drooping Fern was taking effect. Vex swayed, caught himself with a hand on the cot.

"Unfair," he groaned. "To make that offer to a man when he can't act on it."

"Ahh. There are plants that can fix problems of that sort."

Vex lay on the cot, one arm thrown over his head, but he paused and cut her a narrow-eyed smirk. "No," he murmured, his eye fluttering shut. "*That* would never be a problem. Not . . . not when you laugh . . . como unha canción."

Like a song.

Lu's lips opened, and in the stillness of the engine room, she heard herself make a soft, involuntary sigh. Had he intended to say something so sweet to her? Or was it the botanical magic whisking him away from reason and reality?

She repeated the words, a moment of indulgence—and realized he'd said that in proper Argridian.

He was there already, in his mind. In the Church's holding cells.

The stark reality cut through the velvet around Lu's heart. War was coming. Argrid was close. Who knew what the Council was doing? But of all the problems in Lu's world, this one she could solve.

She slid her hand over Vex's arm and started to hum, the song Teo always sang when he was afraid, the one Kari had sung after Annalisa died.

"Dirt and sand, all across the land; the currents are ours, you see. No god, no soldier, no emperor, no king, can take my current from me. Flow on, my friends, flow on with me; together we flow as one. No god, no soldier, no emperor, no king, can erode what we have done."

❖❖❖

Slowly, the memory tonic worked. Vex remembered Aerated Blossom after breakfast one morning, Croxy at sunset one night. He knew there were others, but Lu scratched up a list of the plants that would counter the ones he'd recalled, to get started on those. Vex whisked the list to Edda, who would continue to hunt for plants while she spied on Pilkvist's crew.

There was no news of Milo Ibarra.

Vex knew he and Lu were starting to go mad. They

couldn't see the sun in Backswamp, but that didn't stop them from counting the days. How close were they to Argrid's arrival?

More than a week after they'd made their plans with Cansu, Lu, Vex, and Nayeli readied to go to New Deza. It was way longer than Vex had wanted to wait around in Backswamp before they went to Lu's mom, but Edda kept pressing them to give her time—*"Who knows what chaos will find you in New Deza? Remember, you're a wanted criminal and Lu broke you out of prison."*

They couldn't wait any longer. But Vex feared they had waited *too* long, and so the morning they decided to leave, it was too damn perfect that Nayeli flung herself down the *Meander*'s hatch.

"Edda just dropped this off." Nayeli tossed Lu a vial of Powersage—it would combat the Aerated Blossom. "And she said to let you know that the crew she's on has a trip scheduled for tonight."

Vex splayed his hand on the tabletop next to Lu as she put the Powersage into boiling water. He whipped his head to Nayeli. "What? *Tonight?* Where?"

"They're meeting a ship off the coast."

"Tell me it's one of their own."

"If it was, would they need to meet up with it in the dark, with little warning?"

Vex wavered, relieved he could blame it on Shaking Sickness, not his desire to plunge the *Meander* into a forgotten corner of the island and leave all this behind.

They'd waited too long. All their hope hung on that letter Lu had sent to her mother, but had it been enough to convince the Council to do anything? If Vex hadn't listened to Edda and had just gone to New Deza without her for protection, would Lu have been able to change anything?

Vex shared a look with Lu and almost said all his worries out loud—until he saw her face, gray with horror.

"Tonight?" She spun on Nayeli. "We're supposed to have more time until—"

But she stopped. Pilkvist's two-week timeline had been a stretch.

"All right." Lu gathered herself, pulling up her unbreakable shield. Vex balked—how could she do that? He was ready to drop to his knees and scream his terror to the planks of his boat, and he knew she was just as afraid. "We must tell Cansu. Maybe Cansu's raider reached my mother with the message, and she's already sent support? Just because we haven't heard anything or weren't able to go doesn't mean the Council won't help."

The Budwig Bean Vex had been using to communicate with Cansu sat on the table, and Nayeli snatched it. "I'll tell her." She slipped into the hall.

Lu leaned closer to Vex. Out of instinct or intent, he wasn't sure, but he didn't so much as breathe too harshly in case it would make her move away.

"I'm sure your mother has help coming," he whispered. "If the Council is only a day or two away, we can scout the ships tonight and get information—find out how many ships, how many weapons. I doubt Argrid will attack the moment they land. Maybe the Council heard about the approaching ships through their own sources? They could already be moving on it themselves."

"The Argridian diplomats will likely be filtering information. They could have kept the ships' approach a secret," Lu said. She dropped her gaze to the floor. Each day that passed without Cansu's raider not returning from New Deza or Edda finding Ibarra intensified the worry line between her eyebrows.

Lu looked up. She blinked in surprise at how close Vex was—he could feel her shoulder against his chest, the rush of her exhale on his face.

She didn't pull back. God, he wasn't even touching her—one hand was flat on the table, the other in his pocket—but his blood thickened. Every time she let him this close, it was like she'd granted him permission to experience something guarded and secret and downright amazing.

He soaked it up in case this was as close as she ever let him get.

A *thump* in the hall made Lu jolt back. Vex turned to see Nayeli sagging against the doorframe.

She looked at Lu. The sorrow on her face made Vex step forward, like he could take the brunt of the news she had.

"They're not coming," Nayeli whispered.

Lu seized Vex's arm. He wasn't sure she knew she'd done it.

"What?" Lu asked.

"Cansu's raider got back to the sanctuary. Barely escaped New Deza with his life." Nayeli shook her head. "He never even got close to the Council. The Seniors sided with Argrid two weeks ago and ratified the treaty."

Lu choked. "What? No—my mother said she would delay it. She said she would fight—"

"The councilmembers who resisted the treaty are under house arrest." Nayeli's eyes shifted to Vex, like she couldn't stand to look at Lu as she talked. "The Council has declared stream raiders enemies of the state. The Council isn't coming. They've declared war on us."

❊❊❊

"Lu?"

Vex's voice pulled her back to the surface.

"Adeluna," he said, and she felt her hand on his arm. He stayed steady, and Lu couldn't release him, not now.

"Since it's just us," Nayeli continued, no emotion in her voice, "Cansu wants us to move before Argrid gets a foothold here. Or more of a foothold, at least."

Vex frowned and asked, "What does she think we can do against Argridian warships? If that's what's coming."

"Blow them up. Send a message to Argrid that not everyone on the island is willing to bow to them like—"

Lu heaved forward. "*No*—we need to scout the ships. What if they aren't warships? What if they aren't even from Argrid? It could be a misunderstanding. There has to be a peaceful solution. I have to believe we can convince the Council in time to ally with the raiders and stop Argrid again. *I have to.* I cannot live in a world where Argrid could destroy us so easily. Please."

She said the last word to Vex. She wasn't sure why—not for permission, not for guidance. But that word came, and she wanted him to assure her that she was right.

Vex nodded. "All right," he said. He looked at Nayeli. "Tell Cansu we're gonna scout the ships off the coast tonight. We're not giving up. We'll find out what they are, where they're from, and if they're Argridian, we'll—" He paused, his face going pale. "We'll find proof. Something to convince the Council that raiders aren't to blame in all this."

Even if they had gone to New Deza, as planned, it wouldn't have been enough. They *needed* proof now, not testimony. They needed Milo, or documents, or a captured Argridian soldier who would confess all. This was their best chance at stopping the war.

"Argrid can't win the war, even with magic, if Grace Loray unifies." Lu gained traction, her eagerness growing. "They fear it, otherwise they would not have gone to such lengths to break us apart. We have to try."

Nayeli bowed with the weary exhale of someone who knew the odds.

Only one syndicate would fight the Argridian invasion. Argrid might have a small military, but it had taken every syndicate and all those who called themselves Grace Lorayan to stop them during the revolution.

Grace Loray could lose the very freedom its citizens had worked so hard to earn.

Lu didn't know what to do with her emotions, and as Nayeli used the Budwig Bean to pass on their plans to Cansu, Lu moved back to the table.

Her limbs worked by memory until she knocked over a vial, her hands shaking.

Vex wrapped his fingers around her wrist. His other hand settled on the back of her neck, a whisper of a touch that shot comfort down her spine. She leaned against him, but all she saw were words flashing in her mind:

The war is returning.

Everything I did, the lives I took, the horrible acts I committed, meant nothing.

❋❋❋

Edda gave them the Mecht boat's current location so they could trail it out to the sea. She couldn't abandon her Mecht crew without arousing suspicion, but Cansu said that she would get her raiders out to the ocean. It would be a day of travel from the Tuncian syndicate.

Until then, Nayeli, Vex, and Lu would find out what mysterious contacts the Mechts were meeting late at night. They would scout, and get proof of Argrid's conspiracy, and

Lu would do everything in her power to make the Council see reason.

The *Rapid Meander* left the Backswamp village later that afternoon. Nayeli operated the engine room, Vex went to the pilothouse. Lu stayed alongside Nayeli to assist her, and Teo stayed with them to keep out of trouble.

After a few hours, Nayeli said, "We've reached the ocean."

Lu paused in the motion of shoveling coal into the furnace. Teo sat on Edda's cot, flipping through *Botanical Wonders*.

"I'll be a moment, Teo," she said.

He hummed at her in response, idly kicking his legs.

Lu lifted herself onto the deck. Where monstrous arching trees had been interspersed with the swamp's moist, mossy shadows, there was now an expanse of blue, star-speckled navy sky above and froth-capped indigo ocean below. The air filled her lungs with salt and freshness and a churning sensation brought by the wind in her ears and the waves crashing against the boat's hull.

She had seen the ocean a few times, and this undeniable swell of power always awed her. Here was a force that no one could tame or break.

The *Rapid Meander* sped along, smoke streaming into the dark sky. The late hour worked in their favor, giving them the advantage of stealth when they doused the lanterns. Other steamboats sailed ahead of them, lights low—the Mecht boats, one carrying Edda.

An hour later, the steamboats they followed dove around an inlet. New silhouettes nestled alongside tufts of rock far off the coast.

In the pilothouse, Lu shifted at the door. "Ships."

"Only one country has sails like that." Vex's posture was rigid at the helm.

Lu forced herself to say the word they were thinking, to not fear it. "Argrid."

28

THE THREE STEAMBOATS they followed headed for the largest of the ships hidden among the rock outcroppings. Lu braced herself in the pilothouse's doorway and counted the clusters of masts—three belonged to brigantines, two-masted vessels equipped for speed and protection; and two belonged to galleons, behemoths of transport and comfort.

No warships. But it was hardly reassuring that this fleet was not sent to destroy them—who was on those ships? Why were they here? Were more ships waiting off the coast?

Lu's resolution not to let Nayeli blow up the ships hardened. They needed information. No matter what Cansu said, or what Lu herself had feared, war had not yet come. They could still stop this without violence.

The *Rapid Meander* slowed as Vex maneuvered them around the jagged rocks. The steamboats ahead faded from sight, night welcoming them into the embrace of the hidden gathering.

"Two main ships," he noted.

Nayeli had joined them on deck moments after the Argridian ships came into view, the furnace well stocked with coal and Teo safely belowdecks. "The big one will be full of activity as soon as the Mechts show up," she said.

As if on cue, a single lantern flared to life on board the largest galleon. It flashed twice, then was joined by a second lantern, the lights low enough that, had Lu not been paying attention, she would have dismissed it as starlight.

"Plus Edda'll be with them, so she'll keep an eye out for things there," Nayeli added.

"Things," Vex echoed. "Plants. Or weapons. Or news of ships beyond that we can't see."

"They aren't warships," Lu countered. "This won't end in bloodshed. We can handle anything else."

Vex gave her a disbelieving look. "Bloodshed isn't the worst thing that could come from those ships. Who do you think's on them? Happy diplomats come to celebrate the peace treaty and leave with smiles on their faces?"

Lu clamped her lips, wrestling her fear into submission. But Vex set her mind spinning. The king could be on one of those ships. His son. High-ranking generals with orders to ready the island for incoming waves of soldiers. Or perhaps these ships had come at Milo's behest, and he was aboard one, gloating in satisfaction of his impending victory over Grace Loray. What did they have to stop him? Cansu's syndicate and the Seniors under house arrest?

Lu's hope wilted, the last feeble petal on a dying flower.

They could stop this. They could board those ships, find proof, take it to the Council—

Her plan echoed, focusing her mind.

Get aboard a ship. Find proof that Argrid did this. Get to the Council.

Lu was a soldier. She was a spy. This was what she did— gathered information, took it back to her parents. Her body and mind functioned on that instinct, but beyond it, she was fraying.

Lu pointed at the smaller galleon, off to the right and farther back. "We'll start there."

Vex plowed the *Meander* in that direction, weaving behind rocks to put space between them and the brigantines.

The smaller galleon was docked at the farthest rock, as though its captain found the proceedings boring and wanted to waste no time leaving once the order came. Vex brought the *Meander* around the ship's port side, the right edge of the vessel flush with the rock. He dropped the engine as low as it would go, the eternal slosh and groan of the ocean covering its hum, and as the boat drew closer, a struggle raged in Lu's body.

She hadn't felt this mix of emotions since her missions during the revolution. Anticipation, bright and nauseating and exciting, paired with an exquisite dread. But it was that dread that climbed over all else, towering above her drive, her resolve.

Milo Ibarra could be on that ship.

Vex killed the engine. The galleon's hull bulged with four floors of portholes, arranged in decorative rows that, Lu suspected, would glint with polished copper in the sunlight. But those decorations would be their way in—climb the moldings, flip over the railing, and search each floor for news of Argrid's next step or Elazar's progression or Milo . . .

"Nay, keep the *Meander* hidden behind some of those rocks. We'll signal you when we need to leave. But if things turn bad, get to safety." Vex gave the order behind Lu. She didn't move, her shoulder fused to the pilothouse's frame. "Lu and I can handle this. Can't we?"

Lu's eyes went to the galleon's silent deck.

Hire Devereux Bell to find Milo Ibarra—it had been her only plan.

She hadn't thought this far ahead, with all that had happened. To the moment when they would find him, and Vex would assume she'd accompany him to get Milo—she wasn't a lady now. She was who she used to be. A spy. A murderer.

Milo would see her, brandishing weapons, defiant, vicious.

Lu spun away from Vex. "No. You go. See if Milo is on board."

Vex gave her an odd look. "Ordinarily I'd be flattered that you think so highly of my skills, but that's not all we're here for. Ibarra's important, sure, but he's not the—"

"This is what I hired you for," Lu told him. "I infiltrated far worse places with far less information, and as a *child*, no less."

Lu threw herself at the hatch, getting one hand on the ring to open it before Vex stopped her, his boot on the door.

"Why do you think Ibarra'll fix this? What's he gonna do, confess all he's done?"

Lu looked up at him. "Under the proper circumstances."

Vex dropped back. His demeanor changed, arms slack, eye narrowing. The boat rocked as Nayeli moved closer, while Vex looked tragic and exhausted and furious all at once.

"What, exactly, are the proper circumstances?" he asked.

Lu's heart thundered, her mind roaring yet empty. Ocean spray stuck hair to her cheeks, made her palms clammy and her whole body cold.

She'd wanted to find Milo Ibarra, to drag him back to face the Council. But Milo wouldn't confess—he'd never confessed anything he'd done.

But he would this time. Lu would *make* him.

That wish sprouted in her belly. Roots dug into her legs, leaves unfurling in her chest and up her mouth until she parted her lips and knew, if she let the wish grow, she would laugh. What fragments she had left of herself would clatter out of her fingers, and her wicked, terrible wish would make her pain disappear, because she wouldn't exist after it was fulfilled. She would be as bad as Milo.

But she wouldn't feel anything. She had wanted that for five years, to not *feel*.

Lu looked up at the galleon, tears hot.

"Lu," Vex tried. His voice told her he hadn't moved closer, as if knowing that any motion right now would set her off. "What's happening? Why do you care so much about Ibarra—"

His question broke. Lu opened her eyes to see that Vex had bumped into the pilothouse's wall, his mouth agape.

"What?" Nayeli prodded. She didn't know Lu's story like Vex did.

Lu saw on his face that he'd made the connection. She couldn't stop his realization, and that loss of control freed her to say words she had never admitted aloud:

"He was the Argridian commander, the night they attacked the rebel headquarters."

Vex's hands opened, closed into fists. "You've been sitting by him in Council meetings." His voice grated. "Letting him live. Letting him *be near you*."

"I haven't allowed him anything," Lu refuted. "He doesn't know who I am."

Vex panted. "He doesn't . . ."

Nayeli seemed to feel the gravity in this situation, even if she couldn't place it. "Gods, if you find him on board, just kill him."

"You're damn right," Vex said. He lunged toward the galleon, one foot on the railing of the *Meander* before Lu grabbed his arm.

"I need him alive. Not for redemption—to stop a war."

Vex's eye patch was toward her so she couldn't read his face, but the muscle in his arm coiled under her fingers.

"If I faced the people who did what they did to me," Vex started, "I'd kill them. I've dreamed of it for years."

He looked at her, and it surprised Lu to find not anger on his face, but sadness.

Vex twisted so he held her arm as she held his. "You're asking me to let him live, knowing what he did to you. You want me to show him *mercy*."

"I don't want to kill him," Lu admitted. "I want him to break. That's what I most fear. If I see him on that ship, without propriety holding me back, I won't—" She stopped, chin dropping. "I won't survive the things I'd do to him. I could never look Teo in the eyes again, or pretend to serve this island with dignity. I'd be what I was during the revolution. I *cannot* be a murderer again."

She didn't weep as she said this. She told him, and let the words hover.

Vex didn't show any reaction. Not shock or pain. "For what it's worth," he said, "I know you aren't capable of being what your parents turned you into again."

"How could you know that?"

He smiled. "I didn't become what people wanted me to be either."

He drew her closer before letting go so she could retreat. She didn't. "We're stronger than they could have dreamed. *You* are stronger. Come with me or don't—it's your choice."

With a wink and a smile, he leaped from the *Rapid Meander*, grabbed the lowest porthole, and began climbing the galleon.

"Go," Nayeli said. "You'll hate yourself if you stay here."

Lu looked at her through the pilothouse's window. "I could hate myself if I go, too."

Nayeli shook her head. "We both know that's a lie."

A wave broke on the railing, spraying foam across Lu's boots.

If she followed Vex onto that ship, and the person she fought so hard not to be resurfaced, she would hate herself. But if she stayed and hid in the engine room with Teo, she would hate herself more, for the fear she would continue to let rule her life.

Lu adjusted the satchel around her shoulders, checked

her weapons, and propelled herself onto the side of the galleon. No time to think; no time to worry.

Nowhere to go but forward.

❋❋❋

Vex was glad to have this bright spot of hatred for Milo Ibarra as he climbed the exterior of the galleon. He focused on that, where his mind wanted to spiral out of control.

He recognized this ship. It was one of Elazar's.

No—Ibarra. Find Ibarra. And murder him.

He wouldn't, though, for Lu's sake. But god, give him ten minutes alone with that disgusting excuse for a man, and he'd have Ibarra begging for death.

Vex heard a rustling against the waves crashing, and when he looked, Lu was climbing up the ship below him. He hadn't expected her to stay on the *Meander*—she was the strongest force he'd known. She'd find a way to get through.

But seeing her eased a knot of tension. He wouldn't have to board this ship alone.

This ship. One he'd been on before.

Vex kept climbing, unable to tell whether he was shaking from his illness or terror. He and Lu would find Ibarra, or other proof of this insanity, and get off before anything happened. They'd stop the war before Argrid could sink its claws back into Grace Loray. Before—before—

Lu plopped onto the deck seconds after him and scurried over to where he crouched behind a longboat. Even terrified, he couldn't help it. He grinned at her.

"I figured I couldn't let you go alone," she whispered. "You are, after all, dying of a condition that makes you unstable."

Vex rolled his eye. "Had to bring that up, did you?"

They both faced the deck. Three guards could be seen on the rear quarterdeck, two more pacing along the fore-castle deck. The main deck dipped between the two, low enough that Vex and Lu could hide along the wall, sneak to the central hatch, and drop belowdecks without arousing attention.

"We should start with the lower decks," Lu whispered. "Work our way up. Take anything you find—correspondence, vials that could be Elazar's test potions, *anything*. We'll have to go to the Council after this no matter what."

She moved before Vex said anything. Not that he could have.

Staircases lined the wall below the quarterdeck, a door between them—the way to the captain's quarters. The central hatch was ahead of that door, a straight shot once the guards on the forecastle deck turned.

Vex slammed next to the door seconds after Lu did, panting like he'd run laps around the deck. She grabbed his wrist, and while it was probably to make sure they timed their sprint to the hatch, Vex leaned into it.

Lu shot forward, Vex stumbling behind.

The central hatch thudded open. Light flooded the main

deck as a man climbed the steps.

Lu froze, cursing. But it wasn't Milo Ibarra.

The man held a lantern to illuminate some paper he was reading. He didn't notice Vex and Lu until he stood on the main deck.

He snapped his head up. Lu drew a blade, the knife catching the lantern light with a flash.

The man didn't look at her knife—his attention was rooted on Vex. Who stared back, seeing through six years of absence, of dreams, of pain and death.

He remembered this ship. He remembered standing on it with his father and this man, who had been a boy not much older than himself, before the world burned to ashes in front of a cheering crowd—

Vex was aware of Lu looking between them. "Vex? What—"

The man didn't shout or raise an alarm. He said a name, soft and imploring, from a hundred lifetimes ago.

"Paxben?"

29

BEN WAS SEVEN, clambering through the gardens of Rodrigu's mansion in Deza. Ahead, a hedge rustled and a body leaped through—a thin, wispy boy two months younger than Ben but a whole head taller.

"Got you!" Paxben shouted, and hurled a harmless cluster of leaves at Ben's chest.

Ben laughed as it fluttered to the ground.

"No, act like it's Variegated Holly! You're supposed to do this!" Paxben flailed, eyes dipping back so the whites showed. He stuck out his tongue, which made Ben giggle more.

A shadow passed over them. "Where did you learn that?"

Ben looked up at his uncle Rodrigu and sobered. Paxben, though, never sobered, a wellspring of energy that Ben got to wade in.

"At the University," Paxben told his father. "It's magic. I

know about other ones, too. Drooping Fern and Eye of the Sun and Croxy and—"

"Paxben," Rodrigu reprimanded. "You shouldn't speak of these things."

"Why not?" he whined. "You speak of them all the time!"

Later, Ben would think back on interactions like this and realize Rodrigu's intensity hadn't been righteous condemnation. It had been fear.

Ben and Paxben were twelve, and they joked about his name, Pax*ben*, and how it bound him to Ben more than Rodrigu was bound to Elazar.

"You'll help me when I'm king too," Ben said as they sat on a bridge in the University's complex, feet dangling over a gurgling brook.

Paxben folded his arms, body woven through the railing as Ben's was, and rested his chin on the cushion his elbows made. He was quiet for too long.

Ben started to worry until Paxben beamed at him.

"Of course," he said. "I'll be right next to you. You'll be the best king."

Ben shook his head. "Not better than my father."

Paxben kicked his legs faster. "I'll take over my father's position. We'll be irmáns, side by side, helping Argrid."

Ben grinned. "We already are irmáns."

Brothers.

Ben was thirteen, crouched against the keyhole to his father's study.

"Rodrigu freed war prisoners . . . he bought and sold Grace Loray's evil magic . . . he was an ally of our enemies, a traitor to the crown, a tool of the Devil . . . and his son was, too."

They wouldn't let Ben see either Rodrigu or Paxben in the holding cells. Defensors barred him at the door, Elazar comforting him with a hand on his shoulder.

"I tried to reason with your uncle and cousin," Elazar said. "They are beyond redemption. The Pious God rewards those who uphold his purity at the cost of great personal suffering. We must expunge Rodrigu's and Paxben's souls, Benat, and the Pious God will bless you for the pain you feel."

Ben didn't see either of them until the burning. Elazar allowed him to watch from as close as he liked—*"For catharsis,"* his father had said. Ben stood at the front of the horde.

"Nos purificar!" people screamed. *Purify us.*

Others, "Queimar os herexes!" *Burn the heretics.*

Ben watched Church defensors drag Rodrigu out of the wagon they used to transport the condemned from the holding cells. He was no longer the vivacious mountain of a man who had thundered after Ben and Paxben as they played hide-and-seek in the gardens. No longer the resolute politician who had guided Elazar through the ongoing revolution on Grace Loray. He was now what the Church had uncovered his soul to be: impure.

Purple bruises rimmed both eyes. Lacerations and dried blood covered his body. He stumbled, so weak that defensors had to carry him.

He didn't speak, though, until they dragged out Paxben.

Bile rose in Ben's throat. Paxben spat and kicked against the defensors. Shackles bound his wrists and cloth covered his mouth, drawing Ben's attention to the marking on Paxben's face. No, not a marking—as Paxben fought, the blood-covered bandage slipped, revealing gashes through his eye.

Rodrigu screamed. Begged. "Let him go! Asentzio, for the love of god, don't do this—"

Ben looked back, over the long expanse of people between the front of the crowd and the steps of Grace Neus Cathedral. There his father stood, too distant for Ben to see if he reacted to Rodrigu using his first name.

He was glad that defensors had gagged Paxben.

Defensors flung Rodrigu against a stake and looped rope around his body. He turned toward Paxben, who had to be tossed back into the wagon so the defensors could regain control.

"Let him go!" Rodrigu shrieked as they yanked a bag over his head.

Defensors dragged Paxben out of the wagon again, a bag over his head now too, dishonor defined. They tied him to a stake next to his father, and a defensor with a torch approached. The smoke stung Ben's nose.

The man passed Rodrigu but didn't light his pyre.

Rodrigu's hysteria broke. *"DON'T KILL MY SON!"*

Ben drew in the stench of smoke, holding it when his stomach heaved.

"They are heretics, Benat," his father had said before they'd left the palace that morning. *"As you watch, remember that. We will be blessed from the pain of sacrificing them."*

Ben watched his uncle and cousin burn to death. He imprinted every flame in his mind and used the heat to scald out the pain—if the Pious God could make blessings come from that pain, he didn't want it. Nothing good was worth Paxben's and Rodrigu's deaths.

Ben had watched them burn. He had watched them *die*.

It was a dream, standing on the deck of the *Astuto*, the world drenched in black but for the lantern in his hand that chased the shadows from the faces of the two people before him.

A woman he didn't know, and a man. Ben had spent six years trying to forget that face, and it was older now, so maybe it was a trick—but his heart pushed out a name that was a prayer he'd sworn to never utter again.

"Paxben?"

The man—*ghost*—smiled, because Paxben would smile, because few of Ben's memories of him existed without a radiance that rivaled the sun.

Reality rushed at Ben and he shifted back, bumping into

someone coming up the stairs behind him. Jakes settled a hand on his hip. Ben didn't have the strength to push him off.

"My prince?" Jakes said. "What—"

Chaos. Jakes shouting, "Intruders!" Lanterns illuminating the deck and weapons rattling and feet pounding.

Paxben's sad, broken smile remained.

"Ben," he finally said. Defensors grabbed his arms. "Irmán."

30

THE ARGRIDIANS STRIPPED them of their weapons and Lu's satchel, which she forced herself to let them take. She could replace the objects within, even the family stone from the Tuncian sanctuary. Still, she hated the thought of the Argridians having it.

The cell where the defensors imprisoned her and Vex was clean, unused, letting Lu feel only annoyance at how close they were to the *Rapid Meander*. Through that wall, up, within swimming distance. Had Nayeli heard the uproar? Did she know the Argridians had caught them?

Focusing on those minor things helped steady Lu. The last time she had been at the mercy of defensors had been during the revolution, when Tom had scalded into her mind the importance of avoiding anyone wearing navy uniforms with the white curved *V* and crossed swords.

Now not only was she a prisoner of the Argridians, she

was at the mercy of the Crown Prince himself. The man who had recognized Vex.

Lu listened as the defensors' footsteps receded up the wooden stairs before she rounded on Vex. He had gone pale, his eye on the hall before their cell's bars as though he expected the prince to materialize at any moment.

Anything Lu had been about to yell died to a soft whisper.

"That wasn't a ruse? You weren't playing along to buy us time?" Her voice broke. "You truly know the *Crown Prince of Argrid*?"

Vex nodded. "Yes."

A real response. Not a quip or a wink or a vulgar comeback.

"He called you Paxben," Lu tried.

Vex came to with a piercing glare. "Paxben died six years ago."

Six years ago. The revolution had been underway, so any news that did not directly involve the war hadn't taken priority. But Lu remembered her parents and other leaders giving a moment of silence one morning—the king's brother had led a cell of revolution sympathizers in Argrid, they'd said. Defensors had discovered his treachery and burned him, along with his son.

Lu hadn't cared. Why should she mourn the death of an Argridian royal when she watched his people destroy her island every day?

"Rodrigu." She said the name her parents had whispered.

Vex closed his eye, the name driving into him as though she'd screamed it.

"Your father," she guessed.

Which made Vex the cousin of the Crown Prince of Argrid. The nephew of the king.

✦✦✦

Vex had always found it fitting that he'd left Argrid on a ship. When he'd landed on Grace Loray and been shoved into one of the Church's prisons, he'd felt as though the foundation of the earth had turned to water. Nothing was solid. Nothing was secure.

Until he'd gotten out of that hell and found his own future.

He wasn't Paxben. He was Devereux Bell, notorious stream raider, wanted the island over. He hadn't survived everything he'd been through only to be taken down by . . .

He remembered the look on Ben's face. Shock. *Hope.*

"I know what you're thinking," Vex said, meeting Lu's eyes with desperate certainty. "I'm not an Argridian spy or a Church plant. My uncle wanted me to be—that's why he faked my death and dropped me on this island and waited to see whether I'd live or die. Well, I didn't do either of those things. I became someone else."

"You had to obey him, though"—Lu filled in the pieces—"because he poisoned you. He was looking for the cure too. Like you said—"

"I'm no more loyal to Elazar than you are to Milo Ibarra,"

Vex snapped. "That's all. It doesn't change a damn thing."

Lu deflated. "It does, Devereux."

Devereux. He relaxed.

"Does your crew know?" she asked.

He nodded. "It was how I met Edda. She was in the same godforsaken prison where Elazar dumped me in northern Grace Loray. We got out together." His tension eased. "Nay didn't care. She's got her own painful history, as you've seen."

Footsteps thumped down the stairs. Vex went rigid, his mind blanking, and he was more grateful than he could say when Lu angled in front of him. As though she might soften the force of whatever was coming.

A contingent stomped down the hall. The defensor who had raised the alarm led the way, and when they stopped, he hesitated as though he was reluctant to reveal his charge.

But Ben shoved him away. "Defensor Rayen, leave. Now. All of you. Get out."

Each word was a dagger in proper Argridian, the heft and point of a man who would be obeyed. Vex was almost impressed. Last he'd seen Ben, he'd been a timid, obedient boy who'd have jumped into the ocean if Elazar had asked it of him.

The defensors filed out. Rayen bowed. "My prince," he said, and stalked up the stairs.

Water hummed against the hull as Ben stepped up to the cell.

A tangle of nerves compelled Vex to get a handle on this situation. He moved around Lu, keeping his posture relaxed as he leaned one shoulder on the bars.

"Leadership agrees with you," Vex said in Argridian.

Ben's face went rigid. "Six years."

Vex's heart sank into his gut.

"I watched you burn." Ben gripped the bars in tight, white knuckles. He didn't pay any attention to Lu, his energy on Vex. "I made myself stand there until you were nothing but a charred corpse. And that's all you say to me?"

"What should I say?" Vex hated that his voice broke. "Your father is a tyrant so blinded by religion that he had your uncle murdered and your cousin banished?"

Ben's lips parted. Vex waited, expecting him to scream *Heresy!*

But he didn't. He put his forehead to the bars, eyes closed. "He's here."

A long, slow drain tapped out Vex's resolve.

The last thing he'd seen in Argrid had been his uncle, standing on the steps of Grace Neus Cathedral, moments before he'd had Rodrigu burned. Every time Argridian bullies showed up and threatened Vex, he'd done whatever they'd asked him, because all he could see when he closed his eye was Elazar. Standing under carvings of sins and Graces. *Smiling.*

A spasm swept over Vex, jarring him so hard his teeth rattled, but he covered it by raking his hand through his hair.

Ben felt the vibration along the bars and looked up.

"The defensors sent for him," Ben continued. "He's likely already climbing aboard."

He walked away, padding back up the staircase.

Vex stiffened, as though every muscle was linked—again—to his cousin. His irmán.

They'd snuck into the kitchens in the middle of the night and eaten so many imported chocolates that they'd been sick for days. They'd climbed up as high as they could in the Grace Neus towers and dared each other to crawl out on the cupolas. It had devastated Vex to think Ben could be like Elazar, but Ben hadn't come to see him after Vex had been arrested, or when he and Rodrigu were on trial, or when they waited in the carriage outside the cathedral's jeering crowd.

"You can't expect Ben to betray his father," Rodrigu had told him. Vex had known the truth in that, because he was manacled in a carriage next to his own father, ready to die for him. But Elazar was *wrong*, no matter that he was Ben's father. Ben had to see that. He would see it, and stop this, because they were irmáns and that mattered, too.

Vex slammed his eye shut now. Goddamn it, he would not give in to this. He didn't have to feel the emotions from that past because it *wasn't* Devereux Bell's past—or so he'd been telling himself, every day, sometimes every minute, for six years.

Another shudder crept up Vex's back, but he didn't have the energy to hide this one.

Lu moved next to him. He looked at her and winced in realization.

"I should've . . . negotiated. They'll kill us for trespassing on their ship." Vex swallowed. "Especially now. If Elazar is here . . ."

Argrid had come to finish the war for Grace Loray. The worst of everything they'd feared was happening—

But Lu didn't say anything. She fingered his shirtsleeve.

Vex's heart faltered. "Lu, you don't have to—"

She snaked her arms around him, her chin resting on his shoulder. Shock paralyzed him, but he regrouped, holding her as if she'd dissolve if he touched her too hard.

She stayed until he relaxed. Until they both did.

❧❧❧

Ben kept his self-control even when he saw Jakes on the next level, waiting for him.

"What did you say to him?" Jakes asked. "Pious God help us, how is this possible?"

Ben wanted to scream. To shove Jakes away from standing *so close to him.*

But all he said was "Remember your place, Defensor."

Jakes came to a halt, and Ben left, rushing for the middle deck.

He shoved his way into the laboratory. Gunnar's cot was made despite the late hour, shadows flashing over it as he walked the length of the chain that hooked his ankle to the wall. Jakes's doing, claiming that if Gunnar had repented, he must earn his freedom.

Though it made working with Gunnar like working alongside a leashed, feral wolf who could, if he one day chose, combust into flames.

Gunnar whirled when the door opened. The candle flame on the table heaved.

"What happened? There was shouting." Gunnar's hands clenched, relaxed, clenched again, seeking a weapon that his servant uniform didn't have.

Ben ignored him, slammed the door, and stumbled forward. He caught himself on the table along the rear wall, and a vial of Alova Pipe fell over with a clank.

Paxben was alive. His cousin was *alive*.

Too much had been taken, too many foundations had given to sand, for Ben to trust this.

A vial smacked into the side of Ben's head.

He shot a frown at Gunnar, who held another empty vial, poised to throw. His chain didn't let him reach the whole room.

"What happened?" Gunnar asked with the inflection of a man trying to speak to an insect.

"Nothing that concerns you."

"I am on this boat. It concerns me. We are attacking now?"

"No."

Gunnar said a word in his language that Ben had heard him utter at least a dozen times before. He took it to mean *asshole*, *idiot*, or some combination of the two.

A knock on the door, and it opened, framing Jakes in the doorway. He spared Gunnar enough attention to see that his chain was fastened.

"Your father is waiting for you in the captain's quarters," Jakes said.

Ben crossed his arms, feigning indifference. "And Paxben?"

"Being brought up now."

Ben nodded. "Tell my father I'll be there soon."

Jakes hesitated, clearly expecting to escort Ben, but after a long pause, he left.

"Benat," Gunnar said when the door closed. With his heavy accent, it came out more as *Ben-jay*. "Do not leave me here without information!"

Ben got halfway to the door before he took pity on Gunnar.

"My cousin has risen from the dead," he said, glad it sounded as unbelievable as it felt. "Which is miraculous, considering the Church burned him for heresy six years ago."

"Heresy," Gunnar parroted. "You can use him. How?"

"Use him? He was dead—I watched him *die*—"

Gunnar shrugged. "Church tried to kill him, and he survived. Either Church let him live or your father did. This could change things."

Gunnar was right, damn him.

Ben had been lied to. He knew that by now—but he'd assumed he'd uncovered the extent of the lies.

Elazar had staged the death. It was the only explanation that made sense, but gaping questions remained. Paxben had been caught in Rodrigu's treason. He clearly held no loyalty to Elazar—unless Paxben's defiance had been a ruse.

Ben needed to figure out where Paxben's loyalties did lie before Elazar truly had him killed, or manipulated this event to benefit himself. But doing so meant plowing through the other emotions that crowded Ben's chest like boulders in a valley after a landslide.

A vial rebounded off his sternum, this one hard enough to leave a bruise.

"Go," Gunnar boomed. "I did not agree to wait here, letting the enemy win battles!"

Another vial, but this time, Ben caught it and whipped it back at Gunnar before he left.

Moments after his cousin had resurfaced, he was planning how best to use him.

Paxben was right. Leadership did agree with him.

31

THE MAIN DECK was alive with defensors, those from the *Astuto* as well as a dozen more from the *Desapiadado*, the first sign that Elazar was aboard. Most sent Ben sharp salutes and calls of "Prince Benat" in cracking tones.

Elazar wanted to know he was approaching.

The captain's cabin was under the quarterdeck, a spacious chamber with tables for charting and mahogany shelves of nautical equipment. Thick carpets and padded chairs made the room comfortable, elevated by gold trimmings and a replica of Argrid's symbol in polished wood on the back wall. Ben had spent little time here, entrusting the voyage to the man Elazar had selected as the *Astuto*'s captain, so it didn't feel as intrusive as it might have seeing Elazar take over the finest room on the boat.

Jakes stood at attention by one of the large windows shuttered to hide the lights within the room. The rest of the defensors here were from Elazar's own guard. Elazar himself sat behind the desk under the decorative crest of Argrid, speaking with another defensor.

The door behind Ben closed. Elazar looked up.

Ben spoke first. "I thought we were working together now."

Apparently, he was going with anger as his guiding emotion. Harder to play off, but he was barely hanging on to composure enough to be angry, not sobbing.

Elazar's eyebrows lifted.

"You kept him alive," Ben pressed on. "You had an agent on Grace Loray, one who could have been useful in doing the Pious God's work, and you—"

It was a guess, a wild, furious stab into the night, so when Elazar held his hand up, Ben froze with terror.

Elazar lowered his hand. "Your cousin was too erratic to be useful. I didn't inform you that he was alive because there was nothing to gain from it, and it has been clear for some time that the Pious God wishes me to do away with him. He will now be dealt with."

The lanterns around the room were thick squares of glass with gaps to feed oxygen. But Ben tasted bitter smoke, ash filling his lungs.

The man beside Elazar cleared his throat, and Elazar stood. "Of course—Benat, as you have pointed out, it is beneficial to you to know the moves of the Pious God on Grace Loray. General Ibarra has been instrumental in our plan."

Ben refocused on the man his father had been speaking

with. Not a defensor. Ben had seen General Ibarra only once or twice, as Ibarra had spent most of his time on Grace Loray, leading the war charge. Last Ben had seen him, Argrid's nobility had gathered to send off the contingent bound for the treaty negotiations in New Deza.

Ben nodded at Ibarra, then realized he'd have to react more if he wanted to hold his cover. "General, I thank you for your service. It is not an easy war to fight."

Ibarra bowed. "With you assisting us, we will at long last fulfill Argrid's great destiny on this godforsaken island."

But Elazar was already talking. "My contacts have proven true supporters of the Pious God and have delivered us plants for your use, Benat. Defensors are unloading them now."

Ben had to forcibly pull himself away from memories of the headiness of smoke, burned corpses, and Paxben's smile. "Your contacts?"

Elazar waved behind Ben. The door opened, a burst of sea air chasing away some of the smoke stench. "The Mecht stream raider syndicate. Thanks to their visit, we have convinced them to aid us. They have given themselves over to Argrid and the cause of purifying the world."

Ben's mouth opened. The Mecht stream raider syndicate? A visit?

The memory hit so hard he fought to stay upright. He saw visitors weeks ago—the Mechts they'd begged for aid hadn't been diplomatic officials, as Ben had thought, as

Elazar had *told him*. They'd been raiders from Grace Loray.

"Praise the Pious God," Ben said, the words cutting his tongue.

"Indeed. Ah, here we are. Benat, Ibarra, you are dismissed."

Ben turned, numb.

And stopped.

Paxben, wrists and ankles in manacles, shuffled into the room. The girl trailed him, her dark features bent in an ironclad expression of ferocity.

Defensors prodded Paxben to stop paces from Elazar and Ibarra, behind the desk. The girl stumbled into Paxben and pressed her hand on his back to right herself.

Her eyes shifted over Paxben's shoulder, to Milo Ibarra.

"No," she said, ducking behind Paxben. "No—"

Defensors yanked her forward, ignoring her pleas. She dropped to her knees as Ibarra bowed his farewell to the king, his eyes skimming over Paxben.

The look of victory on Ibarra's face increased with a bellowing laugh.

"Why, Devereux Bell," he said. Paxben lunged as Ibarra stepped around the table, but defensors kicked the backs of his legs, sending him to his knees. "I heard you'd escaped."

"Who?" Ben asked.

Ibarra dropped his gaze to the girl, who caved forward—not in submission, but more like she was trying to hide. "A stream raider nuisance on this island," Ibarra said. "The man your dear returned cousin pretended to be."

Ben couldn't see Paxben's face, but wanted to, to see if the new name matched what his cousin had become.

"What I don't understand is who *she* is," Ibarra continued. "One of my informants said his lovestruck daughter freed Bell. But that girl is nothing but a meek lady, not a—"

Ibarra stopped. He crouched and ripped the girl's head back, his fist tangling in her hair. Elazar did nothing to stop him—why would he? They were prisoners.

Ben fought the instinct that wanted him to dive forward. On the edge of his awareness, he saw Jakes, against the window, watching the situation. Watching *him*.

When Ben refocused on Ibarra, he had to blink twice to clear his vision, because this fuming, red-faced man couldn't be the same self-confident general from before.

Ibarra shot to his feet, staring at the girl as his lips curled back over glinting teeth.

"Adeluna Andreu," he said like he was trying to rearrange the letters to make something new. "You conniving bitch."

❅❅❅

"One of my informants said his lovestruck daughter was the one who freed Bell."

Lu's mouth dropped open.

One of my informants . . . his lovestruck daughter . . .

Pieces of her resolve had been chipping away since she

had revealed her past to Vex. But that had not been destructive so much as recognizing the ache of wounds from long ago.

This was the final tap on fragile glass. The last bullet to take her down.

She was coming undone.

"I'm so sorry, Lulu-bean. I'm sorry this happened to you. It shouldn't have happened—"

Her father had brought the news of the storehouse that had taken their soldiers away from the headquarters the night of the final battle. He had constructed most of the rebels' plans, their attacks and how many soldiers would fight. Kari and others had orchestrated the alliance with the stream raiders. Tom hadn't known of that until it was done.

Milo continued talking, and Lu came to with an aching jolt. He knew who she was now. Who she *really* was.

"—spy during the revolution," he was telling the king. "A useless coward of a girl who ran away during the final fight. She tried to make a fool of me."

I did make a fool of you, she wanted to say.

The king flicked his hand up, cutting off Milo, and Vex shifted toward Lu.

Elazar squinted at her with a level of calculation, as she might study a new plant. *How can I use this? Or is it of use to me?*

"I've heard stories of the final battle." Elazar touched a look to Milo. "The stream raiders sided with the insurgents.

If I remember, it was *you* who ran that night. But that is no matter."

It was. In the way Elazar scorned Milo, stepping around him, focusing on Lu.

The fractured pieces vibrated in Lu's body, her heart catching itself on things she was helpless to undo.

"You were the girl. The one they tortured," Elazar said.

"No," Vex responded. "She's a member of my crew. She's—"

"Every word out of you is toxic, nephew. The Devil's impurities have infected you." Elazar cupped his hands to his chest. "But your life has not been forfeit, praise the Pious God. You have brought me the final key to our salvation."

Vex's face pinched. Lu watched him, unable to bring herself to look at Elazar, whose voice carried the lilt of a man entrenched in insanity.

"You gave this girl treatments," Elazar said. "More than enough to strike her down with Shaking Sickness within the year, according to you, General Ibarra."

Lu rocked, caught herself. This was new information— she knew already that ingesting large amounts of plants caused Shaking Sickness, but the dosage controlled how quickly it killed people. The more plants a person had, the quicker the condition would claim them.

Her throat convulsed.

Lazonade. Awacia. Croxy. More, and more, until her

mouth had burned and her stomach had felt scraped raw. *Too much*, she had known even then.

"Yet she survived. Again, according to you, Ibarra."

Lu looked up at Milo, who stood off to the side. "Yes," he stated. "It's her, my king."

Elazar smiled. "Then we have indeed been delivered."

"Father?"

Lu had forgotten the prince was in the room.

"My son." Elazar clapped the prince on the shoulder. "You will figure out how this girl survived the disease that comes from magic overuse. With that information, you should have all you need to create the tonics as ordained by the Pious God."

Vex had told her Elazar was desperate for the Shaking Sickness cure—but seeing the joy on the king's face made Lu realize with horror how dangerous she was.

She knew how to cure people when they had too much magic. She could keep test subjects alive as Elazar tortured them in his experiments. Permanent magic was not impossible—the Mechts had manipulated Eye of the Sun in such a way—so he might, one day, figure out how to make any magic permanent.

With Lu's help.

"But, Ibarra." Elazar didn't look back at him, his eyes going in an unspoken command to the defensors behind Lu. She heard them move, reaffirming their position, and Milo rose straighter. "You said this girl was the daughter of one of your informants, and yet you didn't know her identity. Your informant didn't tell you that his daughter was the girl from that final battle, and that she had miraculously survived without succumbing to Shaking Sickness. Why is that?"

"I—" Milo's jaw bobbled open. His eyes fell to Lu with an accusatory glare, as though he was realizing the true weight of her presence in his life.

She had made him look a fool when he'd been unable to break her as a child; she had made him look a fool now when she'd proven his inability to recognize details. And, more, his inability to control his informants.

Had Tom known the gravity of what Lu had endured? Either he hadn't realized what it meant that she hadn't gotten Shaking Sickness, or he'd protected her.

Neither option gave Lu relief. She saw Tom smiling at her in a moldy cellar.

"Kari doesn't know about this enemy. It will be so helpful to her, to the war. This is why you're my Lulu-bean—because you can keep a secret so well, it's as if you took a magic plant that sealed your lips. Now, just a quick trip. You won't see a thing, I promise."

Lu had murdered for her father. Had spied for him. Secret missions that Kari hadn't known of, because Tom had stroked her head and smiled at her and *loved her.*

She had told herself they were enemies—she killed out of self-defense, but once, it had been intent. She had reasoned it all away as Tom had told her.

"They're enemies, darling. Their deaths will help the war."

But which side of the war had it helped? Who had she killed?

She heaved, her stomach folding inside out—but as she bent double over herself, she became so aware, too aware, of how she was kneeling before Milo.

"Clear the room," said Elazar. "Not you, Ibarra. We must discuss your shortcomings. Benat, do what you must with this new tool. Defensors, dispose of my nephew."

The prince made a trill of objection. "We may yet need him, Father. Let him live until I can figure out the girl's compliance."

Elazar nodded. "Bring him to the cells, then."

As the room awoke, Milo's glare remained on Lu, a hatred that she drowned in.

She was at his mercy, again. Manacled and a prisoner, with guards grabbing her arms, the prince saying, "To my laboratory. Chain her with my assistant."

Suddenly it was five years ago, and she huddled next to Annalisa, watching as fate hunted her.

No, she'd thought that night in the headquarters. *Whatever fate is coming, it is not Annalisa's—it is mine. Mine alone.*

She had known she deserved few of the good things she had gotten. Her skin was too soaked with blood, stained in ways she could never wash out—and that had been when she thought she'd killed people who at least deserved it, in some awful way.

But now.

What had she done? Had she killed innocent Grace Lorayans, threats who Argrid wanted out of the way? Had she murdered people who might have helped the revolution end sooner?

As Lu looked at Vex, seeing the wild panic in his eye, she went without a fight. The Argridians would try to use him against her if she fought, so she wouldn't. She needed to hold out long enough for Cansu to rescue him.

Tenacity settled over her, suffocating but familiar. She had always known her fate, the last few years when she'd pretended to have a normal life. There it had waited, a shadow on the outskirts of her every thought: the knowledge that she did not deserve ease and normalcy. She had made this her future the moment she had obeyed her father.

Now that she knew the extent of what she had done, a strange calm descended over her. This was what she deserved, punishment and pain. It was righter now than it had ever been.

Vex's panic raged when she stood. He scrambled up, held back by defensors.

"Don't give in to what they want!" he cried. "Lu! *Lu!*"

They took her back out into the briny air. Lu twisted her hands so her palms faced up, holding pools of moonlight.

"Fight!" Vex cried behind her. "They'll destroy you!"

But she knew the truth. *I've been destroyed for years.*

32

BEN SHOULD HAVE gone after the girl. Adeluna, Milo had called her. For the sake of his cover, he needed to march to the laboratory and examine her, or pretend to, to pick apart how she had kept herself from getting Shaking Sickness.

Which did pique Ben's curiosity. *She kept herself from getting Shaking Sickness? How is it possible?*

Ben hung back outside the captain's cabin until the defensors hauled Adeluna and Paxben belowdecks. Jakes talked with Elazar's men near the railing, so Ben stayed by the door, counting the waves that broke, listening to his father berate Milo Ibarra within the closed room.

He reached twenty waves, and moved.

Two defensors guarded the cells, on the level above outside the hatch. They came to attention when he approached.

"No one is to disturb me," Ben told them, shutting the hatch as he descended.

Stupid, what he was doing. But he was desperate.

Paxben stood in the center of the same locked cell as before, hands slung in his pockets, posture relaxed. When Ben stopped outside the cell, he saw his cousin shiver.

"What'd you do with her?" Paxben asked.

"She'll be safe. I promise. I—"

They were alone. For the first time in more than six years.

"Paxben, I'm—"

"Vex."

"What?"

"My name." Paxben looked as though he was trying for ease, but his words came out hard. "It isn't Paxben. It's Vex, or Devereux, if you like."

The name got stuck in Ben's throat. "Fine. I need to tell you—"

"Wouldn't kill you to put some furniture in here," Paxben cut him off again. "Even the cells in New Deza have benches."

"Would you—"

"I suspect these aren't made for long-term prisoner accommodation, though."

"Pax—Devereux!" Ben grabbed the bars of the cell, fighting to keep from shouting and alerting the defensors above. "Would you listen to me? I need to apolo—"

"No." Paxben met his heave forward. "No, Ben. You don't need to apologize, or help me, or do anything. Don't throw your life away on me. I won't let you."

Ben's jaw bobbled open. "You're trying to protect me? Why?"

Paxben chuckled dryly. "He's your *father*. You love him. But I know you love me too, so I'm not making you choose. I never wanted to put you in that situation."

"Never wanted to—" Ben closed his eyes in realization.

That was why Paxben had never told him of Elazar's madness. Why he had never invited him into Rodrigu's plotting. The Ben who Paxben had known would have cried heresy and run to Elazar, asking his father if it was true. Ben had had to watch Rodrigu and Paxben die to realize Argrid wasn't perfect.

"I was so stupid, Pax," Ben whispered, not caring that he'd said the wrong name. He wasn't talking to *this* Paxben—he was talking to the one from years ago, who had struggled as Church defensors dragged him to the stake but had never once screamed for Ben's help. Not while Rodrigu had shouted for Elazar. "All this time, I let it happen. I was guilty, and afraid, and I didn't think there was another way. I gave up."

He opened his eyes and grabbed the bars.

"I helped kill people," Ben continued. "I helped kill *you*. I might not be able to do anything to stop them, not yet, but I'm not ignorant anymore. I'm sorry, Pax—Devereux. Vex. Whoever you want to be. I'm . . ." Ben deflated, head bowed. "I'm sorry."

"It's about damn time."

Ben blinked to find Paxben grinning. Of all the reactions he'd expected—angry yelling, sulking resentment—a smile had not been one of them.

"I told my father"—Paxben faltered, saying the word with a discernable hitch—"that you'd be better than Elazar. The whole time we were helping the rebels? I was doing it for *you*, you idiot. I knew you'd be a king worth fighting for."

"I've barely begun to make amends for everything I've let happen," Ben argued. "And you're speaking of kingship? You've seen how far Elazar's reach extends."

Paxben nodded, solemn. "I know."

"Of course—I didn't mean . . . I don't know what to do. Our country is ill. Where is the source? What do I do to heal it? And you come back." He blew out a breath. "I realize more each day how little control I have over anything."

Paxben offered a weak smile. A cracked memory of a time long past.

"I wrote to you," Paxben whispered. Then laughed at himself. "I knew I'd never send the letters. But I needed to talk to you. I told you about your father's plans and what my father and I had tried to do. I told you about the night they raided our estate. I told you about the Church's holding cells, and what they did, and how—" Paxben's hand went to his eye patch. Ben's gaze landed on it, and he realized that he'd let himself ignore it.

Not to embarrass Paxben, he thought. *Or not to wallow in my own guilt?*

"I told you everything," Paxben continued. "I imagined you reading the letters. I imagined you understanding, and I've had this exact conversation with you so many times, Ben. I imagined everything you could say to me."

"Even this?" Ben waved at himself, at the fearful, incapable man he was.

Paxben grinned. "I always told myself I'd be so damn relieved you were on my side that I wouldn't care. We could conquer anything together."

Ben's grip on the bars went lax. The cell melted away, the ship and Grace Loray beyond, nothing intruding on a moment Ben had never thought he'd get again.

"Irmán," Ben said, his throat swelling.

I've missed you.

Paxben's smile faded. "Para sempre," he returned. *Forever.*

I've missed you, too.

❊❊❊

The room where the defensors deposited Lu was on a high-enough deck that it had porthole windows letting in the moonlight. In that dimness, Lu could make out tables of supplies, cupboards glinting with vials. The familiarity of a laboratory would have been comforting if she had been capable of feeling anything beyond the shackles grating her wrists and the memories of everything her father had told her.

The defensors bound her to a chair and left, shutting the door so the only noise was the quiet shushing of waves beyond the walls.

Behind her, chains rattled.

Lu shot up straighter, unable to look too far behind. Had the prince gotten to the room before her? Would her interrogation begin already, in the dark, when she couldn't see any of it approaching? Her pulse hammered. Though she wanted to use her normal methods of inducing calm, she bit back the desire—Tom had taught her those methods.

The chain clanking was followed by a voice, hoarse and rich, accented with the Mechtland lilt. "You caused the chaos on deck."

Lu clenched her hands on the chair's arms. Not the prince. He'd said something about an assistant, hadn't he?

If he had a Mecht as an assistant, the prince could be close, too close, to making magic permanent. But if the man was his ally, why would the prince have chained him?

The Argridians could be playing on her sympathies to get her to share secrets.

She stayed silent.

The Mecht grunted at her refusal to speak. "Fine."

A long while passed before the laboratory's door opened. In that time, Lu heard the splash of water and bark of orders—Elazar leaving and taking Milo, she hoped.

The door squealed open and the prince entered, light filtering from his lantern. Defensors attempted to follow him, but he shut the door on them as if their mere presence annoyed him.

The chains behind Lu rattled, the Mecht prisoner rising up.

"Gunnar—has she spoken?" the prince asked, his eyes on Lu.

"No."

The prince set the lantern on the table beside Lu along with something that he dropped with a dull *thunk*.

Her book. *Botanical Wonders of the Grace Loray Colony.*

"I haven't seen one of these in years," the prince whispered, speaking, unsurprisingly, in proper Argridian. He adjusted the flame higher, casting light on his face and the equipment on the table beside him. An impressive arrangement, one organized by a mind that understood botanical magic more than Lu would expect of an Argridian. Especially the prince.

The prince caught her appraisal but didn't smile, shifting so he leaned against the table.

"I'm Ben," he said.

Lu frowned. But it was better than *prince*, as though she owed him allegiance.

"You are Adeluna Andreu. Or Lu," Ben continued, "I've been told."

Confusion made her frown retreat.

He pressed on, tired, like he had single-handedly rowed here from Deza. "I have something I would like to propose to you."

Her nostrils flared. "I will not help the—"

"Not for my father. For me. Or, well, for the rest of the world. I'm not that arrogant."

Behind her, Gunnar huffed.

"You have no reason to trust me," Ben said. "But do you trust Pax—Devereux?"

Lu kept her face blank. Her body, still.

Ben leaned forward, knocking *Botanical Wonders* back as he moved. "He said to tell you to—" He rolled the words through his mouth. "To jump backward off the water-fall?"

Lu's stiffness released with a single shift of her head. "What did you say?"

Ben smiled. "To jump backward off the waterfall."

Her breath quickened. "He didn't jump."

Another smile, stronger, gaining traction. "No. You pushed him."

Only she and Vex had been on the cliff that night. Not even Nayeli had seen.

Vex trusted Ben.

As though easing to the edge of that cliff, Lu said, "All right, Ben. What is your proposition?"

"My father wants me to find a way to make magic permanent."

Lu knew this already—Vex had told her.

"You want to do that?" she asked.

But Ben shook his head. Then stopped and squinted.

"I want to cure the world of my father. He gave people Shaking Sickness. I mean to show everyone that I can cure it, and that he can't, and neither can the Church."

Lu looked away, at the equipment spread over Ben's table. "Have you?"

"What?"

"Have you figured out a way to make magic permanent?"

"That isn't what I want to do," Ben pressed. "I want to cure Shaking Sickness. You know what the cure is. If you help me, we can—"

Lu's face went hard, emotionless, her body responding in kind. "Whatever good deed you think will change anything, you're wrong. This is war."

She hadn't said that aloud yet. Not in the machinations, the search for Milo; not in the prejudice and threats toward raiders; not even when Elazar had been on this ship, on Grace Loray's shore.

There had to be a peaceful solution. We sacrificed too much for peace.

But she knew now. There had been no sacrifice. The war had never ended.

She had been a fool, in so many ways.

Lu let go of her collected, demure politician demeanor. She let herself once again become the girl of blood and secrets who had spent her childhood listening to her parents plan battles and discuss death over breakfast.

"If you want to stop Elazar," she started, "you'll need to do more than discredit him by healing the people he's hurt.

He wants permanent magic so he can have an unstoppable army of defensors—but how will he convince his devout soldiers to accept—let alone ingest—magic?"

She suspected what Elazar would do, but she waited for Ben's answer.

He stared at the floor in thought. "He'll say it came from the Pious God. He'll say it wasn't botanical magic, but blessings for those of purity."

Lu nodded. When she was younger, she had left these sorts of plans to her parents, relaxing in the knowledge that the burden went to someone else. But she had heard enough of their plots and listened in on so many of their meetings—she could do this.

Her father had made her very capable.

And Kari? Had she known the truth?

Lu couldn't bring herself to wonder. There was no solace in knowing, no help in the answer. All she needed right now was to plan. To be a child of the revolution.

She smiled, though it made her feel hollow. "We'll make potions. We'll take Powersage, and make strength permanent; we'll take Aerated Blossom, and make flight last longer than one breath. Elazar won't be able to claim permanent magic is a gift from the Pious God, not if we make permanent magic first and tell everyone that it came from Grace Loray's botanical plants."

Ben's face drained of color. He looked behind her, at Gunnar, and his hesitation made Lu lean forward.

"You can, can't you?" she asked. "You can make all magic permanent."

Ben shook his head. "No. But between the three of us, we can figure it out."

Gunnar stayed quiet, his silence weighted. Lu didn't care. She was beyond reason. She was utterly broken.

"Then I'll help you, Ben," she said. "I'll help you destroy your father."

And mine, too.

✤✤✤

Defensors escorted Lu out later, leaving Ben alone with Gunnar and the book that had turned up in Lu's things. The book the Church had burned for the same reason they had burned Rodrigu—heresy.

Ben had agreed to escape this ship with Lu and Vex. To go somewhere safe—Lu had described a stream raider haven in a port north of here—with them, help Lu make permanent magic, and reveal it to the world before Elazar could claim it as a gift of the Pius God.

Relief surged through Ben's veins with a momentum he hadn't expected. It plowed into his worry, six years of holding himself in perfect check, and cracked apart the armor he had built of obedience and piety and carefully selected sins.

He had agreed to irrevocably turn on his father. No more hiding. No more lying. No more holding his breath waiting to be discovered.

Paxben was alive, and Ben was well on his way to being *free*.

The lantern didn't light every corner of the room; darkness sheathed Gunnar near his cot. Ben stayed where he'd been throughout the conversation with Lu, on the edge of the table, ankles crossed.

He lifted his eyes to Gunnar. "You have nothing to say?"

Gunnar didn't move. Not a shift of his shoulders, not a flex of his jaw.

"You have me here to keep you from getting too close," Gunnar said.

"Yes."

"Stop, Benat. Don't do this with her."

Ben-jay, Ben parroted in his head.

Ben peeled his eyes away from Gunnar. They had spent almost two weeks on this ship, with Gunnar watching his every move and making unexplained suggestions to keep Ben from figuring out how to make magic permanent. Two weeks, and Ben had given himself that time, expecting some great revelation to occur to him, one that would make everything right.

But this—making magic permanent with Lu, and revealing it before Elazar could take credit for it—was the only thing that might effect change. His plan of curing Shaking Sickness had felt weak, even to him. Something like that wouldn't be enough to change an entire country's beliefs and stop a war.

"This is different," Ben told Gunnar. "This will stop my father. Your people use magic like this all the time—"

"Yes," Gunnar cut in. "That magic is still burning the Mechtlands."

Ben winced. "I'm sorry. We can use it to help your people, too. If they had—"

Gunnar sighed. "No, Benat." He moved into the light. His expression of severity sent a chill over Ben's body. "You have a good heart, I see now. But you are making a weapon. Only death will follow."

✵✵✵

Once Ben left, Vex fully expected defensors to kill him, despite Elazar agreeing to let him live.

That agreement had been a lie for Ben's sake. Elazar wanted his nephew dead—Vex'd known that since the courtroom in New Deza, when he'd seen the Argridian diplomats. He'd *felt* it, deep in his soul. Argridian pawns of Elazar's, leading a charge for Vex's death at the hands of the Council? Way too convenient to not be intentional—and not surprising, either.

But Vex hadn't been afraid until now. Until he was here. Trapped under his uncle again.

He wouldn't escape Elazar twice, and knowing that brought him close to passing out.

But defensors only came to move Vex to what was more or less a closet on the middle deck. They put Lu back in the original cell, he guessed—they'd keep them split up to use as leverage against each other and drive them crazy with uncertainty.

Damned if it wouldn't work.

Vex forced himself to sit on the floor of the cramped closet. Only a sliver of light peeked under the doorframe. He could hear defensors breathing outside, but otherwise, silence.

Ben didn't believe in Elazar.

Six years of Vex telling himself he was an idiot for writing letters to someone who existed only in his memory. Six years of moving on with his life, because he couldn't expect Ben to turn on Elazar. If Ben had risen against his father, Elazar would've killed him.

Vex leaned his head against the wall and smiled up at the blackness.

For the first time in years, he let himself remember what it'd been like to hope that Argrid would get better. He remembered his father spinning stories of tolerance, encouragement, and growth, and how Vex had pictured it happening: he and Ben, standing side by side. He'd killed that dream the day his father had burned.

But now. Elazar still had endless power—and Ben had power, too.

Maybe Vex would survive this. Maybe every piece of who he had once been wasn't dead.

33

DEFENSORS DIDN'T COME for Lu the first day, nor the second. They brought her food and water and left her to stew alone in the cell, where she imagined what scenarios might be playing out beyond the ship.

Nayeli had figured out something had gone amiss. Where was she now? What had she told Teo? They had not made a plan for this scenario, should Vex and Lu not return. Perhaps Vex had his own arrangement with his crew for such an event. But Cansu was on her way, and bent for war, no doubt. Had the Argridians captured Edda on the Mecht crew as well? Her crewmates had no reason to suspect her. Surely a rescue was coming.

Did the Council know of Argrid's presence off Grace Loray? Or had the Argridian diplomats and their allies concealed that information? What of the councilmembers who opposed Argrid—were they still under house arrest? Or, worse—who was against Argrid, and who else, like Tom, was an Argridian agent?

Lu wanted to rip the planks of the cell apart for some way to expel the pressure in her chest. She pictured her mother's face, relived everything Kari had said, or done, or hinted at, looking for holes, comparing it to Tom's deceit. She pictured Branden, the loyal captain of the castle guard. She pictured Annalisa's mother, Bianca, who claimed she had fled Argrid but died of the disease that Elazar was giving to people—some of whom he let remember.

She pictured Annalisa. Young. Innocent.

How deep did the deception run?

"Lu!"

A voice yanked her from sleep. Cold sweat washed over her, her body awakening somewhere unsafe before her mind could remember why.

Time was impossible to determine in the belly of the ship, but Lu blinked through her fog, noting the absence of any breakfast tray. Not yet morning.

Her eyes landed on the person outside her cell, expecting it to be a guard, or Ben—

But she dove forward with a startled sob. "Nayeli!"

Nayeli beamed. She wore black head to toe, her dark hair knotted against her scalp. Her hands wriggled in fingerless gloves, fast at work picking at the pouches strapped across her waist. But her attention was on Lu, her eyes round and happy.

"I gotta say, Lu, in the short time I've known you, you've ended up in a lot of cells."

Nayeli withdrew whatever plant she'd been searching for. Lu eyed it, amusement warring with disbelief.

"No," said Lu.

"Yes," giggled Nayeli.

Footsteps pattered down the stairs. Lu gripped the bars, rigid—until one more person came into view. Edda.

"Where's Vex?" Edda asked, eyeing the other empty cells.

"How are you here? Where's Teo?"

"Teo's far away, under guard with Cansu's raiders. This ship had an early-morning shift change. Two defensors are unconscious. One more . . . can hopefully swim." Edda paced up and down the hall like she was the one caged. "Hurry up, Nay—we don't have long before this goes to shit."

Nayeli made a sharp croak of achievement and lit the plants in her palms. "Back up, Lu!"

"Nayeli!" Lu tried again. "You can't—"

Edda saw the plant. "Stop! I can get the keys—"

"Oops! Too late!" Nayeli sang and threw the plant at the cell door.

It wasn't Hemlight, which she had used to free Lu and Vex from the Mechts.

This was the far more dangerous, far more *destructive*, Variegated Holly.

***

All the things Ben had planned with Lu—fleeing to safety in a raider syndicate; making permanent magic before Elazar did—hinged on Ben's singular task of getting himself, Lu, and Paxben off the ship.

Doing so had proven problematic.

No one from the *Astuto* ventured to the shore, despite how close they were. Supply runs, when needed, transferred goods from the shore to Elazar's ship to Ben's, but never did a boat go from the *Astuto* to the island. Intentional— the prisoners were aboard the *Astuto*. Having a predictable escape route would be stupid.

When he sent a letter via Jakes to Elazar, Ben found that even he was not allowed to go ashore.

"I request a solid workspace, free of the ship's damp and constraints," Ben had written.

"It is not yet time. Finish your work, at least one permanent potion, and we may proceed. Have you broken the girl yet?" Elazar had responded.

Ben crumpled the letter, feeling the distrust in his father's words.

His cover was precarious. One wrong move, and Elazar could cry *Heretic Prince* and restrain him as a true prisoner.

Three mornings after Paxben's arrival, Ben bolted upright, dreams of plants and fire scattering in the wake of a noise that didn't make sense. His back screamed in agony from where he'd fallen asleep over his table, *Botanical Wonders of the Grace Loray Colony* serving as a horrible makeshift pillow. He rubbed out a kink in his neck, noting first the low light of dawn, then Gunnar, standing, the muscles across his bare chest strained with tension, the thin blanket from his cot pooled around his feet.

"What—" Ben stared at Gunnar's clan mark. From this view, it looked like a sunburst, rays curling across his sternum and into the top ripples of his abdominal muscles.

"Unchain me," Gunnar demanded. *"Now."*

Ben shook his head to clear it. He'd heard a *pop*, only louder.

An explosion from the lowest deck.

Ben flew to his feet, yanking the keys out of his pocket.

"They're keeping Paxben in a storage room down this hall," Ben said as he bent to Gunnar's chain. "We have to get him. If something's wrong, he'll be the first target to blame."

"It came from below. Lu?" Gunnar bounced in anticipation, stretching his fingers. "I said you should talk to her again. She planned her own escape."

"We don't know that."

Ben looked up. The intensity of Gunnar's heat held Ben immobile, like pyre flames drawing him in—and sunbeams stroking his face. They hadn't been this close since the holding cells of Grace Neus Cathedral, when Gunnar had been the one on his knees, his chin in Ben's hand.

Gunnar dropped his head, tangles of blond hair brushing the top of his clan mark. He shot Ben a look of annoyance. "Have you finished? Princes do not know how locks work?"

The lock came free with a *click* and Ben stood, returning Gunnar's annoyed look with one of his own. But he felt the flimsiness of it.

Above, a bell tolled. Feet pounded—the ship awakening amidst a volley of gunfire.

Whatever was happening, they needed to use it, as they had used everything else.

"We fight now," Gunnar said.

He waited for confirmation, but Ben knew that if he said no, Gunnar would shove him down and storm out of the room, an unstoppable fireball. Already the temperature around him had spiked, drawing sweat along Ben's forehead.

Gunnar didn't seem worried that he was wearing only the pants of his servant's uniform. He extended his hand and birthed a flame in his palm. The orange light flared in his eyes, their color the blue of a sky at storm.

"Yes," Ben said, wanting to retch, wanting to scream. "We fight."

Gunnar smiled, the first time he had given Ben something other than a glower, and it was as incapacitating as his heat.

"Finally," Gunnar said and sent fire blasting at the door.

※※※

Lu dove into the corner of her cell as the lit Variegated Holly hit the bars. A dome-shaped explosion erupted, brilliant white light flaring in a blast that rang in Lu's ears. Debris sprayed across her, bits of metal and chunks of wood—but, thankfully, no seawater.

"You could have killed us!" Lu shouted, her ears buzzing. She clawed her way to her feet, analyzing the mess that had once been her cell door. A gaping, smoking hole now, it was littered with pieces of itself—and larger chunks of iron had embedded in the seaside wall.

Nayeli didn't acknowledge any of these dangers. In fact, she was *giggling*.

Edda flew up from where the explosion had thrown her. "Nay, you dumbass!"

Nayeli waved her hands at her ears. "Can't hear you. Explosion was too loud."

Edda glared at her as she hobbled over to the hole in the cell. "Where's Vex?"

The realization settled. They might have had the secrecy to find him—if Nayeli had not, quite literally, blown it away. But as Lu started to yell at her again, bedlam carried. Voices raised in orders, warning; an alarm bell tolled in the rapid pattern of a call.

Lu's eyes went to the ceiling, hearing the expected footsteps thundering down to investigate the explosion. But beyond that, another noise came, faint yet distinct.

"Gunfire?" Relief washed over her. "Cansu!"

Nayeli cheered, but they had no time for further explanation. They shot up the first set of stairs, sidestepping the two unconscious defensors Edda had mentioned, and made for another staircase that would lift them to the middle deck. The closer they got to the main deck, the more mayhem would reign.

Lu jolted to a stop as shouting intensified, words she could make out now:

"Port side! Coming around the stern! More approaching from the shore!"

"Does Cansu have enough raiders?" Lu asked. But would any number of steamboats make a difference against Argridian brigantines and galleons? Cansu's syndicate was the only group on this island fighting Argrid—they couldn't afford to lose anyone in battle.

Nayeli shrugged. "Not taking on. Distracting."

"Which is why we have to *move*," Edda said. "Cansu won't be able to hold on for long, and we don't have Vex."

Lu shook away the parts of her that wanted to sort through the larger goings-on in favor of their imminent survival. Ben would know where they were holding Vex. And they couldn't leave without Ben, too—Lu needed him, if she was to have any hope of stopping Elazar.

"The laboratory," she said. "This way."

Lu shot up the staircase, intending to veer left down the next deck.

The defensors who had come to investigate the explosion barred her way. But what stopped Lu cold, her feet on the edge of the stairwell's hatch, was the man who led them.

Milo pointed a pistol at her.

34

ABOVE, THE FIGHTING intensified. Gunfire came alongside shouting—and in the distant parts of the ship, Lu heard the clank of metal rotating, readying.

Cannons.

Lu put her hands out, feeling her own lack of weapons as Milo aimed his pistol at her. Behind her, Nayeli and Edda filled the hall, sighted by pistols in the hands of the defensors backing up Milo.

"It's over," Lu forced herself to say. "The raiders attacking will take you back to New Deza, and the Council will stop Argrid. It's over."

A bluff. She had no idea how this would end, nor how many of Cansu's raiders there were, nor how many defensors the Argridians had to counter. But that was how it would play out, ideally—Cansu would take at least this ship, and they would drag Milo back to New Deza with a full account of his wrongdoings and the Argridian king's plans. . . .

Lu knew it was a brittle dream. They would be lucky to get off this ship alive.

Milo sneered. "Oh, Miss Andreu," he chided, the voice he'd used when his men had captured her so many years ago, speaking to someone too stupid to comprehend basic sense. "This island is Argrid's."

Once, Lu might have corrected him. *The island belongs to its people!*

Yes, Grace Loray *did* belong to its people. The ones who had fought for it as Lu had and the ones who enjoyed the freedom; the ones who fled here to escape their own homeland's strife and the ones who came with stars in their eyes and hope in their hearts. This country was beautiful because of the variety of its people, and it was strong for that same reason.

Knowing that renewed Lu's courage. "Let Argrid try to fight. We defeated you once; we will do so again."

"Argrid controls the Mecht raider syndicate, and therefore the southern part of the island," Milo said. "The Council has bowed to us as well. But please, do tell me how you think this tantrum of one raider syndicate will change anything. It proves what Argrid has known all along—that this island is desperate for the Pious God to cleanse it."

Vibrations rang through the ship as a succession of explosions detonated—cannon fire. They came a breath before the door behind Milo and his men, the one leading to Ben's laboratory, blew off its hinges.

Lu lurched back into Nayeli. Milo's men toppled away as a roar of flames poured through the doorway, fire licking the air with searching, hungry fingers.

Through the flames stepped Gunnar, his face bent to match the fire he controlled. He turned right, away from Milo's men and Lu's group, and flicked his hand at passing bundles of flames to snuff them out.

Behind him, Ben braced himself on the doorframe, coughing. Half of Milo's men recovered, rushing to Ben or tearing after Gunnar down the hall.

Milo leaped to his feet, pistol swinging to Lu again, though he shouted over his shoulder, "My prince, are you harmed?"

"No," Ben hacked. "My assistant was defending me—we heard the attack. Stand down!"

Milo faltered, his pistol lowering. "What—"

Fire flared again, and three of Milo's defensors screamed at the end of the hall. A *thud*, a shout, and Gunnar stomped back through the building smoke.

Only two of Milo's men remained, divided between Ben's call to stand down and Milo's posture of attack.

But Lu saw who was behind Gunnar, a shadow in the smoke, and she moved.

She threw her body into Milo, knocking his hand into the wall. The pistol clattered from his grip and she swiped it up, kicking out his legs and sending him to the floor. Nayeli threw Hemlight at one of the remaining defensors while Edda elbowed the other in the face. They went down, taken out long enough for Lu to press on for the stairs, her pistol leading the way up to the main deck.

Dawn cast a flushed net over the golden-blue sky, a too-gentle backdrop. Commanders shouted to reload, aim, fire; defensors cried, "Huzzah!" when cannons struck targets or "Duck!" when Cansu's raiders fired projectiles. The rock outcropping that the galleon had docked next to rose as high as its starboard railing, leaving the top of the deck and masts unobstructed for attacks from both sides.

Cansu's steamboats peppered the water between the Argridian armada and the shore of Grace Loray, dots amid rolling waves of blue. Two of the brigantines had gathered around Elazar's ship, but Cansu's steamboats didn't focus there—they skirted the jagged rocks for hiding spots around Ben's ship. Against the size of the galleons and the lethal precision of the brigantines, it would not be a battle. It would be a slaughter.

As this war would be, if Elazar got his permanent magic, and no one on Grace Loray united to stop him.

Lu paused, gun limp, near the central hatch. Nayeli came up on her right, her fingers fluttering around bundles of Hemlight and Variegated Holly. Edda filled in on Nayeli's other side and had drawn knives. Gunnar, Ben, and Vex joined them, Gunnar already holding balls of fire in his palms, Ben with a drawn sword, and Vex with a smile and a wink, as if those were weapons enough.

Defensors began to notice them as Milo burst through the central hatch with his battered and burned men. They gave Lu's group a wide berth, not bothering with intimidation now that they had the upper hand. Milo wiped blood from a trickle down his chin and sneered at her.

She needed another play. Something to give them one last boost against the Argridians training dozens of weapons on them.

❖❖❖

Tension wound around Vex and his group like a net yanking them to the surface. It'd break at any moment—a stray bullet, a battle-blind defensor eager to protect his prince.

Ben spun to him.

"Take me hostage," he hissed.

Vex gave him a dumbfounded look. "What?"

Lu heard, too. She looked beyond him, at the defensors holding their positions.

"They don't know you've turned," she whispered. With no more than that, she smashed Ben's back to her chest. He'd been holding a sword, but it drooped as Lu jammed the barrel of her pistol to his temple.

Well, this was not a situation Vex had expected.

The defensors had, though. They looked more murderous now that one of the prisoners had outright threatened their prince.

"Lower your weapons!" Lu shouted. "Move to the starboard railing!"

The railing that the ship had docked along the rocks. The port side would be free—

Shit. They'd have to jump overboard to escape.

The defensors didn't move. A rifle cocked, the click like thunder.

"Now!" Lu shouted, pressing the pistol a little too convincingly to Ben's head.

"Do it!" Ben ordered, wincing.

The defensors obeyed, lowering their weapons and moving. One man, though, watched Ben with a heavier weight than the rest of the soldiers, like he'd already planned something.

Lu twisted, pulling Ben backward across the deck. Their group reached the railing opposite the defensors, and Vex snuck a peek overboard.

The water was empty, but he'd bet his life that a boat was hiding behind one of the nearby rocks, watching for them. It might well be his life that he'd have to bet, too, free-falling off a ship like they were about to do.

Vex swallowed.

"We swim?" someone asked. The big Mecht.

"Don't worry," Vex countered. "There's a boat."

"There is no boat."

"Trust me, it's there."

The Mecht growled. "There. Is. No. *Boat.*"

"Looks like you're not the only one afraid of heights," Nayeli said. She hopped onto the railing and leaped into the abyss beyond the ship with no hesitation, sinking elegantly into the crashing waves. Vex's throat closed, but she surfaced and started for the nearest rock. Sure enough, a steamboat listed out of the shadows, Cansu at the bow, a pistol in each hand.

Edda waved for Vex to go next. Lu would have to be last, to hold Ben as collateral for as long as possible.

Every other fear scattered, and Vex reached for Lu.

"Lu, give me the gun—let me—"

Lu turned to him for one second. One goddamn second, and Vex's panic rushed through his body before he knew why.

※※※

Jakes moved.

He dove across the deck, drawing his sword, swinging wide. Lu shoved Ben to his knees to protect him from the blade's swing and so she could falter back.

Ben didn't realize what he'd done until the steel of his sword rang where he caught Jakes's blow.

His heart hammered, crushing into his ribs. Behind him, the remaining members of his group didn't move, the whole of the deck caught in the crash of his and Jakes's blades.

Jakes's face went wide with shock. "Ben—" he started.

"Jump!" Ben hurled himself forward, catching Jakes off guard enough that he stumbled back.

The defensors on the starboard deck reacted, racing forward to resume battle. Cries ripped from throats, boots pounded on the wooden planks, and all Ben could do was hope that the rest of his group had heeded his call and jumped off the deck to safety.

The answer came in a blast of heat—Gunnar. A wall of fire washed a handful of defensors backward with screeches of agony, and Ben used the distraction to heft his sword and counter the swing of an approaching attacker.

He'd destroyed any chance he had of pretending not to be the Heretic Prince. However this battle ended, his world would not be the same.

✤✤✤

Lu braced herself on the railing, gun at her hip, Edda tugging on her other arm. Below, waves thrashed Cansu's boat as Nayeli beckoned from the deck.

She needed to jump. Ben's sacrifice would only give them a short delay.

Next to her, Vex watched Ben, his face grim.

If they left, Ben would be condemned for helping them. More than that—if Lu left this ship without him, this war would swallow her up.

Lu's consciousness tore away from the chaos. She saw Edda dive in front of her, back-to-back with Vex as they fought off defensors. She saw Milo across the deck, shoving defensors out of his path, his sword drawn and his eyes on her.

A Tuncian steamboat fired a ball of Variegated Holly close enough to make all on deck duck. It bounced off one of the masts with a rocking explosion, leaving the mast teetering, not taken out.

Lu grabbed Edda in the pause. "Get Vex off this ship," she told her. *Begged* her.

Edda met her eyes, but Lu moved, shoving Edda toward the railing. She gave them cover with a shot from her pistol. The defensors dropped back, created room, and Lu wanted to look at Vex.

But she couldn't. Not now.

She had the cure for Shaking Sickness—a way to protect them as they experimented with Grace Loray's botanical magic.

Ben had the start of permanent magic. He'd figured out on his own that making concentrated magic increased its potency.

Together, and with Gunnar's begrudging help, they would find a way to make magic permanent. Powersage, for muscular strength; Bright Mint, for mental function. Healing. Speed. Defense. *Everything.* Like Elazar wanted— but they would use it to escape and show the island, the world, that they had no need of the Church or Argrid. They had no need to fear any attacker, for they had the defense, and they could build a world on their own strength.

With that arrangement, Lu had secured her own future as well. To do this, to save her island, she would become as transparent as Grace Loray had come to be. Only its truth remained, the fact of what it was: an island of outlaws, of raiders, of sinners. Of Grace Lorayans in as many sizes and shapes as there were plants in their rivers.

But Lu needed Ben to create the permanent magic. And, selfishly, she needed Ben to find the cure for Vex. He would know, or be able to determine, the plants used by the Church, the ones Vex couldn't remember even with help.

The little girl in Lu, the one who had wanted so badly to help the revolution, cried out at the chance of still being able to help her island. She could make up for what she had done.

She owed Grace Loray that. She owed it everything.

Lu spotted Ben in the fray, two men deep. Gunnar neared him, igniting defensors, swinging punches, and throwing kicks.

"Go, Edda!" Lu screamed, twisting back once. *"Get him off this ship!"*

Vex heard her. Edda—loyal, determined Edda—grabbed him and heaved him back, but Vex dropped his heels into the wood.

"Stop! LU!"

Nothing else mattered until the Argridians could no longer use Vex against her. Until every member of his crew was off this ship and *safe*.

Lu ignored Vex's cries and searched again for Ben, rotating the now-empty pistol to use as a club. She would take down the defensors nearest Ben with Gunnar's help and haul him out as Edda hauled Vex, and they could leap off together.

Fire shot through her middle, stabbing from her belly to her spine. Lu's jaw dropped open as her mind scrambled for a sensible solution—had Gunnar burned her?

But she blinked, focused, *breathed*.

Milo threaded his arm around her back, holding her as if in a waltz, while the orchestra played rifles firing and cannons blasting and men dying.

"I would rather see you dead than escape me again," he whispered, pressing his lips to her ear. The motion twisted the sword in her belly, gouging deeper, but pain didn't come.

She had felt this numbness before, spreading out from a single point, immobilizing one limb, then another—

Lazonade. Milo had tipped his sword with Lazonade.

All the horrible things Lu had done came back to her, demanding recompense here, now. She let free one foolish whimper, and Milo held her closer.

"Shh," he purred. "You didn't weep as a child. Tears don't become you."

"Lu!" Vex shouted, but she couldn't turn, couldn't see.

Milo slid out the blade and released her. Lu dropped, the Lazonade's numbness cresting over her. She told herself she should be writhing, she should feel *something*—

"ADELUNA!" Vex screamed.

As she hit the deck and Ben dove for her, lifting her

head in the crook of his elbow, she saw Vex, by the railing. Edda held him back, and the panic on his face was so potent Lu almost rescinded her order. *No, let him stay, please, don't leave me—*

Edda, her face a mask of agony, hefted Vex overboard as she jumped. Defensors flung themselves at the railing, firing after them into the ocean.

Lu felt his absence through the Lazonade. She felt the ache of watching Vex leave her on the deck of this ship, knowing that that was the last time she would see him, and that he would die now, too. She wouldn't be able to save him.

Lu whimpered again, and the ship rocked—or no, it was her vision, spiraling and fading. The world melted into colors, the blue of the sky, the orange of Gunnar's protective fire blasts, and red, somewhere—on Ben, her blood squishing through his fingers.

"We need her!" Ben shouted. "We need her!" Fainter. Farther.

A rush of images. A flutter of sound.

And then, a void.

Acknowledgments

Here we are, darlings. The start of a new series. And while I have a plethora of people to thank for getting me this far, I would be remiss if I began this mushy letter of gratitude to anyone other than YOU.

You, reader, who have either followed me from the Snow Like Ashes series or grabbed this book anew. You, reader, who make this journey possible with every excited tweet, every loving email, every GIF-filled review. I am so grateful to you for giving this book a chance, and for letting my little world become your little world. I hope you got what you needed—and maybe a few things you didn't need, too.

Firstly, thanks are due to Kristin Rens, editor extraordinaire, who continues to "be the reason my daughter is so stressed" (as my mother says). But stressed in the best way. In the "SHE'S RIGHT—WHY IS SHE RIGHT" way that is the mark of a great editor. My books are always better after they've been pushed through your sieve.

Mackenzie Brady Watson. When people talk about finding the perfect agent, they mean you. I am thankful every day that you chose me to be your client, and I strive to make art that lives up to you.

The Balzer+Bray/HarperCollins Children's team: Kelsey Murphy; Michelle Taormina, Alison Donalty, and Jeff Huang, who gave me yet another unbearably glorious cover; Renée Cafiero, Mark Rifkin, Allison Brown, Olivia Russo, Bess Braswell, Sabrina Abballe, Michael D'Angelo, Jane Lee, and Tyler Breitfeller.

I have to call out some specific readers/bloggers/friends by name: Melissa Lee; Rae Chang; Ben Alderson; Branden (his generous Aleppo donation earned him a role in this book as captain of the Grace Loray castle guard); my resplendent War Council who carried over their passion from the SLA series, particularly the incomparable Melany; Julia Nollie; and so many more, too many more, I am bleary-eyed with gratitude for how many names I could list here. You all continue to make this career worthwhile. Thank you.

Writer friends, near and far and everywhere in between: Kristen Simmons (WIFEY), Evelyn Skye (pirates are, like, sooo much better than ninjas), Lisa Maxwell, Kristen Lippert-Martin, Olivia, Danielle, Anne, Claire, Akshaya, Janella, Madeleine, Samantha, Natalie, Jenn—again, I am blessed beyond belief to have made so many friends through this industry that my publisher is playing the proverbial "wrap it up" music.

To my family. Kelson and Oliver—you are places of calm in a profession that demands chaos. My parents, Doug and

Mary Jo, for still acting like this is my debut book. To Melinda—you're not in this book, but hey, it takes place on a tropical island! Aunt Brenda (affectionately G2A), for letting us invade your house. Nicole, Uncle Ed, Cousin Lillian, and all the extended, wonderful members of my family who continue to be proud and excited and text me pictures of people reading my books—I could not ask for a more supportive, loving group to come from. Y'all are good people.

To Amy Egan, for listening to me complain and still being my friend afterward.

And finally, to C. S. Pacat, Seth Dickinson, Valerie Tripp, Michael Dante DiMartino, and Bryan Konietzko, and all the other authors, creators, and artists who make me fight, every word, to be half as good as they are.

Turn the page for a sneak peek at the sequel,

THESE DIVIDED SHORES

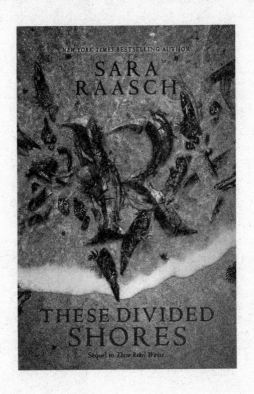

I

"TO ENSURE THE good of every Grace Lorayan, we, your Council, have unanimously voted to relinquish control of the island to His Majesty Asentzio Elazar Vega Gallego, King of the Pious God–Blessed Nation of Argrid, Eminence of the Eternal Church."

Even though Vex and Edda weren't on the side of the castle that faced the courtyard, the councilman's voice reverberated with perfect clarity. Last time Vex had been in New Deza's fortress, he'd come as a prisoner—and he'd rather have been locked in the dungeon again than been subjected to the pristine acoustics of the servants' halls.

He darted behind Edda, flying past windows servants had opened to usher in the lake breeze. All the windows really let in was the stench of sweat from the crowd in the front courtyard and the bleating words of a representative from Grace Loray's Council.

"Cansu and Nayeli are sure they found her?" Vex hissed. "They *see* her? I don't want to hear this speech again. If we're dallying here on a hunch or a rumor—"

Edda adjusted the Budwig Bean in her ear. One of the benefits of running missions with the Tuncian raider syndicate was access to the magic plant, which let two people communicate across great distances. "You planned this whole mission. Having doubts now?"

"I've had doubts about every decision I've made since Elazar set foot on this island again."

Edda's blue eyes softened, but then a maid appeared in front of them. Vex and Edda slowed to a walk. Vex drew the hood of his gray cloak lower, concealing his missing eye, while Edda twisted into the shadows until the maid vanished down the hall.

"The last time we had true peace on this island was centuries ago," the councilman was saying, "when Argrid brought unity to the conflicting immigrant groups that settled here—"

"Nay heard guards outside her room mention her by name," Edda assured him. Spots of pink touched her pale cheeks. "Just because Ben wasn't here doesn't mean this mission won't—"

Vex shoved by her. "Won't be a complete waste?" he snapped. "Yeah, we didn't find my cousin. We weren't able to save the people scheduled to burn today. But here's hoping we free Kari Andreu—that'll fix our problems."

A sack of galles had bought Vex and Edda access to the list of prisoners due to be burned today after the councilman finished his speech. Ben's name hadn't been on it, but eleven other people's names were—and defensors had them lined up at the base of the councilman's platform, watched by a crowd, with no way for Edda and Vex to save them.

Part of Vex hadn't expected to find his cousin, just as he hadn't at the last three burnings he, Edda, and Nayeli had scouted. Ben had made himself a traitor after helping Vex and Lu try to escape his father's ship two weeks ago, but he was still the Crown Prince of Argrid. Elazar wouldn't let priests kill his son like a common criminal. He'd make an example of him instead.

Even so, Vex didn't stop scouting the burnings. Ben had to be *somewhere*.

But god, it'd only been two weeks, and Vex was exhausted to the bone.

Edda caught up to him. Vex expected her to punch him in the shoulder for being irritable, but she walked next to him in silence as if he was a brittle creature. Which pissed him off.

"Threats darkened Grace Loray's shore only when the stream raider syndicates rose against Argrid," said the councilman. "What we perceived as aggression from Argrid was in fact defensors countering the attacks from stream raiders. All this time, we blamed the Argridians when they were as much victim as Grace Loray. The true enemy, the cause of our combined ills, is the manipulative, evil stream raider syndicates."

ARGRID IS EVIL, Vex screamed in his head. *ARGRID IS THE ENEMY, YOU LYING SACK OF CROCODILE SHIT.*

When Grace Loray was discovered centuries ago, it became a free-for-all settlers' paradise. People from the five Mainland countries had come, filled it up, and lived in moderate tolerance until Argrid decided to seize control and attempted to regulate its magic. To counter Argrid's forceful claim, immigrants from the other four countries had each formed syndicates to protect their own.

They had been right to. Argrid had tightened its grip on Grace Loray, outlawing the magic plants that grew in the island's waterways and burning anyone who disagreed with the Church's doctrine. Rebels had fought off Argrid and instituted a democracy—but even that failed when Argrid infiltrated the Grace Lorayan government.

Now Argrid was back. Instead of forcing its standards of purity and magic-abstinence on the whole island, it had singled out one group: stream raiders. Lawless thieves hated by any who weren't raiders themselves. Which made them perfect unifying scapegoats.

"Raiders hoard deadly magic," the councilmember continued to the all-too-silent crowd. Why weren't they screaming in fury? Why weren't they *outraged*? "Raiders pillage and destroy in the name of defiance for defiance's sake. Soon, you will not have to live in fear. The Council has allied with

Argrid to purge Grace Loray in pursuit of our joint goal: a war on raiders."

Vex's lungs swelled. Variations of this weak-ass speech had introduced every execution he and his crew had infiltrated these past two weeks, as though any words could diminish the horror of people burning to death.

But *people* weren't burning, not this time. *Raiders* were burning.

A spasm swept over Vex and he stumbled. His Shaking Sickness spells were getting harder to hide, as though his body knew his one chance at a cure had been stabbed to death on the deck of the *Astuto*.

The thought of Lu hit him like scalding water, and he caught himself on a window frame. Beyond his trembling fingers, a cloudless blue sky capped the island's tangle of deep green jungle. Breaks in the trees spoke of the rivers that wound across the island, with long plumes of steam rising over boats. Below was the castle's garden.

Edda put her hand on his shoulder. "You all right?"

This was the place he and Lu had escaped from weeks ago. He had to be standing right above the window he'd yanked open and jumped out with Teo on his back. Lu had been downright furious at him for bringing the six-year-old along, but what else could he have done? She had to admit that the journey had been good for the kid—

Vex scratched at the rough indigo sleeve of his stolen servant's uniform. *Good.* Sure. If *good* meant Teo sitting in a shack in Port Mesi-Teab. Since Vex had gotten back without Lu two weeks ago, the only person Teo had spoken to had been Edda. But when Vex asked her what he said, she'd told him, *"He's a kid. He doesn't know how to deal with what's going on."*

Vex's heart throbbed and he shook off Edda's hand. "I'm *fine*. Let's go."

Edda gave him a look of disbelief. She fiddled with the Budwig Bean and her face got distant, as though she was listening to a voice echo down a tunnel. "We're on the third floor now. Servant's hall on the south side." A pause. "Second door? Which—oh."

Nayeli poked her head through a door, stray black curls bouncing in rebellion from the beige knit cap of her own servant's uniform. She looked at Vex, the sympathy in her eyes saying Edda had told her, at some point, that they hadn't found Ben. But she didn't press for details—wouldn't, around Cansu. The fact that Vex was Argridian royalty wouldn't go over well among stream raiders, so as far as anyone else knew, Vex was just looking for his cousin. Not his cousin, the Crown Prince of Argrid.

Cansu pushed her way into the hall. "Two guards outside her room. Easy to eliminate."

"Eliminate?" Vex gawked. "Stand down, Cansu. No bloodshed if we can help it."

"We need to take out as many enemies as we can when we have the chance. You know Argrid wouldn't hesitate to stick knives in our backs."

"We aren't Argrid," Vex snapped. "And we aren't your raiders, either. No killing."

Cansu's golden skin reddened. "You gave us the castle's layout. You gave us the *basics* of the plan. But don't you dare go getting it into your head that you're in charge of this mission."

"Oh, and you are?"

"You bet your unaligned ass I am."

White-hot loathing descended over Vex. This was why he'd never joined a syndicate—he wasn't about to follow orders with no questions asked. On a good day, he'd have laid into Cansu until someone—probably he—ended up bleeding. But with the added fury and grief and terror of Elazar's takeover, Vex couldn't have stopped himself.

Nayeli could stop him, though. She shot forward as he opened his mouth, and one hard look from her sent his insults sinking back down his throat.

"So help me," she started, "I've had enough of you two and your verbal pissing contests. Cansu's in charge because we're using her syndicate's resources, but gods damn it, we aren't killing anyone. Now let's get Kari before I change my mind on that last bit and *kill both of you.*"

Cansu flicked her short flop of dark hair out of her eyes and plodded back through the door.

Vex stayed long enough to sulk at Nayeli. "Sorry," he mumbled.

She should've rolled her eyes and called him an idiot for challenging Cansu. But she gave him the same look that Edda wore, one filled with apology and sorrow.

Vex stomped after Cansu. Enough of this. Enough *pain*. He couldn't handle it.

Tall windows lit an ornate hall of marble and gold. Cansu stood over the collapsed bodies of two soldiers outside a closed door.

"Cansu! Goddamn it—"

"They're only unconscious." Cansu waved her fist. "Stop. Questioning. Me."

Vex snarled at her, but Nayeli slid between them. "Gods, *stop*." Her dark eyes went to Vex and she motioned at the door. "You want to be the one to—"

"Yeah." No. But he walked up to it and tried the handle. Locked. Which he made quick work of with picks from Cansu, and when the gold-lined door opened, he took a step inside—

Something iron-hard swung him around and trapped his neck in a vise grip.

Vex yelped, but the sound weakened into a choked gargle.

"Wait!" Nayeli shot into the room after him. "Kari, right? We're friends of your daughter! Let him go—gods, now I see where Lu gets her temper."

"Adeluna?" The grip released. "How do you know her? Why are you here?"

Vex stumbled away, clutching his neck, half certain it was indented now.

"Rescuing you," Cansu said as though it should've been obvious. She shut the door and marched across the room to yank open one of the balcony doors.

A gust of hot lake air swirled in, along with sensations that reminded Vex of memories from another life. Smoke. Fire. Screams.

"Today we commit the following raiders unto the Pious God's mercy" came a different voice. A priest, likely, to oversee the proper disposal of heretics. "Vina Uzun; Branden Axel—"

He kept reading off names. Kari must've recognized one, because she pressed a hand to her chest, rocking forward.

"Can we get out that way?" Nayeli asked Cansu, as if people weren't dying.

"The escape boat's in the lake," Cansu said. "You have that Aerated Blossom?"

No one saw Vex falter. He'd planned their way *into* the castle—steal servant uniforms and sneak in with the crowd that had come to see the burning—but all he'd known of their way *out* was that an escape boat would be waiting. But this was how Cansu planned to get to it—she'd loved his story of how Lu had used Blossoms to jump off the Schilly-Leto waterfall. Vex had been terrified. But Lu—she'd been fearless.

The crowd in the courtyard let loose a pained wail. Vex

felt a blossom of relief that the burning repulsed them, despite their silent, dangerous agreement earlier. Their complacency about Argrid's seizure of power was surface level.

"Who are you?" Kari demanded. Her face showed her calculations just as Lu's did. "Stream raiders? From the syndicate associated with Tuncay? Are you here on Cansu Darzi's orders? Has my daughter become entangled with the Tuncian syndicate?"

"We're not here on Cansu's orders," Cansu said. She turned from the balcony. "I *am* Cansu. The absurdity of a raider Head rescuing a Senior Councilmember is not lost on me, but that's why we're here. Because your daughter, along with these idiots"—she gestured at Nayeli, Vex, and Edda—"convinced me that the best way to stop Argrid from overtaking the island is to unite the Council and raiders and everyone who calls Grace Loray home. Figured Kari the Wave would be the most capable person to do that."

The Argridians had put Kari under house arrest—but she meant a lot to Grace Loray, so they hadn't killed her. She was Kari the Wave, a nickname she'd earned during the revolution because of her guerrilla-style ambushes that had whittled away Argrid's forces. The only reason the rebels had beaten Argrid the first time was because Kari had gotten the volatile, bickering stream raiders to ally with each other, becoming a force too powerful for Argrid to defeat.

Between border skirmishes, burning each other's steamboats, and other messier crimes, relations among the raiders had always been tense. Vex knew, for instance, that Cansu hated the "thieving" Grozdan syndicate with "the intensity of nigrika"—a Tuncian spice so hot Vex hadn't been able to taste anything for a solid two days after he'd eaten a pinch. If the raider syndicates had any hope of unifying to stop Elazar again, they'd need an intermediary, like Kari.

But the deeper reason Vex had suggested freeing Kari was because he knew Lu would've wanted it. It was that simple. That selfish.

Vex's vision faded. He lost sight of the room in favor of a sword, shining with Lu's blood, dripping scarlet circles on the deck of a ship—

"Other councilmembers can help." Kari composed herself, spine straight, again like Lu. "They are locked in rooms along this hall. They can be trusted to—"

"Trust? What do you know about *trust*?"

Kari snapped a look at Vex. Edda and Nayeli did, too, but Edda's focus went back to Kari, and Vex could see her thoughts spin. Should she intervene?

Vex didn't care. He hadn't meant to speak. But here he was, staring at a person who was as responsible for Lu's death as the man who'd stabbed her.

"Devereux Bell." Kari's fingers curled into fists. Last she knew, her daughter had freed him from prison and run off with him. "What do you—"

"Who do you think you can *trust*? Your husband?"

"Vex," Edda tried.

Kari's face went gray. "I only recently learned of my husband's deceit—"

"Stop acting so goddamn proud." Vex's arms shook so hard he had to cross them. "If you'd realized earlier that your own husband was a fucking *spy*, Lu might not be dead."

The last word hung on his tongue. He wanted to say it again, let it stick to someone else.

Kari's lips parted. "What did you say?"

He saw Lu's body slip to the deck of the ship. Her eyes searched for him, her face shocked and scared and alone, with just Ben to hold her, because Edda threw Vex overboard.

He'd left Lu. He'd left Ben, too.

"I said she's dead," Vex growled. "Lu's *dead*. Thanks to you and your husband."

Kari dropped onto a chair. Her silence was worse than if she'd started weeping, grief so tangible on her face that a fierce stab of guilt punctured Vex's heart.

"Or maybe you knew about your husband all along," he spat at Kari. "Maybe you're a spy too. Maybe you're glad Lu's gone. You're as guilty as—"

"Paxben!" Edda cried.

Vex's body went stiff. That name from her—that name *at all*—struck him dumb.

Edda grabbed his arm. "You have to stop. You can't drop this on someone!"

"But it was dropped on *me*!"

Deadly Magic, Double Crosses, and a Dangerous Quest

Don't miss this action-packed fantasy series from *New York Times* bestselling author Sara Raasch!